The Rhythm of my Soul

ROSEHEART BALLET
ACADEMY
BOOK 1

ELIN DYER

The Rhythm of My Soul
Copyright © 2021 Madeline Dyer
All rights reserved.

Madeline Dyer, writing as Elin Dyer, asserts the moral right to be identified as the author of this work.

First published in December 2021 by Ineja Press

Cover Design by Sarah Anderson Designs
Interior Formatting by Sarah Anderson Designs

Editing by Ineja Press

Paperback ISBN: 978-1-912369-34-8
eBook ISBN: 978-1-912369-33-1

The author can be contacted via email at
Madeline@MadelineDyer.co.uk

ELIN DYER

The Rhythm of my Soul

INEJA PRESS

For Grandad

ONE

Taryn

I wait by the curtain for my signal and try not to faint or be sick or wet myself. I mean, I should be used to this. I've been a ballet dancer since I was six, and I've lost count of the number of times I've waited backstage, just as I am now. But this is it. *This* is the most important pas de deux of my life, the dance that will decide everything.

Across the other side of backstage, by the opposite curtain, I see Teddy, my partner. He's dressed in white tights and a dressy shirt—also white—which make him look like Mr. Darcy, even if he's playing Romeo. My Juliet outfit—a simple, cream leotard with a white chiffon skirt and glossy, white tights— matches his in that I don't think it's quite right for *Romeo and Juliet.* Madame Cachelle wanted to try something different.

Teddy makes eye contact, nods at me. I nod back and pray that the butterflies in my stomach will go away, even though Madame says butterflies are good. *They're a sign you care, my little gems, a sign you're not over-confident.*

I breathe deeply. I can do this. *We* can do this. Me and Teddy, because I know him like I know myself. We're in tune, and when we dance, we're one being. Three years ago, when the diploma program paired us together in our main pairs—the pairs we'd be dancing in for at least half of the training program, matching us on height, weight, and ability, to make lifts easier—I never expected how close we'd get. How in tune we'd become. There's an old saying that Madame doesn't like—that each dancer has their dance soulmate. Madame says it's *a load of tosh*, because a good dancer needs to be able to dance with many others. Schedules may change at the last minute, or an injury may mean the prima ballerina ends up dancing a pas de deux with someone other than the male principal. We have to be flexible, and Roseheart specializes in pas de deux. While Teddy is the dancer I'm most familiar dancing with, I've also danced with every other male undergrad at some point—and that's how I know that Teddy and I are matched in a way that doesn't compare when I dance with others. I want to keep dancing with Teddy. So long as this goes well, I will. If we get into the company, Teddy and I will be performing together for the duration of the three-year contract with Roseheart Romantic Dance Company—and possibly longer after that, depending on renewals. Sure, we'd each dance with others too, but Roseheart is unusual in that it favors dancers dancing with their primary partners.

Behind me, I hear Madame fussing around. Normally she's in the front row of seats, but given the importance of this performance, she's back here, keeping time, giving last-minute encouragements, and reminding us that we're all *amazing little gems.*

She taps me on the shoulder, twice, and I breathe in her spicy perfume.

Get ready.

As if I need to be told.

I turn and nod at Madame. She's nearly fifty, but you wouldn't know it looking at her. She's in shape and still performs one of the best arabesques I've ever seen. Now, backstage under the edgy lighting, she's all dark eyes and glossy, dark skin. Her heart-shaped face is smiling as she gives me an encouraging nod.

On stage, the music changes, gets softer and softer. I turn back and lift each foot up in turn, tapping the ribbons on my Repetto Alicia pointe shoes. Three taps for good luck. So far, it's always worked.

The petit rats—the younger dancers of the academy—are leaving the stage, exiting via the other side door. They traipse past Teddy, and I see how he's now completely focused on the music. He'll be counting down the seconds it takes the stagehands to wheel the gargoyles on in the near darkness.

Because this is it now. It's time for the balcony pas de deux—the performance that will get Teddy and I the places with the Roseheart Romantic Dance Company, allowing us to dance alongside the professionals in their fall tour in nine weeks' time—and in the many performances after. It's what every dancer at this academy wants: twelve dancers will graduate each year, but only two are accepted into the academy's company. The rest will audition for other companies or be selected straight away by scouts based on this performance—but the roles outside of Roseheart will nearly always be solo roles. Roseheart is the only company in Europe that focuses exclusively on duos and pas de deux; it's unusual in that its board only accepts a new duo at a time, never singles. And being a professional dancer—and proving to Mum that it's not all a waste of time and that yes, I had to go to this school in particular—is everything I've ever wanted.

As the pianist drops an octave, I make my entrance. My Alicia shoes give me confidence. Repetto is one of my favorite pointe shoe brands, and these ones have a three-quarter shank that gives extra flexibility, molds well to the arches of my feet, ensuring better weight distribution than some of my other shoes. I always dance well in my Repettos.

The lights on the stage are bright while those over the audience are so dim that I can't see who's in the front row, but I know: Roseheart's company director, the board members and directors and managers from other companies always want the best seats. Behind, there'll be various members of the academy's staff and groundkeepers, along with our sponsors and the families of dancers. And, of course, there are the journalists. I try not to think about them. Just as I try not to think about how my mum isn't here. But that's okay. I'd be more unnerved if she was.

This year, *Romeo and Juliet* is the academy's end of year production. All the students are involved, from the youngest petit rats to the seniors and the diploma undergraduates. Across the three years of the diploma course, there are thirty-six undergrads. Six girls, six boys per year. As Romeo and Juliet, Teddy and I are the favorites to be accepted into Roseheart's company. I let that knowledge fill me, use it to boost my confidence because when I'm confident—not over-confident, mind—I always perform better.

I dance onto the stage, trying not to look into the audience in case I see the journalist who made my life hell, and meet Teddy halfway. This pas de deux is one of my favorites. I know the Royal Ballet's performance of it by their principal dancers, Yasmine Naghdi and Matthew Bell, off by heart, but our routine is different, darker. Our choreographer, Rai-Ann Lockhart, wanted this performance *to have a touch of danger,* and Madame thought it would be excellent to dress Teddy and I in white and project cobwebs across the stage and us. Since we got an upgrade backstage on lighting and special effects, Madame's been all about including it in *sophisticated and appropriate* ways. Sam, the tech guy, has been run ragged the last few weeks. But the modern technology does add to our performance.

The pianist strikes darker notes to match the flickering spiders dancing across my skin, and there's a sense of fire between Teddy and I as we move and wrap each other in emotions. There's rawness and desperation, a fear of our characters forever being kept apart and doomed to loneliness and insanity where our minds will be eaten, as we capture the frustration of being star-crossed lovers.

Or, at least, what we think it would feel like.

Dancing with Teddy is seamless—it always has been. We just fit together. There's no gap between where he begins and where I end as we perform. We're one being as we command the stage, capturing more and more passion. The tempo rises as I spin away from Teddy, pirouetting. Five seconds to go until we fly back together and finish the pas de deux with the kiss.

The kiss I'm trying not to think about.

There are two statues on the stage, actual statues made of stone. Both are carved into gargoyles, chosen because the academy's artistic director said it would enhance the gothic undertones of Rai-Ann's choreography and Madame's vision, and in the first three seconds of the five, I dance around the statue on the left, knowing Teddy is doing the same on the right.

You are corresponding with these creatures, asking them for their advice on whether you should embrace this romance, knowing the dangerous consequences such an act could have.

Two seconds to go.

And this is it.

I look up and lock eyes with Teddy, ready to run to him and embrace my Romeo, where we will transition into the most spectacular of lifts. But then Teddy trips, surges forward, and—

I see it happen in slow motion. See how he soars forward, see how shiny his forehead is as he slams headfirst into his gargoyle. I've already started my run toward him, because my body is almost on autopilot because I know this routine off by heart. And maybe part of me thinks Teddy will right himself in time, will get up and carry on and meet me for the lift so we can end with the kiss—but he doesn't.

He slumps down the gargoyle.

The audience gasps.

The pianist stops, a heaviness holding the air. There's just my pounding heart, my feet now slapping on the stage, my ragged breaths.

I reach him and drop to his side. "Teddy?" My voice shakes, and he's not moving. I touch his shoulder, but my hand looks strange with the spiders still projected across the whole of the stage, and it unnerves me, makes me freeze as I just stare at him.

Others run onto the stage. Madame and Rai-Ann and Ross, the physio. I hear other voices, so many I don't know or can't recognize, as hands shove me back. The lights over the audience go on. The company directors' faces suddenly look like caricatures, grotesque and growing, stretching.

Words fly around, and I'm trying to get back to Teddy, to see if he's okay, because it still doesn't look like he's moving. Unconscious?

Ross barks directions at someone, and then I hear Alma, one of the other soon-to-be graduates, calling for an ambulance. Ballerinas and danseurs race around, some looking scared, others excited.

Excited?

"Teddy? It's okay." Somehow, I get to him, and I'm holding onto his arm, and he's still not moving. He's so...still.

"Back now, Miss Foster. Give us space."

"Here, come on." Sibylle, my understudy, touches my shoulder then leads me away. I must be numb because I let her, even though we're not friends and I don't like people touching me. Not unless it's during a performance, because then it's art. This is just...unnecessary. But I don't say anything.

We walk past the front row of the audience, where everyone is standing. Somber faces and hushed voices, stretching back, row after row. I scan all the faces, searching for the journalists, but I can't see her—Adelaide James, the reporter who tried to turn the world against me, but I'm still nervous. The academy's security should keep her out, but she got in before.

"Such a shame," the Roseheart Company Artistic Director says. A tall man with a twisty moustache. Mr. Aleks. I recognize him from the staff photo board at the entrance of the company's main building. He never bothers himself with the academy, only attending the end-of-year production each year to see which two dancers Miss Tavi will choose to join the Company. I've heard Mr. Aleks sits in on many of the company's first-division's training sessions and rehearsals, only occasionally bothering with the second and third divisions, but Netty Florence Stone—the company's female principal who dances in the first division—told Teddy once that you only really hear from Mr. Aleks if he's not happy.

Next to Mr. Aleks, Mr. Vikas nods. Madame already introduced us to him earlier this year. He's the company's third-division ballet master and he's been at Roseheart for twenty years. He works with a choreographer, and together they have the most contact with their dancers. He's the one who trains the third-division ballerinas and danseurs, the division that all the new recruits automatically go into. Suddenly, it feels important to me that I know all of this, exactly how the company works.

Miss Tavi, the woman in charge of selecting the new recruits and who corresponds closely with Madame Cachelle regarding the third-year undergraduates' progress across the final year of the program, nods to Mr. Aleks and Mr. Vikas. "Definitely a shame," she says. "We'd have taken the two leads for sure, otherwise."

We'd have taken the two leads for sure, otherwise.

Otherwise.

"So, who do we replace the boy with?" Mr. Vikas says, looking at Miss Tavi, and I can't believe they're still thinking about this. "We need Miss Foster."

I jolt. *Replace the boy?* So, I won't be dancing with Teddy in the company? My throat feels like it's closing up, like there's not enough room in it to be able to breathe.

"We should wait to see if Mr. Walker is seriously injured," Miss Tavi says. "He may be able to dance with us after all."

Mr. Aleks shakes his head. "We have to decide tonight. It's the way it's always been done. Mr. Walker can always audition for a space next year with a new partner if he's not seriously injured. But we need to focus on this year and who we are admitting. Miss Tavi, who's the male second choice?"

Mr. Vikas and Miss Tavi both peer at her clipboard. She's been making notes on us.

"Mr. MacQuoid is the understudy for the male lead role," Miss Tavi says. "Madame Cachelle and the other ballet teachers say he is above average. And he did perform well in his role as Benvolio tonight, from what we saw."

Xavier MacQuoid. I inhale sharply. Dancing with Xavier is okay. He's strong. Really strong, and he's got good technique. But he's not Teddy. But if dancing with him as my primary partner is now the only way I can get into the company, I'll do it.

I turn and see Xavier behind me, listening intently. His eyes shine. When Teddy was in the picture, I know none of the other guys expected to have a shot.

"But Miss Foster is not above average," Mr. Vikas says. "She's *exceptional*. As is Mr. Walker. We need the accepted duo to be well-matched." He clears his throat. "Asking Miss Foster to dance with Mr. MacQuoid would limit her potential and create an unbalanced pairing."

I hear Xavier's breathing quicken, but I try to ignore him, try to forget he's here.

"Yes, we had that problem a few years ago with Miss Radnor and Mr. Barnes," Mr. Aleks says. "It made their performance too clunky. We then couldn't give Mr. Barnes the roles he deserved, and she held him back."

I hold my breath. Mr. Barnes and Miss Radnor—Tom and Clara—were both let go of after a year, their contract being dissolved. There'd been uproar at the time, especially as Tom was very talented, but the board insisted both had to be let go. Roseheart follows strict rules, left by our founder, and it is cutthroat here. Nonetheless, Tom went on to have a successful career with a Russian company. I never heard of Clara again—her name was tainted by this. She'd have secured solo roles for sure with other companies had she never been accepted by Roseheart and then let go, her reputation tarred. Because after Roseheart, Clara couldn't get any auditions at all.

"Can we bypass the duo admission rule?" Mr. Vikas asks. "Because I want Miss Foster in our company."

Sibylle edges forward, standing next to Xavier. She's the other understudy for a main role. My understudy.

"I want Miss Foster, too," Miss Tavi says, and she looks to Mr. Alek. "I'm happy to bypass the duo requirement if you think it'll work?"

He shakes his head, then twists the ends of his moustache. "We do that, and we'll lose funding from our main sponsors if we don't follow the wishes of the late Mrs. Roseheart."

"So, what do we do?" Mr. Vikas throws his hands up in the air. "I don't want to miss out on Miss Foster, but I strongly advise she's not paired with a lesser dancer."

"Well, if that's not a choice, we admit the two understudies as a duo," Miss Tavi says. "Or we admit no one."

"We admit no one," a new voice says. A man I don't know—someone with a lot of weighting? "This is a moot point you're all discussing. We can only admit graduates—and as this ballet did not conclude, we have no graduates."

My stomach sinks. No graduates.

It's all…over.

TWO

Taryn

The other third years don't know what to say to me. Or to each other. Peter's on the phone to his dad, shouting manically about how none of us have graduated because *a dancer messed up*. I shoot him dagger-looks at that, but it doesn't solve anything. Usually, the twelve third years would be invited back on stage at the end, and we'd all officially graduate before finding out which two are joining the company. But none of that is happening. The company staff made it clear enough.

Right after that, Madame Cachelle and two of the classical ballet teachers shepherded us away from Mr. Aleks, Miss Tavi, Mr. Vikas, and the other man whom I didn't know. The academy doctors were ordering for the room to be cleared, and I could hear distant sirens.

I didn't even get one last look at Teddy. There were too many people around him.

"I don't think the company should've been discussing who'd get the places right then," Sibylle says. "Not with Teddy still unconscious. It was insensitive."

"Well, he's ruined all our careers," Peter says, his red face like thunder.

Then he walks out the common room, leaving just me and the other third-year girls here. I'm not sure where the rest of the guys went anyway. It's not like we usually talk that much anyway, but now there's a strange atmosphere between us all as we all try to both look at each other and look anywhere else.

Me and Sibylle and Ivelisse are sort of a unit because we room together, while Alma and Freya and Ella are the other unit. We rarely talk to each other, but we also rarely talk among ourselves. We've never really tried to. Each of us has friends outside of dance—or at least I pretend I do, too, because they're always talking about their non-dancing friends—and while we are mostly civil at the academy, we're not close. No one really is, because we're competitors.

But now, all of a sudden, they try to speak to me, try to reassure me as I text Teddy for the fifth time, and their words are like empty husks, disembodied petals. Alma hands me a cup of tea—a drink which I notice has the ends of several strands of her golden hair dipping into—but I spot the dark glint in her eyes that I'm sure she's trying to hide because she's keeping the rest of her face neutral, expressionless. Alma has never really liked me, been jealous ever since I ranked higher than her at the end of the first semester in the first year. And now she's not graduating because of my dance partner, and I'm sure she'll somehow blame it on me.

Hell, I bet they all are trying to hide their anger or annoyance or… or how they hope to benefit from it. Teddy's accident—caught on camera as the performance is always filmed—will mean we will be in the dance media a lot. Even companies who didn't attend today and normally never bother with us will likely watch the showreel because people do like watching people get hurt. The sheer number of 'funny' YouTube videos prove that. Our showreel, if Teddy's accident is in it, will get *way more* views than it usually does. This would inevitably lead to some of the dancers here getting offers of roles and auditions from companies who wouldn't normally watch our tapes, even despite us dancers having no formal graduation from Roseheart Ballet Academy. We heard about it happening before, how injuries caught on a showreel will mean more eyes on all the dancers. Something similar happened at a New York ballet school. They had a dancer get injured two years ago in a show and their video made the school famous. I heard how almost all of the undergraduates had offers flying in for various company positions.

So, pretty much all the third years could benefit from Teddy's accident—except me, because dancing with Roseheart is all I've ever wanted. And Teddy won't benefit either, obviously.

"There are other companies that would love to have you, Taryn," Ivelisse says. She's Puerto Rican, and she's got great skin, perfect teeth, and a perfect tone to her voice. I'm sure she could narrate children's books or something. Her voice is just that soothing. My voice on the other hand isn't, and I've never even thought about what I could do beyond dancing at Roseheart's company. "You can still dance as a soloist somewhere else. We all can."

Ivelisse's trying to give me a reassuring smile. I don't think I've seen her smile, not since before she developed anorexia. That just seemed to zap the happiness from her. But she's trying to be positive for me—even though she hasn't graduated this evening either—and I appreciate that.

Freya nods, but she doesn't look up from the screen of her phone. Ella's next to her on the couch, massaging her own foot. She's always getting in-grown toenails, and I watch as she flexes her toes. Her skin is dry and cracked, and a thin line of blood appears across the knuckle of her big toe as she forcibly exercises it.

Ivelisse is right. My career isn't over. Solo positions are easier to get. Due to the lack of male ballet dancers in most companies, there are far more solo female positions or group roles than vacancies for females who are mainly part of a male-female duo. But my career with the Roseheart Romantic Dance Company will be over. And Roseheart is the company I always wanted to dance for. There's something that just encapsulates me about romantic dance and romantic ballet especially. And you'd maybe think it wouldn't, given I'm aromantic and asexual—but once I step onto the stage, I can play hopeless-romantic characters, and

I become caught up in the romance of the dance, the beauty of it. It just speaks to me, gets inside my soul, and curls up there, promising never to leave its home or me during the performance. But I can't imagine feeling these feelings when it's not a performance, when it's just me. I've never been in love, never felt romantically or sexually attracted to someone.

Maybe I love the romance of dance because it's the only romance I feel I truly understand, even if part of me is still desperate to fall in love, to have that connection with someone. And all the online groups for aro people say people like us can still have a connection with others, and beautiful relationships, but I'm just not sure that that's me. I mean, Teddy is aroace too, and he's the one person I could only ever imagine myself in a queer platonic relationship with—that is, a relationship that's more intense than what people generally assume a friendship to be, but that isn't deemed to be sexual or romantic by those participating in it—but then again, I'm happy as I am. Single. I don't really feel that need to find someone, even though I know a lot of other aro people do want a partner. Ballet gives me that feeling of partnership anyway, and I don't think I need it beyond dance. Perhaps because dance is such a big part of me.

I love dancing with Teddy, in particular, so much more than the other guys on the diploma. He and I actually discovered the terms 'aromantic' and 'asexual' together in our first year. Finding those labels existed was like being welcomed home, being assured that there wasn't anything wrong with me. And learning it all alongside Teddy, at the same rate as him, just made us even closer. Besides the few people I've talked to online from the aroace groups—and some of those are anonymous—he's the only person who knows I'm aroace, and I'm the only one who knows he is. We both decided that announcing it to the world could backfire for us career-wise when we both want to be part of Roseheart's company, which even has *romantic* in its name.

Only now, we never will.

My bottom lip wobbles. I know I should feel bad that I'm thinking of my lost career instead of Teddy's health when he's being blue-lighted to hospital. I shouldn't be thinking such selfish things when he's my best friend. It's just another example of how my selfishness hurts people. I close my eyes. Teddy isn't the first person I've lost.

No. I'm *not* losing him. He will be fine.

He isn't Helena.

But he is injured. And everyone knows that affects me. Being in Roseheart's Company is all I've ever wanted.

Still, girls like me don't deserve nice things.

I take a sip of the tea Alma gave me. It's tepid, at best, and faintly tastes of chamomile. There's something grainy at the bottom of the cup. Alma is a massive fan of expensive loose-leaf tea, and I have to admit I am touched by her gesture and generosity. I've never seen her share it with anyone.

Sibylle—the girl I share my dorm with, alongside Ivelisse—snorts and I realize they're all talking. Then Sibylle glances at me. No doubt she can tell I'm close to tears.

A loud shrilling sound fills the air, making me jump. It's my phone. A glance at the caller ID tells me it's my mum.

Oh no. I'd forgotten she'd be phoning.

"Taking this outside," I say to the others, waving my phone at them.

Out in the corridor, I take a deep breath. It's not that my mother and I don't get on exactly. It's that there's too much between us that can never be said. Too much heartache.

"Hi, Mum."

"Taryn. It's finished, now, yes? You said it lasted three hours?"

The ballet. Right. "Yes."

"And did you get it?" Despite everything, how we disagree on me doing ballet still, there's hope in her voice. So much of it, like it's flowing out of her. We may not speak much, but I know she thinks about me a lot. Sometimes, speaking is just too difficult.

It's easier for Mum this way, compartmentalizing her life into the before and the after. At home with her new boyfriend and my little sisters, she's in the after. I'm a reminder of her old life. And so is ballet.

She begged me to stop, after Helena. Said it was too difficult—difficult for her and that it'd be difficult for me. Mum never outright mentioned the cost of my tuition and all my pointe shoes and the private and expensive physiotherapy I'd needed up to that point alone, but of course I was aware that that was another reason she'd prefer me to stop.

Mum said we all needed a fresh start, a clean break, with no reminders—as if she could forget that *I'd* be a constant reminder, my face a mirror for what we'd all lost. And ballet—it was Helena who'd been interested in it first. We were twins, so of course we ended up doing it together.

And now it's just me.

"The girls have been so excited." My mum rambles on, telling me how my sisters have been telling all their friends. "They said you're just like Angelina Ballerina, and they won't stop reading those books again. They found your old copies, you know. And they keep asking their dad to stream it onto the TV too."

It's clear she's talking about the girls, my younger half-sisters, to distract herself, to calm her. She's nervous. And now I have to tell her that I didn't manage it. That all the money she poured into me going to this academy—which was far more expensive than all the others—is for nothing. I have to tell her I failed, and that it was through no fault of my own.

"I…" My throat feels too thick.

"Taryn!" a voice screeches.

It's Tessa. My five-year-old sister. Then there are hushing sounds and a crackling, before Tessa's yelling, "I knew you could do it!"

"Tessa, darling, give the phone back to Mummy. Come on now…" Mum speaks in a softer tone to Tessa than she does to me now. I notice it immediately. Then Mum's back, talking to me. "You got in then? I didn't hear exactly what you were saying to Tessa, but that's wonderful!"

It's suddenly too hot in the corridor. The air is too sticky, too humid. *No*, I want to say. Only I can't. I can't say the word.

"Yeah." My voice is weak.

What the hell are you doing?

"That's wonderful, Taryn! I knew you'd do it. We all had faith in you. Congratulations. And how great that you'll be getting your own salary now. So independent."

My head spins. "Thanks, uh, I've got to go."

"Oh, yes, of course. Meeting with the company, now, right?" Mum asks, and it tugs at my heart. I hadn't thought she'd been listening properly when I told her at the end of last year what would happen after the final show of year two.

How it should've gone… Me and Teddy, taking our final bows. Mr. Vikas and Miss Tavi and Mr. Aleks conferring for twenty minutes with input from Madame Cachelle before then getting on stage and calling the names of the pair being accepted. An hour or two to celebrate before the induction and company greeting, typically held late at night, where we would've officially met the company dancers and signed our first contracts with Roseheart Romantic Dance Company, ready to start training with them after the weekend.

"Oh, I won't keep you then," Mum says. "You'll be wanting to celebrate. And this is great, Taryn. We're all really happy for you."

My deception—my lie—sits heavily in the pit of my stomach, and I feel empty after Mum's said goodbye, empty as I head back into the common room. Seeing the sympathetic faces of my peers makes me immediately glad that they didn't hear my lie.

"We were just saying we should get some dinner," Ivelisse says, standing up. That's not something I ever thought I'd hear from her mouth any time soon, unfortunately.

Here, a lot of the stereotypes about ballet dancers being concerned about their weight and starving themselves are unfortunately true. Way to fight back against misconceptions, Roseheart! Ivelisse is probably the worst one for this, and I know I shouldn't say 'worst' like it's a choice or like she can be compared to others with EDs. It's not something she's chosen to have, it's an illness, I know that, and eating disorders shouldn't be compared. I've heard the therapists say that you can't say one case is more severe than another, especially when low weight isn't the only indication. But Ivelisse's the only one who has a full schedule of appointments with the Roseheart nutritionist, a Roseheart therapist, and many other appointments with doctors at the local hospital, while the rest of us just have monthly guidance sessions on nutrition and check-ins with the academy nurse as needed.

Ivelisse gives me a small smile. Her lips stretch too thin as she does. I suppose it's not just she who rarely smiles. Many of us don't. Even when Teddy and I were told we'd be dancing the lead roles in *Romeo and Juliet*, I don't remember smiling. Only careful nods and promises to do the academy and company proud.

Alma says she, Freya, and Ella will get food later—as if staying in our dorm units is important now even for this—

but Sibylle, Ivelisse, and I head outside, to the main academy block where the canteen is. I'm not keen on getting dinner in front of Ivelisse and Sibylle because I worry about what they're thinking when I carefully select my food—that I'm unhealthy and maybe they even think I'm fat because I'm curvier than them. I'm always super aware of their eyes on me and my plate.

I have fructose malabsorption. My body can't process fructose, the sugar found in fruits and a lot of vegetables, and in regular table sugar too. It means that a lot of desserts—including ice cream—are out for me, but it also means I can't have a great deal of fruit, and I have to be almost as careful about vegetables. Only one to two servings a day of berries and cantaloupe, or half a small banana, and the only veggies I can tolerate without getting severe pain and stomach problems are Brussel sprouts, capsicum peppers, and cucumber. So, most of my food intake is made up of dairy, potatoes, brown rice, lean chicken, and fish. Compare my carb, protein, and dairy-heavy plate with Ivelisse's carefully selected piece of chicken, tender stem broccoli and one cherry tomato, and it's obvious who's having the feast.

The dining hall is abuzz with talk about me and Teddy. *Of course* it is. There may only be thirty-six undergrad students across the three years of the diploma, but Roseheart offers some of the biggest and best ballet training programs for children aged four to eighteen, and the lower school has nearly three hundred students in total. Dancers ranging from petit rats to seniors are everywhere.

"I heard he's *dead*," one younger student says, her eyes wide. Her voice is a ridiculously loud stage whisper. She speaks theatrically with her hand in front of her mouth. "He had a brain aneurysm in the ambulance and—"

My glare stops her short. She pales and doesn't move, frozen to the spot.

But Teddy can't be dead!

"Shut up," Ivelisse hisses at her, while the other young dancers make inhaling and shushing noises. "You don't know a thing." Ivelisse turns to look at me. "They're just making it up. You'd be the first the teachers would tell if…if something has happened."

Would I though? Would the school tell me as soon as they know? Would the hospital even tell the school immediately? My heart rate rises, and my chest tightens. I want to run, but I can't. I know that. I glare at the younger girls. I can see the excitement on their faces. Cheeks flushed and bright eyes. Like they want something bad to have happened. They want gossip. And this is all that this is to them—*gossip*.

Sibylle glances back at me. "He's not dead." Her German accent is thicker than ever. It's always like that when she's worried. We may not be close friends, but we all know how to read each other.

I nod and clasp my hands together, dry wringing them. *Teddy is fine. Teddy is fine. Teddy is fine.*

We sit at the table nearest the door. The three of us. Feels weird. Sure, we've sat together before, kind of have to when there aren't that many tables and we tend to sit in year groups, but now Ivelisse and Sibylle keep looking at me and then sharing glances with each other. Like they're worried.

I check my phone again. There's a message from Grandad: *So proud of you. Well done!* I smile, but it makes me sad that I'm deceiving him, too.

Still nothing from Teddy though. I have his dad's number, and I wonder about texting him. Because while his dad wasn't in the audience, he'll have been notified about this, right? He'd have more info than I do at the moment, surely?

We get our food, and the canteen fills up. At a table across from us, Xavier, Peter, and Robert sit. Advik and Charlie join them a moment or so later. The remaining male undergrads are subdued. I hear Teddy's name in their conversation over and over again—very different to their normally rowdy conversations. A couple of them still sound annoyed about how none of us have graduated now.

"Maybe we'll perform the show again tomorrow," Advik says.

My heart sinks. Without Teddy, *I* won't be performing. I couldn't even take on the more secondary role that Sibylle was performing with Xavier earlier today, without a partner, and I can't see that they're going to boot out one of the other girls.

Xavier, Sibylle's partner and Teddy's understudy, tells Sibylle they must do an extra practice together tonight, but she just frowns at him.

"Not appropriate," she says, glancing at me.

After Ivelisse's finished eating, she excuses herself to go and meet with the academy therapist. She has these sessions every weekday after the evening meal.

"You coming to the lounge?" Sibylle asks me, despite the look of annoyance on Xavier's face.

I nod. Nothing better to do.

"I am sorry, you know," she says, linking arms with me. The gesture feels odd. "You did deserve the place. You and Teddy both did."

I thank her.

The lounge is on the other side of campus, near the studios. Not many people are in here tonight. It's only for the diploma undergraduates, those aged sixteen and above. Thirty-six of us in total, equally divided between the three years of the program. The first and second years must mostly be in their dorm rooms tonight, or still in the canteen.

Unlike our dorm common room, the lounge has a gaming system, a pool table, and a large TV screen. Xavier and the other boys immediately monopolize the three forms of entertainment, leaving Sibylle and I to sit on one of the sofas. I sit first, and she sits right next to me—another reminder of how unusual this situation is. Usually, I'd be sitting here chatting to Teddy or reading one of the biographies I love or scrolling through Facebook to see what my mum is up to.

But Sibylle starts telling me about the latest episode of Eastenders, and how she thinks she looks a little like Shona McGarty, with her pale skin and dark hair, and it's sweet that she's trying to distract me. I nod and agree with her as I send another text to Teddy: *Really hope you're okay.*

His lack of any kind of response is making me increasingly more nervous now. Is he still unconscious, like he was when the rest of us were ushered out of the academy's theatre? Have doctors worked out what's wrong? Is he in surgery?

That last thought doesn't make me feel any better, but before I can dwell on it, the lounge door opens and a flock of girls enter—Freya, Ella, Alma, and two second years. Then Ivelisse joins us a few moments later, her face kind of pinched in like she's struggling not to cry. I wonder how the therapy went.

"Any news on Teddy?" Alma asks me.

Freya and Ella are silent, but I can tell they're both listening as they perch on the arms of a sofa a few feet from the one Sibylle and I are on.

I shake my head. "Not yet."

A teacher from the lower school steps into the lounge, which is a surprise both because the lower schoolteachers rarely come over here and because teachers in general leave us be when we're in the lounge. This teacher is tall and thin with lots of lines on her face. I don't know her name, but I think she teaches English—the lower school students have regular academic subjects alongside ballet—and she pauses in the doorway.

That's when I see what's in her hand—the hand she's holding up in front of her. A pregnancy test.

"I need to know whose this is," the teacher says. "It was in the toilets by the library."

The boys have stopped playing their games, but the teacher's looking at me and Sibylle.

"Well, it's not mine," I say.

"Or mine." Sibylle laughs. "I wouldn't be so silly as to leave one lying about if it was."

Finally, the teacher looks away from us and focuses on the next pair of girls. Freya and Ella both shake their heads.

"Not mine," Alma says.

The second-year students shake their heads.

"Why would it be one of ours?" Ivelisse asks. "You just said you found it in the lower school."

"I am asking all our girls," the teacher says. "And the library serves the whole academy and company, not just the lower school."

But like any of us ever go down there. We avoid it at all costs. Not just because the librarian is crabby, but it's weird going back there. Like we're younger than sixteen and still in school. Whenever I've wanted to read books—mostly memoirs and biographies written by ballet dancers—I've ordered them through the local bookshop rather than request them from Roseheart library.

"Is it yours?" The teacher is looking at Ivelisse, and I realize she's the only one who hasn't answered the question.

"No. But I'm sure if I was ovulating then my whole medical team would be thrilled." Her voice is dry.

The teacher doesn't say anything more, just gives a small nod and leaves.

Peter rolls his eyes. "Wouldn't like to be in the pregnant girl's shoes right now." He mimes a gun by his own head. "And, seriously, if it's a guy here who's got a girl up the duff, he should've been more careful. Plenty of girls out in town you can hook up with."

The academy has a zero tolerance for pregnancy, and, amazingly, the exclusion rule applies to both the girls who get pregnant and the boys who impregnate them. Two years ago, there was a pregnancy in the school, and the girl in question—a rich dancer named Fran—wouldn't confirm who the father was, leaving the staff certain he was a danseur here. She was excluded immediately, and when his identity became known, he was also asked to leave.

The chatter of the room turns away from Teddy and toward this new gossip, but I can't concentrate on it. All I can do is focus on my phone and pray Teddy will reply, so he can prove me wrong. Prove the bad feeling in my gut wrong.

Because something serious can't have happened to him, can it?

THREE

Jaidev

"I do not care." Avril says the words with so much venom and ferocity that I actually recoil. Look at me, a grown man scared of the woman who adopted him and raised him for the last fourteen years.

But Avril *can* be scary. Hell, everyone here says it. Madame Troisière is *formidable* and *angry* and a lot of worse words that the others use. Only I don't normally see this side. Even last year, after the.... Well, even after *that*, when I told her I wouldn't be joining the Paris Ballet Company but instead would be enrolling on the school's training course to become a ballet teacher—to teach kids' courses, as then I wouldn't even need the higher qualifications—she wasn't angry like this. No, then she was amused, and then she was insistent that I was in shock because I clearly hadn't thought it through. And she was right, as it happened—why would they let someone with a criminal record work with children? I ended up just staying at her school, doing another year of general training and studying dance-teaching in my own time, but with no goal to strive toward. But the point was Avril wasn't even angry then, and that was a way more stressful time, what with the cops constantly around.

So, I thought the sharing of my decision today would go smoothly. Easily.

But I guess there's only so far you can test any human. Even if she is your adoptive mother.

I lean back in my seat. The fabric is too soft. Hell, everything in this room is too soft. Avril and I have vastly different decor tastes. Her whole office is furnished with feathers and felts and fluffy wall tapestries.

"You are really going to waste all this training? All this money?" She shakes her head, then mutters something in French. She still thinks I don't know French swear words, which is kind of amusing since I moved here with my grandmother when I was five. I learnt French swear words at the same time my French peers at school did. But Avril made sure that I kept speaking Vietnamese, paid for classes for me, and encouraged me to read Vietnamese literature; a lot of the time, I'm sure she expects me *only* to swear in Vietnamese.

She narrows her eyes on me and gesticulates wildly. "And what will it look like to the other companies, if my own son decides he does not want to dance at all anymore?"

"Look, I've thought about it long and hard." I lift my head, making eye contact with her across the desk. Maintaining good posture is important to her, even in arguments. Don't want to give her another reason to complain.

"No, you have not. You are rushing into this. You are just scared."

"I'm not scared. I just don't want to be a dancer."

Well, that's a lie. It's not that I don't want to dance. It's that I can't be a dancer anymore, not *now*. It's too painful. And I definitely can't be a dancer or even a teacher here, in this school, even over a year later, because there are too many memories.

Memories of *her*.

I've tried, really tried, but I can't do this to myself anymore. But when I was poring over notes on didactics and different dance styles, I felt like I was breaking. Not just because I wanted to be in the studio, improving my own dance with a solid goal to aim for, but because I was still at this school, expecting to see *her* every time I looked up from my books or stepped into a studio. I need a clean break, even if everyone else will think I'm the least deserving of it.

I breathe deeply. "You always pushed me into this way of life. Into dance."

"You loved it." Avril is quick to counteract, as always.

"You never gave me another choice. I want to find out who I am." I clench my hands together. "I need to do this." Maybe I'll even go back to Vietnam. Find my roots, again, however much of a cliché that sounds.

"What you need is to stay here," Avril says. "Don't let the rumors get to you."

"I'm not." I'm not even sure what rumors she's talking about—as far as I knew, those eventually stopped a few months ago, but I guess fires are easy to relight.

"Good, because they'll die down again soon," she says.

Great. Just what I want to hear. I shift my weight in the chair, then straighten my spine. "I don't want to dance anymore. I'm sorry, Avril, but I'm nineteen. You cannot make me stay here against my will."

"Against your will?" She snort-laughs, then fiddles with the silver necklace at her neck. The catch is faulty and the number of times she's nearly lost it is ridiculous.

She's still not taking me seriously, that much is clear, and it annoys me. It's always been like this, I suppose. Avril getting her own way regarding anything to do with me. The only difference before was we were on the same page. She fought on my behalf, got me roles I never thought imaginable, got me a place at her school only a couple years after she became my guardian when she discovered I loved dance, even though I hadn't been up to the standard of the others there. I'd never dared or wanted to go a different route before. I'd assumed that defying Avril was a path just meant for Bastien. Not me.

"You need to think carefully about this, Jaidev. You need to understand everything I've done for you, how I've dedicated the last thirteen years to your career and how—"

The telephone on her desk rings. It's red and retro, and I've never heard it ring before. Thought it was just a model.

Avril answers it while keeping her sharp eyes on me. "Yes, Cherie, send him in."

No more than a second later, the door to Avril's office opens and Mr. Maxim enters. He's one of the board members and wears duster jackets that look overly long, even for him with his six-foot-five frame.

"Avril, there's been a, uh, development. I've got Madame Cachelle from Roseheart Academy on video-link in the main gallery." His eyes cross to me, and I get the sense he's really boring deep into me. Mr. Maxim is always like that. Creepy. "You'd better come quickly."

"I am in the middle of something with my son," Avril says, shooting him a dagger look. I hear the annoyance in her voice—not just at being interrupted, but also that he called her 'Avril.' She hates anyone at the school using her first name, even Mr. Maxim. She should always be *Madame Troisière*. That's what I call her at the school, and sometimes it's easier to call her that in private too. She refers to me as her son, though she's never told me she wants me to call her 'Mum'. I know she doesn't want to put that kind of pressure on me, and she's also scared about seeming like she's trying to replace my own mother.

"This is *about* your son."

I go cold. The last time there were calls about me I was...

I close my eyes, determined not to think about that time with the police calls and flashing lights and...and *her*. Lying broken.

I didn't mean to do it.

"Jaidev, we are not finished," Avril says, and she sweeps her way out of the room, her long skirt swishing behind her.

I stay seated where I am. I know better than to assume this means I've been dismissed.

My phone buzzes. *Want a joint? Got one spare.*

It's Bastien, my mother's son. I should clarify, he's her biological son. The Troisières adopted me when I was six. I was already living in France, as at the age of five, I'd been orphaned by a car crash that killed both my parents when we lived in Hanoi. My bà ngoại—my grandmother—had, at the time, been in the process of moving from Vietnam to Paris, due to the recent death of her husband—my ông ngoại whose name I share. She'd wanted a fresh start, even more so after she lost her daughter and son-in-law too, and with my parents gone and she being my only living grandparent, she took me with her. For that year, before Bà Ngoại passed away, we'd lived in Marseilles. Not exactly the place she'd wanted to be, but we were happy, and she came to love the French port and the sea.

For a long time after my adoption, Bastien didn't seem to like me as I turned out to be the ballet dancer that Avril wanted her biological son to be. But when he realized that my dancing took the focus off him—and stopped Avril pushing him into a ballet career too—he softened to me. Now we're sort of friends.

If him asking if I want a joint is what friends do.

Bastien has a drug problem. It's the elephant in the room that none of us ever talks about. Avril's tried to silently sort it, sending Bastien to three different rehab programs in two years, after she found it wasn't just weed he was using but heroin too. But as far as I know, that's the extent of her support. I've never even actually heard her say anything aloud about Bastien's illness. I only found out she was funding the rehab when he told me it with a shrug and a strangely wistful, "Maybe she still cares about me after all."

No, I'm good, thanks, I reply to his text. I still find it weird he offers me drugs, given he doesn't want Avril to know he's no longer clean. I could easily rat him out, but I owe him. When things were difficult, two years ago, after the incident, Bastien was there for me. Of course, Avril was there too. But she wasn't the one who stopped the death threats. That was Bastien.

You sure? His reply is instant. *I'm in the neighborhood*, he adds.

Neighborhood. It sounds so American. When Bastien left Avril's ballet school aged eleven, she paid for him to attend some prestigious school in California. He may have spent five years there and been back in France for just five years since then, but he now speaks both French and English with a bad American accent. I'm sure he puts it on. It annoys Avril.

I shove my phone in my pocket and look around Avril's office, trying not to think about what she and Mr. Maxim and a ballet teacher from that English school could possibly be talking about regarding me. Is it those rumors Avril mentioned?

My stomach feels too heavy, uneasy. It always does when I think of that sort of thing. I stand up and pace a little. Need to distract myself.

I examine the photos on Avril's walls. Most of them are of me. Me, in lead roles in *Black Swan* and *Giselle* and *Sleeping Beauty*.

I wait several more minutes. Avril doesn't return, but it's getting hot in here. I adjust my collar. I am dressed smartly. A suit. I thought Avril would take me more seriously in this attire when I came to break the news to her.

The gallery isn't far, and after a while, curiosity starts to get the better of me. I could just head over there, see if I can hear anything…

Opening the door and listening carefully for sounds in the corridor makes me feel like I'm being sneaky. But the hallway's silent.

I tiptoe out. My new leather shoes squeak a little. I walk slowly and carefully to the end of the corridor, then turn right. Still no sight of anyone—but voices! I can hear voices, Mr. Maxim's droll tones, and Avril's voice too. She sounds excited.

I speed up and reach the door to the video-link room. It's shut.

I press my ear to the door.

"Jaidev will do it," Avril says. "*Of course* he will. He would not be stupid enough to pass up this opportunity."

Do what? Huh. The hell I will—whatever it is!

I grit my teeth and shake my head. No. I've had enough of her controlling me. This is my life, and from now on, I'm going to be in charge of it.

FOUR

Teddy

I am floating. Floating through water. I am weightless, like how I've always wanted to be when I'm dancing. Because I have no body now, and it's a relief. It's just me. Just me…

Theodore!

The water's warm, and there's a part of my brain trying to tell me I'm swimming, even though I'm not. I'm dancing. Pirouetting now, in blue lights and memories and twisting time.

Theodore!

There it is again. I frown. That word.

No, not a word, a name.

My name.

And suddenly the name has a shape. It is a paper airplane coming toward me, cutting the water cleanly into two sections until I'm in the gap between two giant walls of water.

"The anesthetic is still wearing off," a voice says. "It'll be a while until Theodore can communicate with you as normal. He may be able to hear you though."

"But he will be able to?"

"Yes, hearing is one of the first things to return."

"No. I mean communicate as normal. Once he's fully awake."

There's a pause, and I realize they're talking about me. Even if I'm not sure who they are. Or if they're actually here. Or where I am, because it's like everything's floating and moving.

"Sorry, that was poor use of…" The voice trials away, and I'm unsure if the man's stopped speaking or if the words are just floating in a different direction. But then he's back, speaking stronger. His voice has an almost strident tone to it that grates against my ear canals. "As my colleague said earlier, the CT scan showed no serious brain injury, but we won't know the extent of Teddy's concussion, until he is awake. Then he'll be able to give us more of an idea and we can do further assessments. The swelling from the nasal manipulation should also reduce soon—we were lucky that we were able to do that before the usual swelling from that injury occurred. Normally we have to wait several days… And his cardiologist will be in touch soon too with the…"

The words drift off again, but I've heard enough. Just those two dreaded words: *brain injury.*

Sudden awareness pours over me. It's cold. Cold wherever I am because my skin is goosepimpling and I am *cold*. But I can *feel*. I have a body. A body that isn't wet, that hasn't just been floating and dancing through a beautiful ocean.

A body that's lying down. Something firm beneath my spine.

A hospital—suddenly, I can smell it. Too clean and artificial. Antiseptic.

"But…but he's my boy," the other voice says.

Dad.

It's Dad. My heart speeds up—and it's a weird sensation suddenly knowing both that you have a heart and that it's speeding up. But my dad is here. The man I haven't seen in…in ages. I don't know how long. Can't think. But where's Mum?

Dead.

The word bites me.

My eyes open, and it's strange because it's like it just happens. Like I'm not in control of it. Of anything. I can't be. Not in a world where my mum's not here and—

Bright lights. Wires. Machines. Screens. Faces.

I'm processing everything, but slowly. There's a lag. I'm aware there's a lag. And my heart…my chest feels heavy. And my face…my nose. Something's not right with my nose.

"Theodore? Oh, Theodore, boy! It's okay."

The man to my right looks both like my dad and not. His face is too lined and his hair too gray. He presses cool fingers to my forehead, and then the other man—one with a pale face and a navy-blue uniform—is speaking to me in slow and careful words, telling me that I'm in hospital, that there was an accident.

But I don't want to listen.

I don't want to hear. I don't want those words to be funneled into my ears because they can't reach my brain.

Because if they do, they'll burrow in too deeply into the pink fleshy textures and grow roots. They'll become permanent, and it'll cement what I can feel.

That whatever has happened is bad.

That I won't dance again.

That I'll never dance with Taryn again.

Taryn. My heart squeezes. Taryn with her cautious personality in everyday life, but who transforms into an ethereal being when she dances. Whose soul wraps around mine because we recognize each other and we're the same. The best of friends. Partners.

The doctor clears his throat. "You've suffered extensive—"

"No," I shout, and my volume surprises me. Is that because something is wrong with my head?

I think my voice surprises everyone though, because my dad and the doctor step back. Through the window at the end of the room I see staff looking. All at me.

I think I liked it better when I didn't have a body.

"I don't want to know about a head injury. Head injuries mean I can't dance." My words taste strange.

"Theodore, we will of course be doing more tests. It was quite a bang on the head that you took, and we have also managed to fix up your nose, but those are not the main concerns," the doctor says.

Not the main concerns?

"Ah, there she is." The doctor points to my right.

A Black woman has entered the ward, and she marches straight over.

"Theodore Walker?" she asks, her voice chipper.

"It's Teddy." I try to sit up a bit, but there are wires all over me and sticky things on my chest. Dad tries to stop me, a hand on my shoulder, but I push him away.

"You're Dad, I assume?" The woman looks at him, and Dad nods. "Excellent." She pulls the curtain around my bed, sectioning us, her, and the man in the navy-blue uniform off from the rest of the ward, from the rest of the world.

The man has a clipboard now, and I'm not sure where it came from.

"I am Dr Reimbert," the woman says. "Consultant emergency cardiologist here."

Cardiologist. That's…that's serious. My stomach does a loop-the-loop motion, and I stare down at the wires attached to my chest with sticky pads and tape. Suddenly, I'm aware of a monitor bleeping away. It's right next to my bed.

"So, Teddy, we've got results back from the ECG and the heart echo we did. We did the echo when you were still very woozy from the concussion because the ECG showed abnormalities. You might not remember any of this as you were taken through for the general anesthetic after to have your nose sorted out."

I don't. There's…nothing but water and oceans in my memory, and I know that can't be real.

Dr Reimbert leans forward. "Tell me, do you have a history of shortness of breath, chest pain, or dizziness?"

I shake my head. "No. I'm a dancer." The only times I get dizzy are when I'm pushing myself too hard, when I've been in the studio for hours before breakfast. Then, I get dizzy. But that's just normal.

Dr. Reimbert nods and then leans even closer, so I can see clumps of mascara on her eyelashes. "Any arrhythmias you're aware of in daily life? That's abnormal heart rhythms. Faster or slower? Jumpy?"

I stare at her. "No… I mean, my heart speeds up when I dance, but that's normal. Right?"

"Teddy, I have concerns. I want to book further scans for you, and I want you to see a specialist consultant. I've also requested an MRI at this point, so we should get a time through soon for you. But the results we've had so far show a thickening of the heart. And I'll tell you what I suspect: there is a condition called Hypertrophic Cardiomyopathy. It can cause symptoms, but equally it can go undetected—until there's a serious problem. It's rare, but many of the people who end up diagnosed with it in adulthood have no symptoms until a major event. HCM causes problems with the electrical system of the heart. We believe it could be the cause of your earlier blackout today."

"Blackout?"

"Well, some of your teachers reckon you tripped and that's why you hit your head, but it's possible that it was a blackout. That you were unconscious *before* you hit your head, and the blackout was what made you actually fall."

I frown. I can't remember… I was waiting backstage… The final show. And then there's nothing but water. Oh, lord.

What happened? Did I mess it up for everyone? Or maybe we finished the show and…

"What?" Dad splutters. "A heart condition? He can't have a *heart condition.* He's a professional dancer."

The words, from Dad's mouth, any other time would've been a blessing. Dad's never seen my dance as anything professional. Just girly. Hearing his words now is strange because there's pride in his voice. Pride and fear.

I know what's coming. Even before Dr Reimbert opens her mouth again, I *know.*

"I'm afraid it's very likely that Teddy's dancing days are over."

"But you're not sure that it *is* this heart condition," Dad says.

Dr. Reimbert tilts her head to one side. "We know there is an abnormal thickening of the heart, Mr. Walker. We also know Teddy may have had a blackout. A specialist cardiologist will know more, but I can tell you a lot of people with HCM don't get diagnosed until they're in their late teens or twenties, as they don't get symptoms until there's an obstruction or cardiac event. And a lot of those who get diagnosed after a sudden collapse or cardiac event *are* young athletes because an exercise-heavy lifestyle puts too much strain on a HCM heart."

"What, so everyone with this condition finds out like this?" Dad says. "This is absurd!"

"Not everyone," she says. "It is genetic and when we diagnose an individual, we like to test family members too. That's most often how young children are diagnosed with this condition. But we know there are people out there undiagnosed. And, Teddy, initial tests are indicating this as a diagnosis. We will know more after further tests. We will have the MRI, as I already said, and I'll refer you for genetic testing too. We are especially concerned about your heart's left ventricle chamber, and I'm going to speak to a senior cardiologist at a different hospital who specializes in HCM, but I'm going to suggest we go for diagnostic catheterization if that's okay with you?"

I stare at her. Suddenly, everything is too loud in here. The buzz of machinery. Nurses' voices beyond the blue curtain. Dad's breathing.

"What's diagnostic catheterization?" Dad asks.

"It's a procedure we use to look at how well the heart is working," Dr Reimbert says. "It isn't required for a diagnosis of HCM, but we are concerned about the flow of blood through the left ventricle, so this will give us more information on how much obstruction there is, and we can also gather other data as well."

Obstruction?

"I... No," I whisper. "I can't have this. I have to be a dancer."

Taryn's face fills my mind.

Dr. Reimbert shakes her head. "Teddy, I have strong suspicions that you do have HCM and dancing again, at such a high level as I'm assured you dance at, could very well kill you."

FIVE

Taryn

An hour later, everyone seems to have decided the pregnant girl is one of the blond twins in year nine because those two are always going out with guys who look way too old for them—like, seriously, these men even wait at the school's gates for them, and it's a bit creepy, men in their twenties waiting for their teenage girlfriends to get out of school.

"I can't believe the board hasn't done anything about that yet," Ivelisse says with a yawn. "It's creepy."

"What can they do though?" Xavier asks. "Those guys look scary. And even though the school gives us the code of conduct and we have to sign the rules and stuff, they can't actually tell us what we can do in our spare time, only say what will happen if pregnancy happens."

"Yeah, but if they're underage," Freya says. "And year nine is what? Fourteen? Fifteen? God, I can never remember now. Seems like so long ago. But they should do something."

"Yeah. It's illegal," Sibylle says.

Several of us nod in agreement, and I check my phone again. Still nothing from Teddy.

"It's so unfair though that this girl's going to lose her opportunity here," I say. And "And the guy too, if he's a student here." Because it's not just a 'have the baby and come back later' kind of deal. It's a 'you're pregnant and you leave us forever' deal.

Sibylle's frowning deeply and looks like she's about to say something, but the lounge door creaks open. It's Rainie, Madame's assistant. She looks around for a moment, then her eyes fall on me. She beckons for me to get up. I do and cross the room.

"They want to see you in the boardroom," she says, her voice low.

They? I frown, but Rainie doesn't say anything more.

I feel everyone's eyes on me as I leave the lounge and follow Rainie. My heart hammers all the way.

The door to the boardroom is open, and Madame is just a foot or so inside. "Ah, there you are. Come in."

At the board's table, the other ballet teachers are there along with Mr. Aleks, Miss Tavi, Mr. Vikas, and the management team for the company. I know most of them by face, but there are a couple of people I do not recognize. I bow my head to them all.

"Please, sit down," Mr. Vikas says.

I sit.

"Taryn, my gem, we have received word from the hospital," Madame says, and then she pauses, and my head is pounding and my heart is squeezing as I wait for her to say something. But the pause goes on and on—who the hell pauses this long?—and I start to wonder if that rat was right. Have they called me in to tell me that Teddy is dead?

A lump forms in my throat, and I try to swallow it, but saliva goes down the wrong way, and I choke. My eyes stream, and I'm spluttering as one of the women I don't know rises and gets me a glass of water—seemingly out of nowhere.

I gulp it back, and it makes me nauseous. Oh God, I don't want them to say the words.

"I'm afraid Teddy has sustained a severe concussion and a broken nose—which he's just had surgery for. But initial scans have also indicated a previously unidentified, serious heart condition." Madame's voice is sincere.

A serious heart condition? I gulp again—because that seems to be about all I can do now—and stare at her, stare at them all. Visions of Teddy strapped up to heart monitors and beeping machines that write spiky graphs on crinkly paper fill me. They're so at odds with my other visions of Teddy—his lean, muscular body, how he can lift me with no problem, how he goes to the gym seven days a week, how health conscious he is—it just doesn't seem right. Or real. How can Teddy of all people have a heart condition?

"Is he…is he going to be okay?" My voice is barely audible. I am shaking. I mean, the heart's pretty important. But isn't dance supposed to reduce your chance of heart problems? Still, maybe that advice assumes that the dance is moderate. What we do isn't moderate. It is intense. It's our lives. It's always been our lives.

"He is in a stable condition at the present time," Mr. Vikas says. "We believe there is however a question of whether it will be safe for him to dance again at any level, let alone ours, given the high impact nature of ballet."

"And we have no doubt, Miss Foster," Miss Tavi says, her doleful eyes on me, "that you would've won the place on the tour with our company, should it not have been for Mr. Walker's accident. We have had our eyes on you for a long time. As you know, you're the strongest female dancer in the graduating year. We have two spots available, and as you also know, the two who join must be partners. Mr. Walker is not going to heal in time, if at all. And you and Mr. Walker are partners."

I frown. "Well, I already know I can't join as a solo dancer." Unless they're going to make an exception. Because Roseheart is the only company I know of that doesn't accept solo dancers.

"That is also correct," Miss Tavi says.

Next to me, Madame clasps her hands together. Her silver rings flash under the harsh neon light-strips.

I frown. Have they brought me in here just to rub it in? They could've easily just updated me on Teddy's condition outside the lounge. They didn't need to have the whole board watching my reaction and witnessing my disappointment over my own future.

Miss Tavi clears her throat. "We have two months of training before this year's fall tour starts, and we have to decide *today* which of the graduates will join us—we always decide on the evening of the grand ballet so we have adequate time to train our new dancers for the tour. And this is where we have a problem. We want you, Miss Foster, and Mr. Walker was by far the strongest of our male dancers. We have discussed it at length, and even the next best would not be a suitable companion for your ability."

I don't break eye contact with Miss Tavi, just wait for her to continue. Because she has to be about to say something, something important. Else why bring me in here at all?

"There is one option. The Paris Ballet School."

My heart sinks. A position there as a soloist? "Thank you, but I'd rather —"

"Let me finish." Miss Tavi's voice is clipped. "The Paris Ballet School has a dancer who is of exceptional quality. Mr. Ngo graduated a year ago, but then when he was about to audition for a company, he surprised everyone and switched to a teacher-training course instead, so he never entered any company, though he never completed the teacher-training either. Madame Troisière tells me that he has now changed his mind again and wishes again to dance professionally. And he has no female partner."

My head spins. "So, I could partner with him?" I ask, breathless. A dancer joining the Roseheart Company who wasn't trained at our academy is unheard of—but is this one tradition they are willing to break? It has to be, if they're telling me about it. And the Paris Ballet School has a good reputation. Several of the ballet teachers here either did some training there or were in their company before they turned to teaching. "Yes, I'll do it, definitely."

I know I shouldn't be so eager. I don't even know who this dancer is. I've no idea if we'll complement each other, because some dancers just don't. And the Paris Ballet School follows the French ballet style—different to the English. I mean, he'll be able to adapt, I'm sure—Alma was classically trained at a French school for two years after she moved from Germany, and she had to take classes at Roseheart for a whole year before she could start the diploma here, to really get used to the English style. The difference isn't as big as some of the other ballet styles—Vaganova and the Royal Academy of Dance probably have the biggest style difference. But trying to do all this *and* dance well together in time for the fall tour, well, that's almost a ridiculous goal. But if this is the only chance? And Mr. Ngo has to be better than the other male graduates here, for the company to suggest it.

"We will run the lead up to the fall tour a little differently this time," Miss Tavi says. "While, usually, we'd have welcomed our chosen graduates to the company by now and have contracts signed, we will take both you and Mr. Ngo on immediately but on a more temporary basis."

Temporary? My heart pounds. But this is better than nothing.

"You will train together for the tour. And with the rest of the company dancers. The fall tour is *A Midsummer Night's Dream*, and the two of you will do a pas de deux for it and also be background dancers within at least two other scenes. You have eight weeks to work together on this and learn how to be partners. At the end of the eight weeks, if we are happy that you together uphold our standards in a final assessment on August 26th, we will officially welcome you to Roseheart and you will join us formally and have contracts issued—I'm told, Miss Foster, that your eighteenth birthday isn't until the end of August, so you'd still need a guardian's signature on it, too, for those few days."

I nod.

"Then that would give us a week between permanent contracts being issued and the tour starting."

"But if the two of you do not pass the final assessment," Madame says, "you will both return here. You will have another year to work together, and with the next year of graduating dancers, you will perform in the Grand Show, competing for acceptance into Roseheart's Company."

They're looking at me. Everyone is looking at me. "Oh, right. So, the understudies aren't being selected?" I don't know why I'm saying this, like I'm trying to put the idea in their minds.

"Understudies are chosen if the lead couple do not perform adequately in the final show, or if one of the leads chooses not to accept the contract with us, and if we are satisfied with the understudies' performance quality," Mr. Vikas says. "But you performed well, Miss Foster, and Mr. Walker's performance was out of his control. We want you. You are a better dancer than your understudy, and we believe that you may still be a better dancer with Mr. Ngo than the pair of understudies are. You're quite talented, Miss Foster, and we are willing to give you this chance."

Miss Tavi looks at me. "Do you accept it?"

I can hardly breathe. "Yeah, of course. I'll do it. We will do it." Me and this Mr. Ngo, whoever he is.

Tight-lipped smiles are exchanged. Maybe it's not just the dancers who can't smile properly.

"There is one small matter to address, Miss Foster," Mr. Aleks says, speaking for the first time. His voice is light and fluttery. "I need your assurance that should you and Mr. Ngo not make it to the tour this year, that you will indeed do another year's training here. Which includes another year's fees. We have heard from Madame Troisière that Mr. Ngo has confirmed he will do this, as his intention is to dance in our company. We want him and we want you. If not this year, then next. We cannot have you two dancing for eight weeks together, if you're then not going to return to the school for the next year. It simply wouldn't be fair on Mr. Ngo, expecting him to get used to yet another dance partner, and you are matched to his ability whereas the other girls are not. So, in that case, we'd admit you next year *alongside* the top duo of next year's third years."

Two couples being admitted in one year. Wow. They must really want me. They're giving me this chance now, and if Mr. Ngo and I don't manage it, we also have a chance next year. I daren't ask what would happen should we fail next year.

I can't even think of that possibility.

"Of course," I say. "I agree. Yes."

"You'll have no issues paying the fees?" Madame's eyebrows are raised. She knows how I struggled to get the funding for this year in time.

"We need your word, Miss Foster, that you can pay the fees for an extra year—because in all likelihood that is how long it'll take you and Mr. Ngo to dance fluently together. The eight-week thing is a last chance because the company wants you for their *Midsummer* tour. But it's not a guarantee."

"Of course not. I can pay for next year." Another year here? My heart pounds. It won't come to that. It won't. Somehow, I'll get in. I have to. I'll get onto the fall tour, and then I also won't have lied to my mum either.

"Excellent!" Mr. Vikas says, clasping his hands together. "In that case, meet me outside Studio 4 tomorrow at 1pm. We'll do a Saturday session. It will be your first practice with Mr. Ngo. He will be arriving at the airport shortly before then, but Madame Troisière assures me he'll be ready for training upon immediate arrival at Roseheart."

SIX

Taryn

I know tomorrow's a big day. A last chance kind of thing. That I should be resting and trying to sleep. I need to do well tomorrow in my first dance with this Mr. Ngo, whoever he is, but instead of resting and allowing my body to recuperate, I scroll through article after article on my phone about apparently healthy people suddenly dying from cardiac arrest with no warning. Because a serious heart condition, like what Madame was saying, surely has to mean that's a possibility. Teddy could've *died*.

The blue light of my phone's screen sends a hazy aura over the whole of the dorm room, but neither Sibylle nor Ivelisse says anything. I know they're awake though. Ivelisse is doing push-ups and scrunches that she promises her doctors she's not still doing, and Sibylle's listening to heavy metal on her earphones—loud enough that I can tell it's Slipknot. And I'm learning the statistics, the terrifying numbers of just how many people die. I tell myself that me doing all this research means I do care, that I'm not selfish. Then I wonder if it doesn't matter because if I'm only doing this research so I don't feel selfish then my intentions aren't genuine.

At two forty-five, Ivelisse gets into bed. Sibylle's still awake, now reading from her kindle—which I suspect is a distraction because she must be upset about the company's decision to give me a second chance, meaning her chance of joining Roseheart is over, as I thought it was only fair to tell her as gently as possible once I knew. Though shortly after I'd told her, Madame announced that all the third years had officially graduated despite the circumstances. Everyone had cheered then and begun applying for auditions with other companies. As Roseheart students, we're allowed to stay here until the end of August, and most choose to do this because daily training is important for any professional ballet dancer, regardless of the company you're in. The ideal set-up is to have a seamless transfer to another company between graduation and your last day at Roseheart. Then your training isn't compromised at all.

My eyes are growing heavier and heavier though, and I'm just falling asleep when my phone vibrates, jolting me from that strange half-awake state. It takes a moment for my eyes to focus and read the WhatsApp notification. A message, from Teddy.

You okay?

Oh my God. *He's* the one in hospital and he's asking *me* that?

I sit up, the mattress creaking, and type furiously, demanding to know how he is and what's happening. *They've barely told me anything*, I add. Maybe he wouldn't have wanted Madame saying anything. He might want to be the one to tell me.

I hold my breath as I wait. He's typing.

They think it's hypertrophic cardiomyopathy. But they need to do more tests.

I immediately Google what hypertrophic cardiomyopathy is and feel the dread in the pit of my stomach get heavier and heavier. It's surprisingly close to what I'd already been reading about.

But you're okay? Right? I ask.

Yes. But I'm sorry, T. You've lost out on a place because of me.

Hey! It's not your fault. You've got nothing to apologize for. The important thing is that you're okay. Honestly, Teds.

And I tell him about the second chance I've got, typing so quickly I almost mistype every single word.

I wait for his reply.

The app tells me Teddy has seen it. He doesn't reply. And I don't know what that means.

SEVEN

Jaidev

A loud rapping on my door wakes me, and I've only opened my eyes for two seconds before a figure storms in.

"Hey, you can't do that!" I rub my eyes, then sit up straighter. "Avril!"

"I told you, Jaidev! I told you to be ready." She waggles her finger at me. "I expressly told you to meet me in the foyer at eight. Did I not? And is it not five past eight now?" She makes a high-pitched noise at the back of her throat—something she only does when she's really annoyed. "We are leaving for the airport and—"

"And I told you I'm not doing it. I'm not dancing again." I glare at her. "Can you get out of my room now? You've no right to do this."

"We are going! I am not having my students—my own son—look fickle and unprofessional in the eyes of Madame Cachelle. I am sure some of Roseheart's teachers think our school produces sub-par dancers compared to theirs, but you have the chance to redeem us because they know you are good, and you will speak well of our training there."

So that's what this is about. Avril's school. Her reputation. Not me. I fold my arms. "But I'm not doing it. I told you, I'm not dancing."

We had a whole huge argument about it last night, right after Mr. Maxim opened the door of the video-link room and I practically tumbled over the threshold, having been listening a little too intently. I was fuming and I told Avril then—told all of them—that there was no way I was doing it. In fact, I told them I was moving out. Today.

Avril had laughed when I told her I'd be staying with Bastien. Laughed like it was the funniest joke in all the world.

Now, she is not laughing. "Just get ready."

"No."

Avril sighs. "This is stupid. It's not like anything big has *just* happened. Those rumors are nothing. So why don't you tell me what this is really about?"

"What it's really about?" I stare at her. "Why isn't it enough when I say that I just don't want to dance? That maybe I'm not supposed to be a dancer, despite what you think."

I pull the duvet around me. There's no way I'm telling her the nightmares have started again or that my therapist—whom she doesn't know I have—thinks it's because I'm still trapped in these walls. How can I ever expect to be free of the past when I'm not allowing myself to move on? I need a break—not just a break from this place but from dance altogether. Because I know what will happen if I'm dancing with this new girl. I'll be remembering, I'll be thinking it's *her*. My flashbacks will restart, not just the nightmares.

I need a clean break. And living in Bastien's trailer with him does sound more appealing than I ever thought it would.

Avril sits on the edge of my bed. "I want what is best for you, and I know this is an opportunity that you need."

"Just stop, okay." I hold my hands up. "You can't make me be a dancer anymore. I don't want to be and the more you go on, the more determined I will get not to do this."

She presses her lips together in such a fine line that her meticulously applied lipstick all but disappears. "Very well." She rises from my bed. "Very well."

She leaves and it's…. it's weird.

I frown. I can't have just won. Not after the argument, the screaming, last night. It would never be this easy.

But she has gone. Left. So, I'm not going to the airport. Not getting on the plane. I won't have to dance with a new girl. I will get away. I really will. A grin spreads across my face, and I grab my phone to text Bastien, to tell him the plan we came up with late last night is really on. We are really doing this. I've escaped. I'm going to be free.

Something silver catches my eyes. Avril's necklace on my bed. Must've fallen off. It's always doing that because she won't get the clasp fixed. Doesn't want anyone else touching it.

It's the last thing her husband gave her before he died. Avril will be distraught if she thinks she's lost it.

Swallowing my pride, I scoop up the necklace and open my door. I call after her, but it's silent. She must've gone already. I grab my dressing gown and run down the corridor, then out to the foyer where the housekeeper's desk is.

"Which way did Avril go?" I ask Lani.

Lani, the housekeeper, points straight ahead, through the big double doors. I race forward and see my mother. The accommodation block is on the edge of the school grounds, right by the road.

I throw the doors open and rush out.

"Avril!" I shout, holding the necklace up.

She's by the road, starting to cross it as she looks back. Her eyes widen and—

A blast of sound—a horn. A red car and—

I scream, feeling everything inside my body contort as the car hits Avril.

EIGHT

Taryn

I get some sleep before my alarm goes off at 7.30, but I'm not rested. My dreams were filled with Helena, my brain imagining what she'd look like now, if the bad things hadn't happened.

If I hadn't caused the bad things.

No. I swallow hard. I didn't cause it. Not like how some people think, anyway. Adelaide James wrote articles on me, painting me as a murderer. *The deadly ballerina. Who will be her next victim?* But none of that was true. Yet I still feel guilty. Because I feel like I did cause it, on some level. Just not in the intentional and direct way that Adelaide James made out that I did.

I'm sorry, I want to say to Helena. *But I promise I'm doing all I can, living for the both of us.*

I like to think she's not angry, looking down at me. That she knows it was an accident, but I can never shake the feeling that she *is* watching me, making sure I'm doing everything right, now.

"You coming?" Sibylle asks. "To breakfast?"

I nod and plaster a smile on my face. Barring one time when I apparently whispered her name in my sleep—most likely during a nightmare—I don't talk about Helena. Of course, after that night, Sibylle asked me who she was, but I shrugged and said I didn't know. I can't have anyone asking questions. She's my secret—my guilt—and she has to stay that way.

Ivelisse has already left the dorm, so it's just me and Sibylle heading downstairs. Alma is at the canteen, eating a fruit salad very slowly and carefully with a spoon. Sibylle and I join her, and I grab some toast. They ask me if I've heard from Teddy, and I update them. But there's a twisting feeling in my gut as I check my phone again. He still hasn't responded to my message about my new partner.

"He'll be jealous," Sibylle says with a shrug. "I mean, he's a man, right?"

"Jealous?" I laugh. "Teddy definitely wouldn't be jealous."

"Yeah, you're not even together, right?" Alma asks, waving a chunk of apple at me. "Or have you been hooking up secretly?" Her eyes suddenly glisten. "Wait, you're not the pregnant one, right?"

I snort. "Definitely not the pregnant one." Teddy and I have never done anything remotely romantic or sexual—beyond dancing together, that is, as Madame is always telling us how the best romantic duets are filled with romantic and sexual tension.

But the thought of me and Teddy being together in any way like that makes me uneasy. The thought of being with *anyone* makes me uneasy—even if at times I feel like I should want a relationship. Like it would make things easier. But I'm lucky Teddy is aroace, too. I can't imagine how much harder it might've been to dance with him otherwise.

Oh God. Mr. Ngo. Chances are he won't be aroace, and now I'll be dancing with him for eight weeks—no, longer. Mr. Vikas is certain we'll be accepted into the company either this fall or next summer.

"Guess it really is one of the blond twins who's pregnant then," Alma says with a shrug.

Pregnant. I don't know why but the word has always made me uncomfortable. I mean even the whole concept of pregnancy, of growing an actual human inside your own body, having life distort you into new shapes, makes me shudder. I know for a fact I never want to be pregnant. I told Teddy that once and he was surprised, saying he'd always wanted to have a family—that wanting to conceive with his partner would be a reason he'd actually have sex. He'd looked at me, like he'd expected me to say the same, but I didn't. I told him I couldn't ever imagine myself having sex, for whatever reason, because I'm sex-repulsed. It's not something I ever want to do. He then he asked me if I was maternal at all and suggested I could adopt in order to avoid having sex, like he couldn't possibly fathom that I wouldn't want kids somehow. But I told him no, that I've never felt that desire to raise children. I know I'm not the only one who doesn't want kids though—aroace or not. You read all sorts of articles online about how having a family 'completes you,' but there are always many comments from people disagreeing—whether it's because they don't want children themselves or can't have them. I know I'm not unusual in that sense, in my preference for not wanting to reproduce, but Teddy just looked at me like I was crazy then.

"Maybe you'll change your mind when you're older," he'd said, and it had annoyed me.

I mean, I know why he said it, because I know he wants children at some point, because he talks about a family in the future where babies are present, but his belief that I will inevitably change my mind really got to me. Like he thinks he understands my future better than I do. I was sure that if a guy had said what I'd said, no one would've suggested *he'd* change his mind.

Now, as we eat breakfast, Alma and Sibylle gossip about pregnancy and sex, and I just try and go along with it and pretend like I too am excited by such talk. I mean, I don't mind them talking about sex. I'm sex-favorable when it concerns others, so long as they're consenting adults, of course. I'm just repulsed as soon as the idea of sex includes me. It does get a bit difficult at times though, especially when they ask me direct questions. They know I've never had a boyfriend, but, before, I haven't really corrected them when they've alluded that maybe Teddy and I are sort-of together. It's easier to do that, to conform to societal expectations and not draw attention to yourself. Especially when you don't know how people might react. By the time breakfast is over, I'm glad.

I've not got the first practice with Mr. Ngo until this afternoon, but I want to spend my morning wisely. I'll call in at the company's choreography office to familiarize myself with the new routines I'll be performing and properly meet Evangeline, the third-division choreographer, and then I'll also get used to the company buildings with their studios. Apparently, they're much grander than what I've been dancing in thus far. I could even fit in some solo training before Mr. Ngo arrives.

The only times I've been in the company buildings until now were when I was running errands for Madame or Rai-Ann or having fittings for costumes. The company always has its own seamstress, and its current one, Allie, joined last year, replacing the elderly lady who'd been the seamstress for thirty-one years. Allie is a lot less scary. I decide to visit her first.

As I step into the main company building, I pass the company's principal dancer, Netty Florence Stone. She walks like how she dances—with flowing lines, elegance, and her head held high. She doesn't acknowledge me as I pass. Maybe she doesn't know me. Or maybe she wouldn't bother herself with someone who might not even join the company.

I reach the costumes room—a long, corridor-like room with rails and rails of clothes and rows of pointe shoes: Gaynor Minden, Bloch, Repetto, Grishko, and so many other brands. The room is divided into sections that are labeled with the names of the company dancers. I allow myself to have a little daydream about my name being on the wall—*Taryn Foster* would look good. *And it should be there*, Madame had said to me.

Then it hits me that I won't be working with Madame Cachelle anymore. Mr. Ngo and I will be working with Mr. Vikas, the third-division ballet master, and Evangeline. And maybe some other staff too. Ballet teachers and assistants. Jitters fill me, and, suddenly, I want to just turn and run back to the safety of the school, the warm embrace of Madame, and familiarity.

But I don't. This is what I wanted. Even if I thought I wouldn't be making this transition without Teddy.

At the end of the costumes department is Allie's office. I knock on the mahogany door.

"Come in."

Allie's heard about Teddy—of course she has—because the moment I step inside, she tells me what a tragedy it is that he was injured. "But at least you've still got a chance." She gives a wide smile as she wheels herself across the room. "And it's so lovely of you to want to pop in and see me first." She reaches for a box on a shelf and then sets it on her lap. It's about the size of a shoebox, and she heads toward me before opening the box.

I gasp as I see what's inside it: a gold, metal star. She offers it to me.

"No, I'm…" My voice wavers. "I'm not supposed to take it yet."

Every new graduating couple gets given two gold stars when they join the company. It's always the seamstress who gives them at Roseheart because the company acknowledges that half of the performance is in the costume, and the previous seamstress started the tradition.

"Nonsense," Allie says. "You'll make it. I know you will."

I give a small smile. Nerves are already getting the better of me; part of me just can't believe I'm here. I don't know what to say now.

"Take it, then."

I take the gold star. It's heavier than I expected. A lot heavier. And it makes me think of Helena, my twin sister. When we were little, Helena had stuck glow-in-the-dark stars all over her side of the room. She loved those stars; said they foretold the future as the both of us were going to be stars.

My throat tightens. Helena always wanted to be a dancer—and I did too, of course, but ballet was her idea first. And because we were twins, we did everything together.

Until we didn't.

"Now, I need to get your measurements. Give Amanda a holler, will you? She can help me. She should just be just out there." Allie gestures vaguely toward the costume room.

Feeling like none of this is real, I head back out and sure enough there is a woman out there. She looks at me, stony-faced.

"You better not mess up this chance." Her voice is clipped. "This has never been done before and as you and your partner will be training with professionals, it's expected that you'll both be up to our standard for the tour. If not, Mr. Vikas will not be happy. He'll have wasted all this time and money on you."

I nod and tell her how grateful I am for the opportunity. She just snorts.

Getting measured up by Amanda and Allie doesn't settle my nerves at all. I know I'm taller than most ballet dancers and I'm curvier too, but Amanda doesn't even try to hide her disdain when she writes down my size. I try not to let it get to me.

It's a relief when it's over, and I escape to explore the rest of the buildings before Mr. Ngo arrives. I find where the practice studios are and the choreography office. There's a small café tucked behind the last studio, and then there are a series of larger studios. A plaque on the wall points left for medical and right for administration. Upstairs are studios 14 to 18 and in the next building across a courtyard are four large ballrooms and the two grand theatres.

I skirt around the ballroom building and find the accommodation block for the company dancers and staff. It's set back a little way, but it looks welcoming. I cross the small grassy area and smile as I see a rose bed. I love roses, and, suddenly, I have dreams of how I'll soon be living in this block, once Mr. Ngo and I have succeeded in securing placements and jobs at the company, and my room will overlook the beautiful roses.

I push open the door of the accommodation block—and come face to face with four dancers. They're beautiful. *Of course* they are. All elegant limbs and delicate features and perfect make up. They're dressed in tracksuits, but I'm sure they've got leotards and tights and maybe legwarmers underneath. Each woman carries a pair of pointe shoes and a water bottle. They stop dead when they see me though.

"What are you doing?" the one nearest me asks. Her voice is like a tropical rainfall.

"Hi," I say, offering a smile. "I'm Taryn."

"You can't come in here," she says.

"Oh, I was just looking around," I say.

"Around?"

"Yeah, the studios. The offices. That sort of thing. I'm Taryn Foster."

The woman nearest me rolls her perfectly-eyelined eyes. "Don't make yourself at home, girl. You're not one of us yet, and I doubt you ever will be, not when you're getting a new partner now. So do yourself a favor and leave us to rehearse on the tour alone. We don't need you messing anything up. And we sure as hell don't need to be getting used to you, only for you to let us down."

My eyes smart. "Oh, I... Sorry." My voice is a pathetic squeak.

"And you need to go," another of them says. "Only company dancers are allowed in here." She makes a shooing motion with her hands and the others laugh. "And you're making us late for our *job*. Off your go."

I try to swallow the lump in my throat as I stare at them. They can't actually mean what they're saying. Only, it appears they do.

I turn away, my shoulders curling. Their laughter rings out behind me.

NINE

Jaidev

Flashing blue lights. Too many people. An antiseptic smell. Floors too smooth. Yellow cleaning signs. Doctors and nurses shouting.

Her mother, here. Scorching eyes. "No! I don't want you anywhere near my daughter."

Firm hands pushing me back. A hard chair. Sympathetic eyes from a woman who doesn't know.

My blood is boiling, ready to split my skin. Everything's moving too fast, and I'm moving too fast. My lungs scream and burn, but I've got to find her, got to see. Need to tell her how sorry I am, how I didn't mean for this to happen, how—

"Jaidev Ngo? I'm Detective Malonson. We need to ask you some questions…"

I take a deep breath. No, that's not happening now. That was in the past. But, of course, sitting here makes me think of it. It's the same. My fault.

"Want another coffee?" Bastien asks. His voice makes me jump. I'd almost forgotten he was here, dressed in scruffy, oversized clothes. His hands are shaking. He's already had three plastic-cups of the hospital's watery coffee. His eyes are bloodshot, and there are deep bags under them. He jumps up. "Yes, coffee. We need more coffee."

Bastien runs off to procure his current drug of choice—though I wouldn't be surprised if he slips outside to smoke a joint on the coffee run—leaving me to sit alone outside Avril's room. All I can think of is the flashback—and how weird it is that I'm thinking of *that* time, rather than when my parents were killed in a car crash. It makes me feel bad that when my mind wandered, it wasn't to the accident that took my parents away. Because I'm sure that's what I *should* be thinking about. Fixating on, perhaps, given the similarities. Thinking how unfair the universe is when a vehicle took away my mother and father and now another is trying to take Avril, too. But, instead, I'm focused on *that* night. When there wasn't even a vehicle involved. The only similarity was the hospital.

Still, I suppose getting arrested makes an impression on you, makes you create connections you wouldn't otherwise.

I stretch my feet out in front of my chair, lifting them off the ground for a few seconds, then check the time. Been here two hours. Two hours since I last saw Avril, when they wheeled her off to theatre. She was awake then, yelling at me to get on the plane instead. Huh, like I could do that.

Bastien arrived an hour later and immediately got into an argument with a nurse when she couldn't tell him any more about her condition. He'd been warned he'd have to leave if he didn't calm down. But he did calm down, with the help of coffee, and spent the time between taking huge gulps of the liquid speaking on his phone to Avril's sister and mother. They're both travelling over from Normandy now. Should be here by now, really.

My right left jiggles like it's got a pulse of its own as I stare at the wall. The notices seem too bright, too garish, and my eyes glaze over as the memories try to grab me.

No. This is not like this. I'm not going to get taken to the station for questioning. I'm not going to get arrested. This was an accident. It really was.

Shudders overtake my body, and I cover my face with my hands, leaning forward, my elbows on my knees. I take several deep breaths that wrack through me.

She'll be fine. She'll be fine. She'll be fine. Internally, I repeat the mantra over and over—

"Jaidev Ngo?"

I startle at the voice and look up to see a young doctor with a moustache and a sympathetic face. I nod, and then he's speaking. His voice is kind of scratchy, but I get the gist of what he's saying: I can see her.

Frantic, I look around for Bastien but he's not in sight. The doctor gestures for me to follow him, so I do, my phone clamped to my ear the whole way as I leave a voicemail for Bastien. "Avril is awake, I think. We can see her. They're taking me to her now."

A few moments later, the doctor pushes open the door to a private room. I see Avril instantly, in the bed, looking so fragile and small and different. Her skin's got a yellowish tint to it and one of her legs is in plaster and elevated. There's bruising around the right side of her face, and she's hooked up to all sorts of machines.

The doctor is talking to me, explaining about Avril's condition, but I can't really take in his words. Not just because of the shock of this, but because she's glaring at me. Proper glaring.

"What are you doing here?" She frowns. Her voice is an octave higher than usual. "Jaidev, you've missed the plane! That brilliant opportunity, and you've just thrown it away!"

"Avril… You got hit by a car." I stare at her.

Her hair's not in its usual, perfect style. Of course it's not. I feel silly for even noticing it and thinking about it. It's swept back in a loose ponytail now. There's still some dried blood across her hairline. I try not to focus on that.

"Oh, and the world stops, does it?" She tuts and actually waggles her finger at me.

"I couldn't just *go*."

"Why not? That is an amazing opportunity, and it would've elevated my school too. God, Jaidev, when will you ever realize that it's not all about you?"

The doctor laughs and says he'll leave us to it. And of course, Avril's still droning on and on. Unbelievable.

I take a seat next to her bed. "What kind of son would have just got on a plane when their mother had been hit by a car?"

"A sensible one who knew it was nothing."

"*Nothing*?" I stare at her.

"Like one car is going to send me to the grave." She snorts then winces, most likely realizing what she's said. "See, Bastien knows I'm fine," she says quickly. "He's not worrying, not here, missing out on his career. No, he's taking every opportunity to develop it, just as you should be."

I wonder what career she thinks he's developing. "Avril. Please, I—"

"Where's my phone?" she demands. "We can book another flight. I can phone Madame Cachelle and explain about this. I'll have to really reassure her that you are serious about this, that you've not changed your mind about joining a company again. Goodness, Jaidev! Why do you always have to be so difficult?"

She moves to sit up more, but she flinches. Pain flashes across her face, and then everything changes with her. It's like she just…deflates. All the tension and strength in her body drops away. She stares at her plastered leg, and it's like she's seeing the cast for the first time. I see the way her eyes widen, see the panic making itself home in them.

"I'm…" Her voice wobbles as she looks at me. "I'm not going to dance again, am I?"

I can't answer that, and she knows it, I can tell. Her bottom lip wobbles, and I reach for her hand, give her as reassuring a squeeze as possible. Ballet is everything to Avril. Everyone knows that. She's not just an amazing teacher and the head ballet mistress at her school; she was one of France's best ballerinas, having been a principal dancer at two different companies. And she still dances now—Avril's one of the most hands-on teachers at the school, demonstrating full choreographies and dancing in the Paris Ballet School's productions.

Or, rather, she was.

"No, no, no," she mutters, but her voice gets smaller with each word. Smaller and smaller, until it's gone. "I have to dance," she whispers. Her eyes are earnest and watery. "You know what I mean. You feel it. That dread when we can't dance. And I... My leg..." She dissolves into tears.

She's right. I do feel that dread. Because as much as I don't want to dance again because of what happened, part of me also feels like I'll be losing myself if I don't. Like I won't be able to breathe. Even when Bastien came up with our plan, I was still practicing various formations and moves in hidden seconds in my room. It made me feel alive, and I couldn't just stop. Because it was me being true to myself. It's what I need to do. Frustratingly, it's part of who I am.

But I look at Avril, so fragile, so broken in her hospital bed, and I can see it in her eyes: the finality of what's happened. Oh, God. To have it all taken away like this...

But at least she's done it, a voice whispers. *Because what if you never truly follow your heart now and then your chance is taken away? Accidents happen all the time.*

Regrets.

I hate regrets. And life can be short, I know that. Chances can be taken away, demolished, in the blink of an eye.

"Avril." I clear my throat. "If you really want me to dance at Roseheart, I will."

I expect her to immediately say yes. To return to her strict self. To jump at the chance of getting me to do what she wants—what *I* really want. And maybe it won't be so bad, because it would be a fresh start of sorts. A new location. A new school. A new partner who doesn't know anything about me. But Avril just nods, looking up at me with tears in her eyes.

"Do it," she whispers. "Do it for me."

TEN

Taryn

"Taryn! What are you doing in here?" Madame finds me in the common room.

I'm the only one in here, and I've been researching the ballet that the company is going to be performing: *A Midsummer Night's Dream*. After the dancers so rudely evicted me from the company buildings, I made my way straight back here, deciding I wouldn't be setting foot back there on my own without Mr. Ngo. The problem was that I bumped into Miss Tavi on the way, and she told me Mr. Ngo had been delayed—by six whole hours.

"Oh, I'm just researching things," I say to Madame now. Been doing this for a while. It's proving quite interesting, too.

I've always been fascinated by how Roseheart produces modern twists on classics. The diploma and academy productions were always so much fun, but this proposed production of *A Midsummer Night's Dream* looks spectacular. The company is using George Balanchine's choreography and Felix Mendelssohn's music from the 1962 premier of the ballet as the basis for their production, but our choreographers have tweaked a lot of things and added more scenes. There are now more pas de deux in the first act than in the original, and the second act isn't so much a classical dance wedding celebration but rather evokes many of the fantastical elements that are present in the first act in its wedding celebration, with the divertissement pas de deux incorporating stunning costumes of fairies for the two dancers.

I've no idea what part I'll be asked to dance, but the divertissement pas de deux looks amazing. Still, I know I haven't got a chance of being in that role. Not when it'll be my first time dancing for the company, and I'm only here on a temporary basis. I just hope I don't get the role of Helena in *A Midsummer Night's Dream*. I don't feel like playing a character with the same name as my dead sister. I feel haunted enough as it is. And of course, *A Midsummer Night's Dream* was my sister's favorite ballet. Reassuringly though, I know being cast as Helena is unlikely. She's one of the main characters.

Madame shakes her head. "Taryn, my gem, you're part of the company now. You need to be over there—and Mr. Ngo is about to arrive. Martyn has gone to collect him."

I check the time. I'm not too sure who Martyn is, and all of a sudden, I'm nervous about meeting Mr. Ngo too. I know he's older than me and has more experience. What if he also looks down upon me, just as the company dancers too? But I'm also curious about him. Even if he is six hours late.

We walk to the main reception of the company's administration building quickly.

"You go inside and meet him," she says to me. "I just need to check where he will be staying."

I push the door open. No one is there, and I'm relieved. I take several deep breaths, glad to be here first, then a door creaks open from the opposite side of the room.

A lithely built—but clearly very strong—Asian man with neat, short black hair enters the room. He carries a rucksack on his back, and he's dressed in jogging bottoms and a hoody. His trainers look brand new and expensive.

"Taryn?" He smiles at me, but the smile doesn't reach his eyes. He looks tired, worn out, and his eyes are pink.

I recoil. There was a scandal at the Paris Ballet school recently to do with drugs and loads of their ballet dancers needing addiction help. God, if Mr. Ngo is addicted to some substance, then dancing with me isn't going to be his main priority.

"I'm Jaidev Ngo," he says. His voice has an accent, but I'm not sure what it is. I'm hopeless at identifying accents.

"Taryn Foster." I keep my voice guarded as I study him.

He slings his rucksack onto the floor. Inside it, something clinks. "Well, it's wonderful to meet you, Taryn. I understand I'm now too late for a studio session today with you, but we are to start first thing tomorrow?"

I nod. "Yeah. Studio 12 is booked for 7 a.m."

Mr. Vikas hadn't been happy about coming in on a Sunday, but he'd said needs must.

"Perfect. Now, can you show me where to get food? I've only had two cups of coffee all day."

"Sure. We'll just wait for Madame to get back with details of where you're staying."

It's a relief when Madame returns, saving me from wracking my brain for what to talk about. Madame says Jaidev is to stay in Teddy's room. So, he's staying in the school, too, like me. It also means that taking Jaidev down to the academy's canteen is easy—I definitely don't feel like going to the café in the company block, and while I'm sure there must also be a canteen for the company that I hadn't yet found, I do not want to risk bumping into any of those company dancers again. Guess I really will just have to prove my skills to them to get them to like me.

Jaidev grabs his rucksack and swings it onto his back in a movement that nearly has his elbow in my eye, then he thanks Madame.

"Is that all your luggage?" I ask. We're standing by the Kieran MacQuoid memorial—a plaque for Xavier's brother. He was a dancer here, too—before I joined. Eight years younger than Xavier, Kieran was in year three of the lower school when he was murdered. I've never heard Xavier talk about it directly, but everyone here sort of knows even though I can't remember who told me. Kieron was shot along with four other people, when they were out in London, shopping, one day.

Jaidev shakes his head. "My suitcase is being sent later. I hadn't packed it."

I frown a little at that but don't ask, just show him the way to the canteen.

Once there, I grab a baked potato with tuna and a small portion of lettuce. He does the same. I don't know whether to be annoyed at that or not.

Sibylle is sitting at a table with Peter and Xavier. She waves me over.

"Is that him?" she stage-whispers to me.

I turn. Jaidev is now getting cutlery and a glass of water, but he is also looking at Sibylle. He clearly heard her.

"Be nice," I say, feeling strangely protective of Jaidev. I give Peter a warning glare because if there's one person I know who'll be problematic, it's him.

Peter gives me a sickly-sweet smile back. "I'm just simply delighted to meet him."

Xavier doesn't say anything at all, just cuts up his salmon into small, even squares.

But once Jaidev is over here, the tense atmosphere does dissipate and we're all making small talk. I ask him what the Paris Ballet School is like, and he asks about Roseheart's way of doing things. The conversation then descends into general natter about films and *Bake Off,* which Sibylle and Xavier have been binge-watching after their pas de deux rehearsals for months. Peter nods enthusiastically and claims he is the spitting image of one of the contestants, but I don't watch it so I've no idea how accurate he is. I mean, Peter often thinks he's more attractive than he is—Freya and Ivelisse are always saying that.

Alma joins us at this point, and we all talk for a good twenty minutes after finishing our food, and it feels better. Certainly better than how I imagine things would've gone if Jaidev and I had eaten in the company buildings.

"You must excuse me," Jaidev says. He looks to Peter. "Would you be able to show me where my room is?"

Peter looks at me. "Which room?"

"Teddy's."

"Then you mean *our* room," Xavier says. He sighs. "Teddy and I shared."

"Ooh, drama!" Alma says.

Jaidev doesn't look happy about not having his own room, and it's understandable. I don't think I'd want to share a room with someone I didn't know and who was probably annoyed that I was getting a chance when they weren't. That rules were being bent for me.

Because the company *is* bending rules, and I'm aware that it may not be making me favorable in the eyes of others. Xavier, especially. Maybe Sibylle, too, secretly. She's just too nice to show it at all.

Jaidev, Peter, and Xavier leave. The moment they're out the canteen, Alma turns to me.

"Did you hear?" Her eyes are wide and shiny as she lowers her voice. "He's a psychopath. You need to be careful."

"A psychopath?" I let out a small laugh. Then I stop.

Sibylle has frozen.

"Yeah," Alma says. "His mother was hit by a car less than twelve hours ago, yet he's still here. Dancing is apparently more important. If you ask me, *that* is the behavior of a psychopath."

ELEVEN

Teddy

I can't talk to anyone. Not my dad, not my doctors. There's no one. Not even Taryn. She texted again today, several times, and maybe it was stupid but when I saw her name on the screen, I thought it meant she and I would still be connected.

But then I remembered how last night she'd mentioned this other guy. My replacement. And she's moving on. Quickly.

And I'm not.

I'm stuck.

Stuck here, as they need to monitor me some more before I go home. Then it'll be a case of waiting for appointments for the MRI and diagnostic catheterization as soon as they become available. But I can't even think about that. Can't answer the doctors. Not verbally. I just nod.

I don't speak.

"Come on, son!" Dad says as I stare at the hospital food.

It's late, and dinner's been on the tray in front of me for what seems like hours, waiting for me to eat it. Twice, nurses have prompted me, but I'm pleased they're not being insistent. Not yet, anyway.

"You've got to eat," Dad says. "You always used to have an appetite."

Appetite. Like when I used to eat jam doughnuts and cake. When I didn't realize that a blueberry muffin for breakfast had so much oil and fat in it. How I'd eat a chocolate bar at break when I was twelve. I'm just glad I know how to eat healthily now. It was difficult at first—but once I told people I didn't like chocolate and I wasn't a fan of cake, it got easier. People stopped offering me the bad foods and I was able to focus on eating only the right things.

But the memory of being extravagant with food makes my shoulders curl now. And that's how Dad remembers me? Pigging out, like that?

But what does Dad know? *He* was never around. He doesn't know whether I used to eat or not. Only Mum knew. And Roseheart, of course. But not Taryn, because even though I wanted to tell her, I just couldn't. Felt ashamed. As numerous people have already pointed out, I do a girl's sport. Why would I want a 'female illness' as well?

I hate gender stereotypes. Hate it all as I stare at the wilted broccoli next to my battered fish and greasy chips. I don't think the broccoli is organic. The fish and chips, I both want to shove into my mouth and never touch. I both want to tell Dad everything about how food makes me feel—so then he'll stop pressuring me to eat—*and* stay quiet. The conflict is ripping at my seams, and it means I have to move my hands else I feel I'll explode. So, I lift my fork and push a clump of sad, pathetic broccoli round the plate, counting the circular motions.

One, two, three, four.

Counting is a distraction.

Five, six, seven, eight.

Joe, the nutritionist at Roseheart Academy, knows and helps me. I have sessions with him. It's all contained, secret, because I asked it to be. Not like how everyone knows Ivelisse sees Joe way more often than all the others and that she has dieticians and therapists and doctors involved too.

But I'm not going back to the academy. It hits me like a ton of bricks, and I flinch. I feel like I'm being crushed by the realization, crumbling into a fine powder. *I'm not going back there.* I won't get any more help with…with this all. I stare at the food. And I just feel it like it's a certainty. Ballet was what helped me. I had to keep my strength up to keep dancing— Joe kind of made me see that. And not *just* dancing, but dancing with Taryn.

I can't do that now. I haven't got that motivation to keep me eating when my career is over.

Without a word, I push my plate a few inches away. It makes a scraping noise. I can't eat any of it. Not when I'm stuck here—because if I have to eat the fish and chips, I know I'll have to dance. Have to do something healthy to counteract the unhealthy food. And I can't dance with all these people monitoring me, watching me, in here.

"That's all right, boy," Dad says. His voice is forlorn. "You tried. Maybe you'll be hungry later."

I adjust the beanie hat I'm wearing, pulling it down a little. It's comforting, having it on. Even if it is brand new. Dad asked earlier if I wanted anything. I said a beanie and he went out and bought one. "Maybe. It'd be easier if it's something softer." I point to my nose. There are splints around it, and nasal packs in my nostrils too that the doctor explained are required for stability of the septum. Eating is going to hurt.

But, still, even if the food was soft, I know I won't eat. I can't. Not now. I'm too stressed. So, instead, I pick up the information booklet that the doctor left for me this afternoon. The one on HCM. Just looking at the booklet make me feel sick. I flick to a random page. *Living with Hypertrophic Cardiomyopathy: it is vital that a patient diagnosed with HCM takes their medications as required and makes an effort to stay well hydrated.*

Well hydrated. The words blur.

It's not just food I struggle with. All the other dancers at the academy drink a lot of water, but I've always found it difficult. I've never really been able to say why.

A healthy diet is also vital for anyone diagnosed with HCM.

A healthy diet. Well, I do eat healthily, I know that. I'm always super concerned about the quality of food. That's why I couldn't eat the fish and chips, even though part of me wanted to. And the broccoli, though my brain told me it was healthy, just didn't look…right.

But I *do* eat healthily. Even if Joe says I need to eat more, eat a healthy amount, and not cut out certain food groups.

Oh, God. I stare at my arm, try to see it objectively, see if it's thin or not.

What if my lack of water and struggle with food has caused this? Joe was always saying how eating disorders can cause severe problems. *Severe*…like a heart problem.

I plough through the HCM booklet, trying to find a page on causes. Trying to find if I've caused this. But all it says is it's genetic.

Genetic.

I look at Dad. He's peering intently at his phone now. He played football until about ten years ago when he got a knee injury. And Mum was a professional ballet dancer, just like what I want to be. While Mum did die—from falling when rock-climbing on a girls' holiday—neither of them were struck down in their late teens or twenties. Because they don't have this condition.

And that means I can't have it either.

It'll be the lack of water and food that is making me dizzy, and it must explain the arrhythmias and heart thickening, too. That'll be it. I haven't got this condition. I just know it.

TWELVE

Teddy

"I can't believe you got the fittest one!" Peter slaps me on the back the moment I enter my room—which is a surprise as Xavier is my roommate, not him. But there's no sign of Xavier, and Peter is instead bouncing around the room, all red-faced and shiny with sweat.

"Excuse me?" I stare at him, faint irritation stirring in me. I've only known Peter for a week—that's how long it's taken the teachers to decide whom will be matched together for the primary dance pairings—and already he's the guy I like least.

This isn't the first time Peter's been overly loud and raucous when talking about girls. Only yesterday he was boasting about his 'body count.' It took me a good few minutes to realize he was referring to the girls he'd slept with and not people he'd killed.

Sometimes, I feel like I'll never fit in with other guys.

"Taryn. Did you see her—" Peter motions to his own chest. *"None of the other girls have anything like hers, and you've got her."*

It's true. Taryn is curvier than the other girls. I noticed that. Of course I did. But I didn't notice it in the way that Peter and the other boys are laughing about now. For me, it was just an objective observation. But I can imagine what thoughts are going through their heads...and I've never really thought about any girls like that. I notice things, like appearance and physique, but it doesn't make me want to try and seduce them or whatever. Ha, Peter would probably laugh if he knew I was thinking of the word 'seduce' and not something more...rowdy?

"So, did she put out?" Peter asks, breathless.

"Excuse me?" I stare at him.

"You just went to her room?" He gives me a look that I think is supposed to convey something—but what that something is, I don't know.

"I did." I nod. Taryn had this cool idea that each week as we dance together, we should take a photo.

"We should do it no matter what," she'd said, her face flushed and eyes sparkling. "It'll be a record of our progress, and we can see if our acting is also getting better, if we're looking like we're romantically involved by the end of it. See if we can fool the world."

She said the words like it was a challenge, but it had made me nervous. She couldn't have worked out that there's something...different about me. That I've just never felt those feelings. But I do like how she didn't just assume that our romance would be real. In several of the ballet clubs I joined as a young teenager, it turned out all the female dancers wanted to be paired with me for romantic pas de deux under the belief that we'd develop real *romance. And then when I never asked them out, they got angry at me.*

"So did you get laid?" Peter's question jolts me back to my present.

My throat is suddenly dry. "What? No!"

"Third base then?"

I have never quite been sure what third base is. When I asked my cousin a few years ago, he just taunted me for not knowing. "No. We're just friends."

"Just friends? With her?" Peter's eyebrows nearly disappear into his messy blond hair. "What are you, gay?" He laughs, then stops. "Wait, you're not, are you?"

"Would it matter if I was?" I stare at him. It's my best confrontational stare, one that I know makes people uncomfortable.

Peter splutters and looks at anything but me. "Uh, well, no. It'd... just be a waste that's all."

"A waste?" I raise my own eyebrows this time.

"I'd dance with Taryn in a heartbeat. You ever want to swap, just let me know."

"No." My word comes out quickly, and I realize I feel strangely protective of Taryn. She's my friend already, and, although I don't know her well yet, I am sure Peter's words would hurt her. I just know it instinctively. Because Peter's a jerk and women don't like jerks. Or at least they shouldn't. But I've also seen what magazines say, how women like bad boys and that good guys get left behind. Whatever that means. I always think those articles are written by these so-called 'good guys' who have

been rejected by women and so they call it 'being friend zoned'
in an attempt to shame the women.

Peter gives me an odd look. He doesn't say much after that,
but then Xavier, my actual roommate, returns and tells us the
other guys are having a party of sorts in the lounge.

"Just the boys, yes!" Peter holds his hand out for a fist-bump,
but neither Xavier nor I complete the action. "You coming?"

Still, both Peter and Xavier are both going to this party, and
it appears they're going right this very second, so I follow them. I
need to be more sociable, I know that.

The party's by Roseheart's lake, and it's cold. But as I listen to
the other boys with their talk about girls and sex, I can't help but
think these aren't the guys I want to be socializing with. It's like
they're talking a foreign language, all about who's hot, who they
want to hook up with. As they rate the girls on the course—and
all I can think of that's remotely similar is that maybe kissing
could be fun, but not really anything more, which I can't share
with the boys here—I can't help but wonder what is wrong with
me.

THIRTEEN

Taryn

I meet Jaidev at the appointed studio at 7 a.m. the following morning. Mr. Vikas is already there, and judging by how he's sitting, legs crossed at a desk at the side of the studio, with a calm countenance and not a hair out of place, he's been here a while. I glance at the clock. I'm not late. Jaidev's only just unzipping his orange hoody, revealing his training vest. Alma's words return to me, and I look at Jaidev. As he takes a swig of water from a sports bottle, he doesn't look like a psychopath—and I'm pretty sure him being here while his parent is in hospital doesn't make him a psychopath either. But still, Madame Troisière *is* in hospital. In the dorm last night, Sibylle, Ivelisse, Alma, and I looked up the accident. A vehicular collision, and yet Jaidev is here.

"Are we ready?" Mr. Vikas's voice makes me jump, and I turn, flustered. "Then let's warm up."

I put my duffel bag at the side of the studio and then adjust my shoes. Whereas I wore Repettos for the *Romeo and*

Juliet performance, I now have one of my pairs of Grishkos on. I pretty much stick to these two brands, and this particular pair I've been dancing in for nearly five weeks now. They're my comfiest pointes at the moment, customized *just right*, but they are softening a bit. I baked them in the oven for a bit, a few nights ago, in preparation for what I hoped would be my first practice with Roseheart Romantic Dance Company as a professional, as one of them. I always find baking them works better for me than the hardening spray, in extending their life.

I settle myself at the barre. My reflection stares back at me. The barres in the academy studios aren't by mirrors, but these are. It's disconcerting, having myself watch me. Judging me.

Jaidev joins me at the barre, three feet along. He looks casual and relaxed. I look…well, scared. And nervous. And like I'm trying too hard. Jaidev looks much more relaxed, like he's at home here, comfortable.

I glance at Mr. Vikas, feeling my face heat up. The mirror confirms how red I'm going. I hadn't realized Mr. Vikas was going to be here for mine and Jaidev's first dance.

Mr. Vikas instructs us on our warmup and then asks to see some movements. "Solo. Taryn first," he says.

I breathe a sigh of relief that we're still dancing solo for now—for some reason having an audience makes me even more uncomfortable about my first dance with Jaidev than actually going first for a solo, with both of them watching me—but there's not much time to pause, because then I'm demonstrating an arabesque, as instructed by Mr. Vikas

"Extend the working leg more," Mr. Vikas says. "And now let's see that foot"—he points at my supporting leg, the one I'm standing on—"in demi-pointe."

I shift my position, so I am standing on the ball of my foot, rather than being flat or en pointe.

"Good," he croons.

Mr. Vikas asks to see allegros, and I perform my best assemblé, sauté, and soubresaut. Once I've done these three, there's a pause, and I wonder if I should also do some of the other allegro moves, but then he nods.

"Entrechat quatre and fouetté rond de jambe en tournant, please."

Fouetté rond de jambe en tournant makes me want to laugh. Whenever Teddy heard that phrase, he'd roll his eyes. "Us normal folk just say fouetté," he'd say. "Makes them sound really pompous saying it all."

But it doesn't sound pompous inside the walls of the company. It sounds right, proper. This is professional ballet.

I perform the moves, and this is then followed by the request for a ballotté—not my favorite as the classical movement requires both coupé dessous and small developpés. I struggled with ballottés for a long time when I was younger, trying to perfect the rocking and swinging movement, but now I manage it on the first go, using a ninety-degree leg extension.

"And with forty-five degrees?" Mr. Vikas requests.

I oblige.

He gives me a few more instructions, then nods and turns to Jaidev. "Now, you."

Mr. Vikas asks Jaidev for assemblé soutenu en tournant before leading into a complex series of combinations. I think Jaidev's definitely got the harder requests, but he pulls them off well. Only twice does Mr. Vikas correct his arms and adjust his general posture, reminding him, "We're not in France now."

Watching Jaidev dance is almost magical. He moves like silk, yet there's strength to his dance too. No wonder they think we can do this in eight weeks.

I breathe deeply, already knowing the liability is going to be me. Jaidev is amazing. He's almost inhuman in his ability to become these movements. But we all know it's a sign of the top dancers. The best ballerinas and danseurs have this ability to transcend the apparent limits of the human body.

"Now, together," Mr. Vikas says.

My heart pounds as I join Jaidev in the center of the studio. He's still barefoot. I'm not. After a moment, Mr. Vikas orders Jaidev to get his shoes on too. Jaidev pulls out a pair of soft-soled leather slippers.

Mr. Vikas takes no prisoners as he directs us in our first dance. Jaidev's hands are hot whenever he touches me, but his grip doesn't shy away from me. Not how Teddy's did when we were first paired up. We don't talk to each other, me and Jaidev, just listen to Mr. Vikas's instructions.

"Look in the mirror as you dance this part," Mr. Vikas says. "Notice your lines, the movement. Jaidev, see how Taryn draws out that arm? You need to lean in further. We need symmetry. And, Jaidev, you still look like you're dancing at the opera. You need to learn this. We haven't got time for basic errors."

"I understand," Jaidev says. "I was just speaking to Madame Cachelle yesterday evening, and she is allowing me to take part in one of her intensive courses on the English style. I will also take extra classes with the Academy's charactère tutor as I feel that is a current weakness of mine."

Mr. Vikas just grunts.

We dance for almost an hour before Mr. Vikas announces a break. He disappears out of the door a second later, leaving me and Jaidev out of breath and staring at each other. I push back stray, sweaty tendrils of hair that have escaped my bun. Jaidev reaches for his water, takes four sips. I don't know why I count them.

I retrieve my own water from my duffel bag, then find myself looking at Jaidev again. There's something about him that means I can't take my eyes from him. He just looks so powerful, strong.

"Is... Is it true about your mother?" I ask, and my voice cracks a little. Hastily, I lick my lips. "Is she in hospital?"

Jaidev nods, a crisp and clean movement. "I don't want to talk about it." He sits down and takes one shoe off, then grabs plasters and bandages from his rucksack. The knuckle of his big toe is sore and inflamed.

"Oh, uh, I'm sorry."

"Just dance, okay?" he says, looking up at me. "That's what we're here for." He grimaces as he applies a plaster. "We have to get this right." His voice is dark, and it… There's something else in it.

We have to get this right…or else.

No. That's just me being dramatic. Jaidev's not mean or anything, is he?

When Mr. Vikas returns and talks us through combinations that feature in Evangeline's choreography for our pas de deux, I feel so nervous I can hardly remember his words. My dancing is slow and clumsy, and I know he notices. And Jaidev too. He's grimacing by the end of the practice.

"Well, it'll take time," Mr. Vikas says, glaring at me. "And practice."

Oh, dear lord. It's laughable, thinking I could manage this with someone who isn't Teddy. There's no unity with me and Jaidev. No flow of expression or connection. While Jaidev is amazing on his own, I know we're not connecting well. The grim look on Mr. Vikas's face says it all.

"You need to get used to each other. Trust each other. I'll check in with you in the coming week and get you the actual choreography for the tour. In the meantime, work on your core strength and endurance, Taryn. And keep up with the academy's pointe classes until we get you transferred to company classes. Jaidev, definitely take those lessons with Madame Cachelle on the English style of ballet. She's a good instructor." He dips his head a little. "Be sure to improve by the time of the first assessment, else Miss Tavi and Mr. Aleks won't be happy—that'll be around the third week of training."

I nod, feeling strangely close to tears.

"We will, sir," Jaidev says.

I nod again, sure my voice will comprise only of squeaks if I try to use it now.

Jaidev turns to me the moment Mr. Vikas leaves. "See you this afternoon? We can get another practice in then, too, before I've got my charactère class. I can draw up a timetable and color code it for us—can you let me know when you'll be doing your pointe training too? And endurance training. It's good to make a full schedule for all of this. I reckon we can do two full studio practices a day like this, plus specific exercises. And familiarizing ourselves with Roseheart's vision for *A Midsummer Night's Dream* would be helpful, too."

I just nod. He knows what he's doing. But I've never really scheduled my endurance sessions. They've always just been things we've done as and when we can. Sibylle and I would go for runs three to four times a week—sometimes with Ivelisse, too—while Teddy and Xavier would spend extra hours in the fitness room and gym, pretty much every day. The only other sessions that we're scheduled for are the extra classes—pointe and flexibility class for the girls, jumps and strength classes for the boys, and expression for both. I wonder how soon my company classes for pointe and flexibility will start.

Suddenly, it all feels like so much—sure, we had a lot of sessions for the diploma course, but we had two years to make that work. Not eight weeks—and with a new partner. I try not to shake.

Jaidev and I head out into the cool air and automatically I'm walking toward the school buildings. Sibylle and Ivelisse are sitting outside on the steps up to the main block—and just as I reach them, a gaggle of female company dancers step out of the building. Sibylle and Ivelisse move so they can get past. I don't even know why the company dancers would have been in an academy building. They have everything they could need in their own premises.

The company dancers cast long-lashed glances our way. I recognize two from yesterday. One with long blond hair and another with chestnut locks. Both have bright-red lipstick.

The tallest one—who practically threw me out of the accommodation block yesterday—smirks as she looks at me. Then she turns to the others. "Taryn and Jaidev won't manage it in eight weeks. She'd been dancing with Teddy for three years. This is just clutching at straws. We should just redesign the choreography of the tour at this stage and write them out." She speaks loudly, projecting her voice like it's a performance. Maybe she's always wanted to speak on stage, but ballet uses our bodies to speak. Not vicious tongues.

Another nods vigorously. "It's a bit of an insult to all of the other third years who've worked so hard for this for years, if they get it after a few weeks of dancing together. I'm sure they must feel that way."

I freeze. What's she trying to do? Stir trouble? I glance at Sibylle.

"And," the first one continues, looking toward Sibylle. "It's just a kick in the teeth particularly for you, as the understudy."

Since when do company dancers take note of who the understudies are?

Sibylle shifts a little on the steps, drawing her knees closer to her chest. She looks up at the dancers but doesn't say anything. Ivelisse is frowning, her mouth slightly open, like she's trying to work out what these dancers' game is.

The blond dancer takes a step toward Sibylle and points at her. "That's what you and your danseur are there for. And you'd have got in, if you weren't being compared to Taryn. You're easily as good as last year's admissions."

"Hey," Jaidev starts to say, but she stops him with a glare.

She points again at Sibylle. There's something predatory about the way she points. "They're rightfully your places if the lead couple messes up or can't accept the places, no matter what new rule and extension Mr. Vikas and the board are coming up with. Girl, if I was you, I'd be fuming. Not still being chummy with Taryn. I mean, I've seen you chatting and that."

I stare at her. She's been watching me?

Sibylle laughs. The sound is too high-pitched and so clearly a sign of how nervous she is. "Taryn and Teddy didn't mess up though. He got a serious diagnosis." Then she beckons me over. She's smiling, revealing her perfect teeth.

My heart pounds as I approach. Jaidev's following behind me.

The company dancers stare at me. They're like a pack of hyenas—and they all just seem so much better than me. Prettier, skinnier, more elegant.

But they're mean, too.

"Babe," one of them says to Sibylle. "You want to protest this? You should. I mean, we'd have your backs. We'd support you. Just know that. And Jaidev isn't even a Roseheart graduate." She speaks like Jaidev isn't even right here, and that annoys me. "They're just trying to break too many rules this year. They need reminding that this company has *traditions*."

They blow kisses to Sibylle, completely ignoring Ivelisse, and then leave, also ignoring Jaidev and me.

"Seriously? They came over here just to stir shit?" Ivelisse grunts.

Sibylle doesn't say anything now that they've gone, and I don't know whether it's my paranoia or not, but I'm sure that for the rest of the day, she doesn't quite talk to me with her usual warmth. Not that we're ever super friendly, but still, I think she's colder now. Is she listening to the company dancers? Have they planted a seed of doubt in her minds over the fairness of it all?

God, do the company dancers really hate me that much already? And if they're like this already, what will they do if Jaidev and I actually get permanent positions with the company?

FOURTEEN

Taryn

After lunch, Jaidev and I meet for our next practice. I'm full of nervous energy, and I can feel it simmering under my skin. Sibylle is all I can concentrate on. I share a room with her. What if she actually hates me now? And now I'm supposed to be putting my all into learning to dance with a new partner, and the more I realize just how distracted I'm getting, the more frustration builds up within me.

"You've got to keep time better," Jaidev says after I've made the same stupid mistake for the third time in a row. We're only doing light work, given we just ate, and it's stuff I should have no trouble with.

I nod. "I know." Great, he's going to think I'm a rubbish dancer now.

I try to push my worries aside. I can't let those company dancers get to me. If it wasn't for their words, I wouldn't even be thinking that Sibylle hates me now.

Just concentrate!

But I can't.

I just…can't.

I need to pull myself together.

Five hours later, after training that just got more and more intense with every hour, at dinner, I watch Sibylle carefully. She's got red lipstick on. That's the first thing I notice—and it looks good, contrasts with her pale skin. Along with her black hair and the statement glasses she sometimes wears when she gives herself a break from her contact lenses, the look is striking. But seeing her wearing that shade of lipstick makes me start sweating. It's the same as what those company dancers wore.

I breathe deeply, try and tell myself it doesn't mean anything. Sibylle sometimes does wear makeup. And she has a lot of different shades of lipstick. *This doesn't mean anything.*

She talks to the others at the table—Ivelisse, Alma, Peter, Xavier, and Jaidev—but not really to me, and the longer it goes on, the more nauseous I feel.

"How was your day?" I ask at last. My voice wavers. Is this the right thing to ask, when I'm the one who's now dancing for Roseheart's company, even if it is only temporary? And she's… well, I don't know what she's doing. Applying to other companies?

"It was okay," Sibylle says, stirring her food round and round.

I wait for more, but she just pushes keeps her salmon circling her plate. Her eyes are dark, and her knuckles show white with how hard she's clenching her fork.

"Do you want to go for a run later?" I ask. There's still a good few hours before it gets dark, and we often run at dusk.

"No. My Achilles tendon is flaring up a bit."

Alma and Ivelisse make a joke about something, and I catch my name in their sniggers and notice how Sibylle snorts—something said about me? My gaze shoots to Alma, but she and Ivelisse are both laughing. My stomach tightens, and I try to listen as they begin whispering. Their gazes keep crossing back to me, then darting away.

I take several deep breaths and make myself concentrate on my surroundings instead. The harsh clicks of cutlery on ceramic plates. Peter's grating voice as he talks to Jaidev and Xavier about how he's suddenly got two auditions with great companies, and he's sure it's because of the showreel that the academy put out—Teddy's accident is in it to draw in viewers and the attention of other companies, just as I suspected it would be. But then I become too hyper-focused again, knowing why I'm trying to concentrate on the guys' conversation and not Sibylle and Alma and Ivelisse.

Have those company dancers' words really had an effect on Sibylle? On all of them? Because maybe they *were* saying it all anyway, among themselves, about how unfair it is that I'm getting a second chance at getting into the company when the places should've gone to the understudies. They could all really hate me now, especially Sibylle.

I try to push my fear away.

No. Sibylle is my…friend. As much as anyone is friends here.

I zone in on the guys' conversation again. Jaidev and Peter are chatting away, but I notice Xavier's not being friendly with my new partner. Because he's the displaced understudy too? Like Sibylle?

I stir my bowl of plain kefir and oats, feeling sicker and sicker.

"You okay?" Ivelisse asks. Her tone is neutral, her voice oddly clipped.

I nod. "Just tired. I'm... I'm going to go to my room for a rest."

I never really rest, and I can feel their eyes on me as I leave hurriedly. Anxiety swirls deeper and deeper within me. I need to speak to Teddy. He'll calm me.

But he doesn't answer his phone as I ring him when walking to the dorms. He doesn't reply to my texts, and my worries about everything are just getting bigger by the time I reach my room.

I open the door, and—

There's some rubbish on the floor. Bits of paper and—

My mouth dries.

It's not rubbish. It's my photo board. My most precious memories of me and Teddy, lies in tatters across my carpet.

I stare at the mutilated photos, strips of glossy memories. Some have been torn, but others have been crisply cut with scissors. Tears pierce the corners of my eyes. Scissors—that indicates premeditation, doesn't it? Someone really hates me. And whoever it is wants me to know it.

I gulp and look at Sibylle's bed. Then Ivelisse's. I sniff and feel sicker. Could they have done this? Or someone else? With a start, I realize that, barring Jaidev, I could have no friends—or people who don't hate me—at all here now. The company dancers all clearly think I shouldn't be dancing on their tour, regardless of whether Jaidev and I make it work, and now the dancers I've trained with for years probably hate me for getting special treatment.

The small amount of kefir and oats I had managed to eat weighs heavily in my stomach as I gather up the tatters of my photos. My eyes linger on a strip of a photo that I recognize instantly, though I can only see the bright pink of my shirt and Teddy's arm. But it was the first photo, the first photo we took after our very first pas de deux session. Mum had sent me some new practice clothes, loose fitting shirts and joggers and leg warmers. She'd picked the pink shirt most likely for a joke as she had to have known it was my least favorite color. But the morning of the practice, I'd spilled tea over my bed, and my open suitcase had been on my duvet, ready to finally be unpacked properly as I'd been putting it off. I've never been that good at organizing my things. The only shirt to miss the tea was the pink one.

Peter made fun of me for wearing it. I never wore it again, and I took it back home when I went for Christmas the first year. My sisters saw the shirt and they loved the color, so I gave it to them, even though it was much too big for either of them. But, here, that shirt lived on via my photo board. And it became more than just a shirt. It was the start of mine and Teddy's career. The start of our friendship. Our connection.

I try Teddy's number again. He doesn't pick up, so I grab my jacket and change into my running shoes. I grab my purse and navigate to the bus app on my phone. A few minutes of searching tells me which buses I need to get to see him at the hospital. Thankfully, buses run pretty regularly here in London, even on Sunday evenings, and I need to see him. He's my best friend and we help each other. I helped him when he was struggling to cope with his mother's death in the first year, and he knows how much I worry about things. Earlier this year, when we had our formal assessments just after Christmas, I got so stressed, but it was Teddy who was able to keep me sane. We spent extra evenings in the studios, not practicing the performance dances, but choreographing our own fun routines, dances that reminded me why I fell in love with ballet in the first place. And I need his steady reassurance now, his grounding effects. And I should be there for him, too. I should've already gone to visit him, I know that. It's been two days since his accident.

The corridors are silent as I slip out of the school and down the main drive. The air's stickier than I anticipated and within a few moments my skin is tacky with sweat, keeping my jacket pressed tightly to my arms and neck. I reach the bus stop just as the bus comes into sight, and my luck with that lasts when I make my connecting bus in good time. Just forty minutes after leaving the school, I'm walking into the hospital.

I give Teddy's name to the staff at the desk and after a moment consulting their computers, they direct me up to his ward. He's in a private room, lying on his side facing the door. His nose has some sort of splint over it, and I wonder if it's really painful. His eyes are unfocused, and I wonder for a moment if he's actually asleep with them open. Xavier said he does that sometimes.

Teddy jumps as I open the door and then scrambles to sit upright. There are monitors clinging to him, spider-wires stretching to big metal machines.

"Hey," I say, my voice soft.

He's staring at me, mouth open. "You're…you're here? What the hell, Taryn?" He shakes his head, like he's trying to shake away an apparition.

But I'm real.

"*Of course* I'm here." I sit at his bedside. "I should've come sooner. I'm so sorry."

"It's… It's fine," he says. "I wasn't expecting anyone this evening."

I cross one leg over the other, then lean forward. "I was worried, when you hadn't replied to my messages today, and even more so when you didn't answer your phone." My eyes fall on his phone, on the little tray at the foot of his bed.

"Oh," he says. "It…it ran out of battery."

"Oh, Teddy," I whisper. "I didn't think to bring a charger. But I can bring one tomorrow. Maybe I can do it before first practice. The buses are twenty-four hours, right?"

He nods. He looks so fragile. So alone.

"But how are you?" I ask. "I looked up that heart condition. So, what's happening next?"

He shrugs a little. "Still being monitored for the moment—because of the concussion. And they're worried about low blood pressure and bradycardia now as well, but what's new? I've had those for a long time. But they've said I'll switch to outpatient monitoring soon. And then I'll have a diagnostic catheterization to look at my heart—but I don't think it really can be this HCM condition they're talking about."

He sounds so determined, like he doesn't want to believe it could be. And who would want to be told that?

I squeeze his hand. "Does your head hurt? Your nose?"

"My head, not really." His voice is small. "My nose is sore, and my front teeth hurt quite a bit still. The doctor said that can happen after nose surgery though. Something about a nerve that connects to them can get bruised in the surgery or something. But everything feels weird. Being here and not... I just want to dance." His words crack, and I squeeze his hand even tighter, then stop a little. His hand feels more fragile now, somehow. Like I could squash all the bones together, fracture them so easily.

I don't know what to say as I look at him, my best friend.

"Has your dad been to visit?" I whisper.

My gaze falls on a box of chocolate on the tray, next to his phone. It's unopened, and Teddy doesn't like chocolate. That was one of the first things I learnt about him on our induction day when we all went to the canteen. There was chocolate mousse. I couldn't eat it because of the fructose content of chocolate, and Teddy also said he couldn't eat his. Said he didn't like chocolate. I'd thought at the time he'd only said it because Peter had said I was a weirdo for not eating chocolate, that Teddy had been doing this solidarity thing—even though we hadn't yet been partnered together—but it turned out he really doesn't like chocolate. I've never seen him eat any.

Teddy grimaces. "Won't stop fussing. Seems to think this is his opportunity to redeem himself. But he's still a dick."

A small smile comes to my lips. "Yeah."

"So, how is it?" he asks, his voice a bit stiff and his tone oddly formal. "Dancing with your new partner?"

I run a hand through my hair. "Terrible. We're so out of sync, and bar Mr. Vikas and the other company staff, no one seems to think we should even get a place with them."

Teddy swallows a little awkwardly and his Adam's apple visibly bobs. I wonder if he is in fact thinking that, too, sharing that view.

"They all hate me at the company, all the dancers," I say, and I tell him what the women have said to me and how they're trying to ignite fire in Sibylle, make her and the others angry at me. "And then someone tore up my photo board."

His eyes widen at that. "No?"

I nod.

"Oh, Taryn." He reaches for my hand and squeezes it.

Tears pierce the corners of my eyes, and I know I shouldn't be talking so much about myself, feeling sorry for myself, when Teddy's in here, when he may never dance again, but now I've started, I can't stop.

"That's not even the worst of it. I've got to get this position, learn to dance with Jaidev in eight weeks, else I've got to do *another year*. And I can't afford it. And then Mum will find out I've failed."

"Wait. She doesn't know about any of this?"

I shake my head. I don't tell him I lied though. I can't bring myself to utter those words.

"Just breathe," he whispers, his voice soft. "Just dance for yourself, okay?" he says. "You've got to do that. Dancing is how you look after yourself. You've got to do that." He pauses slightly. "You know what happens when you don't."

I feel my face heat up. I don't want to think about that. But I know he's right. I've got to dance. It's fine to dance for the company and try and get this part, but I can't let it consume me. I've still got to dance for *me*.

I manage a smile—just as something vibrates. A phone. Teddy's. The screen has lit up.

So, it's not out of battery after all.

"That'll just be my dad again." His eyes are a little shifty, but he doesn't offer an explanation for his lie.

I don't push him. Maybe he just got mixed up, a voice in my head suggests.

Maybe.

"And that's visiting time over," an unnecessarily cheerful voice says. I turn in my seat to see a young nurse poking her head into Teddy's room. "You can come back tomorrow, dear."

For a second, neither Teddy nor I say or do anything. There's a strange atmosphere in the room, like there's too much tension and it's going to shatter any moment. Then we both sort of jump into action, saying goodbyes.

"I'll be back soon," I promise.

I hug him. He feels bonier than I remember from just a few days ago. Has he lost muscle mass that quickly from being in here? I mean, he can't have been training at all, and we're always told we need to train daily to maintain our skills and fitness. But I hadn't thought he'd lose weight this quickly, and I can't ask because the nurse is ushering me out.

"Remember to dance for yourself," Teddy calls after me, and I'm nearly crying all over again as I leave.

Remember to dance for myself.

That almost seems pointless now, when Teddy and I will never dance together again, and I can't connect with Jaidev. There's no point in dancing at all if I can't get on the tour and make my mother—and Helena's memory—proud.

FIFTEEN

Teddy

"You need to feel the romance of this dance," Madame Cachelle says, readjusting my grip on Taryn's waist. "Look into her eyes because you two are in love."

I snort. I can't help it.

Hurt flashes across Taryn's face.

"I...I've never been in love," I say quickly, to show Taryn it's nothing personal. I mean, the last thing I want to do is hurt her. But then I wonder if this is something I should be saying on the second week of dancing on this program, of dancing with Taryn. We still don't really know each other. We may seem similar so far, but people are like onions—there are layers and layers to one's personality, who they are.

Madame rolls her eyes. "Then, my gem, we will have to teach you what love is. This is a school for a romantic dance company, and ballets, especially classical ballets, focus around love. Taryn, come on, I bet you can help Teddy here. Sometimes, love just comes easier to girls as they do not have as many raging hormones battling in various parts of their body." She shakes her head. "Men, only thinking about one thing."

"Seems kind of sexist," Ivelisse mutters. She's got big, haunting eyes and a mesmerizing kind of beauty—one that has power to it.

"Taryn, look into Teddy's eyes with love and make him feel it," Madame instructs.

If anything, Taryn looks scared as she stares up at me now. Her eyes are so wide and the muscles around her mouth have tightened. Her shoulders have lifted up a little, like she's tensing. I can almost feel her trembling. Is that what love is? I frown to myself.

"Relax," Madame tells her. "Soften your shoulders and extend your lines. And smile, give him a coy look."

"Coy?" Taryn's voice is a whisper.

"You know, when you're trying to seduce your boyfriend but you're pretending you're not," Madame says.

"I've never had a boyfriend," Taryn says.

There's a hoot of laughter from Peter who's nearby, dancing with Alma.

"What do you mean you've never had a boyfriend?" Peter looks at Taryn incredulously, and the sudden closed look she gets makes my heart lurch.

Madame tells him to shh and concentrate on the combinations she gave him to practice with Alma, but he's not listening to her. He just stares at Taryn, who's getting redder and redder on the spot.

"Well, I… I've just concentrated on ballet," she says.

"And quite right too." Madame looks flustered. *"All right, everyone, let's—"*

"So, you're still a virgin?" Peter laughs.

There are sniggers from around the room, and Freya outright laughs. I hear someone mutter, *"What a freak,"* and fury ignites within me.

Taryn looks like she's about to cry.

I clear my throat. *"Well, I've never had a girlfriend."* I glare at Freya then face Peter again. *"It's not that odd."*

"Okay, everyone." Madame's voice is strained. *"If we can all just—"*

"What are the both of you? Gay?" Peter laughs and says it all like he hasn't already had this conversation with me. I frown. Just what is his problem?

"Homophobe," Ivelisse mutters. She looks Peter dead in the eye, then mutters in Spanish.

Madame zeroes in on Peter in no time, condemning his homophobia and saying there's no place for that kind of language in this school. She tells him to step outside. Peter just shrugs and laughs as he leaves. Madame follows him. Even once the door is closed, her sharp words to him ring through the studio, among us, because all of us have stopped dancing now. We hear her tell him he'll be meeting with the academy's board later.

I find myself looking at Taryn. She's staring at the ground and then she crouches to adjust the toe pad in her right pointe shoe. Objectively, I can see she is 'fit,' just as Peter said. She's well-proportioned and her muscles are toned. She's got a symmetrical face and her hair is glossy, pulled back into a tight bun. Her pale *skin is free of blemishes; there are just a few freckles on her face that make her look kind of adorable.*

But adorable *isn't the word I'm guessing Peter and his mates would use to describe her.*

Again, last night, I heard them talking about which girls they wanted *to do. They asked me, and I'd just shrugged and managed to avoid giving an answer. But it made me wonder again why I don't seem to feel what they apparently do.*

My mother's always asking me when I'm going to bring a girl home for her to meet. Apparently, it's weird that at sixteen I haven't already done so. I'm sure that when I kissed Tanya during Year Ten and my friends told Mum, that she was expecting a relationship to form. But it didn't. I just… the kissing was nice enough, but it didn't set off the feelings I thought it was going to. It didn't make me want to do anything else. Nothing ever has.

I wonder if I could take Taryn home to meet Mum one day, if Taryn is the sort of girl Mum would want to meet. But I still can't imagine wanting to do anything beyond kissing with Taryn—and not just with the sex, but also the whole dating thing, too. The idea of going to a cinema or whatever, of romancing her, just doesn't feel like me. *I've never really understood the whole idea of doing conventional romantic things, like dating, but I don't understand why the idea of taking her out to dinner romantically makes me feel something I'm sure is dread. And it's not just about my discomfort around food—because I know I could order a salad with lean chicken— no, it's more about the idea of a date. And not in a nervous way either, like how my cousin said he gets before dates, but it's in an I-don't-want-to-do-this-at-all way because it wouldn't feel right, would feel like I was leading her on, and then guilt would be curdling in my soul. Or maybe that's what it's supposed to feel like. Maybe everyone is faking this. Maybe I just have to do it and get used to it.*

"What?" Taryn says, her voice guarded, like she's holding it close, ready to use it as a weapon. She's standing tall now, her arms folded across her chest.

I realize I've been staring at her. "Nothing. Sorry," I say, because I can't tell her how I've been—and still am—wondering why the other guys feel something I don't.

SIXTEEN

Taryn

On the way back from the hospital, I get off the bus two stops early and walk through the inky night. As I knew they would, my footsteps take me to the graveyard next to St. John's Church. The wooden gate creaks and squeaks as I swing it open. The first time I came here, that sound made me jump. Now, it feels like a welcome.

The whole place feels like a welcome, a sanctuary. For a long time, I've felt more at home out here than in the dorm rooms. Because, here, I am free as I dance along the gravel paths, letting the ambience of the graveyard fill me as I create a connection deeper to the world, to my body, feel the beautiful power of ballet. And it's always like this as I dance for Helena.

Every time I think of her, I try to make it positive. Recalling a good memory. A time when we made each other laugh. Or when we were little and baking cupcakes together, sticking sticky fingers into the bowl of mixture.

I almost can't believe I've lived so long without her. Nearly six years now. It both feels like a lifetime, and it doesn't. It feels like everything and nothing and all that's in between as I think of life before the accident and life after.

The accident I caused.

Darkness creeps into me, and it's trying to stir me up, disrupt my dancing, but when I'm out here, I'm dancing for Helena. It doesn't matter that this isn't the graveyard she's buried in, because I feel like, spiritually, all graveyards are connected. That all souls are present in every single one, and somewhere, Helena is watching me, feeling this dance. This is for her, this routine, just like it always is out here. Well, for her and me, a way for me to connect to the half of me that I lost. And this is all Helena has now, the only way to live through me, to still dance, so that's why I don't allow the darkness and my guilt to destabilize me now. That can—and will—wait for other times, because this is something I'm doing for her.

I dance around the graveyard, losing myself in the feelings, the memories. My sister is everything. Together, we are everything. Identical sisters. And sometimes when I dance by gravestones, I feel like I am becoming her—weightless, and free, and haunting. Or maybe I was her all along. Maybe I'm Helena and Taryn is dead, gone, looking down on all this, and I'm living through myself, both of us at once, dead and alive and everything in between.

Ghosts are a silent audience, and I do my best dances out here, for her, for us, when there's no pressure. Teddy got that.

And I feel it now, feel it getting stronger and stronger as I near the end of my routine. Dancing in the dark, for ghosts, is exhilarating, mesmerizing because it's all about the beauty of movement, about communicating emotions, and creating connections.

And ghosts never comment.

Except this time, they do.

Because the moment I finish my combinations, someone claps a long, slow clap.

SEVENTEEN

Jaidev

In the moonlight, among the graves, Taryn looks almost otherwordly. Her hair's come loose from the bun and half of it hangs in soft ringlets and looser waves around her face. Her height works with her on the dance. I'll be honest, when I met her and discovered she was a lot taller than most other ballerinas—almost my height—I was worried. Very worried. And then when she kept stumbling in our practices, I thought she just seemed a little clumsy. I put it down to her height. She just didn't seem very graceful, and I wasn't too impressed with whom I'd been set up with.

But out here, Taryn is graceful. She's one with the night, the moonlight, the graves, embodying a lost spirit, her steps radiating sadness. There's confidence to her dancing, and she seems more comfortable, more at ease here than I've seen her in the studio earlier today, in either of our sessions.

When she finishes her dance, I clap without thinking. It's just innate, instinctual.

She freezes and then whirls toward me. It's too dark to see her expression, but I'm sure she's narrowing her eyes. Tension fills her posture.

"Hey, it's okay. It's me. Jaidev." I clear my throat, a little uncertain, as I realize what this could look like—like I've followed her to an isolated place. "I wasn't following you. I'd just gone out for a walk and I was trying to phone Bastien, my brother, but I lost the signal. And I came up over here, thinking it'd be stronger, being higher up, you know?" Feebly, I wave my phone at her. "But it's not."

She nods but doesn't relax.

"Your dance was beautiful," I say. "Really breathtaking. And the emotion in it was just… Why didn't you dance like that earlier in the studio? I mean, I was beginning to think you weren't up to my level—" I break off, realizing how arrogant and conceited that sounds.

"I was just nervous," she says, her voice guarded.

"Nervous?" I ask. "Of me?" I hold my hands up. "I'm not scary. I don't bite."

She rolls her eyes—somehow, I see that in the moonlight. It warms me a little, makes the corners of my lips twitch.

"I guess we just have to get used to each other," she says.

"Yes. We do." I shift my weight a little from foot to foot. It's cold. I want to step closer to her, more out of the wind, but I also don't want to scare her. I mean, it could still look like I've followed a lone girl to a graveyard. Even if I had stumbled across her performing the most mesmerizing dance. "We'll manage it," I say. "Despite what everyone is saying."

"*Everyone?*" Her voice rises in pitch. "They... I don't know if they're as against you as they are me, those company dancers, but no one seems to want me to succeed with this."

I take the smallest step closer. "I want you to. I want both of us to."

And it is true. I'm not just doing this for my mother's sake, because I made that promise, or because of my fear of regrets. Watching the beauty of Taryn's dancing and the emotions it made me feel has truly reminded me how much I love dancing—because that feeling you get when dancing, well, nothing can beat it. Seeing Taryn dance makes me want to dance. Makes me want to speak that language too, delve into that world and never leave it.

Avril was right: I need to dance. It was the change of location I needed, not the change of career. Not once today when I danced with Taryn did I think of what happened or of *her*. I was just focused on the moves, the steps, and I was enjoying the adrenaline, the way dancing felt like freeing myself.

And dancing with Taryn could be great. She's trained for years and years, and it's clear she's a natural. I've just seen that. I almost want to ask if I can dance with her now, here, but I don't know if that would seem creepy or weird or something, so I don't.

"You know what some dancers can be like," I say. "Clique-y. But once we prove to those already performing in the company that we deserve to be there, they'll get used to us. They just don't like us because this is going against tradition.

But Mr. Aleks and Miss Tavi and Mr. Vikas are giving us this chance. And the other staff have already accepted us, too. That lady, the costume designer, she was really nice to me. Warm."

"Allie," Taryn says.

"Allie." I nod. "And we'll do this. We'll prove we deserve this, and the others will get used to us being there."

"And Sibylle and Xavier and the others?"

"They'll either come around or they won't." I shiver. "But if they don't, it's not the end of the world. They'll be leaving before our eight weeks is over, anyway. Right?" I'm still not exactly sure how the academy is structured here, but I think that's what someone said. Or maybe I read it on Roseheart's website. As soon as I landed at the airport, I got a taxi over here and continued learning as much as I could about this establishment.

"Oh." Taryn's voice is small. "I... I hadn't really thought about that, not that way. It's... yeah, they'll be leaving."

"So, it'll be okay."

She nods, a little cautiously. Then she smiles and it's a more genuine smile. It's the same smile she had on her face when she was dancing solo in the silver shadows out here, and it makes my heart warm.

"And if anyone gives you any more grief, just tell me," I say. "I'm not going to let anyone upset my partner. Especially when you dance like that."

I think she's blushing and that makes me smile, feel lighter. This could really work.

I hold my hand out toward her. "May I dance with you. Just freestyle it?"

"Here? Now?" She sounds uncertain.

"Yes. I think it'd be good to dance with you here, where we're not being judged by that Mr. Vikas. He is a bit scary. And dancing here, where we can just have fun and feel the joy of it, is something that sounds good right about now." Which, I realize, is an odd thing to say and want to feel in a graveyard. I'm not really religious—my parents were Buddhists but not strict, though Avril is Catholic and imagining what she'd say about this situation makes me smile.

"Oh, uh, okay," Taryn says.

It's a little weird at first, as I start to dance out here, just moving more freestyle than ballet, because Taryn just watches me. But dancing outside, like this, without judgement from those who'll decide my fate, is freeing. And after a moment, Taryn joins in. She dances separately to me, different moves and different timing to my faster pace, but her lines are elegant and flowing and angled toward me.

My steps are light as I adjust my pacing, letting myself connect with her, with what she's using her body to convey. My movements become classical ballet, matching hers. And after a few moments, I feel it, that connection with her. Like we're in sync as we're dancing, sweeping movements under a weeping willow at the edge of the graveyard. Adrenaline and emotion carry us forward.

We move closer together, and it's amazing how ballet has this unspoken way of communicating because we don't even have to confer on what to do. Taryn's movements become slower and more graceful, then she's right by me. I reach out, supporting her as she pirouettes, like this is the start of the adagio of a grand pas de deux. I concentrate on maintaining poise and strength, offering her a steady hand as she finishes her pirouette and uses me as a virtual barre. The strength in her eyes grounds me each time I make eye contact with her, rooting me further to the spot.

We do a basic lift, and then we're slipping out of the pas de deux of classic ballet, letting in more contemporary modern moves, really just feeling the atmosphere again.

I'm breathing deeply by the time we finish, and part of me is overwhelmed by the sheer beauty and feeling of it all. Because if Taryn and I can dance together in sync, unchoreographed, out here in a graveyard, then we can do it in the studio. We can take the *Midsummer* choreography when we're given it, and we can breathe life into it. Our own life.

"We'll do this," I say, smiling.

Taryn nods, her face flushed. "We will."

EIGHTEEN

Teddy

"Hello, Theodore, isn't it?"

Groggy, I blink at the woman who's suddenly next to my bed. I hadn't noticed her enter my room. Well. I was asleep. The clock says it's half eight in the morning.

"Teddy," I say. "Everyone calls me Teddy."

"Hi, Teddy." She smiles. She's got tanned skin and blond hair pulled back into a tight bun—the same style Taryn usually has—and a wide smile that appears to have too many teeth. "My name is Alexandra. Sorry it's such an early meeting here—I'm just fitting this in before my appointments start today, really. I'm one of the dieticians here."

I jolt and sit up straighter. A *dietician*? My mouth dries. I'm fine. And I can't talk to anyone here. It was hard enough talking to Joe at Roseheart—in all the sessions he insisted I had after I'd gone to him worried about the unhealthy food in the canteen—because in each session, the voice in my head was screaming at me that I definitely didn't have a problem like he seemed to think, that I was just making wise choices and that not wanting to put junk in my body was a *good* thing. The voice was begging not to tell Joe anything, saying I was just taking up his valuable time and resources, taking it away from people who really needed the help. Like Ivelisse.

And these past few days, I thought because I'd avoided the doctors here finding out about my fear of unhealthy food that it meant I wasn't really unwell, not like Joe had begun to persuade me that I was, telling me all about OSFED and orthorexia, two eating disorders I'd not previously heard of, and pushing me to see a doctor. After all, no one here had asked me about my eating—even though eating disorders can explain heart symptoms... Last year, Ivelisse had a relapse and was absent for two months—she caught up later, during the summer, and Robert came back for a couple of weeks to dance with her so they could perfect their pas de deux. The rest of the time she was dancing with one of the second-year male dancers who was also taking time to catch up having missed a lot due to pneumonia. But when Ivelisse had the relapse, Taryn told me how she'd found pro-ana blogs in her search history. I didn't really know what they were, but I looked them up and was opened to a world of 'bloggers' who promoted what they called the 'anorexia lifestyle' and promised to 'help' people, guiding them in how to successfully make them people they are proud of. Countless of these bloggers wrote about goal posts. Things to strive toward: *If you end up with orthostatic intolerance or arrhythmias, you're doing it right! You're showing you're in control! It's proof of how disciplined you are!*

Of course, I'd never tried to achieve those things. That wasn't my goal—I am solely concerned with the quality of food, with making sure everything is organic and healthy, but those pro-ana sites taught me that EDs can cause heart problems. Joe's reiterated as much since, when he's tried to make me see that I could have orthorexia—an obsession with healthy eating that has gone too far. He says some doctors classify it as OSFED—Other Specified Feeding and Eating Disorder—rather than a separate disorder in and of itself, but I thought the idea of me having either OSFD or orthorexia was silly. I couldn't possibly have an *eating disorder*. Yet I had begun to wonder if maybe it wasn't healthy to spend *so much time* thinking and worrying about what I ate, especially when most of the other diploma undergrads didn't seem to spend anywhere near as much time planning their meals and fretting.

In the last year, Joe's done a lot of work with me on food education, after I initially went to him with my concerns over the canteen food. I'd told him the cooks needed to switch to more organic food and to offer more meals without carbs. Joe assured me I was eating healthily, but he was wrong. I couldn't eat healthily with what the academy was serving.

"It's not right," I'd said. "We need more free-range chicken available, and I wanted to have salad instead of potatoes, but the cook wouldn't let me. She's giving out all this wrong advice, and I need these healthy foods, not all this poison. Can't you just talk to her?"

Joe had frowned and asked me for more details about my diet.

"Well of course I don't eat dessert," I said, when he'd prompted me share the desserts I ate. "Unless it's fruit salad."

"Because of the calories?" He squinted at me. "Are you counting calories, Teddy?"

"No!" I don't know why but that had annoyed me. "Desserts aren't healthy. Especially the amount of butter the cook puts in her cake."

"How do you know how much butter is in the cake?"

I shrugged. "Because I asked her for the recipe, pretended I was interested in sharing it with my mum. But I wanted an apple, that was all, and she wouldn't let me. And I needed to have an apple because apples are healthy. They're good foods."

"But you need to have carbs—and you've told me you've practically cut out the whole carb group."

"I have sweet potato."

"You have one portion of that a week, Teddy, according to this." He nodded at the list he'd made as I'd proudly reeled off a typical menu—the proof that I was being healthy. Joe shook his head. "No rice, no white potato, no pasta."

"Because I need to be healthy."

"You're not getting enough energy though."

"I am. I eat loads of salad. All sorts of fruit and veg. And chicken. And I don't eat ridiculously small portion sizes of those, like Ivelisse does. It's not about calorie-counting."

"But you need foods from all the food groups. Include carbs and dairy. They won't hurt you."

It didn't matter how many times Joe told me I needed to eat these 'unhealthy' foods, how he said my body needed energy, because I just couldn't do it. And I couldn't see how eating healthily could really be a problem.

But since I saw the page in the HCM booklet about diet and hydration, it's made me wonder. I've always prided myself on maintaining an optimal level of health. Only, if my heart thickening isn't down to HCM, then it has to be something I've done wrong.

I haven't been eating healthily enough. If the genetic test and the catheterization prove it's not HCM, then it's down to me.

"So, your doctors just wanted me to have a little chat with you," Alexandra says, sitting in the chair next to my bed. "Just because they've noticed you're not really eating much."

"I'm not hungry." I grip the edge of the scratchy blanket too hard and stare at the tray at the foot of my bed. My breakfast is on it, uneaten. "And my nose and front teeth still hurt. And I don't really like hospital food, either." Well, my teeth actually feel a bit better now, but I always find it harder to eat when I'm stressed—and this is definitely a stressful time.

I want to scream. It's a tug of war inside me. One team wants to tell them my worries about food, and even what Joe suspects, because I want the reassurance that my food issues haven't actually caused this heart condition or made it worse, yet I also don't want to be told it is HCM because that means no dancing. At least if it is OSFED or orthorexia or whatever causing this, then I can get better, right? I can dance again.

Alexandra gives a small laugh. "That's understandable. And of course being in a strange environment with strange food can make you less hungry too. But we just wanted to check in with you to see if you'd benefit from any supplements."

My stomach drops. *Supplements*. Joe has mentioned those more than once, trying to persuade me to have them. A few months ago, he brought in some starter packs. Fortisip Compact. Vanilla flavor and strawberry. I couldn't bring myself to try them—there was too much glucose and milk in them—and I told Joe I'd try harder to stick to the meal plan he'd given me. Joe had agreed to it, saying that for the time being that was okay, but if I began to lose more weight or my health declined, he'd have to notify health professionals— and my family. I'd vowed it wouldn't come to that, coming up with ways to make myself heavier at weigh-ins by water-loading. After all, Roseheart isn't an ED Recovery Centre where they're more clued up on how sneaky people like me can be. To some extent, I'm taken at face-value, and because I've resisted any official diagnosis, unlike Ivelisse, I'm not taken out of Roseheart for separate appointments.

And that's surely proof I'm not sick anyway, else Joe would just make the appointments for me and tell my dad, regardless of what I wanted. Makes me think that orthorexia can't be as serious an eating disorder as anorexia, when I'm given choices about whether to get help and Ivelisse wasn't—even though we've always been told never to compare EDs.

Or maybe yours just isn't bad enough yet.

I swallow hard. As Alexandra asks me which foods I like and don't like, I wonder if Joe *will* tell others. He has to have heard of my diagnosis by now. Maybe he's said something, hinted at things. Maybe that's why this dietician's really here. Maybe she's trying to confirm what Joe's said. Maybe they're just looking for yet another reason why I can never dance again.

"Okay, well, your BMI is a little low, but it's not too worrying," the dietician says.

A little low.

Not too worrying.

The words suddenly seem like both a relief and an insult. They don't think there's anything wrong with me, so they're not going to make me eat. But for some reason it seems like an insult—like I'm not doing this right, like I'm not healthy enough. Yet it also doesn't make any sense because I don't want to lose weight, not like Ivelisse said she did, when, last year, she broke down crying over eating a forkful salad.

See, that's the difference. She doesn't want to eat anything. But I do. I just want to eat healthy things.

"Right, well I'll be off then," Alexandra says. "I'll let the kitchen know which foods you like. See if we can get something softer as well after the nasal surgery. I'm sorry you were given fish and chips before. That's not good practice. Should've been soups after a surgery like that."

I smile and nod, even though the idea of soup has me recoiling. But I listed fruits and vegetables mainly for Alexandra's list, though I did then add yoghurt and lasagna as a panicked afterthought because I don't want anyone here thinking I've got a problem with food. I need to get away from this hospital as soon as I can.

I just hope I don't get faced with lasagna tonight.

"What… What about ballet?" My voice squeaks, just as Alexandra's almost out of the door. "Will I be able to dance?"

I don't know why I'm asking her when she's a dietician and when I already know the answer, been told it countless times. But maybe I am hoping for a different answer. Maybe she doesn't know much about my suspected heart condition and will give me the go-ahead. And, after all, there's no reason for her to suspect I've got an eating disorder, so she can't limit my exercise on that basis, not like how the doctors last year said Ivelisse would've had to have stopped ballet for a much longer time than two months if she'd continued to lose more weight.

"That'll be a question for your cardiologist," Alexandra says. "I'm sorry I don't know."

But I do.

And I need someone to tell me I can do ballet still. I need that permission to be a danseur, to be me. Everything else is inconsequential.

NINETEEN

Taryn

After a quick morning run—always a great way to start a Monday morning, even if I was alone this time—I'm back in my room and staring at the remains of my photo board again. I've collected the photos up and arranged them in a little pile on my desk. They still make me feel empty, numb, and I still don't know who's done this.

Sibylle is still asleep, bundled up in her bed, even though it's half nine now. Ivelisse is in the en suite bathroom the three of us share, the sounds of the shower on. Neither of them has to get up early now they have no timetabled sessions here.

I watched them a lot last night, Sibylle and Ivelisse, trying to fathom them out, work out if they really do hate me, but I couldn't tell. All I know is someone does.

My phone pings. Email notification. It's from the company. Mr. Vikas's secretary. A lady called Dora. She's emailed me a schedule of company classes for flexibility, point, expression, and pas de deux. *Mr. Vikas will give you your rehearsal timetable—which is separate to this—later,* she writes in the email. *You're expected to attend all the classes in this attached schedule each week and fit in your partnered practices and endurance training in your own time.*

My company classes on this schedule begin later this week. They're mostly arranged in blocks on the same days, keeping other days completely clear—probably for Mr. Vikas's rehearsals and sessions.

The sounds of the shower stop, and a few moments pass as I sort through my various pairs of ballet shoes, trying to decide which to select for my next session with Jaidev. Suddenly, I hear retching sounds from the bathroom. Ivelisse.

I head to the door. "You okay?" I call softly. "Ivelisse?"

I hear her gasping more, being sick, and I grimace. The first thing I think is that it's her eating disorder—but I also remember how upset Ivelisse got last year when she had a stomach bug, and everyone had just assumed it was her eating disorder.

Ivelisse doesn't reply, but there are more retching sounds.

I turn around. Sibylle is sitting up in bed now, looking at me.

"She all right?"

I shrug. "It doesn't sound like it?"

Sibylle frowns and gets out of bed.

"Oh, what happened to your photos?" she asks. "I was going to ask yesterday and forgot. You took them down?"

I watch her carefully, then look toward the pile on my desk. Sibylle's eyes widen.

"You cut them up?"

I shake my head. "Someone did, though."

"Shit." Her eyes are wide. "Who?"

"I don't know."

Her frown gets deeper. "Are you going to report it?"

I watch her even more carefully, trying to read her body language. Does she think I should? Does she want me to—or not?

"You should," she says. "It's vandalism."

"What's vandalism?" Ivelisse asks as she opens the bathroom door.

I turn to her. Her eyes are all watery and her face looks too pale, eyeliner smudged down one side of her face.

"Are you okay?" I ask.

She nods. Doesn't say anything. No offer of an explanation. Just the nod. She's got a towel wrapped around her and I can see how thin she is. So thin it makes me feel uncomfortable in my own body.

Ivelisse grabs some clothes from her wardrobe then locks herself back in the bathroom to change, like she always does. Then I hear her speaking Spanish.

I glance at Sibylle.

"She'll be on the phone. Her mum usually phones around this time. But, Taryn?" Her voice is low as she moves toward me. She jerks her gaze to the closed bathroom door. "Do you think we should tell Madame about…" She gestures vaguely.

"I don't know," I say. It's true that we're asked to keep an eye on Ivelisse, but I don't want to be telling tales on her. Being sick once doesn't mean her ED is worsening. And I don't want to rock our fragile friendship, as much as it is a friendship, anyway.

Even if she's the one who tore up your photos?

But I don't know that it was her. I can't imagine either of my roommates doing it. It could be someone else, and I don't want to burn any more bridges than I already have.

"We should just keep an eye on her," I whisper. Then I grab my soft-split shoes and water bottle. "I have to go now."

The studio is empty when I arrive. Jaidev's not here yet. Part of me is relieved, because I've somehow made myself incredibly nervous about dancing with him again after we managed that connection in the graveyard. Last night feels like a lifetime ago, sort of like a surreal dream that might've never actually been reality.

I change into my practice clothes and warm up at the barre. A few minutes later, Jaidev arrives, and I tell him we won't have long to practice together today as I've got a visiting appointment to see Teddy.

"Okay, but I spoke to Mr. Vikas earlier," he tells me as he takes his hoody off. "And today's our last general practice together before we meet the choreographer and watch the company dancers doing their tour rehearsals. Then we'll work out the exact details of our dance for the tour."

I nod.

It feels weird dancing with him again. Outside of the graveyard, under the harsh studio lights, there's not that immediate sense of emotional connection between us, but we find it after a few minutes. It's exhilarating, realizing how quickly we've formed this. Of course, we're at nowhere near the level Teddy and I were, but it's promising that Jaidev and I are at this stage already.

It makes me think that us being accepted into the company in time for the fall tour isn't such a long shot. That it might actually be achievable.

We train for four hours, then it's time for me to go.

"We haven't finished the routine though," Jaidev says. "Just a few more minutes."

"I know. But I've got to get to the hospital."

"For… for your… friend." He seems to have trouble saying the last word.

"For Teddy. Yes." I give him an odd look then grab my water bottle. "Maybe see you later, when I'm back."

Teddy is my best friend, so I don't know why the thought of going to visit him again actually makes me nervous—way more nervous than I was yesterday. And it's not just nerves I'm feeling. It's guilt. Yesterday I told him that Jaidev and I weren't working—yet now we are. Only Teddy knew about me dancing in the graveyard before, yet he'd never danced with me here. But Jaidev has. I feel like I'm betraying my best friend, like there's this massive divide between us now. Not just because we won't dance together again, but also like we won't be friends, best friends, for much longer as the rift is getting too big. And maybe Teddy knows it too—he lied about his phone being out of battery.

This morning, before I went on my run, I'd arranged to visit him in the afternoon, having phoned up to book my hour half slot with the nurses—apparently, they're very particular on bookings and that—but it doesn't leave me with much traveling time to get there, not now I've done morning practice with Jaidev.

The buses are all running late, and I'm so worried about missing my visiting slot that I end up running. At two minutes before my appointed time, I'm standing outside the general hospital. Just staring up at the building, watching people go in and out.

Move! I tell myself. I've not got time to dally, and I wasn't scared to go in yesterday.

I swallow hard and summon all my courage. I take a deep breath. I can do this.

It doesn't take me long to reach Teddy's ward, and I walk straight past the reception desk, nodding at the nurse stationed there, and toward Teddy's private room. Then I see the door is open and the bed is empty, freshly made. All signs of Teddy have gone.

"He was discharged just an hour or so ago," the receptionist calls to me.

I spin, slowly, feeling like everything is moving around me.

Discharged? And he never told me? I falter. I texted him earlier to tell him I was coming here. I sent the message via WhatsApp too. The app told me he'd seen it—though he didn't reply. I pull out my phone and check again, in case I've missed a message. But I haven't. And now he's... gone. Left. Without telling me.

"Oh, okay." My voice is small. "Uh, thanks."

I leave the hospital, numb. I catch the first bus almost on autopilot and stare at the people around me, laughing, smiling. I grab my phone and call Teddy.

"Hey, Tedster," I whisper softly into the voicemail message when he doesn't answer. "I... I went to see you at the hospital, but they said you've gone... Home?" Is it home he's gone? To his dad's?

I take a shuddering breath. Teddy doesn't even like his father much. Before his mum died, Teddy only really saw his dad a few times a year. For the last few holidays, he's visited him, but he hated it.

But now he's gone there? Gone to a whole world I don't even know. Maybe a whole world he doesn't know either.

I wonder if this is the end of us, of our friendship. If I'll never see him again.

"I... I'm sorry I didn't get to see you." My voice cracks. "But...but stay in touch, okay?"

I walk back to the academy, close to tears. But I know all that matters is Teddy's alive.

TWENTY

Jaidev

"Mate, your phone has been ringing for like half an hour," Xavier says when I return to my room.

"Oh, right. Thank you." I grab it from my bed. Eight missed calls. All from Bastien. Shit. I'd only popped out for a walk. Needed a breather. After my session with Taryn, I attended Madame Cachelle's classes, then ended up having dinner in the canteen with Peter, and wow, that is one annoying guy. All his talk about sex was just getting too much. Especially when he seemed desperate to know about previous relationships I've had. Whether I want to go to the clubs with him round here as there are always lots of 'keen girls.'

I've only ever had one girlfriend. *Her*. Camille. My dance partner.

Darkness shadows me for a moment. I mustn't think about her. About what happened.

I swallow hard and focus back on my phone. If Bastien is phoning rather than messaging, something is wrong.

Majorly. And that just makes my heart pound faster. It has to be Avril.

I take a deep breath and call Bastien. Xavier goes back to his desk. His laptop's open and as I count the rings of Bastien's phone, I find my eyes focusing on what Xavier's doing. He's Googling auditions for fixed-term ballet company contracts in the UK. I press my lips together. So, he's applying elsewhere then. He's accepted that me and Taryn will get the positions with Roseheart, and he's not going to try and change the company's mind, like those dancers were suggesting to Sibylle.

Or he's keeping his options open.

Xavier sees me looking and quickly closes the browser. His desktop photo shows two white boys, arms around each other, smiling at a camera. I think one is Xavier—when he was much younger. And the other a little brother? Both have the same brown hair and dark eyes. Then Xavier closes his laptop. He swivels in his chair so his back is to me, and just sits there.

I walk to the wardrobe and open it absentmindedly as I wait for Bastien to answer—it's just ringing and ringing. My side of the wardrobe is still very empty. My suitcase still hasn't arrived. At the airport I asked Lani to pack for me, telling her what I wanted. Mainly just ballet clothes, but also my father's áo giao lĩnh. It's the only thing I still have of his, and he told me it was his father's before him, and his father's too, and so on, being passed through the generations. I never met my father's father; he passed away of cancer before I was born.

The only grandfather I met, though I was too young to remember, was my mother's father. He was born in Tezpur, on the banks of Brahmaputra in northeastern India, and moved to Vietnam when he met my grandmother. I'm named after him, and I've always felt a connection to him because of it. I smile as I remember how my grandmother told me when I was three years old that I thought he was actually two people, as we used both the Indian and Vietnamese names for 'grandfather' for him. My parents encouraged me to use Ông Ngoại, as Vietnamese was my first language, and while my grandfather often called himself by that name too, every once in a while, he'd refer to himself as Dada—it was what he called his own grandfather in Tezpur. My grandmother laughed once, when on the phone I apparently asked if both Dada and Ông Ngoại would be at her house when we next visited.

Although I don't remember firsthand the grandfather I was named after, I have fond constructed memories of Dada/Ông Ngoại based on my grandmother. But with my paternal grandfather, my ông nội, the only thing I have that links me to him—and my other ancestors from that line—is the áo giao lĩnh, the traditional garment being passed down father-to-son. It also makes me feel connected to my father too, and I often wonder when my dad would've chosen to give it to me. Instead, it became mine when I was orphaned, left to me in the will, and my bà ngoại kept it safe for me until I was about twelve. Then she presented it to me, this fine collared robe that felt like a lifeline, a way to connect with those I'd lost.

The ringing on the line stops, and Bastien's voicemail finally kicks in.

"Bastien, I got your missed calls. What's going on? What's happened?" I can't keep the worry out of my voice, and I pray he'll return my call soon.

Next, I phone the hospital Avril is in. International calls are expensive, and she texted me right after I arrived in England telling me not to call. That she'll have a nurse call me if it's important, otherwise we'll just connect on messenger. We have been exchanging messages and small updates, yes. But Bastien's missed calls have me worried something's happened with her. As I wait for staff at the hospital ward to answer, I check Messenger. No messages from her there.

Xavier swivels in his chair. It creaks. He looks at me and then around the room. It's a poky little room, with two twin beds crammed in, two desks, and one shared wardrobe. Apparently other rooms have multiple wardrobes, but not this one. There's no en suite here either. We share a bathroom at the end of the hall with six others.

At last, the ward answers, and in French I ask if Avril's okay. They assure me that she is and that she may even be able to go home next week, with help.

"Home? I… I'm not there. I'm in England," I tell them.

"Will anyone be there? We've got another son in our records. Bastien Troisière?"

"Yes, uh, he lives near her."

"So, he'll be able to help?" the nurse asks.

"I hope so." My voice is small. I mean, Bastien will. He's getting better now.

"Great," the nurse says. "We'll be in touch with him anyway closer to the day we plan to discharge your mother."

"Great," I say.

Bastien won't let her down. He can't. Not when she's always there for him. For us.

TWENTY-ONE

Taryn

The next morning, Jaidev and I arrive at the dance studio to find Evangeline, one of the company choreographers, waiting for us. She talks us through the overall choreography for Roseheart's version of *A midsummer Night's Dream*, outlining the main differences between this and the classical productions of it.

"And here's the cast list," she says, handing us a piece of paper.

Jaidev and I each take one edge of it, holding it between us.

My eyes widen. We're the dancers for the divertissement pas de deux, as well as each being on stage several other times, including in the big ensemble dances of the second act.

"Oh wow," I say. We are the divertissement dancers? That amazing choreography where we get to be fairies?

Evangeline is grinning. "It's certainly a special dance. And very popular roles."

"And you trust us for this?" Jaidev asks.

"Prove to me that it was the correct decision," she says. "We don't want your understudies being chosen instead."

I look at the names of the divertissement understudies, but they're unfamiliar to me. My eyes glaze over as I glance at the rest of the cast list. The character of Helena is being played by Li Hua Zhao—she was the female graduate from the diploma last year. But aside from her and Trent—the male graduate last year—I don't really know any of the other cast. The principals aren't in this production, but this is the third-division's tour. The company produces three different ballets at all times. The third division is where new dancers start—and where they remain for years if they don't get better.

"The lead roles of Oberon, Titania, and Puck are being played by those at the top of the third division," Evangeline says. "That's Harry Hesketh, Victoria Simmonds, and Pierre Garnier. They will be center stage in the majority of the main scenes of both acts, along with Marion Lazear who is playing Hippolyta, and those selected for the roles of Theseus, Tatiana's cavalier, Hermia, Lysander, Helena, and Demetrius." She points at each role on the list. "You'll meet them all later today."

"Today?" I stare at her. My stomach twists at the thought of meeting the company dancers properly, of having nowhere to run, even though Jaidev told me yesterday that Mr. Vikas said this was coming up. Oh God, what if any of the female dancers in this production are those dancers whom I've already met?

"Yes," Evangeline says. "The whole cast for this tour will be here this afternoon for group rehearsals. Understudies too—we do a round-Robin system for understudies in all our divisions. So, Li Hua Zhao and Trent Mason are also understudies for Oberon and Titania, as well as being Helena and Demetrius, and…" She points to more names, then tells us so many more roles and names that I can't keep up. "You'll get a better idea of the flavor we're going for with this telling of *A Midsummer Night's Dream* after today, too. And Mr. Vikas and Miss Tavi will be here too."

She has us work on our divertissement pas de deux, barking instructions at us. The choreography is ambitious, and it's the first time we've really done a lot of lifts. Jaidev stumbles twice and I nearly miss my footing at one point as I run toward him ready to be swept up off the ground, ready to fly. I can't imagine how amazing this would look with the fairy costumes.

"Are you nervous about meeting the others?" I whisper to him when we stop for a break. Evangeline has already stepped out to go and pick up the training and rehearsals timetables for us that she says Mr. Vikas has been working on.

We've got ten minutes until Mr. Vikas and the other company dancers arrive.

"It'll be fine," Jaidev says. "Try not to be nervous." He cups my face in his hands, and I don't like it, the physical contact. It's unnecessary now that we've stopped dancing. "I'm just going to make a phone call," he says, starting toward the door. "Been trying to get through to my brother since yesterday, you know? And I also need to find out where my suitcase has gone."

He leaves me alone in the studio, and I find myself thinking about Helena—I always think about her when I dance, but of course this ballet in particular was her favorite because there's a character with her name in it. I breathe a sigh of relief that I wasn't selected to play Helena, but still I'm thinking about her now. About what it would be like to have a sibling my own age to worry about. I mean, I have my little sisters. But I don't really know them. Mum had the oldest four years ago, with her boyfriend Giovanni. The second one two years after. I was already living away at a ballet school then. It's like they're a family unit, the four of them, and I'm just extra. If Helena was still here, things would've been different. There'd have been two of us. We wouldn't have both been sidelined.

Or maybe Mum never would have gone on to have the other two. If Helena hadn't died, then maybe Mum wouldn't have even met her new boyfriend. He's a grief counsellor, after all.

Grief.

Suddenly, the room seems colder and the mirrors more eerie. My reflection is watching me. I don't like it, so I get up and walk. I need something to do. I stretch at the barre and then retie my hair in a bun, just to make sure it's perfect. I'm sweating a lot, and my stomach feels like its contents are slipping about.

No matter what I do, I feel like too many eyes are watching me. I don't know why, when I'm completely alone now. It's stupid. Just me in here now. It's my head that's the crowded space.

But then I can't stand it. I need some fresh air. I slip outside, into the corridor. No signs of Jaidev or Evangeline, nor Mr. Vikas. Or any company dancers. But the air's still stuffy and stale, just like in the studio. So, I follow the corridor to the left, to where there's a little courtyard with rose bushes planted in a neat row. I head out there, gulping the fresh air in too-big chunks that make me nauseous. I let my hands dangle, my fingertips brushing the top of a rose bush. The fleshy pads of my thumbs press against sharp thorns— almost hard enough to draw blood, but I stop myself.

God, I don't even know why I'm reacting like this. This is what I wanted, to be a dancer in this company. And if Jaidev and I get accepted, I'll be dancing in ballets with them all the time. They'll have to be nicer to me. And they will be, once they get to know me.

And I have to give them this chance to get to know me.

I take a deep breath.

"It'll be fine," I say, as if I can expel all my unease through saying the words aloud. Like the words are a dog that'll chase my fears away. Because I know exactly what I'm scared of: of being ostracized, of being laughed at, of being excluded.

Of failing.

I head back into the studio. Suddenly, I want to be in there when the dancers arrive. Not arriving afterward. My steps are shaky as I make my way into the studio—

I stop as I see what's written on the mirror.

All the blood and warmth and everything drains from my face, my body, trying to pull me down. I feel darkness tugging at my edges as I stare at the lipstick swirls on the mirrors. The words.

I know you're a murderer.

TWENTY-TWO

Jaidev

Taryn's acting weird when I return to the studio. Even weirder than before. Yep, she's definitely overthinking things. The company dancers aren't even here yet. Neither are Evangeline nor Mr. Vikas. We've still got two minutes until the time given.

"Don't worry," I tell her and give her my biggest smile. Bastien finally answered the phone—he's fine—*and* I've located my suitcase. It's been found at Heathrow and should be delivered later today. I pat Taryn's shoulder. "We'll do this."

Taryn doesn't look convinced, she just keeps looking over to the mirror by the large window. "Did you speak to your brother?" she asks.

"Yeah." I laugh. "I thought it was a life-and-death kind of thing with the amount of missed calls he'd left me. But it turned out he'd seen some cute meme of a cat or something and wanted to tell me about it." I look at her quickly. "He's, uh, got problems with addiction, so sometimes he gets really, uh, over-animated about certain things."

Taryn nods. "That must be difficult. You must worry a lot about him?"

Am I worried now? I mean, yes. Bastien had been speaking so fast. Just like how he does when he's high or something. But I'm trying not to jump to conclusions. Bastien can be dramatic anyway, and I'm glad that this was nothing, really. Not compared to any of the reasons he could've been desperately trying to call me.

"Yeah, I worry about him," I say. "He's complicated."

"Family often are," Taryn says, and the way her eyes take on a haunted look draws me in. Makes me want to know more about her and her complicated family.

"Brothers? Sisters?" I ask.

"Sisters." She looks down at her feet, then up again, but sort of behind me.

Thinking maybe someone is arriving, I turn to look. But there's no one there. Just the doorway showing the empty corridor and the wall to the left, by the window, where a large mirror is in front of a barre. There's a faint pink hazy area on the mirror. I frown, don't think that was there before, but then there's not time to ask her about it because suddenly there *are* voices.

It takes a few moments for the owners of the voices to come into view in the corridor, complete with a clatter of feet. The company dancers are here.

A glance at Taryn shows me she's gone deathly pale.

I focus on the company dancers as they enter. They make no attempt to hide that they are looking both Taryn and me up and down with varying expressions of contempt, suspicion, intimidation, and boredom. Only one looks friendly out of the group. There's eleven of them. They sit on a bench along the left side of the room, alternating ballerina with danseur. They're all watching us. The men look about as strong as me, and that reassures me. I feel like I'm on the same level. Good. The women are all focused on Taryn, and I wonder what they're thinking. Several are leaning forward, their eyes slightly narrowed. Two are leaning back though, arms crossed, looking somewhat bored, like they think they're wasting their time. Most of the dancers look smaller than Taryn, who I know is unusual for a ballerina. She's got to be five feet nine or ten, and Taryn's curvy too. These ballerinas for the company look more like the conventional idea of a ballerina: petite and dainty and really skinny—but lithe, strong. I wonder if these women are thinking Taryn doesn't look like them.

Taryn is shaking, and I reach across, squeeze her hand, try to reassure her.

We can do this.

Mr. Vikas and Evangeline enter, along with a pianist.

"Right." Mr. Vikas claps his hands in a somewhat theatrical manner before gesturing to Evangeline and then barking instructions.

Evangeline gathers me and Taryn together and goes over the choreography for the pas de deux we were practicing earlier.

"We'll start with seeing that," she says.

We warm up, Taryn at the barre and me by the barre, stretching, before we rehearse the pas de deux again. It's of moderate complexity and we're not making mistakes, we're just not executing it smoothly yet. But these things take time. And everyone is watching us. I thought the group rehearsal would be just that—a *group* rehearsal, but so far, the company dancers are all just sitting on a bench to the side, watching us. Judging us.

I concentrate fully on Taryn as we dance, try to anyway, but when we finish, and I look at our audience, I see several whispering to each other. One ballerina laughs. Evangeline is standing with her face neutral, arms folded. Mr. Vikas is shaking his head.

"No, no, no, this needs a lot more work." He groans, but then he turns to the company dancers. "Warm up. You all have a vibe together, a way of dancing that embodies the same atmosphere. Taryn and Jaidev need to learn this same vibe. They need to get used to dancing with you."

Taryn looks even more scared as the ballerinas and danseurs get up, and I feel oddly protective of her.

"It'll be okay," I tell her before we're divided up— ballerinas on the left and danseurs on the right.

And then the practice is on. The Roseheart Romantic Dance Company runs things differently to Avril's school. Mr. Vikas has us warm up and perform solo variations, asking us to pair up—ballerinas with ballerinas, and danseurs with danseurs—to give peer feedback. The danseur I'm paired with is called Manuel. He seems pretty sound, respectful. Not glaring at me or anything. I think he's got the role of Theseus in the tour.

"I saw you in *Giselle*," he says to me, smiling. "You were really good."

"Thanks." I pretend his words haven't made my heart drop. *Giselle* was the last ballet I danced in before…

I shake that train of thought away. As Manuel and I perform the various instructions from Mr. Vikas, I sneak glances at Taryn. A ballerina is helping her stretch out at the barre now. They don't seem to be talking much, but at least Taryn doesn't seem to be trembling still.

After the exercises are complete, and a few ballerinas have given Taryn small nods of approval when she does a particularly impressive variation, we turn to group choreography for the ensemble performances in act two. Of course, the company dancers have practiced these a lot before and are nearly flawless, but Evangeline and Mr. Vikas direct Taryn and me.

By the end of the practice, I do feel like I am beginning to understand Roseheart's vision for this version of *A Midsummer Night's Dream*. It's an unconventional portrayal of the story, but all in all, I think it sounds pretty good. Magical, even.

"We will rehearse again tomorrow," Mr. Vikas says. To me and Taryn, he adds, "be sure to memorize the timetables. We have an extensive training schedule planned in order to get the two of you ready in time. When we are putting in so much effort, we expect you to, too." There's a warning tone in his voice, and it almost feels like we're being told off for something we've not yet done.

"Be there bright and early," I say.

Taryn lets out a small squeak and a nod, then we are all dismissed. Taryn scurries out and disappears. I'm unsure if she's desperate to get away from all the company dancers or not. I mean, a couple did look friendly toward her by the end. I think it was obvious to them that she was nervous.

Everyone else exits as I'm grabbing my bag, but one dancer lingers in the corridor outside. A white ballerina with shiny, chestnut hair, creamy skin, and very red lips. Her eyes narrow on me as I approach her. I think she's called Victoria. I heard that name being said several times in practice—usually in gallant phrases of praise from Mr. Vikas. She was playing Titania.

Victoria doesn't move to get out of my way. If anything, she almost becomes more solid. Her eyes darken, and there's tension in her shoulders.

"I know what you did." Her voice is low. "So, you'd better watch yourself. All right?"

The corners of my mouth twitch. "Uh, I have no idea what you're talking about."

"Really?" She raises her eyebrows and lets out a dainty snort. "Let's just say the ballet world is small. People talk. People know each other. People remember. And people like me don't forget when our friends, our *family*, are hurt. When they're *thrown*."

Ice fills my veins. "I didn't throw her."

"That may be the verdict the police made, but we all know. Camille sure as hell knows. And I don't want you at this company, so like I said, you'd better watch yourself and stay out of my way."

I try not to shake. "Or what?"

"Well." Victoria laughs. "Do you really want to find out?"

TWENTY-THREE

Teddy

"You've told the academy I'm not going back?" I stare at my dad, my phone in my hand. The email I just got from Roseheart's administration team is still on my screen. They only just sent it—bang on 9 a.m. I wonder if they typed it up yesterday and scheduled it to send first thing today.

We're so sorry to hear of your diagnosis. Given you were so close to completion of the BTEC Ballet Extended Diploma we will be issuing you with an honorable graduation. It is regrettable that you are not able to attend Roseheart Academy to receive your certificate, but we understand your decision not to return here. We wish you the very best of luck with your future.

"Well, yeah." Dad frowns and looks up from his book— the latest Richard Osman detective novel. He's been dropping toast crumbs on it as he reads. "You only had a month left anyway, and you can't dance. The doctors said that."

I want to scream. Sure, the doctors said that, but they're *wrong*. They don't know me. I have to dance. "You had no right to do that. I was going back next week."

"Next week?" He snorts. "Theodore, you've got all these tests coming up. And that catheterization will be soon, too. It sounds like a big deal. They said you'd need to rest after it."

I roll my eyes. The doctor did say that when they discharged me—because catheterization is an invasive procedure to look at my heart—but none of these medical staff know *me*. I'm strong and I'm healthy. I fuel my body with the right things. I won't need to rest. I'll bounce back quickly. "I need to get back to Roseheart."

Dad puts his bookmark in the book and sets it to the side. "What for?" He swivels his whole body to face me. "You can't dance anymore."

"I... I need to speak to the admissions team." My mind races. Dad's not going to let me go back if he thinks I'm going to dance—and I *have* to. Before, I was thinking I needed someone's permission to dance, but I don't. I just need mine. I know what's best for me. "Roseheart's academy trains choreographers and dance teachers, too. I can do either of those."

He raises his eyebrows. "Spending *more* of my money?"

I glare at him. He *can* afford it. He's a lawyer. A good one. And he owes me—all those years when we had no contact. When he left my mum, he pretty much pretended I didn't exist until she died. Then he saw her death as a second chance to be a father to me. Mum had already set aside a fund to pay for my ballet education, but when Dad took over the parental duties—albeit late and only because of the circumstances—he said he'd pay instead. That the money my mum had left me should be for something else, though he never specified what.

"I can pay it," I say.

"Don't waste your mum's money on this."

"Waste it?"

"Yes, all this dancing. It was different with your mother. She was a ballerina."

"Oh, so it's a gender thing. If I'd been a girl, you'd support it. So, we're back to this old argument."

He clears his throat. "You're not going back. And you're not wasting my money or your mum's on some new course. Got it?"

My shoulders tighten. "It's my life! And it wasn't my decision to have all this taken away from me! You know how good I am at it, or maybe you would've if you'd actually come to any of the shows and got over your sexism." I take a deep breath, try to steady myself. "Ballet is my life. If I can't be there as a dancer then I still have to be there. And I will be. You can't stop me."

He makes a grumbling sound. "I'm trying to protect you."

"Protect me?" I want to laugh.

"Yes! And you've never shown any interest in teaching or what was it? Choreography? Never mentioned those before."

"I didn't know I apparently had this stupid heart condition before." I let out an exasperated sigh. But this catheterization procedure will prove I don't have it. My shortness of breath and collapsing is caused by my eating—I wasn't being as healthy as I thought I was. It has to be that.

I will be more careful of food, making sure everything is organic and that I'm getting the right vitamins and minerals, and I *will* dance again. I mean, I can't not do ballet. Everyone knows you've got to exercise to stay healthy—so it's fine for me to dance. I need dance to keep fit.

Dad opens his book again, then brushes crumbs from its pages. "We'll think about it."

"Like I need your approval."

"I said I'd think about it, Theodore. We're not rushing into anything. Now, you better get some breakfast before we leave."

"Leave?" My heart lifts. To go back to Roseheart? He's surrendered so easily?

"To go to the support group." His voice has an edge in it. "You're lucky the monthly meeting is today for this area. You could've had to wait a lot longer."

The support group. I only vaguely remember the doctors telling me about this, right before I was discharged. I'd just nodded, thinking I'd never go. Dad, on the other hand, clearly has different ideas. God, he's so annoying. Thinking he can stop me dancing and now decide what I do with my day.

"You're going," he says before I can say anything. "It'll be good to meet others with this. Have more of a support network. And you're going to meet new people."

172 | ELIN DYER

"I can go next month."

"You're going today."

"You can't make me. I'm eighteen.'

"Then you should see that this is important." He levels a look at me. "Go to this, and I'll think about paying tuition for a new non-dancing course at Roseheart."

I don't know what I expected a support group for hypertrophic cardiomyopathy to look like, but it wasn't this: we're in a café, and everyone is laughing and smiling. I don't know why I'd assumed everyone would look decrepit and overweight and obviously unhealthy, but several have similar builds to me. Immediately, I feel shame. In the booklet that the doctors gave me about HCM, I read about the misconceptions of the condition. How people think it's caused by unhealthy lifestyles, when in fact it's genetic. And I know I've been doing the same thing. Making assumptions. Judging. Shame fills me.

"Hello, you must be Theodore?" a middle-aged woman with bright purple hair says. She pulls out a seat next to her table.

"It's Teddy," I say, and I hear Dad grumble. He never liked my nickname, said it made me sound soft. Still, I guess ballet makes me seem soft, too.

Dad's right behind me and tells me to sit down in the chair the woman's offered. It's embarrassing him being here, like I'm a little child. I scan the room. I think I'm the only adult accompanied by a parent. Oh God. Even some teenagers are here on their own.

"I'm Tracy," the purple-haired woman says as I sit. "It's so great to have a new face here. Well, new faces," she adds looking at Dad, and her smile gets even wider.

Oh, hell no. I want to disappear.

"So, you've just got a diagnosis, you say?" Tracy asks, her gaze back on me.

"Yes," Dad says before I can say anything. He's already been talking about me. On the way here in the car, he said he'd phoned the group leader to let her know we were coming and to get directions, but he hadn't mentioned he'd been talking about me.

I shoot him a look, but he doesn't appear to notice.

Dad's chatting away to Tracy, like they're suddenly old friends. Old friends who talk about their children's heart conditions—or suspected heart conditions. Tracy has a son in his early twenties who isn't here, and I recoil in horror as I hear how he suddenly went into cardiac arrest when playing football when he was thirteen.

"What do you do?" A high-pitched voice makes me turn, and I find a girl peering at me intently. She's got the palest skin I've ever seen and really fine blond hair that shows a surprisingly pink scalp through it.

"I… uh, I dance. Ballet. Professionally," I add, clearing my throat.

I wait for the reactions of everyone here—because people always say *something* when they learn that I, a guy, am a ballet dancer. But this girl just nods, and no one else seems to be paying attention to me. Everyone is chattering away. Even Dad doesn't appear to have heard because he's not launching in with a you-*used*-to-be-a-dancer correction.

"Cool," the girl says. She stretches her hands in front of her. "You going to keep doing it?"

My eyebrows shoot up. "Well, yeah. I want to. Can I?"

Can I? Why am I asking her permission? She doesn't matter.

She snorts and rolls her eyes. "You'll find a new way to do what you love. You've still got to live." She lowers her voice. "I used to be a jockey. Had to stop that, but I still ride a bit. Just not intensely."

"And that's not a problem for you?" I ask, leaning forward.

She shrugs. "Everyone's affected differently. Doctors don't know why we all have different tolerances. They all advise no strenuous or intense exercise, that sort of thing." She points at a balding guy who's very tall, his height even apparent when sitting down. "He struggles with any uphill walking and has a pacemaker, but she—" She points at the oldest woman here. "She can still jog. It all just depends on the person and how badly affected you are. Your cardiologist will help you work it out, I guess."

"I really hope I can dance," I say. My voice sounds odd to my ears though. *Of course* I'm going to keep dancing. I mean, I'm a fraud sitting here.

"You will." She smiles. It doesn't exactly light up her face—that's just an annoying cliché—but it makes her features almost seem to suit her more. Those thin lips and narrow nose. "Either way, you'll find a way to stay connected to it. If you want to."

I nod.

"I'm Gemma," she says.

"Teddy."

"I know." She rolls her eyes. "Tracy gathered us all early to say you were coming and how we mustn't all try and talk to you at once." Her eye roll gets even deeper, and I don't know whether to be alarmed or embarrassed by this news. It just makes me want to disappear through the floor even more. She laughs. "And Tracy is a fan. Well, she reckoned it was you."

"What was me?"

Gemma laughs. "She recognized your name when your dad phoned up. She's mad about ballet and said she saw some performance you were in last year. *The Nutcracker?* Up in London?"

I nod. Last Christmas. This is the first time though someone has indicated that I'm a celebrity. "This just gets more and more embarrassing."

Gemma laughs. I'd thought she was fifteen or something, but the longer I look at her, the more I realize she's probably older. Maybe even my age.

"Tracy told us not to mention the ballet as you won't know what your future is yet."

"But you still asked?" I raise my eyebrows.

"I asked what you did, kind of without thinking. You just looked so lonely sitting there." She shrugs. "Done now, though, innit? But you're cool. Cooler than a lot of others here. I mean, all some of them want to talk about is medical stuff. And I get it, we're all a very rare breed. Ha. But I want to talk about normal things, too, and I think you do, as well?"

"Uh, yeah," I say.

"Good. I like people-watching." She nods over at an elderly couple by a window on the far side of the room who don't appear to be part of the HCM meeting. I have to twist a little to see them. "I think they're drug dealers."

I burst out laughing. "What?" That couple looks the least like drug dealers I can imagine.

"It's always the unexpected ones," she says with a knowing look. "Trust me, people surprise you all the time. They have these huge secrets you'd never expect. Secrets they'll do anything to keep hidden away, festering, rotting until they turn their whole beings bad."

Gemma is…intense. High energy. But fun, I guess. I can't help but smile, and for the first time since getting this stupid probably diagnosis, I feel a little better. A little calmer and at home.

But still, I don't feel a kinship with these people. They actually have this condition. I don't, and the tests will prove it. After all, they can't have diagnosed me that quickly. And the hospital was quick to say they *suspected* this but that the diagnosis needs confirming. If the scan they did really showed thickening of my heart, then there's another explanation.

There has to be.

I will get better. It's my food issues, how I'm still not being healthy enough, that's causing this. Nothing more.

TWENTY-FOUR

Taryn

I know you're a murderer.

I can't get the words out of my head. No matter what I do, how I try and distract myself, I can't stop thinking about the message. Someone here knows.

I try to concentrate on ballet—I mean, that's what I've been doing for the last twenty-four hours, since someone wrote that on the mirror. For what has to be the thousandth time, I tell myself the message is nothing. It's just a joke.

Just a joke.

I mouth the words over and over again and try not to think about the threat. Because no matter how much I try and persuade myself it's a joke, I know it isn't. It's a threat. Someone here knows what happened with Helena, and this is a warning. And it has to be linked to me getting this extra chance to get into the company. I know people clearly don't want me here, and this threat tells me that one of these people—or more—knows my secret and is prepared to use it against me. Expose me? Tell everyone if I don't back out. Is that what they're trying to get me to do?

Frustration pulls through me. I'm in one of the school's practice rooms, where I feel more comfortable than in the company's studios, at the barre. I need to work on my core strength, and I've been here for nearly an hour now.

My heart pounds. Who can possibly know this?

None of the company dancers were outright nasty in the practice earlier. A couple were even sort of nice to me, especially Li Hua. But Marion and Victoria are both two who were mean before, and while they were civil in the practice to me, I was wary. They'd be the obvious choice in trying to frighten me away—but how would they know about my sister?

I mull over it all, going through dancer after dancer, trying to work out who could know, but nothing solid comes to mind. Just because dancers might think it's unfair I'm getting this chance, it doesn't mean they're behind the threatening message. That could be anyone.

And the number done on my photo board? That could be the same person as the lipstick threat—or someone else. I didn't even see anyone in the company grounds yesterday right before the message was written, when Jaidev and I and Evangeline were there and just going out for a break.

Jaidev or Evangeline?

My mouth dries, and I grip the barre harder. No, it wouldn't make sense for Jaidev to be behind the message. He wants to succeed with me. He wouldn't want me being distracted. So that leaves Evangeline. I mean, I don't know her but that wouldn't be professional at all. And I can't imagine her doing it. Something tells me it's a dancer. And probably someone who knows more about me than I suspect, because I don't talk about Helena. That brings me back to my roommates. I know I apparently whispered Helena's name one night, so I guess it could've happened more than once. But only my roommates would've heard that—and I still can't imagine Sibylle or Ivelisse writing that message. And it wasn't their handwriting. I frown. I can't remember exactly what the lipstick writing was like, but I'd recognize Ivelisse's loopy scrawl and Sibylle's uniform hand anywhere. I'd have known instantly if it was either of their handwriting, wouldn't I?

The door to the studio creaks open, and I turn to see several petit rats from the lower school enter. They stop when they see me.

"Sorry, we thought we'd booked this room?" one of them says, her voice faltering.

"I'm just going." I grab my duffel bag and gather my things, suddenly desperate to get away from dancers who could be threatening me. I mean, logically I know it's very unlikely to be these girls as I don't even know them.

But I just want to be on my own.

It doesn't take me long to get to my room, and I throw my duffel bag at the foot of my bed, then head to my wardrobe. In the bottom left corner, there's a box, and I pull it out carefully. Put it on my bed and open the lid. I just want to look at them. Because they're Helena's shoes. The last pair she wore. Repetto. She'd been dancing in them for maybe a couple of weeks before she died, and she'd dyed them a burnt-orange color. Very distinguishable.

"I'm sorry," I whisper.

But the moment I open the box, I realize it's too much. The fabric of the pointe shoes is breaking down, the left more worn than the right. And they look like they've just been taken off, or they're about to be put on again, waiting to be danced in once more.

I can't look at them, not now. It's too soon, still too soon. Always too soon.

I close the box quickly, feeling sick and shaky as I tuck it back into the wardrobe.

I need to get out of here.

"Hey, Mum?" My voice is soft, tentative, as I hold the phone to my ear, as if I'm afraid my own mother's voice will somehow leap out of my phone, flicking into my ear canals like a serpent's tongue, and hurt me.

"Taryn. Uh, hi." She sounds as uncertain as I am.

I rarely phone her. It's been this way for years. Whenever we have spoken on the phone, it's always been her phoning me after an important event. I let out a long breath and lean against the tree trunk. I'm back at the graveyard, and I'm not sure why. Normally, I come here to dance for Helena, not to phone my mum.

"How are you?" I whisper.

There's a crackling on the line. I imagine how wide my mum's eyes will be now. The uncertain look on her face.

"I'm good… We're all good." She hums a little under her breath—something she always does when she's nervous. "Congratulations again, darling, on getting the place with the company. I know how much you wanted that."

My heart squeezes, as if the lie is wrapped around it. I want to tell her everything. Tell her about Teddy's injury and his diagnosis, about dancing with Jaidev, how the company dancers hate me, the threatening lipstick message, and how I lied. How everything could come tumbling down if I don't make the tour. How I'll need to find tuition for another year.

"The girls are very excited about it," Mum says. "They've been telling all their friends about their amazing big sister. They really are proud, you know. I am, too."

A fuzzy feeling wriggles through my nose, and my eyes smart. I take several deep breaths and try not to cry as I stare at the gravestones ahead, the shapes of them. It's the first time Mum's said that. Since Helena, we haven't really talked properly. I even avoid going home as much as I can, because when I'm there, I'm a ghost wandering the empty rooms, staring at my mother from afar. There's been this distance, and I know I remind her too much of Helena. I mean, there's no way I can't.

But there should be two of us dancing at Roseheart—and that's why Mum never comes to shows here. Says she finds it too difficult. Once, I tried to make it easier, saying maybe

Helena would've chosen a different ballet school, but we both knew she wouldn't have. We were inseparable.

I press my free hand into the dry earth and wonder how things would've gone if Helena was still alive. If we'd have been competing against *each other* with our partners to get Roseheart Romantic Dance Company. If I'd have beaten her or if she'd have beaten me.

I wonder how different things could've been. If her presence could have had wide-rippling effects. Maybe Teddy wouldn't even have been a dancer here at all. Maybe the whole cohort for the diploma would've been different. So many things could've been so, so different.

"Thanks." My voice is choked, and I have to swallow several times. I pull at the dry grass, at the few stubby blades that are poking out of the earth by the tree roots.

"I'm glad you're doing what you want," she says. "That's important. And we miss you." It's added like an afterthought and her tone is different, harder. Her walls have gone back up.

"I miss you, too," I say. It's been a good year or so since I saw her. A fleeting visit back home to the house I grew up in. "Hopefully, I'll see you again soon."

"Yes." Her voice hitches. "The girls would like that. Moo's always talking about her famous sister now."

Moo. I don't even know which of my little sisters that nickname applies to.

"Well, I must go," I say, still staring at the gravestones. Their shapes are moving, blurring under my unfallen tears.

"Mr. Vikas wants to get another practice in this evening. For the tour."

"Ah, yes. Of course." She sounds relieved that our conversation is ending.

I am too.

After the phone call, I stay in the graveyard though. Just sitting here, feeling the cold seep into my bones. I've never felt so alone, and my instinct is to text Teddy, but I know I can't. Things are different between us now.

"I've got no one," I whisper into the darkness.

TWENTY-FIVE

Taryn

"This Teddy… your last dance partner. You talk about him a lot," Jaidev says, the next day.

The two of us have just finished an intense practice this morning, and we're sitting in the canteen. And I'm sore. During the practice, I was still thinking about the threatening lipstick message, worrying still that I hadn't got rid of enough of the lipstick because it turned out wiping it off a mirror was really quite difficult. I wasn't concentrating properly as Jaidev and I did a lift because we were in the same studio and I thought the smeary pink mess on the mirror was still way too obvious and someone was going to notice it. I pulled a muscle in my lower back as we landed. I don't think Jaidev noticed though. Or Evangeline. Luckily, the other company dancers weren't there—the next time I'll see them is tomorrow, when I'm transferring from academy classes to company classes. Classes where I'll be dancing with just the women. Where I won't have Jaidev by my side.

Jaidev's staring intently at me, waiting for my answer. *Teddy, right.*

"We danced together for two years. Primary partners." I shrug. I didn't think I was always talking about Teddy. But then I realize I did mention him twice this morning, during the practice with Jaidev. Just little things that I can't even remember now. Nothing important.

Jaidev nods. "And were you… together?"

Together? "As in…?" My eyebrows shoot up, and I nearly choke on my forkful of jacket potato.

"Boyfriend and girlfriend," he says, and he says the words so… so casually. Doesn't stumble on them at all. Not like I would.

I shake my head. "No. Just friends." But using the word 'just' for what me and Teddy have makes me feel bad. Like I'm minimizing whatever it is, because it's more than friendship, even if it's not romantic or sexual. Because we were *best* friends. We were connected. Even if we aren't now.

Jaidev nods, shovels more food in. Doesn't say anything more and I don't ask, because conversations like this always make me more uncomfortable.

There's a flurry of movements by the canteen doors, and I look up to see Sibylle entering with Freya and Alma. Her face is flushed, and she makes a beeline straight for me.

I freeze.

"Oh my God, Taryn!" Sibylle's voice is high-pitched, and she practically throws herself into the seat next to me. "I've got an audition! Next week! And it's with Berlin State Ballet!"

"Oh, wow! That's amazing. When did you apply?"

"Just after Teddy's accident—when they offered you this second chance, because I knew you'd get it, and I'd been going to apply there anyway, as soon as the end of year show was finished," she says, making room at the table for the other girls to sit down.

She applied then, thinking I'd get this position with Roseheart? So, it can't be her who's trying to unnerve me in order to get my place instead. Not when she thinks I'm definitely going to get it and has made alternative arrangements.

"What have you got to do for the audition?" I ask.

"They want a variation from a classical ballet—auditioner's choice. Have to let them know today which I'm going to do though, so their pianist knows. I'm thinking of doing one from *Giselle*."

"You should totally do that." Alma's voice is cool, crisp. She holds her hands carefully up from the table so they're not touching anything. "Just painted my nails," she says by way of an explanation, but she doesn't look at me.

Is she jealous of me? Still thinking it's unfair I get this chance? Even though she never really had a chance at getting into Roseheart's company.

"Are you applying anywhere?" Jaidev asks her.

Alma shrugs. "Of course. But I'm waiting for auditions to open again at some of the American companies."

"I'm going on for more training first," Freya says.

"You are?" This is a surprise to me.

"Yes, I know Roseheart does both classical and contemporary, but I just want to do classical. Really get good at that. Because although the company dancers here are good, don't get me wrong, proper classical ballet *is* harder. I'm looking at a course in Germany."

I can't help but think that's a dig at me. Like I'm choosing the easy route by trying to join the company. Not that it is easy. No, this is just Freya trying to unnerve me. She's always been like that anyway.

"There's a great classical program at Avril's school," Jaidev says. "You should look there, too. They have a lot of connections with the classical companies, too, in Europe."

"Can you give me a referral?" Freya bats her eyes at Jaidev.

"A referral?" He sounds surprised.

"Yeah, like tell her you've seen me dance and I'm really good."

A small line appears between Jaidev's eyebrows. "But I haven't seen you dance."

She rolls her eyes. "Put your fork down and come with me." She stands, her chair legs scraping the linoleum floor and holds her hand out to him—practically right in front of his face.

Jaidev looks at me for half a second, his eyes wide. Alma snorts.

"Come on." Freya twitches her hand.

He takes one last mouthful of his food before rising. Freya practically pulls him from the room.

"He's going to have to tell Madame T that she's the best dancer in the world now," Alma says.

"Yeah, and then Madame Troisière will wonder why he's dancing with you and not her," Sibylle says, looking at me. "But, honestly, you're so much better."

"How is it going, dancing with him?" Alma asks, her voice careful and poised like a snake.

"We're getting there," I say, thinking of the graveyard dance. That was a connection, but we still haven't yet been able to replicate that intensity and connection fully in the studio.

"Maybe it'll take longer than you think," Alma says. "Maybe it's just fairer if none of us joins the company this year."

Sibylle shushes her. "Anyway." She frowns. "Have you seen Ivelisse? She said to meet here round about now, and she'd help me look through *Giselle*. I've still got to decide which variation I'm doing."

"Well, she's not here," Alma says. "Probably making herself sick again."

"What?" I stare at her.

Sibylle freezes.

"Well, yeah," Alma says. "I mean, I kind of thought it was just anorexia she had, but maybe it can change. She's been sick *so much* lately."

"Purging can be part of anorexia though," Sibylle says.

Alma shrugs. "But have you seen the amount of ginger tea she's gone through recently? The common room is nearly out of the Pukka teabags, and they're my favorite to have, when I've run out of loose leaf."

"Ginger tea?" I say blankly, thinking of the other morning when I heard Ivelisse being sick.

"Yeah, for nausea." Alma rolls her eyes. "When you purge, it makes you *so* nauseous. One of my sisters was bulimic. She was nauseous *forever*. She even had GERD from it."

"GERD?"

"Gastroesophageal reflux disease. It's pretty nasty. All about stomach acid coming up and stuff."

I set my fork down. "Do you think we should tell someone? I mean, we should, right?"

Sibylle nods. "We could mention we're worried about her, to Joe? I don't think we can go straight to her dietician or therapist. But he could."

Alma tuts under her breath. "She's not going to like you ratting on her."

"She's our friend, and we're looking out for her," Sibylle says. She looks to me and I nod. "Maybe we should check our room first though?"

"For what?" I ask.

"Evidence," Sibylle suggests, her voice tentative.

"What, like a diary that tells you she is bulimic now?" Alma laughs. "What kind of world do you think we live in?"

I glare at her. "Can you not make a joke of all this? It isn't funny."

Alma snorts. "But, I mean, what *are* you looking for?"

"Scales," I say. We're not supposed to have scales in our dorm rooms. That's one of Roseheart's policies to try and prevent eating disorders and obsessions with weight forming. But last year, when Ivelisse began to relapse, she snuck some scales in. Madame found them under Ivelisse's bed.

There were other things too, things we only realized were signs after Ivelisse was really unwell. She had an app on her phone where she logged what she was eating, her laptop history showed visits to various blogs and sites on extreme dieting and weight loss, as well as pro-ana pages, and we found a lot of stashed food in her wardrobe. Food from various meals that she'd somehow slipped off her plate unnoticed and hidden instead of eating.

If Ivelisse has started purging too now, I don't know how that might change what we could find—but there'd be something, wouldn't there? Maybe air freshener or something to cover up smells?

"Well, let's go," Alma says. Her eyes have lit up like she's enjoying this too much. She stands.

I glance at Sibylle. "It feels a bit like snooping, though."

"Yeah, but we are concerned." Sibylle pushes her hair back. She's wearing it loose for once, and it's a sleek black curtain that dips below her shoulders. "And we can't really tell Joe unless we're actually certain about this."

It feels bad as the three of us head to the dorm room. Like we're all in conspiracy now against Ivelisse, but Sibylle keeps reminding me how we're doing this to help.

"Like an intervention," Alma says.

I get my keycard out and let us into the dorm building, then we head up the stairs to the second floor where the third-year girls' rooms are. The keycard unit by our room flashes as I swipe my card, and I open the door.

Everything just looks the same as earlier, and Ivelisse's not here.

"Wonder where she is," I mutter. With the semester officially being over now, it's not like the others have scheduled timetables, so Ivelisse could have gone off pretty much anywhere. Not just in the school grounds but she could be on a day trip. Or at an appointment.

"Let's start the search, then," Alma says, heading straight for Ivelisse's bed.

"I'll check the bathroom." I head there, mainly so I can shut the door and just stand here. It feels wrong, doing this. And I know there's nothing to find in here. Only our shampoo and conditioners in the shower cubicle, and then toiletries and disinfectants under the sink.

After standing here for a few moments, I head back out. "Nothing in there."

I freeze as I see Alma holding the box with Helena's shoes. My wardrobe door is open.

"Hey," I say. "That's mine!"

"What is?" Alma holds up the box and shakes it. "There's nothing in here."

Nothing? My heart pounds, and then I'm running the few steps to my bed. I skid onto my knees, crashing into the bed frame, and pull the box from Alma.

It *is* empty.

I lunge for my wardrobe, poring through the contents in there, but there are no shoes. I turn, looking around the room.

"What is it?" Sibylle asks.

"Uh, some shoes. Repetto pointes," I say. My voice doesn't even sound like me now. "They've…they've gone." I pull a hand through my hair. Have they been stolen?

"Oh, come on, there are loads of shoes." Alma points to the side of the room where several pairs of *my* pointes are in a messy row. Each of us has about three or four on the go at any one time, in various stages of breaking in.

"They're not those ones… These are…special."

"Special?" Sibylle asks.

My sister's. Helena's. But I can't say the words. Neither of them should know about Helena. No one here should. But someone does. The lipstick-threat writer knows, and now they've done this. It has to be the same person.

Revenge.

I know you're a murderer.

"If something's been stolen, you should report it," Sibylle says.

My gaze snaps to her. The person who stole them wouldn't want it reported, so she can't be behind this. Unless she's bluffing.

"For a pair of shoes?" Alma laughs. "Come on. You probably just left them somewhere else. Or in your warm-up booties?" She points to where my pair of Uggs sits by the door. When I'm wearing full costume for performances, I wear Uggs over my pointes when not on stage to keep my pointes and tights in immaculate condition.

"I didn't," I say. I know I tucked the box with Helena's shoes into my wardrobe before I went to the graveyard yesterday. And they were definitely in the box, then.

"Let's go," Sibylle says.

"I thought we were searching for Ivelisse's diary or something?" Alma says.

Sibylle tells her we can still do that later and adds that it may well become a search bigger than just our room if my shoes have indeed been stolen. Roseheart doesn't tolerate stealing.

We find Maggie, a housekeeper for our dorm, and report it to her. She says she'll tell Madame and to try not to worry, that they'll turn up again soon. Probably by the evening. Someone may have taken them, thinking they were theirs: "A lot of you girls have Repetto shoes, you know."

Only—they don't turn up. Evening draws in, and there's no sign of it. Madame's been on the case, alerting everyone to my missing shoes. Several people say the same as Alma, that pointe shoes aren't that important, but I can't correct them. Because I need to be watching people's reactions. The thief has to know the significance of the shoes, and they're going to be watching me for some sort of confirmation. Setting up this hunt for them does kind of confirm it to them anyway, I realize, but I don't want to be getting upset more than I already am. I need to be calm. I need to figure out who's watching me, who's done this.

Because someone is out to get me, and something tells me this won't end here.

TWENTY-SIX

Teddy

"I can't believe they've got to interview me for this course." I yawn as I speak into my phone. "And now I'm just so nervous."

The train tumbles, and early morning light streams in through its windows. I can't believe how quickly Roseheart offered me an interview. I only contacted them yesterday morning, the day after the HCM meeting at the café, and they said to come in today for an interview.

"It'll just be formalities," Gemma says, her voice a little muffled, like she's underwater. "You'll get it, anyway. They'd be mad not to want you. You're crazy good. I watched those videos you sent."

I smile. Last night, I sent her clips from last year's production of *La Bayadere*. Taryn and I didn't have super prominent roles as it was mainly about showcasing the third-years' skills—and the winning couple, Li Hua and Trent, were amazing. But Taryn and I did have a short pas de deux and I also danced a routine with all the male undergrads from both years of the diploma. I was proud of the showreel and clips at the time, and now they're even more important to me because I can't watch this year's one. I messaged Xavier about it, and he told me there is a clip of me dancing at the start of *Romeo and Juliet*, before the balcony pas de deux, but that most of my presence on the showreel is centered around my accident. I can't bring myself to watch any of it.

"Still, I'm surprised Madame Cachelle didn't just put a good word in for me and let me bypass the interview or something," I say.

I'd be lying if I said I wasn't nervous for the interview. Of course I am. I don't really know anything about being a choreographer, and now I have to convince the teachers of that course that I do. And I have to manage it. I have to go back there.

Gemma chats on and on, until we lose the phone signal when my train goes into a tunnel, right before my station.

It's weird getting off the train without my luggage. I've done this journey many other times, but it's always been when I was going to Roseheart as a dancer. When I had my audition for the ballet diploma, Mum drove me. She was full of smiles and encouragement. Telling me how proud she was that I was a dancer just like her.

It doesn't take me long to walk to the right area of town, and then there it is. *Roseheart Romantic Dance Academy and Company Grounds.* The sign is as polished as ever, and it makes me feel slightly sick.

The could-have-beens flash through my mind.

"But I can do this," I tell myself.

I *can*.

"I must admit, I was surprised to hear from you so soon," Madame Cachelle says. Next to her, the two choreography teachers nod.

I hadn't realized Madame Cachelle would be in on this interview at all, but I suppose it makes sense, given she's told the two choreography teachers that she can vouch for how dedicated I am.

"It's not unusual for a dancer to retrain after an injury," Madame continues, "but we didn't even realize you were out of hospital, Teddy."

"Yes, it was just a few days there," I say. Did they really expect me to be there for over a week? "But I just wanted to get back here."

I look around. We're in one of the offices on the third floor of the academy's admin block. There's a large rectangular table in this room; I'm on one side of it, and the three teachers are seated in even spaces along the other side. Four large glasses of water were poured as I sat down, and I stare at the glasses now. I'm the only one who's not touched theirs, despite how dry the roof of my mouth now feels. I can't even remember when I last had a drink.

"I told you Teddy is very dedicated," Madame says to the two choreography teachers.

I've only seen them around the academy a few times before. They teach in a different block to where the ballet diploma was mainly taught, but I recognize them. Mrs. Nolan is full of smiles and has a warm face, and Mrs. Walters looks like a much older, more weathered version of her.

"So, what is it that made you choose choreography in particular?" Mrs. Nolan asks.

The truth is I picked the choreography course because the only other course Roseheart offers that isn't focused on ballet is dance-teacher training. I've never thought of myself as a teacher, and I was sure that Madame would've realized that. I figured I had a better shot with the choreography course. Plus, I think there's less overall dance in the choreography program than the teacher-training, and I don't want to not be accepted if the teachers think my HCM is going to be a risk. From the research I did online, this choreography course is pretty much just theory based for its first year, improving knowledge on steps and moves—which I already know anyway. The second year has a module on directing other dancers and that one requires some actual dance as you demonstrate to the cast. Same for the third year.

But the second and third years are so far away, and I just need an excuse to be back here. They can't be monitoring me all the time, outside of studying. Just the thought of getting back into a studio makes me feel lighter, more like myself. I can keep training, keep up my stamina until the doctors realize their mistake and formally discharge me and correct my records. Then I can go ahead with my actual dance career.

And if I'm at Roseheart when my medical records are corrected, then surely, they'd offer me a place somehow at the company. Maybe I could even train next year with the then-final-year students. The thought of learning new routines with a girl who isn't Taryn doesn't make me too happy, but it'll be worth it. Because then once me and this new girl are accepted into the company, Mr. Vikas will decide that I *should* dance with Taryn and be her primary partner. He'd be silly not to. And this Jaidev guy can dance with the girl whom I graduate with. It'll all be sorted, and the world will be back to how it should be.

I clear my throat. Mrs. Nolan, Mrs. Walters, and Madame Cachelle are still waiting for my answer. "I've always been fascinated by the stories that ballets tell. And I want to learn more about this role. To be able to design a ballet in that way and infuse my own creativity would be amazing. And it would help keep me connected to the one thing I love most."

"And you don't think you'd find it too...stressful?" Mrs. Walter asks.

"Or tempting?" Mrs. Nolan adds. "Being around ballerinas and danseurs all day? We'd want this to be a comfortable and safe environment for you, so we have to consider the impact on your mental health that this could have, being so close to doing what you once used to do."

What you once used to do. I don't like the way those words sound.

"I'd rather be here than not," I answer, honestly. "I've spent the last two years at Roseheart, and it's become my life.

Even before here, I was at ballet schools. I need to be in the ballet world."

The teachers all nod.

"Well, as you know we've got some time before the new year starts," Mrs. Walter says. "We ask that all prospective students for the BA Choreography course submit a portfolio of choreographies. While we can accept a smaller portfolio if the candidate has strong dance experience, we will have to ask for a portfolio of some sort from you."

A portfolio? I feel blood drain from my face. Suddenly, it's like the room is colder. I've no idea what a choreography portfolio looks like.

"We can also give you some material to read ahead of the Choreographic Practices module, which may also help you in putting together this portfolio," Mrs. Nolan says. "And I'm sure you'll have no trouble producing it. With Madame Cachelle's glowing reference, yes, we'd love to have you on the choreography course. Please just make sure to submit the portfolio two weeks before the start of the new academic year, and we'll be good to go."

"That's no problem." I flash a smile, even though my heart is suddenly pounding. That's just over a month to get it sorted, I think. "I can definitely do that."

"And we will of course require medical clearance for your enrolment on this program," Madame Cachelle says.

"Medical clearance?" My skin prickles. It's too hot in the office. Too crowded. Too much body heat radiating from the four of us.

"Yes," Mrs. Nolan says. "To check that choreography is a viable career. Depending on where you end up, some schools and companies will have their choreographers regularly taking on very active roles within the dance, pretty much performing whole routines in time, in order to show the dancers how to do it. We have to be careful with your health."

I force a smile. "Of course."

"Then, all being well, we'll see you at the start of next semester."

The start of next semester? That's September. And suddenly it does feel too long—especially when I'm here now, when the ballet studios are practically within touching distance.

They're all looking at me. The interview's over, and I should be going.

"Uh," I say, looking at them all.

"Yes, Teddy?" Madame Cachelle rises swiftly. "Are you not feeling well? Shall I get—"

"No, it's not that. I'm fine." I swallow quickly. "It's… I know this is unconventional, but can I stay this summer? Just until classes start—because I've got a lot of studying to do. I only know choreography from a dancer's perspective, and I need to learn more about the portfolio. I just really want to make this work."

"I'm sure something can be arranged," Madame says, smiling. "We'll let you know when we've got a room available. But it should be soon."

Soon? Not…today?

"I can't share with Xavier anymore?"

"Our new dancer is there now," she says.

The new dancer. *Jaidev.*

I try not to scowl, try to smile. "Oh, uh, can I ask where my belongings are then?"

"The housekeeper should know," Madame says.

I thank them all as I leave, even though I'm annoyed. Not just because they seemed to try and erase all evidence of me having shared with Xavier the moment I was carted off, but that I also didn't buy a return train ticket. I assumed I'd be staying at Roseheart. And now I've got to go back to Dad's…only to return 'soon.'

My belongings have been shoved into cardboard boxes and stuffed into a store cupboard. Brilliant. The housekeeper gives me an apologetic look but assures me they'll be safe until I'm back.

"Back?" says a low voice.

I turn to see Joe, Roseheart's nutritionist. He is smiling, but it doesn't quite reach his eyes.

"How about we catch up in my office," he says, looking at his watch. "I've got a good half hour before I'm teaching."

The air around us is heavy and oppressive, and it's clear to me there's no choice but to follow Joe to his office on the second floor. We seem to get there too soon.

"Take a seat."

I do. The same seat I always sit in. The bench at the side of the room. There are three different types of seating to choose from—a small armchair, a classroom chair, and a bench—and picking a chair always feels like a test I don't understand. I chose the bench the very first time, and then the next time I wondered if it would mean something if I then picked a different seat, so I went for the bench again— and every time afterward.

"Well, it's certainly a surprise to see you back," Joe says. He's in his late thirties and is a stockily built man. Muscular. He told me once he used to play rugby professionally before a knee injury ended his career.

"I'm enrolling again. Choreography course."

He leans back in his chair. It's a leather swivel chair next to his desk. He never sits behind the table. I read somewhere that some teachers do that to look less formal and some therapists do it to seem more on the same level as their patient. As the nutritionist, I guess Joe's kind of both. Or, at least, that's how he acts. He's the only teacher who is like the choreographers and costume staff, in that the prefers us to use his first name.

"Well, that's good," he says. "It's good to have a goal." The light in his eyes gets more intense. "But how are you?"

"I'm fine."

He gives a small smile. "It's okay to tell the truth, Teddy."

My shoulders tighten. "I am telling the truth."

He brushes some lint off his shirt. "I know about the diagnosis. The heart condition. But did you tell the doctors about the OSFED?"

About the OSFED. Like that's what I have. He sounds so sure. And it's weird how part of me is still against it while the other half is sure I have some sort of eating disorder as I need that to explain the HCM misdiagnosis. It's confusing.

"Because it's important doctors are aware of the whole picture," Joe continues.

"They do know." The words burst out before I can stop them. They are birds flying round, making me dizzy, and it's like part of me is leaping about, trying to catch them. But they're always just out of my grasp.

"Good," Joe says. "And you're getting help with this, too?"

"Yes."

"So, what are they doing?"

"Doing?" I squint at him.

"To help? These doctors?"

"Oh, I'm having a catheterization soon. And I've got medication as well." Well, they gave me tablets for the HCM, but there's no point in me taking those given it's a misdiagnosis. They'd do more harm than good.

"And for the eating?"

"Therapy," I say. "Guided support sessions." I wrack my brain, trying to remember all the support Ivelisse gets. "Dietician, too." At least that one is sort of true. I did have that one meeting with Alexandra.

"Good. That'll help," Joe says. "I'm pleased."

My eyes fall on the scales in the corner of his office. When I look up, I realize he's seen me looking at them. For a second, I think he's going to ask to weigh me now. But he doesn't. He just nods.

"Well, it'll be good to work with you again in September."

"Work with me?" My voice is a squeak. He only needs to work with the dancers, not the choreographers, right? Unless he suspects I am going to be dancing? Could he realize this HCM is an incorrect diagnosis, too?

"Yes." He smiles an easy smile. "I'm here for *all* the students at Roseheart—and all the professionals, too. Don't worry, Teddy. You won't be on your own with this."

TWENTY-SEVEN

Taryn

"Well, are you coming in or not?" Marion holds open the door to the studio, sighing dramatically. She taps her foot. She's wearing Bloch pointes—and also what has to be half a bottle of perfume. "We haven't got all day."

Going into the room, with all the company dancers circling, is not appealing in the slightest, even though Li Hua is in there too and she gave me an encouraging smile on her way in while I just hovered outside the doorway. The tutor isn't here yet, and I look down the corridor, to see if there's any sign of her.

"We have to warm up before the pointe teacher gets here," Marion says. She rolls her eyes. "God, it's like you're not even a dancer."

There's a chorus of snickers from inside.

To say I've been dreading this is an understatement.

I slip inside and take a place by Li Hua at the barre. She gives me a quick smile but turns to talk to the woman next to her—with a jolt, I realize it's Netty Florence, the female principal dancer. Oh my God, I'm in a class with Roseheart's best ballerina. A quick glance around confirms that what has to be *all* the female company dancers from all the divisions are in this class, not just those on the *Midsummer Night's Dream* tour.

Nausea and anxiety twist my stomach into knots. I don't know whether this should make me feel better or not. There are at least fifteen women here who aren't on the fall tour with me, who may not know about the vendetta that Marion, Victoria, and maybe others too still have apparently built against me. There's a chance more will be friendly here, just like Li Hua is. But there's also the chance that word spreads as fast among the company as it does in the academy. I sneak glances at them: petite women with slender yet strong arms and legs. With a jolt, I realize I'm the tallest dancer here. Probably the biggest too.

But then a woman enters who's bigger than me, and my heart lifts as I stare at her. She's wearing a crisp shirt and smart trousers. Has she got her leotard and tights on underneath? Just as I'm thinking how much better it'll be for there to be two dancers who aren't really skinny but have more curves than a lot of companies think is acceptable for ballerinas, the woman takes a seat behind the piano in the corner of the studio.

The pianist. I try not to let my disappointment show and concentrate on putting my pointe shoes on, starting with the left foot. They're a newer pair and they're very hard still, not broken in properly. I freeze. Why didn't I bring another pair? Especially for my first pointe class with the company. I should've brought a pair I know I'm comfortable dancing in. I want to make a good impression; prove to these dancers that I deserve to be here.

I grab my second shoe—and something catches my eye. Something red on the underside, near the toe. My mouth dries. A pushpin. Someone's stuck a pin in to try and injure me? My head spins. I haven't left these shoes unattended since I got to this class, so this has to have been done up in my room. Ivelisse or Sibylle? Alma? Or one of the company dancers went into my room? But how would they know I'd pick *these* shoes?

I hook my fingernail under the head of the pushpin and start to lever it out. I'm going to have to check all my shoes now, every time I dance. Maybe I'd better warn Jaidev too.

"That's Madame Jean," a voice whispers just as I've got the pushpin in the palm of my hand.

I turn to see a ballerina behind me, smiling. A heart-shaped, tanned face framed by dyed blond hair. Then I realize the instructor's in here now: an Asian woman in her mid-forties. Just standing at the front of the room, she's got a sense of elegance and authority.

"Ah, right. Uh, thanks." My voice is weak, uncertain. I'm not sure what to do with the pushpin. I don't want to draw attention to it, let all the dancers here know that someone has tried to sabotage me because then it might put more ideas in their heads.

"She's the pointe specialist," the dancer tells me. I'd guess she's probably around thirty or so. I don't recognize her, but then I've only been at the academy for three years, so she must've graduated a long while before that—if she joined the company at eighteen, starting the diploma at sixteen years of age. Some dancers start the diploma here a little later though, like Alma. She's two years older than me.

The dancer holds her hand out to me. "I'm Nora. And just ignore Marion and Victoria." She rolls her eyes. "They're the resident idiots here who think they're queen bees. We're not all like that. Most of us are actually decent people, but those two just like making some people's lives hell."

"Is it always like this?" I ask. "For the newest dancer?"

Nora tilts her head to one side. "Mostly. I mean, it wasn't last year, with Li Hua joining. Marion took an instant likening to her—though I think it was kind of racially driven because right before then, she'd talked before about how all of her friends were white and that it didn't look good. Then she was chummy with Li Hua right away—well, until Li Hua became friends with others instead. But it has been a bit like this before. When Clara was here, she had it rough, before she and Tom left."

Ah, yes, the mismatched duo. Unbalanced. What Xavier and I would've been.

"But I think you've got it worse," Nora says, her voice sympathetic. "A lot of the dancers here don't like change. Marion and Victoria are all about tradition here, and they don't like that you've been given special treatment."

Special treatment. I wince at that. But I haven't actually done anything wrong. I danced well at the end-of-year show.

"And they also don't like that Jaidev's here," Nora says, lowering her voice. "I don't think the guys mind too much about it. But Victoria in particular is pissed off. Heard her saying how Jaidev doesn't belong at Roseheart because he didn't train here. I think she's just worried the board's going to change the setup here and start taking auditions from dancers trained elsewhere. Because he's the first one here to break the mold. Yet she's not around him all that much—not compared to you. And maybe she sees you as the reason he is here. And it's easier to take stuff out on a girl than a guy, a lot of the time."

Well, this isn't making me feel any better.

"But don't worry." Nora pats my arm, and I want to recoil away from her touch but force myself not to. "She wouldn't actually do anything to harm you."

No? I think. *Well, someone put that pushpin in my shoe.*

Nora steps up to the barre, and as she warms up, I'm trying to work out if Victoria or Marion could've tried to injure me. I have seen them in the academy grounds, after all, when they were trying to rile up Sibylle. They could've gone into my room. But how would they get a keycard?

"I hope you're all nicely warmed up," Madame Jean says. She's got a slight French accent. "We will start in thirty seconds."

I look around and realize everyone is warming up at the barre or stretching. And I'm just standing here like a lemon.

I grab the trainers I wore to walk down here and drop the pushpin into the left one, praying I'll remember to remove it before changing back into them. Then I begin warming up too, next to Nora. I copy what she's doing—plié, relevé in first, then plié, relevé in second—like I suddenly don't know what to do without the guidance.

"Okay, ballerinas." Madame Jean claps her hands. "Let's begin." She nods to the pianist in the corner, and she starts playing.

What follows has to be the most challenging pointe class I've ever endured: a torture combination of revelés, followed by tendus and enchappés at the barre, before we move into the center and perform revelés, sous sous, enchappés, pirouettes, and walks. When Madame Jean isn't happy with a move, she gets the dancer to perform it again.

Somehow, I manage to do all of mine in a satisfactory manner, despite my nerves, and her only feedback to me is a sweet smile. Victoria, on the other hand, stumbles slightly during a pirouette and her enchappé in the center looks a bit rough, a bit sloppy.

"Do it again," Madame Jean instructs her over and over.

When Victoria eventually manages it, she shoots dagger looks at me. I try to ignore her, but part of me can't help but wonder how she got one of the lead female roles in *A Midsummer Night's Dream*. So many of the dancers here—including many also in the same tour—are clearly better than her in this class. Still, in that first group rehearsal, Mr. Vikas seemed over the top in giving praise to both Marion and Victoria. Maybe it's favoritism.

Madame Jean has us finish with bourrées, and then we're just stretching again, warming down. My feet are surprisingly sore after those intense ninety minutes. I change into my trainers, the pushpin in my hand.

"You may as well give up," Victoria hisses to me as we leave. "Roseheart is a company built on tradition. My great, great grandmother would be fuming."

Great, great grandmother? So, she's related to the founder. That's why she doesn't like me, and that's why Nora said tradition is important to her and Marion.

"Yes," Marion says, coming up behind her. "And you're not going to do it—you and Jaidev. You'll see that soon. You're just embarrassing yourself, and you're only going to give us more work when the ballet master and director realize you're not up to this. Then we'll have to change everything, so things make sense without you."

"Oh, go and get a life," Nora says loudly.

"It's all right for you," Marion tells her. "You don't have to dance on the same tour as her."

"Ignore them," Li Hua whispers to me, slipping into step next to me.

"Yeah," says another voice. Netty Florence. "They both know you're better than them, and they're threatened. That's all it is."

A warm, glowing feeling fills me. The female principal thinks I'm better than Marion and Victoria, and she's sticking up for me!

"Thanks," I say, and the warmth only grows.

"We're going for a run later," Li Hua tells me. "Me, Nora, and Netty-Flo. Want to join us?"

I blink. A run with them? "Sure." I hope Sibylle and Ivelisse won't mind. But I have to make friends in the company now. Both of my roommates will be leaving in the next few weeks, anyway.

"Great." Netty Florence smiles, and I wonder if I'll soon be calling her Netty-Flo. "See you in thirty mins? Down by the gates."

"Sure." It seems to be the only word I can say now.

The ballerinas head off, and I'm smiling, not even the memory of Marion and Victoria's harsh words can dampen my spirits now. The female principal is accepting of me!

But when I return to my room and assess all my pointes and flats, my mood darkens. Because in the toe of *every* right shoe is a pushpin.

TWENTY-EIGHT

Jaidev

"Hey, Jai!" a voice calls across the gym, and I look up and see a Black danseur beckoning me over. I recognize him from the rehearsal session for the fall tour. I think he was dancing mainly with Li Hua.

I'm not a fan of my name being shortened, but I let it go. The danseur reminds me that he's called Trent—which is just as well as I've forgotten nearly everyone's names—and says we've both been selected.

"For what?"

"The photoshoot." He wiggles his eyebrows in a way that makes him seem rather camp.

"Photoshoot?"

He looks amused. "Yeah, there's always one being done. Or it feels like there is. Mr. Aleks just sent the memo round. We're all to meet by the gates."

"All? How many of us?"

Trent looks at the list. "Six of us. All guys. Pretty impressive you've been selected for this already, mate.

Must've made a good impression on Mr. Aleks. Right, so go and get some canvas flats. Old ones, mind. Nothing too good or expensive. It's an urban shoot, in the heart of the city. And those pavements and all that gravel really tears up the soles. Wear trainers for the most part, though. We've got to meet in half an hour."

"What clothes?" I ask.

"Just says urban. Usually means a black hoody and dark leggings. Bring jogging bottoms too. I've got to find the other guys now, but you know where to meet? The gates by the south edge of the grounds? Where Mr. Aleks goes to smoke, thinking no one notices."

Trent leaves, and I hurriedly go to my room. Luckily, Lani had packed a black hoody and plenty of leggings and jogging bottoms among the other clothes and garments I asked her to pack. Only got two pairs of canvas flats though. I grimace. Well, I'll have to order some more anyway. I'd assumed Roseheart would have a shoe store, like at Avril's school, but apparently each dancer here just sources their own shoes themselves.

I change quickly and head down to the gates, my flats in my hand.

Taryn is already waiting there. She's dressed in a hoody and leggings, too. She's wearing trainers, but she doesn't appear to have pointes or flats with her.

"You're doing the shoot, too?" I ask, frowning a little. I thought Trent said it was all male dancers for this.

"The shoot?" Taryn squints at me.

I explain what Trent told me.

"Oh, no. I'm going running. With a few of the dancers. Including Netty Florence, the principal." Her voice holds awe, but I can tell she's still disappointed not to have been chosen for the shoot.

A few minutes later, ballerinas arrive and greet Taryn. Li Hua and Netty Florence and another ballerina I don't know, one with blond hair. They all greet Taryn warmly, and I'm glad. Victoria's not among them—good. I feel protective over Taryn, of course, but since Victoria gave me that odd threat, I've felt uneasy every time I've passed by her. And I know that's what she wants—to unnerve me. I mentioned it to Xavier the evening after it had happened, and he'd just shrugged and said I should expect some backlash when Roseheart are changing their rules to give me a chance with them.

"But is Victoria violent?" I asked him.

"Violent?" he spluttered, then laughed. "You don't need to worry about a woman. Men are stronger. Just be glad it's not a guy who's made this weird threat. You wouldn't want a guy going against you, right? I know I wouldn't."

"But she could make my life hell."

He shrugged. "Probably all just talk and nothing more. I mean, she wouldn't want to do anything that might jeopardize her career with Roseheart. She's got too much to lose."

Now, the others for the shoot are arriving. Five danseurs.

"Good luck," Netty Florence blows a kiss to Hamza, the male principal. I'm pretty sure they're together.

Then the women are off, running. Taryn looks back once, a quick flick of her head, and I raise my hand to wave.

"You are smiling so big right now," Trent says. "You totally like her."

I feel myself blushing.

"Hey, there's nothing wrong with that," Hazma says. "The ballet masters and mistresses always say the couples with the best chemistry and connection actually are together in real life. And it certainly works for me and Net."

"If you're interested in her, you should tell her," another of the guys says. I think his name is Pierre.

"Yeah, ask her out or something. Be brave! And if she feels the same way, it'll also improve your dancing. I mean, you two've got your work cut out anyway," Trent says. "Eight weeks can be pretty standard for us to learn a new routine, especially for the Christmas shows as we only learn those dances after the fall tour is over—but we're not dancing with a completely new partner, then."

"Or getting used to the English style of ballet," Pierre says. "It took me a good six months to feel I was fluent in the English style. My arms just kept wanting to do the French thing instead."

"Yeah, so if you like her and she likes you, makes sense to get together," Hazma says. "You'll be all loved up and have a shortcut to nailing your pas de deux and getting a permanent contract at Roseheart."

"So, you going to ask her?" Trent's eyes are wide. I didn't think someone could possibly look as excited for something than he does now.

Am I? I don't know. I mean, I do like Taryn. I know that. She's quiet and sensitive, and when those female dancers were being mean to her, it really upset me. I feel protective of her, and *of course* that just makes me think of how protective I got over Camille, when we were together. How beautiful our relationship was.

And how it ended.

"Jaidev Ngo, you're under arrest for…"

But I also can't stop thinking about Taryn—and I know I could really like her, just as I liked Camille. I can't forget how ethereal Taryn looked dancing in the graveyard—or how amazing it felt dancing with her there. There was something magical and beautiful about our duet in the moonlight, among the graves.

But before I can answer Trent, Mr. Aleks appears with two photographers in tow.

"Let's do this." His voice is clipped and I'm sure he couldn't look any unhappier even if he tried.

"Okay, do another of those twisty things," one of the photographers says. "All of you at the same time."

Mr. Aleks's frown deepens even further.

We're on a rooftop—one of the tallest buildings in this part of London—and it's cold and windy up here. I'm not a fan of heights to be honest, and every time I'm asked to pirouette or leap, I have visions of misjudging the space and somehow stumbling too close to the edge.

Of course, it doesn't happen, but I'm glad when the photographers suggest we do some more ballet outside storefronts. On the ground. Much better.

Half an hour later, we are running through the same combinations and moves, over and over, the cameras clicking away. Quite a crowd gathers to watch us outside Selfridges on Oxford Street. Mr. Aleks takes over from the photographer in instructing us, leaving the photographers just to operate the cameras.

Members of the public are taking photos too, videoing us. And I like the attention. I've not been photographed as a dancer since the accident, last year, and I'd forgotten how it feels. How it fills me with confidence.

I find myself wondering what Taryn will think when she sees these photos. Part of me wants her and the ballerinas to jog past us here, to see us, even though I'm almost certain they'll have chosen a route that's not directly through a built-up part of London.

Ten more minutes pass, and then it's another change of location. In the mini-bus, Hazma nibbles an energy bar.

"Damn," Pierre says, showing the guy next to him one of his flats. "Practically worn it right down."

"I hope that's not a good one," Trent says. "I did tell you."

"Yeah, yeah, I know."

Mr. Aleks just keeps frowning.

"Is he always like that?" I whisper, leaning toward Trent.

He nods. "When are artistic directors ever happy? They've always got something to scowl about. Anyway." He looks at his watch. "We've got ten minutes until we're at the next location, so that gives us plenty of time."

"Time?" I frown, not getting what he means.

"To plan out exactly how you're going to ask out Taryn, of course!"

TWENTY-NINE

Taryn

The next week passes in a blur. Sibylle leaves in a cloud of excitement for her audition. Jaidev and I attend classes and the full-cast rehearsals and keep practicing our divertissement pas de deux—though suddenly things feel…different between us. I don't know why, but he keeps smiling at me. Keeps looking like he's about to say something, but then he doesn't. He just focuses on the pas de deux, or whatever training we're doing or sometimes he focuses on the couple who are understudies for the divertissement. They've mainly been standing on the sidelines of our pas de deux rehearsals, learning our choreography.

In my pointe and flexibility classes, and during the fall tour rehearsals, Marion and Victoria keep making digs at me, though nothing more happens to me. They just really seem to hate me, so I conclude that one of them has to be behind the lipstick-mirror note, my destroyed photo board, and the pushpins in my shoes—I just can't imagine either Ivelisse or

Sibylle doing those, and besides, both of them seem to have accepted they're not going to Roseheart. Sibylle messages me from the hotel she's staying at for her audition—she's staying there for quite a few extra days and uses lots of exclamation marks to tell me about her sight-seeing—and Ivelisse asks for my opinion on which routine she should record for a video audition at one of the Russian companies. I give her advice and even help her record it, even though I'm not sure a Russian company is the best choice for her; they nearly always favor the stick-thin, almost skeletal-looking ballerinas and it worries me, the idea of her being around so many really thin dancers. Would that worsen her anorexia, make her compete against them to be the skinniest? We never found any 'evidence' in our room to suggest her eating disorder has worsened, but we're not doctors or therapists, and I know we don't know all the signs. Still, I don't think she's been sick since. That must've just been a one-off, despite what Alma thinks. Sibylle wasn't worried really when I last talked to her about it. Alma, on the other hand, said she *was* worried, but her eyes had lit up, kind of like the idea of being worried excited her because she thought it equaled drama.

Still, I always assumed that Ivelisse would go back to the US when she graduated. Not just because she always complained about how much paperwork she needed to fill out to be able to study abroad, but also because her immediate family is in New York. Then again, I don't know whether they're close.

Helena's shoes still haven't turned up. That's one thing that's really getting to me. Whoever is targeting me has to have taken them. I wonder if they've still got them, or if the pointes are now in landfill somewhere, mangled and dirty. I want to ask my new friends Nora and Li Hua and Netty Florence if they've noticed any new pointes appear in any of the dorms, but I also don't want to be accusatory. Those dancers may like me at the moment, but I don't want to seem like I'm complaining and trying to get Marion and Victoria in trouble. It could easily get back to them, and they already hate me enough as it is.

I need to see if I can search Marion's and Victoria's rooms one time, I know that. See if I can find Helena's shoes. But how? I was already frightened away from their accommodation block two weeks ago, and I'm not the kind of person to break in—even if I could walk through the main doors—and snoop. I felt bad enough with the plan to Ivelisse's things with Alma and Sibylle.

"Hey, Taryn," a voice says, startling me, just as I'm outside Studio 14, waiting for Jaidev for our next practice.

My eyes widen as I turn. That *voice*.

And I see him. See his soft brown eyes and the way he's smiling.

"Teddy!" I squeal, and I run to him, hug him.

He grunts, makes a soft *oof* noise.

I pull back. "Are you okay? Did I hurt you?"

"I'm fine." He smiles. He hasn't got the nose splint on now, and his nose looks pretty good—but apart from that, he looks…different. But I can't put my finger on what it is. What are you doing here, Teddy?"

"Teddy?" Jaidev's voice makes me stop. I hadn't realized he'd appeared, but now he has stopped next to me. "Well, it's nice to meet you."

Teddy raises one eyebrow. "Jaidev Ngo, I presume?"

Jaidev nods and then wrings his hands together a little.

I turn back to Teddy. "What are you doing here?"

"I'm just on my way to see the housekeeper," he says.

"You're nowhere near housekeeping," Jaidev says. And he's right. We're in the company grounds.

Teddy shrugs. "I thought I'd come by the studios. Try to surprise you."

I cannot stop smiling, and I'm aware I probably look weird. My face is even beginning to hurt from the effort. I don't even care that he barely replied to my messages "But you're back?" I ask. "Like, properly?".

He nods. "Well, choreography course. I'm doing extra lessons this summer before it starts in September."

"So, you can't dance anymore?" Jaidev asks, his voice clipped and strange. He folds his arms. He's still standing right behind me.

I give him an odd look before turning back to Teddy.

"Not for the moment," Teddy says, his voice thick.

"Oh, it's just so great you're back," I say.

Jaidev taps my shoulder. "Come on, we need to practice."

"Just give me a moment," I say, a little irritation pulling through me.

"Why don't you go in and start warming up?" Teddy says to him. "I won't be a minute with Taryn."

Jaidev doesn't look happy as he enters the studio without me, but I barely concentrate on that. I just look at Teddy. Teddy who's *here*. Who I never thought I'd see again. Who I thought I'd lost my connection with. But I was wrong. Teddy and I can recover. We're best friends. Of course we can.

"Does he know?" Teddy asks me.

"Know?" I raise my eyebrows. "What?"

"About who you are." He lowers his voice. "Ace and aro."

"Uh, no." I let out a half-laugh. "Why would I tell him? That's my own business."

His gaze is cool. "I don't need to be allo to know that man likes you, is attracted to you. And he's getting ideas."

"He's not getting ideas." I shake my head. Honestly, the idea is absurd.

"Good," Teddy says, "then I've got nothing to worry about."

Nothing to worry about? I frown, but I can't ask anymore because then Evangeline arrives to run through our choreography to see if any tweaks are needed at this stage.

"See you later," Teddy says, and he leaves.

The whole practice with Jaidev has me trying to work out what Teddy meant, why he would think that Jaidev is into me, and what Teddy means about nothing to worry about. But, honestly, it's like everyone is speaking a language I don't know. Even Teddy.

THIRTY

Teddy

I don't get it. I've identified the emotion I feel around this Jaidev guy, and it's jealousy. But I don't get *why*. Well, I know it's because he's with Taryn all day. But I'm not sexually or romantically attracted to Taryn, so it makes no sense why I'm feeling like this.

Still, I know you can get jealous when your friends become close to others. At primary school that happened. I was best friends with a boy named Johnny and then a new kid started. Ed or something, his name was. He replaced me in Johnny's books, and I was furious. So jealous. Ed came in the way of me and Johnny.

And, yes, this is the same. This is what Jaidev is doing. He's replacing me. He's coming in the way of me and my best friend. Or maybe my stupid diagnosis has already done that. I mean, I did kind of ghost her for a while—but that was more of my coping mechanism for dealing with all this ridiculous heart stuff. Still, once that gets sorted out,

Roseheart will have to let me dance with Taryn. They'd be ridiculous not to. And then things will go back to normal with me and Taryn.

I arrived earlier today, and my room is on the same level as the first years studying the diploma. At least I haven't got to share though, and I think quite a few of them are leaving for the holidays shortly anyway, wanting to see their families. Only a couple are staying to keep training the whole summer.

I make my way over to the housekeeper's office. She told me to meet her here at two o'clock and she'd go through the boxes in her store cupboard to check which ones are mine. Apparently lost property gets put in there too.

It doesn't actually take long to sort it out, and within an hour, I've got my clothes unpacked and in my new wardrobe. Fondly, I look at my pairs of canvas flats. I touch them, feeling the fabric, and suddenly I know what I need to do now. I'd planned to start my choreography portfolio today, but this is more important.

I head back to the company buildings and ask for directions to the choreography office. A teacher gives me directions, and then I'm there. The door is ajar, but there's no one there. Maybe all the choreographers are all in rehearsals. So, I slip inside, my heart pounding.

It doesn't take me long at all to find the choreography for Jaidev and Taryn's pas de deux for the tour—it's even labelled with their names. I take a quick photo of it on my phone. I need to learn this. My appointment for the catheterization is next week. It'll prove I've not got this condition, and then I'll be able to make a proper case for replacing Jaidev. After all, he replaced me. We're supposedly interchangeable.

I have to see if I can still dance with Taryn this year. And if I already know the steps, that will make it easier.

But looking at the steps written out is completely different to being taught it. I frown at the many different arrows and scrawled notes. I need to watch it being performed.

The door to the choreography office clicks softly as I shut it, and I make my way back to the studio Taryn and Jaidev are in. There's a window in the door and through it I can see some big French doors opening out onto a courtyard. There are heavy curtains drawn part way across the door, and shrubbery outside. A perfect place to watch from.

It doesn't take me long to settle there, pretty much hidden by the plants. I'm confident Taryn, Jaidev, and the choreographer won't see me. But I can see them. It's enthralling, watching Taryn dance, but every time I catch sight of him, my mood darkens. It should be me.

It *will* be me.

I make notes on my phone of their pas de deux, and I strain my ears to hear the choreographer's instructions. But no matter how hard I try and listen, the woman's words are just a faint muffle.

"Well, well, well," says a voice behind me.

I jump and turn to find a woman with chestnut hair and red lipstick peering at me.

"What have we got here? Are you spying on them?"

"It's not what it looks like," I say, my heart pounding. I try and move away from the French doors, but my legs have half gone to sleep and I stumble.

"Oh, and what do you think it looks like?" she asks. Then she frowns. "Wait, you're Teddy Walker?"

I nod. "I am."

"So, what are you doing?" Without warning, she snatches my phone and peers at my notes. "You're learning their pas de deux?" Her eyes shine.

"I'm just making notes," I say.

Her lips press into a thin line before twisting into a garish smile. "We'd much rather have *you* join us than him." Disapproval drips from her voice like treacle. "Jaidev thinks he's all that, you know? But you *deserve* to be here."

"Yeah?" My voice wobbles.

"My name's Victoria Simmonds," she says. "I'm a direct descendent of the Rosehearts."

"The Rosehearts?"

"Yes. I have a lot of influence around here. And we both want the same thing here, so we should help each other."

"You can help me get into the company?" I ask.

She nods. "Of course. That space is yours. You're definitely better than Jaidev, and, well, you're better than a lot of the male graduates. You're the one who should be here." She touches my arm, giving it a little squeeze, like she's trying to feel my bicep. "So, have we got a deal?"

"Yes." I'm breathless. This is great. Perfect.

She smiles. "I will be in touch with instructions." She taps away on my phone before handing it back. "There. Now you've sent me a text, so we've got each other's numbers."

She disappears as quickly as she came, and when I go back to the French doors, the studio is now empty. Their session has finished—but mine is just starting.

I head inside. I've been getting out of shape, because although I'd been trying not to eat Dad's junk food, I had to have something—he kept insisting, and I couldn't risk him taking me back to the hospital. So, I wrote down everything unhealthy that I ate and worked out exactly how many sessions at the gym and how many at the studio I'd need to do to remedy all the badness I put in my body.

And soon, everything will be exactly as it's supposed to be.

THIRTY-ONE

Jaidev

"So, how is it going?" Avril asks over FaceTime on Sunday. "Have they offered you a permanent contract yet?"

I laugh. "Not yet. We've got our first formal assessment next week. Week three. Both the ballet master and the artistic director will be watching." I paste a smile onto my face, trying to seem confident and relaxed, but I'd be lying if I said I wasn't nervous. I'm actually bricking it, and I know Taryn is too. "How's Bastien doing, looking after you?" I ask, mainly to change the subject.

Avril's been out of hospital for a week now.

She snorts and moves her phone, showing me the plaster on her leg. "See these doodles? That's what he's been doing."

The video image is blurry because she moves her phone so fast, but I'm sure they're not just 'doodles.' Bastien is an artist, and if he's decorated Avril's cast, that's a good sign. Because that usually means he's not high. He only draws when he's clean.

"But he's helping you with everything, right?"

"Yes. He is. But there's only so many times you want your son helping you to the bathroom. This leg is just such a pain, Jaidev. I can't even get up off the toilet on my own. It's so embarrassing."

"It's fine," I say, mainly because I don't know what to say.

"But tell me about you. About the ballet. Your new partner? I want to know everything."

I can tell by her tone of voice that she's sad she can't dance now and may never dance again. She wants to experience it through me now, and isn't that the least I can give her? And so long as we don't actually talk about the upcoming assessment, I can manage that.

"She's called Taryn."

"Last name?" She twists around and a moment later I see her laptop in my phone's screen.

"Avril, you are not Googling her right now, are you?"

There's a tutting sound. "*Of course* I am. Well, searching for her on YouTube. I need to know who my son's career rests on. Now what's her last name?"

"Foster." To be honest, I am sure Avril already knows these details. She was on video-link with Madame Cachelle discussing it all. But Avril does this kind of thing a lot, pretending not to know something so it can be told to her again.

"Right… Let me see. Ah, here we go. She had the lead role in this year's *Romeo and Juliet*. The showreel's here. Let me just watch this."

I resist rolling my eyes. The soundtrack from the showreel drifts over, sort of distorted by the connection. I've already watched it. The moment Teddy falls made me wince the first time I saw it.

Teddy.

I do not like him, but I think it's mainly a defensive thing. Ever since he arrived here, two days ago, he's been super bristly toward me, which of course just puts my back up. We've been locked into glare-offs and some sort of weird competition for Taryn's time. Of course, as I'm training with her, I've got the most time with her, and we tend to eat together too as the intense scheduling requires weird break-times. When we can't eat a great deal right before a practice and we're not finishing now until super late—around nine o'clock each night, because we're fitting in our pas de deux rehearsals, group rehearsals, our individual classes, and endurance sessions—we end up eating one big meal daily around half-nine, which is close to a whole day's worth of nutrition. Earlier in the day, we're subsisting almost entirely on energy bars and the odd snack. It's nearly always the same when we've got to train for eight or nine hours a day. Eating a lot before training just doesn't work because we end up needing to wait a while before we can dance so we can avoid cramps. So, most of the dancers I know alter their routine to allow for one big meal in the evening in the leadup to a big performance or tour. Well, that didn't apply to a couple of the girls at Avril's school. They were convinced one big meal would cause weight gain, so they barely ate any kind of proper meal during the intense training periods. Their ballet really suffered for it, and last I heard one of them was still in in-patient psychiatric care.

At Roseheart, the canteen stays open until ten, but no one else uses it at the time when we're there—except, last night, for Teddy. He appeared. Taryn and I have gotten into a routine of sitting opposite each other at a small table, chatting and laughing as we make fun of Victoria and Marion in hushed whispers with wide eyes, like we're scared of being overheard. But the moment Teddy joined us last night, the whole atmosphere just changed. He squeezed himself next to Taryn and just stared intently at me.

Teddy kept mentioning things that had happened last year, trying to get Taryn to talk about those instead, like he was actively attempting to exclude me from the conversation. Taryn, bless her, did her best, trying to include me, giving me little summaries of the things that happened, her eyes quickly darting between me and Teddy.

"You're a better dancer than Theodore Walker," Avril says. "Even before he had this accident. I mean, yeah, he's good. But you've got better…. energy. And I'd bet you're stronger too. Did you see the lift they did at the start of that showreel? To the untrained eye, it looks spectacular, yes. But his arms were shaking just a little. A danseur should not look weak when he lifts his partner."

Partner. Is that what they are, Teddy and Taryn? More than just dance partners? I mean, I asked Taryn and she said no, and I even asked Xavier too, who said they just seemed like really good friends. But maybe Teddy wants them to be more. Thinks they're more, even? Last night, he sat so close to Taryn that their arms kept brushing. She pulled back a little, scooting to the left, but he had then just filled up the space she'd made, sort of stretching more toward her. He'd met my eyes then, and there'd been a hard glint in them. In the end, I'd wanted to physically push Teddy away from her, to give her the space she'd so obviously wanted.

I do like Taryn; I can't deny that. Earlier, Trent messaged me asking if I'd asked her out yet. Being me, I hadn't. Not just because I'm worried—but because of what happened with Camille. After the accident, I vowed I'd never let anyone get hurt by me again.

Maybe I should just leave Teddy and Taryn to it… Just see her only for the rehearsals. I could always buy a pot noodle to have in the evenings and use the kettle in the common room, leaving the canteen for the two of them.

"Ask Roseheart to film your next dance with her," Avril says. "I can help, too. Give feedback."

"Avril." My voice is a warning tone. "That's not necessary."

"Nonsense, you're my son. Now, what is the scheduling like? And the food? The food is important. You need the right fuel."

"The food is fine." And it is good, I know that. Roseheart has its own nutritionist and aside from organizing the menus and working with the cooks, he also teaches nutrition lessons. I heard every student in the academy has to attend them, and you can have individual sessions too, if you want.

The company uses the same nutritionist, but sessions aren't mandatory unless the company doctor is concerned about you.

Hmmm. Maybe I shouldn't plan to have pot noodles instead of a decent evening meal. That most likely wouldn't help my dancing.

I talk to Avril for a little more, then tell her I need to go. "Another rehearsal, with Taryn."

"Break a leg," she says. "Not literally." She laughs, but it doesn't ring true.

I'm still thinking about that laugh—the hard edge it had—when I meet Taryn in Studio 11 fifteen minutes later. It's late, and the lights have been turned off. She flicks them on, and the bulbs flicker. We wait for the lighting to sort itself out, but it doesn't. Just keeps dimming and flickering. It's a bit like candlelight.

"Shall we just go for it?" Taryn asks. "I don't know if any other studios are free. There were only a couple left by the time I booked it, and they often fill up quickly anyway. They always do."

I nod. "This will be fine." The lighting shouldn't be a problem anyway. I know the Roseheart dancers are used to performing in strobe lighting for some of the contemporary ballets they do. I've not done that before—Avril's school is much more classical based—but I need to get used to dancing with distracting lighting. Not that this mild flickering is that distracting, but I have to start somewhere.

Taryn looks determined and strong as she warms up at the barre, pointe shoes on. In this studio, the barre isn't by the mirrors—they're over by the right, but someone has drawn a dark, velvet curtain in front of them. I join her, warming up, and then we rehearse a couple of specific moments from the pas de deux, before doing a whole run through of the choreography. It's an extra session we have decided to do. Not a timetabled one, given our upcoming assessment, and there's something almost special about us both being here, untimetabled, choosing to spend extra time dancing together.

There's something magical about dancing with her in the flickering light, with no music. Just the sounds of our feet, our breathing. My skin almost sears every time she touches me, and a warm, glowing feeling fills me, just makes me want to keep dancing with her forever.

By the time we reach the end of the pas de deux, I feel sad it's over. That our moment has finished.

But we keep meeting for these moments—these intense dances that feel so, so magical. From Monday to Wednesday, we pack in more and more rehearsals alongside our busy timetables. And we're getting better, I can feel it.

"I think we're ready," she says, the evening before the first assessment as we finish our pas de deux. Her eyes are bright, and they make me smile. "It's magical, isn't it, that dance? How amazing is it going to look in full costume?"

"Yes." I want to reach across and hug her—but I don't. I've noticed now that she doesn't really like people hugging her. She even looks uncomfortable when people touch her arms. The only time she's at ease with contact is when we're dancing, and that just makes our pas de deux seem even more special.

So, I just give her a wide grin—so wide I feel like I might burst. I turn to get my shoes and change out of my flats. And that's when I see something written on the edge of the studio mirror peeking out from behind the velvet curtain.

"What's this say then? A love note someone left?" I laugh—suddenly very much hoping that it isn't a love note left by Teddy for Taryn—and grab the curtain, give it a firm yank.

I hear Taryn's sharp inhalation of breath, and then my eyes focus on the words written on the mirror in red lipstick.

I go cold.

I warned you before. You shouldn't be here. I know what you are. You don't belong here.

THIRTY-TWO

Taryn

The company board holds a meeting first thing the next morning, Thursday 21st July, the day of our first assessment. Every single company dancer is packed into the theatre, alongside all the staff: teachers, artistic staff, medical and wellbeing teams, administration, housekeeping, hospitality, cleaners, the board members, and directors.

A man is on stage who I think is Mr. Eldridge, but I'm not sure. He's the current owner of the whole institution, and I think I've only seen him once before.

"I will not tolerate racism of any kind at Roseheart." His voice booms.

Jaidev is next to me, and his left leg is jiggling. He thinks the message was aimed at him. He got so quiet when we saw the words. His face paled, and then he barely spoke. I hadn't even realized at that point that it would've looked like racism if it was directed at him. Because I knew straight away it was a message to me from Victoria or Marion. They don't want me here. Somehow, they know about the accident that caused Helena's death, and they think it was murder. They think I did it, and they want me to leave.

Just as I was about to say we should just clean it off—not realizing the impact it would of course be having on my partner—Evangeline came in.

"Thought it was your names down on the system for this studio. Doing an extra practice? How's it going?" The moment she saw the message on the mirror, her face fell. Her whole posture tightened, as if someone was pinching in. "Who did this?"

"We don't know." Jaidev's voice shook.

Evangeline shook her head. She got her phone out and snapped a photo. "Just in case whoever did this tries to erase it by the time I get others in here. Come away, you two. We need to investigate this. It is serious."

I wanted to say it wasn't as serious as she thought. It was directed at me, not Jaidev. But of course she'd think it was directed at him, an Asian dancer joining a company that is still predominantly white. In the diploma, Ivelisse was the only Latin American dancer, Advik the only Asian dancer, and there was a Black dancer named Will in the first year of the course. That was it. Everyone else was white. Looking around the theatre full of company dancers now, I realize there's overwhelming whiteness here, too, not just in the academy. Out of maybe sixty professional dancers, I can see maybe six or seven who are non-white. That's ten percent, I realize with a jolt. The same applies to the teachers too—or the ratio is even smaller, in fact. The French pointe teacher, Madame Jean, is the only teacher I can see who isn't white, just as Madame Cachelle is the only teacher for the academy who isn't. I don't know how I didn't realize any of this before. Shame fills me. Maybe in the academy, it was because I was friends with Ivelisse and often danced with Advik, and was taught by Madame Cachelle, that I didn't really notice the lack of diversity beyond them.

I focus back on the words being said.

"A full investigation into this will be carried out. I urge the writer of this message to step forward and turn themselves in," Mr. Eldridge says. "We will be looking through CCTV footage, and if we find the person before they've confessed, the repercussions will be greater. This is not the first time we've had racism at this institution, and just like then, it will not be tolerated."

Not the first time? I breathe in deeply. Maybe the lipstick messages *were* aimed at Jaidev, rather than me, and are racist after all. That first one was also left when we were both practicing together. And there have been none left for me when I've been using studios on my own—or when I've alone anywhere else.

But someone *did* steal Helena's shoes, rip up my photo board, and put pushpins in all my pointes and flats. I look at Jaidev. I haven't told him about those petty things done to me or about Helena's shoes. Maybe there are things being done to him he's not told me about. Maybe we're both being targeted, but someone has brought his race into it?

I feel sick. Then I think about the message left the first time. *I know you're a murderer.*

But Jaidev isn't a murderer.

I mean, is he? He can't be. Just as I'm not either.

But Alma did call him a psychopath, the voice in my head reminds me. But that means nothing. That was just Alma being Alma. Or Alma being racist.

"We will be searching rooms," Mr. Eldridge continues.

"They're going to be looking for red lippie," a ballerina near me says. "But most of us have that."

There's a lot of murmuring.

"And if no one has turned themselves in by this evening, we will be getting the police involved," Mr. Eldridge says. "Just to emphasize to you the seriousness of this matter."

There's almost a collective intake of breath from around the room, but several people are nodding.

Mr. Eldridge wraps up the assembly and says schedules are to resume for the day. This morning, I've got a flexibility class, followed by a run with Sibylle—who's now back from her audition—and Li Hua, then a class with the expression teacher, *and* a fitting session with Allie, the seamstress. She emailed earlier to say the first draft of my costume for the fall tour is ready, and to come by after morning classes. Then it's lunchtime—though I doubt I'll be eating much, given my assessment with Jaidev is this afternoon.

I move with the other female dancers toward the studio for the first class, the flexibility class. No one is really talking. A few of the girls look scared. I notice Victoria wiping her lipstick off onto the back of her hand. Actually, quite a few girls are doing it. A lot are wearing various shades of red. I mean, Sibylle even has that color, and I know I do too; one of last year's performances required all the female ballet-diploma students to wear it. It's not an unusual color.

The morning passes quickly, and all too soon I'm in Allie's office, knowing I've only got less than an hour before the assessment starts. She's smiling as she shows me my dress for the tour—a beautiful, dark garment with sleek, shiny black feathers that make up the skirt. The feathers have an iridescent quality hue as she turns them from side to side.

"And these are the wings," she says, showing me a pair of fragile-looking wings.

They're mainly black but have a blue band along the outer edges of all four wings and remind me of a Blue Banded Eggfly butterfly—Helena and I had a book on different butterflies when we were younger, and that one was one of my favorites.

"Jaidev's wings match yours, see?" Allie indicates what I assume is another pair hanging up, though they are wrapped up well in tissue paper and tape, so I can't see the design.

"These are beautiful," I whisper, and I touch the wings. They're soft like velvet, but ultra-lightweight, too. And I wish I was looking at it another day, a day when I wasn't so preoccupied with the threatening lipstick notes or the impending assessment.

I try my dress and wings on, and Allie makes notes of alterations needed. I'm glad Amanda isn't here this time so there are no comments about my size, because I'm sure she'd say I wasn't dainty enough to be a fairy in this magical divertissement pas de deux.

Next, I head to the canteen. I can hardly eat anything, so I cut lunch short, having only half a rice-cake with some butter. Jaidev isn't there, and Teddy just keeps trying to talk to me. I tell him I've got a headache and want to rest before my assessment.

Up in my room, I pull Misty Copeland's memoir, *Life in Motion*, from my bookshelf. I've read it countless times already, and the pages are well-thumbed. The margins are covered in my pencil scrawl as I made notes on the first couple of times, I read it. I was analytical then, trying to pick out things Misty said that could translate to me. Things to make me a better dancer. Because Misty is amazing. She only started ballet when she was thirteen, and now she's one of the most famous dancers. Not only did she start late, but she's a Black dancer—and reading the words of marginalized dancers suddenly seems more important than ever.

So, I let her words fill me, until it's time to be assessed.

I'm a bundle of nerves as Jaidev and I meet in Studio 13. Unlucky number thirteen. Great. I try not to let superstition get the better of me, but Helena died on a Friday 13th and since then I have always paid attention to that number.

Mr. Vikas and Mr. Aleks are already here, as are Evangeline and a pianist I don't know.

"Warm up quickly," Mr. Vikas tells us. "Mr. Aleks hasn't got long here."

We do—but warming up with the scrutinizing eyes of both the ballet master and artistic director on me isn't easy, I'm self-conscious and very aware that I'm trembling. I glance at Jaidev. His eyes are focused as he warms up next to me, also at the barre.

"Just relax," Evangeline whispers, and the door opens, revealing a tired-looking Miss Tavi.

But I can't relax. This is like one of those nightmares I got before every exam and assessment in the academy. I never get these nightmares before the performances or shows, even that last one which was also an assessment for graduation and an audition, but that had a different vibe to it. Whereas this is exactly like the formal academy assessments midsemester, where the teachers watch and frown, where you're trying to swallow your nausea and concentrate on remembering your combinations. Where you're waiting to be told if you're good enough to get a lead role in the main production. Where every student in the room is just as nervous while also trying not to show it.

"Okay, let's see the divertissement pas de deux, then," Mr. Aleks says. He stands at the front of the studio, his arms folded across his body.

The pianist starts playing, just like that. Jaidev and I scurry to our starting positions. My chest rises and falls too quickly, too sharply. There's a rushing sound in my ears. My blood feels too heavy in my legs, weighing me down. My stomach twists.

Then we begin.

I'm concentrating so hard, trying to remember the choreography, trying to keep time, trying to match my timings to the music, trying to keep character, trying to maintain my connection with Jaidev, trying not to look at Mr. Vikas or Mr. Alex or Miss Tavi or even Evangeline, though she's smiling. I'm just trying to get through it. I feel clumsy as I dance, even though I know I'm managing it well. Despite how much my head is spinning, I'm not making mistakes.

Evangeline claps when we finish. I am giddy, breathless. Jaidev gives me a smile, then runs his hands through his hair. It almost feels surreal that we've finished, that we've got through the whole routine.

Miss Tavi nods.

Mr. Vikas clears his throat. "Good."

Good?

I look at him, trying to read his body language. Some teachers say 'good' as their highest mark of praise, but for others, it's the level that's only slightly above 'satisfactory.'

Mr. Aleks strides forward. He makes a considering noise then turns to the ballet master. "Technically, it's strong. They're both up to the standard for the company, but it's wooden emotionally."

My heart sinks. *Wooden emotionally.*

"It's lacking romantic connection between them." Mr. Aleks casts his eyes over me and Jaidev. "Their romance isn't believable, and it's affecting the fluidity and emotion of their dance."

Technically strong, but lacking romantic connection. I take a deep breath. I never had that problem with Teddy. But *of course* me and Jaidev have got this problem, and *of course* we're lacking intimacy and emotional connection. We've only been dancing together for two weeks.

"We'll do it," Jaidev says. His voice is eager, earnest. "We'll practice until we've got this. We won't let you down."

"Good." And with that, Mr. Aleks sweeps out of the room.

Mr. Vikas gives us some specific technical feedback on various parts of our pas de deux and suggests we book in for some extra character lessons together, too. "Learn to create a connection if there isn't one."

We both nod.

Evangeline says she'll be back later for our scheduled choreography session, and then it's just the two of us.

"It could've gone better," Jaidev says. His eyes are sad, and I realize just how much he wants this too.

"It didn't go *badly*," I say. "Technically, we are good. Good enough for the company."

"But wooden."

I shrug and try to focus on keeping my voice light. "We can't be harsh, though. We have to focus both on what we've done well and what we need to improve."

He just shrugs, then crouches and pulls off one of his canvas flats. "It's the romance, Taryn. The romance is the problem." His voice is low, and he looks up at me through his dark lashes. "That's what we are missing. We are not believable in our romance when we dance because we do not have any romance."

"It takes time," I say. "It always does." I mean, Teddy and I connected quite quickly, but it wasn't instant. Maybe a month or so. It's just been three weeks.

"And time is what we do not have." He makes a strange noise in his throat, sort of like he's clearing it but kind of like a growl too. "But maybe there is a chance, if we can…make it real?"

Make it real? I stare at him. I don't understand what he's meaning. You can't just make romance real because you want to. *I* can't do that.

He smiles, tentatively. "I like you, Taryn, and I believe you like me, too. So… So what if we got together? We could just try it—and it would help our dance, and we'd get this connection that the artistic director wants. It would help us get the permanent contracts here and…" He trails off, then looks away.

"I…uh…"

Getting together with Jaidev? Not just for dance, but for…a relationship? That's what he's meaning. I don't know what to say. My head spins. He's attracted to me? And he thinks I am to him? He's presuming my romantic orientation, maybe even my sexuality, just like that? But then again, maybe those who are on the ace and aro spectrums are the only ones who'd consider that someone might *not* feel those feelings. But, still, he thinks this is acceptable to do, to propose something like this? He's admitted he likes me, and he's using our professional situation to try and further his own goal—of what? Wanting to sleep with me?

"I…" I literally can't speak. It's like I'm shaking inside. Teddy told me his dance partners before Roseheart all wanted relationships with him, and it made it awkward to dance with them afterward.

I stare at Jaidev, almost unable to believe he's done this. It's already awkward enough at times between us, and if we even get this contract, I'll be dancing with him for years. And if we don't get it, it's still another year of dancing with him at the academy.

Oh, God.

"Taryn, I'm sorry."

"I've got to go." I grab my bag and leave the studio.

THIRTY-THREE

Taryn

I am running, feet slapping linoleum and then stone and then grass, then linoleum again.

"Hey, Taryn, wait up!"

I turn, tears nearly filling my vision, and see Teddy. At least it's not Jaidev, but I still don't want to talk to Teddy. I just want to be on my own.

"Not now!" I call.

"But I'm… Hey, what's the matter?"

I don't turn back to him, just keep running. "I'll see you later, Ted. Just not now."

I head to my room, feeling both too hot and too cold. How dare Jaidev put that pressure on me! How dare he presume anything! I'm not attracted to him. Just because I can see he's conventionally an attractive man, strong and muscular with a good jawline, it doesn't mean I want to be with him. And I wouldn't be with him just to get a role either—even if it *is* a position I've wanted forever. I'm not going to do something I'm not comfortable with, and right now, I don't want a relationship at all. Yet, of course, relationships are what so many people *do* want, and I also know that most people want sex, too. My breathing quickens. I thought Jaidev and I were friends. But this whole time, has he just been after one thing, and assuming that I'd say yes because he's attractive and because girls don't usually say no to him?

"Hey." A voice makes me jolt. In the haze around me, I hadn't realized Ivelisse was outside our room. "Taryn?"

I don't want to be crying in front of her, in front of anyone, but here I am doing just that.

"What's happened?"

I cry more—and I don't know why this is upsetting me so much. Why I'm flitting from anger to sadness to despair, why I'm showing so much emotion. Because I know it's over now? I can't dance with him.

"Taryn." Ivelisse smooths my hair back from my face and leads me into our room. She sits me on my bed, then hovers in front of me.

I put my duffel bag down and find myself telling her in gulps and stuttered breaths, that Jaidev wants to be romantic with me—maybe even more—to improve our dance. It sounds silly saying it like this—*be romantic with me*—but I just can't think of the right words, the way to express everything I'm feeling. And *of course* I don't want to say I'm ace or aro. I still want to hold that close to me. It would be different, if I'd already signed a contract with the company, but I haven't. And they could decide not to offer me a contract because I'm aroace, even if they wouldn't say that was their reasoning. I can't risk my orientation becoming common knowledge before I'm ready and have secured the job of my dreams. Only then can I come out as an aroace dancer—if I want to.

"So, you're upset because he asked you out?" Ivelisse blinks slowly. The corners of her mouth twitch up a little, though I think she's trying to keep her expression neutral.

"Yes."

"Because it's not genuine? Like, he only wants to be with you to make sure you get the places with the company?"

I nod. "And now it's going to have ruined everything."

"Why?" she asks.

"Well, I can't dance with him now. It's going to be too awkward."

Ivelisse laughs. "Dancers dance with their exes all the time—you always get dancers getting together, especially at schools. And most schools don't even have primary partners like we do. They have to dance with exes and maybe their exes' new partners. And that might be awkward at first, but they do it because ballet is important. It's their career. It is what they are, what they have to do. And *this* isn't even that. Jaidev will get over the rejection, I'm sure."

I gulp. "He'll think I don't want this as much as he does, that I'm not willing to do what he is."

Ivelisse shakes her head. "You say that like he'd be having to endure something, too, in being with you. Taryn, honestly, this just feels like an overreaction. You've got this amazing chance here, and you can't *not* dance with him because of this."

I breathe deeply, looking at her, and start to calm down. Maybe I acted hastily, leaving the studio like that. I mean, Jaidev doesn't know I'm aroace. He would've just assumed I felt the same way, right? Especially if he's used to his female partners falling at his feet.

"I'm sure he didn't mean to upset you," Ivelisse says. "He's really sweet, from what I've seen. He seems like a decent guy, unlike Peter." Her tone darkens and she clenches her hands into tight fists.

"Peter? What's he done now?"

"Didn't you hear him last night in the lounge?"

I shake my head. "I wasn't there. Had an extra practice."

"Well, he was making rape jokes." Anger flares in her eyes. "And even Xavier and Robert tackled him about it, and he was just all like, *ha ha, it's still funny*. And it really wasn't, you know?"

"He's just awful. When's he leaving?"

She shrugs. "I don't know. I just hate him more every time he opens his mouth. Like, how can he even think that's okay to say?"

I curl my fingers. "I—"

My phone rings, startling me. I dig it out of my bag and look at the caller ID.

Mum.

I frown. Mum only phones after big shows to see how I got on. She can't be phoning to see how the assessment went because she didn't know about it. She thinks I've got the part.

Unless she did somehow find out and knows I lied?

My mouth dries.

Or she's just phoning me for an uncharacteristic chat, like I did with her?

"You going to answer that?" Ivelisse says.

I lick my lips and press the accept button. "Mum?" My voice cracks.

A sense of dread pulls at my stomach, like it's trying to drag me down.

"Taryn, oh my God. We've… It's your sister. There's been an accident."

Everything stops. The world around me drains of color and then folds in on itself until there's nothing left.

Helena's face. Her eyes. My eyes. A mirror. A mirror not moving.

Peering down from the balcony, screaming her name, my throat hoarse. Screaming pain and fury and blood. Blood, down there. Pooling.

Her hair's fanned out, a halo around her, but the blood is swallowing it, swallowing her. She's not moving. Not moving. Not moving.

I shriek. My shriek splits time. It all fractures and everything's happening at once and nothing is happening.

The neighbor screaming.

Helena's last breath.

"We told you not to go onto the balconies! Now you know why, don't you?"

"Start CPR!"

"That balcony is too dangerous! Why do you never listen?"

"Shannon! The CPR!"

"Why didn't you stop her?"

THIRTY-FOUR

Teddy

"So, tell me about Taryn," Victoria says.

She smiles pleasantly at me, and there's something strangely alluring about her eyes. I can't look away. It's like she's Medusa or something. I don't even know if that's right. Greek mythology isn't my strong point.

"About Taryn?" I frown a little and glance around the studio before looking back at Victoria. "Why?"

"Well, we're going to have both of you in the company, right?" she says sweetly. "So, I want to know about her."

My eyes narrow. I know what she can be like. I asked Xavier for the names of the company ballerinas who were making Taryn's life difficult, believing Jaidev would've said something to him, and he had. And the first name uttered was Victoria's.

"Well, Taryn is the kindest person I know," I say.

She's kind and a genuine person. But there's sadness under her outer layer, I can see it. Anyone can really who looks at her. And I know it's because of her sister. The dead one. The one she doesn't ever talk about.

So many times, I've wanted to ask Taryn about Helena, but she's never told me about her directly. Or at all really. And I don't want to mention her name, be the one to bring her up. I don't know how Taryn might react. I don't want to upset her.

"And what does she want?" Victoria asks.

I frown. My stomach makes a grumbling noise. I haven't eaten or drank anything today, but that's okay because I've got the catheterization procedure later this afternoon, and you can't eat six hours beforehand. "What do you mean?"

"What's her goal? Why does she want to be at Roseheart's company? She wants to be the female principal?"

I laugh. "What girl wouldn't?"

"Woman," Victoria corrects. "Though I suppose she is a girl, isn't she? Still seventeen, right?"

I nod. Taryn's birthday is the last day of August. We'd been told before that any diploma student admitted to the company who isn't eighteen at the time would need a guardian to also sign the contract also. Taryn had been nervous telling her mum that, a few months ago, said she was half expecting her to refuse to sign it. But I'd assured her that that wouldn't happen. And when Taryn had messaged her about it on Facebook, her mum had said she'd do it.

Victoria makes a disgusted sound, deep in her throat. "So, she wants to be principal. Well, well, well. And she's stuck up enough to think she'll get it easily."

"Uh, no," I say. "She'd just be happy to get into the company. We both would be. All we want is to prove that aroace dancers can succeed. That romance can be authentically performed and…" I trail off, feeling too much blood pound in my head, as I realize what I've said.

Victoria's eyes are wide. "Taryn is aroace?"

"Oh, uh. Yeah. I am, too." I rub at my arms. My breathing is suddenly too quick.

"Don't look so worried," she says. "I won't say anything. I'm not heartless."

"Really? You've been making life pretty difficult for her as it is."

She shrugs. "Just rites of passage, isn't it? She'll get over it. They always do."

"I mean it, Victoria. You can't say anything about Taryn being aroace."

"Why would I? I'm ace-spec, too." She tosses her hair over her shoulder then reaches for a hair-tie from her bag

"You are?" I stare at her.

She nods. "Demisexual. Not aro though—well, I thought I was for a while, but then turned out I was demiromantic as well as demisexual. Fell right for this guy, found I was pretty into sex once I had the deep emotional connection to him, *blah blah blah*." She rolls her eyes. "I sound like one of them definitions guides. But, anyway, I'm not going to say anything. Not about that. I know the struggles we all face. Anyway, do you want to learn this choreography or not? We're here to dance. Not talk."

We dance—forty-five minutes of grueling combinations. Victoria is pretty ruthless, and by the time I've finished, I'm nauseous and a little dizzy.

"So, tomorrow then?" Victoria asks as we change our shoes after.

"Oh, uh, no, I can't do then." I look at my phone. Shit. I'm going to be late. "I'll message you!" I yell as I run.

"You still shouldn't have gone back there." Dad's in a mood with me when he arrives to collect me, and that's the first thing he says. There's no *Hello, Teddy, how are you?* or anything nice like that. Just going straight to the point because I went against what he wanted. To be honest, I've been avoiding his phone calls ever since I came back here.

"Dad, please." I haven't got the strength to argue with him. Not when my appointment, the catheterization procedure, is so soon.

It's a 6 p.m. surgery. Check-in is forty-five minutes before. The letter said they're running an extra clinic into the evening to try and clear waiting list times. Not that there's been much of a wait for me. I collapsed on July 1st and now it's the 21st.

"It's too much." Dad drums his fingers on the steering wheel. "Being back here so soon. You're not well. I need to be able to keep an eye on you."

"What. To check I'm not dancing?" I snort, but I'm suddenly aware of everything—how it's cold in the car because Dad's got the air conditioning turned up full blast. How my shirt is scratchy against my chest. How the headache I've been trying to ignore is still there.

"Well, are you?" Dad looks at me, then pulls the car out onto the road without waiting for an answer.

But I still say it. "No." The lie doesn't even make me feel bad because it's kind of meaningless anyway. Soon, this will all be cleared up.

Dad doesn't talk really for the rest of the journey, except to say he's packed an overnight bag for me. As if I'm even going to be staying that long. I'm *fine*. I'll just have this procedure, and then it'll be done, and all this silliness will be sorted, and me and Taryn can dance together again.

When we arrive at the hospital, Dad drops me off because he can't find anywhere to park. A sudden rush of dizziness tries to grab me as I walk into the main entrance of the hospital, alone. Suddenly, I feel weak and small and scared.

Scared.

"But it'll be fine," I say, and several elderly people near me give me strange looks. Right. I'm just the weird teenager talking to himself.

I've got the appointment letter, and I check where to go. My feet drag as I take myself there. There's a lump in my throat that I just can't seem to swallow, can't get it to go away. I imagine that it's the shape of my esophagus now, that extra shape a permanent feature, and it nearly makes me throw up.

One, two, three, four.

I breathe deeply.

Five, six, seven, eight.

I can do this.

I'm fine.

This will prove it.

I have to do this to dance with Taryn again.

I sign myself in at the reception area of the cardiology department. Just seeing that word—*cardiology*—on the wall makes my stomach feel heavier. My breathing is too loud as I sit in the waiting room.

I strain my neck, looking back toward the door, waiting for Dad to arrive.

No sign of him.

Are you coming up yet? I text. *Level two, department C.* In case he's forgotten.

I drum my fingers on my thighs.

Still trying to park.

"Theodore Walker," a voice calls.

A young nurse with a smiley face and clumpy mascara.

And then it's… Then it's happening…

A hospital gown. A blue basket to put my own clothes in. Consent forms. Another nurse. A pen to sign the forms with. Someone laughing, making a bad joke. The doctor in front of me. A bald man with a head that's too shiny. He laughs and says he does these procedures all the time. Nothing to worry about.

Nothing to worry about.

A nurse tells me to empty my bladder. I do so, feeling sick with nerves the whole time. Then I'm led through to a lab that looks too sterile. Like something off a horror film, where people are cut up.

My mouth dries, and I try to distract myself, paying attention to what's going on in here. Two doctors in scrubs. A blood pressure cuff is strapped around my arm. Pens write notes on clipboards. Someone directs me to lie on a table. The flimsy paper creases under me. I try to adjust my hospital gown, to give me some more dignity. Someone laughs.

They put sticky electrodes on my chest. They talk all the time. Their voices are abrasive and grating.

"Are you nervous? Oh dear, you do seem nervous. Your heart rate's gone right up. Just relax."

Relax. I can't relax. My empty stomach churns.

I try to straighten my gown again. More voices.

Then an IV in my arm. A syringe of clear liquid. Just a sedative, they tell me. Because I'll be awake, but this is just to help me to relax.

I'm fine.

But I wish my dad was here, as they prepare the side of my neck for the catheter, swiping it with a cold disinfectant wipe that stings a little with the force applied.

I wish someone was here with me.

"We'll just get the local anesthetic in, before we thread the catheter," a doctor says. "Then we'll begin."

It's a weird experience, the during and the after—because I'm groggy, groggier than I thought a sedative would make me, and it's like time is too thick, like seconds are dragging on my skin, pulling me both forward and back. A nurse is here at one point, saying something, but then she's gone. Dad's here, and then he's gone, too.

Someone's serving food. I can smell it. Grease. My stomach curdles.

But then they're gone. Everyone keeps going.

"Yes, he's still a bit out of it from the sedative, bless him. It can happen, but he'll be right as rain shortly, I'm sure."

Dad's back. I blink. Feel a bit more normal now. More like me. I'm in a bed in a ward. Blue curtains are drawn around, but only half the way, so I can still see some of the room, other beds.

"Sorry, son," Dad says. He pulls at his face, making his skin sag even more as he looks at me. "The procedure confirmed what the echocardiogram showed. You've got hypertrophic cardiomyopathy, but the doctor said they were able to get a lot of data."

Confirmed? No.

It can't be.

My mouth dries. *No.*

Dad's still talking. His lips are moving, but the rushing sounds in my ears are too loud. There's an angry tide inside me taking over, washing everything away, flooding me.

No.

No.

No.

THIRTY-FIVE

Taryn

"Tessa's still not awake." Mum covers her face with her hands, her shoulder shaking, her whole body shaking as I arrive at the hospital waiting room. "Why isn't she waking up?"

I reach out, hug her, even though it's been years. Even though we're not close now. She's smaller than I remembered, somehow, like she's shrunk, her spine curving maybe. She clings to me in a way that hasn't happened since Helena's death. Mum's always the strong one.

Except when Helena died. Then she melted.

No. This can't happen again.

It can't.

I swallow hard.

"Mum, what exactly happened?" Because I still don't know.

She was hysterical on the phone, every time I called from various buses as I was getting nearer and nearer, just screaming over and over about how there's been an accident. Tessa is in a coma, but that's as much as I know.

Mum starts crying harder.

"Okay, where's Tammy?" I ask, looking over her shoulder. I've only just got here. The same waiting room where we waited to hear news on a Helena, even though I'd already known. I'd heard her last breath and seen how she'd shattered. I'd looked into her eyes, and I don't know why, but I remember them as broken glass, as if she had glass eyes. She didn't, and I don't know why that image is so strong.

"Grandad's got Tammy. They've gone to get something to eat." Mum speaks the words against my neck. Her breath is hot, feels muggy. Dense with tears.

There are other people in here, waiting, and several are watching Mum like she's entertainment or something.

I turn her away from them.

"But the doctor said to stay here," she says.

"And Giovanni?" I don't really like my mum's boyfriend, but then again, I don't know him. Every time I've returned home, he's been at work. He travels a lot for that. A lot of the time he isn't even in the country.

Mum rubs her face. The skin below her eyes is red and distorts without snapping back straight away as she pulls at it. "I still can't get through to him."

"What? He doesn't know? About any of this?"

She shoves her mobile into my hand. "You try him. I've got to…." Her face crumples, and then she's running, her massive handbag slamming into her back with every step.

"Mum!"

"Stay here," she cries, turning back to look at me—just for a second. "In case the doctor comes. I just can't…"

And then she's gone. A hollow feeling fills me, getting bigger and bigger, like someone's whittling away my insides. Scraping out my flesh.

Last time, Mum melted into a puddle, became a sodden tissue on the ground that no one could scoop up and get to stand on its own. Now she's fleeing.

Everyone's looking at me, and I sit down. Do I stay here like Mum said? Or go after her? Her phone screen lights up, but it's just a Twitter notification.

Okay. *Giovanni*. I'll call him.

I try to unlock Mum's phone, but I don't know her passcode, so I call him on my own phone. I've had his number in my contacts for years, but I think this is the first time I've ever used it. I press my phone more firmly to my ear. The line rings and rings before it clicks off. No answerphone, so I can't leave a message.

A nurse calls out a name—one I don't catch—but then a woman with a baby on her lap stands. The baby begins shrieking. I try not to show alarm visibly, but I just don't really like babies. And sometimes, I feel like I'm the only person in the world who doesn't like them. I just don't feel maternal.

Even when my sisters were babies, I didn't really connect with them. Well, I didn't really see them. I was away at Roseheart, or at my previous ballet school. I only saw the babies in glimpses, but that had been enough. Everyone else coos over babies, even Teddy. He's always saying how he wants a family one day.

"Taryn!"

I look up as a blur of blond pigtails and a pale blue Elsa dress flies at me, jumps on me.

"Tammy!" I almost feel winded as I hold onto her, somehow not dropping either phone.

In the doorway of the waiting room, Grandad appears. He shuffles, walking with a stick, apparently putting great concentration into each step. He sees me and smiles.

"I'm glad you're here," he says a moment later as he sits next to me.

I lean forward. "What's happening? Do you know?"

He shakes his head and suggests to Tammy that she plays with the kids' toys a few feet away. Then he turns to me. "Where's your mother?" He frowns, looking around.

"She just ran off."

Grandad rolls his eyes a little. "She'll come back."

"So, tell me what's happening? Mum's barely said a thing."

He is breathing hard, wheezing a little. "Tammy found Tessa unconscious. She said she was sleeping, but then your mum couldn't wake her. She didn't call an ambulance straight away. I don't know why. She phoned me, hysterical. I then called an ambulance, and by the time I got there, she said she'd phoned you too. She was in a bad way, calling Tessa *Helena*."

Coldness fills me. I flex my fingers and focus on Tammy. She's picked up a picture book with a red dog on it and is flipping through the pages, frowning. Then she sits down next to the box of children's toys and starts pulling out all the books, one by one. I guess she must like books, but that's as much as I know about her. Tammy has always been the baby until recently. Now she's two years old, I find her a bit more endearing, but I've not really gotten to know her as a person yet. Tessa is two years older. I know more about her. But not enough.

"Has Tessa got any medical conditions?" I ask Grandad.

"Not that I know of." He reaches across and places his hand on top of mine. "I'm glad you're here. I know it's difficult for you, being back here."

I nod a little. I don't want to focus on that. I look toward the door, as if Mum is going to reappear.

"Should I go after her?" I ask.

"Let me. You just stay and watch Tammy. A doctor's going to be back any minute, I should think. We've been waiting two hours, and they'd said it would only be an hour. Ring me as soon as a doctor is here, and I'll come back."

Grandad ambles away. I ring Giovanni again, but still no answer. I call Tammy to me and hug her tightly, because I think this is what I'm supposed to do. She babbles to me about the book clenched in her hands. *Sleeping Beauty*.

"Like Tessa," she says. She's smiling, looks happy. She doesn't realize how serious this is—and none of us actually knows what's happening. Not knowing is the worst.

When we were last here, me and Mum and Grandad, we were waiting on news of Helena, and it was agonizing, but deep down, we knew. They'd been trying to save her, Mum and Grandad, giving CPR until paramedics arrived and took over, trapping her into their ambulance. But I'd known, when I was sitting here, waiting for news. I had that gut feeling. I'd seen Helena's body, broken. I'd heard how raspy her breathing was—and when it had stopped—before Grandad had arrived and shouted to start CPR.

I'd known what was coming then. But this time? This time, I'm in the dark. I don't know what's even happened with Tessa. Nobody seems to.

My phone rings, startling me. Giovanni.

"Taryn?" His rich voice is full of concern. "What is going on? I've got many missed calls from Shannon, Bob, and now you."

"It's Tessa," I say. Tammy, next to me, looks at me with wide eyes. "I don't know exactly what's happened because Mum's hysterical, but we're at the hospital. Tessa is in a coma, I think, and I'm with Tammy now, in the waiting room. I only just got here, maybe ten minutes ago, and I haven't seen a doctor yet."

"Oh God." There's a long pause. "Pass me onto Shannon."

"Mum's not here. She got upset and ran out. Grandad's gone looking for her."

He swears under his breath. "Right. Text me details of the hospital. The postcode and address. I'll leave work now."

I hear him shouting to his secretary, asking her to book him a flight.

"I'm not going to get there until this evening but call me straight away if there's any news. And get Shannon to call me as well, as soon as she's back."

"I will."

Giovanni ends the call. Tammy looks up at me, sucking her thumb. Her eyes are filling with tears, almost in slow motion. Then one trickles over and runs down her face.

"Is Tessa going to join Angel Helena?" Her voice cracks. "I don't want Tessa to go there. I want her to play with *me*."

Angel Helena.

I didn't even know that's what they call her.

"Shhh," I say. "It'll be okay. Tessa will be fine, Tammy. It'll be okay. We'll see her soon."

Maybe the worst part of saying those words is that I don't know if they are a lie, and the weight of that possibility wraps around me tightly as I text Giovanni the address.

Almost an hour later, a doctor emerges. He says Tessa is awake and recovering, says she had a critically low blood sugar level. He says it's most likely diabetes. They'll keep her in for tonight. Mum is back now, subdued and tearful. She says she and Grandad will stay at the hospital overnight and Giovanni should arrive here at about nine. She gives me keys to the house, asking me to take Tammy back as it's almost midnight now. Tammy is now asleep on my lap, and I nod.

The bus back is quiet. Tammy and I are the only people on it, until a heavily pregnant woman gets on. The driver pulls the bus away from the stop before she's had a chance to sit down, and the woman lurches to the side, stumbling. I reach out to grab her, to help, but I'm too far away. As it happens, the woman half falls into a seat.

"Are you okay?" I call.

She turns, looks a bit shaken, but nods.

"She has a big tummy," Tammy whispers into my ear, then buries her face into my neck.

I don't know whether to say it's because there's a baby in there, because what if there isn't? Alma says one of her sisters has endometriosis and at times is so bloated from it that strangers ask her when she's due. "It's the most upsetting thing, too," Alma told me once. "Because she's struggling with infertility due to scarring on her womb or something, and she's had three rounds of IVF. And then strangers assume she's pregnant. She's practically in tears when that happens."

I definitely don't want to assume anything. I'm uncomfortable just at the thought of making someone uncomfortable. But then seeing pregnant people has always made me feel queasy as well. I'm not exactly sure why or when it started—or if anyone else feels this way. I mean, it must just be me because everyone says how wonderful pregnancy is. Pregnant women are always complaining about strangers touching their bellies—so it must just be me. I can't imagine anything worse than reaching out and touching a pregnant belly.

Would it feel soft or firm? Can you, like, feel the baby underneath the skin?

I saw a video a few months ago on Facebook. It was one of those progress videos where a short clip was filmed each week to track a woman's pregnancy. At first, in the early weeks, she looked pretty much normal. You wouldn't have known she was pregnant. That only started being apparent by week nine in the video, only ever so slightly, and for the next few weeks she had a small bump. The kind of pregnancy bump that I thought looked nice. But then it ballooned. Her belly became wider than she was, and all I could think was that it looked like an alien, this thing stuck on her abdomen.

I scrolled through all the comments, curiosity getting the better of me as I read all sorts of loving comments professing this pregnant woman's beauty. And that was when I knew for sure there must be something wrong with me, because by the thirty-week clip, I was repulsed.

The thought of something—*someone*—growing inside me or anyone just made me feel sick. I broke out in a sweat, feeling lightheaded and dizzy. I had to stop watching the video.

But I often get this sense of repulsion, looking at bodies. Not just pregnant bodies. *All* bodies. Sometimes I get weirded out by what the human form is like. Like how weird it is that we're just these torso lumps on two spindly legs. How we have a huge blob on top for our head, and two arms. A couple of times when I've been people-watching after ballet has finished and it's the next group warming up, seeing them contort their bodies like that has made my stomach queasy. Made me think of grease pooling in my gut, and I've had to take several deep breaths.

Everyone in the ballet world seems to think that the human form is beautiful. It's art. And so, I don't know why

I'm like this—because when I dance, it feels like I'm *beyond* my body. Like I'm transcending my human limitations. Dancing with a partner feels intimate and emotional and perfect. When I'm purely in the zone, I forget that we are sacks of muscles and flesh and bones, encased in skin. We're art and stories and emotion.

But sitting on this bus now, with the pregnant woman several rows in front, it's not art, not for me. It's flesh and blood and bone growing, transforming.

I have to look away before I feel any queasier.

Tammy says she's hungry when we get back, and I am too, even though it's nearly 1 a.m. I make Tammy and myself a snack, figuring it can't do any harm, and we stream an episode of *Peppa Pig* as we eat. I reply to messages on my phone from the Roseheart dancers—Ivelisse and Li Hua—even though it's late. Ivelisse will probably still be awake anyway.

I stare at Jaidev's message. *I'm so sorry. I didn't mean anything by it. It was just a suggestion, and I didn't mean to put any pressure on you.*

That almost feels like a lifetime ago. I reply, telling him it's fine. I mean, it has to be. Maybe I was overreacting too. And right now, I've got more important things to worry about.

It's strange being back here. The house with the plush, blue carpet and the same scent in the air fresheners and all the balconies.

The *balconies*.

I close my eyes. No. I can't think of them. But *of course* I can see the door to one. The glass door. There's no curtain in front of it. The house is old, several hundred years, but there are four balconies. Two on each side of the house. One on each level. The living room, the kitchen, and upstairs, two of the bedrooms. I wonder if Mum has had the railings replaced with stronger ones. Safer ones.

Or maybe the doors stay permanently locked. I can't bring myself to try one of the door handles.

Tammy and I are on the sofa. The same sofa I'd curl up with Helena on. It's more stained now, the fabric worn thin in places. Over there, by the log burner, is where we'd sit to warm our hands on cold winter's nights while Mum would tell stories. Our favorite stories were the ones about our dad. She had all these amazing tales about the stuff he was doing—but really, it turned out that we were conceived as a result of a one-night stand. Mum said she'd had a phase where she was out every night, meeting men, and she's never said it, but I don't think she knows who our father is. I'm pretty certain he doesn't know. And so, neither do we.

But we always had Grandad, Mum's father, and he said he'd be our dad too. He was. He taught us to ride our bicycles when we were little. He took Helena fishing when suddenly she decided she wanted to go, even though he'd never been before. He'd pick up coloring books for us and felt-tip pens. And he bought us our first pointe shoes, when we were both a couple of years into ballet and the ballet mistress at the first school had said we were finally ready to go on pointe.

On the mantelpiece, above the fireplace—now cold because Mum never lights it until the first day of October—there are four photographs. I'm first, in the white frame. Then Helena in the blue frame. Then Tessa, the green frame. And Tammy, the orange frame. Four girls smiling. Each photo was taken when we were two years old, so it almost looks like we should all be the same age now or something. There are no photos showing the age gaps. Always individual ones, I notice. And no photos taken after Helena and I were older than five are no display.

But the four photos just emphasize how there should be four girls here. I can almost feel Helena's presence in the room, and I daren't look toward the balcony doors in case I see a shimmer of her.

Quickly, I head into the kitchen, telling Tammy I'll wash up and then it'll definitely be bedtime, so she doesn't see me cry.

THIRTY-SIX

Jaidev

"You actually told her you should get together to improve your dance?" Trent stares at me, with one eyebrow raised, then bursts out laughing.

"Yeah. And then she didn't even show to the practice late yesterday evening or this morning." I pause. "I mean, I texted her and said sorry, and she said it was fine, but I'm pretty sure she is avoiding me. Didn't see her at dinner last night either, or lunch today."

"Mate, sounds like you've really upset her. How exactly did you word it?"

I recall what I said, with what I think is pretty much a word-for-word recount. Trent just shrugs in the end though. No words of wisdom.

"Just have to wait and see."

Waiting doesn't exactly make me feel good. I want to be active, doing something, but I also don't want to flood Taryn's phone. So, it looks like I'll just have to wait for her to come back.

It's easy enough doing this, keeping myself busy. Luckily, there are no formal rehearsals with Taryn and Evangeline, and it's just my solo timetable this afternoon. But I wonder when Taryn will show up to any of our own sessions again, the ones we scheduled in ourselves for extra practice.

I busy myself with classes. I've got three this afternoon—leaps and jumps, and two with Madame Cachelle on the English way of dancing—before endurance and gym. As I'm walking to my first class, taking the outside route that passes the main gates of the grounds, I see Ivelisse. She's walking with her hood pulled up, hands deep in the pockets of her leather jacket, heading toward the gates.

"Hey," I call out and she jumps. "You seen Taryn?"

"Yeah, she's gone." Her voice sounds thicker than usual.

Gone? "Gone?" My eyes widen. Has she... did I scare her off completely?

Ivelisse nods. "Family emergency. Yesterday."

"Wait, what?" I rush toward her. "What's happened?"

"I don't know," she says. "But look, I've got to go. Got an appointment in the city, and I can't be late."

She scurries off.

I message Taryn quickly, asking if she's okay and if there's anything I can do. I almost expect an immediate answer, but there's not. Even a few hours later, there's still no reply from her.

Hazma leans toward me as he adjusts his foot and rubs it. We're in the gym. "Did anyone come forward yet?"

The lipstick threat. I shake my head. I can't help but think it's Victoria. I mean, I know she wants me out of here, but I also can't assume it is her. Just because she made it clear she didn't like me, it doesn't mean she'd leave a racist note.

"No one's said anything to me if they have."

"Unfortunate that it happened right before your assessment, too," he says. "But don't worry. We'll find out who did it." He gives me a grin I think is supposed to be reassuring.

After I've finished for the day, Mr. Aleks finds me to say the police are here and want to talk to me about the threatening message. At first, I think it means they've found something, but a few minutes into the conversation with the detectives, it becomes apparent they've got no new information. They're just trying to *ascertain the facts,* as they say.

"We are aware of the previous incident you were involved in," one of the officers says. She's white—they both are—with dark hair pulled back into a neat ponytail. "And we know you were cleared of any intent in that."

Intent. Like I'd want Camille to be hurt at all.

My mouth dries. I nod and look around the room. Mr. Vikas's office. At least I'm not in a station right now.

Or a cell.

"Do you think it is reasonable to assume that the person threatening you here also knows of the incident?" the other officer asks. She's older, and I think she speaks with a Manchester accent, though I'm still a bit unsure with all the British accents.

"I don't know," I say. "It's more of a you-don't-belong-here message than one that sounds like it refers to something specific. They haven't mentioned anything in the message that would indicate that."

Except Victoria knows. She definitely knows.

The officer nods. "We have to look into anything it could be related to."

My chest tightens. "Anything that would mean it's not racist then?" I ask. "That would mean I deserve a message like that?"

"That's not what we are saying. And we will be looking into this very seriously, I can assure you."

"Well," I say. "There is one person here who knows about Camille. Victoria Simmonds. She made it clear to me before that she knows about…about what happened. She said it to my face."

"What did she say?"

I think back. "That I'd better watch myself."

The two officers share a glance.

"So, a clear threat then."

"Well, yes."

"And do you think she'd leave a cryptic message, too? To warn you?"

I shrug. "I don't really know her. I don't like her, though. She's making my ballet partner's life difficult too. Constantly undermining her in front of other dancers."

"That's…" The older officer looks at her notepad. "Taryn Foster?"

I nod.

"Okay, then." She closes her notepad. "We'll look into this more. Try not to worry. We'll find out who it is."

Will you? I want to shout, but I don't. I don't trust the police, and I don't feel kindly to them.

Not after they arrested me for murdering Camille.

THIRTY-SEVEN

Teddy

Sometimes, I feel like the whole world is going on around me, moving at breakneck speed, but I'm stationary. I'm stuck in one place, and I can't move. There's no one else with me, because everyone else knows how to run fast, to keep up. They don't get left behind. But I do.

Minutes blur into hours and hours blur into days, yet it also feels like nothing is happening. Doctors talk to me. Sometimes at the hospital and sometimes on the phone. They say words like *implantable cardioverter defibrillator* and *pacemaker*. Then the air is cold, and trees are whispering. The engine of Dad's car is rattling. We've gone out for a drive. My neck is still sore from the procedure. He stops at a petrol station, buys himself a coffee and donut. A water and a donut for me. I don't touch either. Then it's cold at home, despite the heating turned up high. I cannot get warm.

Dad makes me soup. "You have to rest a lot," he says, and he keeps saying it and bringing more and more soup.

Heinz cream of tomato and cream of chicken and minestrone. God, doesn't he know that cardiac patients aren't supposed to have a lot of soup? So much cream and saturated fats and fluid content and salt. I mean, did he not even read any of the booklets from the hospital? Because, sure, I'll go along with his pretense that I've got HCM if it means I can eat more healthy foods with less arguments from Dad.

But Dad just doesn't understand. "Soup's good for ill people," he says, and nothing will change his mind on it.

One time, the soup has cheese on toast with it, but I just stare at the little puddle of grease sitting in a dip on the cheese and all the white bread, and after that, Dad eats it and cooks no more cheese on toast for me, but still the soup comes.

I weigh up my options and eat the tomato soup most of the time when it's served because Dad doesn't seem to know what a salad is. The alternatives of cheese on toast or the hot dogs and burgers he makes himself (minus any salad) seem worse to me. So unhealthy. I tell him I don't like chicken soup and I don't, not because of calorie intake or anything but because that one just seems way too unhealthy. And I need to eat healthily.

I eat the minestrone, carefully picking out the shells of pasta and stacking them on the wide rim of the bowl. I build forts with the pasta, a huge fort all around me that protects me from everything bad.

Xavier texts me. I try to reply, but then I let slip to him that Victoria thinks I'm the best of the male graduates this year. He doesn't reply after that, and I can guess why. Xavier never likes losing.

Victoria's texted a lot, too, demanding to know whether I'm even serious about the plan if I can't show up for sessions. How can I reply to her though, when she's not lost what I have?

The moment I learnt what the catheterization procedure confirmed, that was when the falling began. Me falling into myself, into this place where everything moved around me, where pasta became a fort shielding me. Where I'd lost everything.

Gemma texts me a lot. I can't reply to her messages. I can't do anything, can't talk to her. It's too painful because I know what she gave up, being a jockey, even if she is still around horses. And I don't want to give up any part of who I am.

I *can't.*

I'd rather die than never dance again.

I'd rather die.

Dance and die or not be me…

I stare at the tartan rug on the living room floor, turning this over and over in my mind.

There's a photo of Mum on the table, even though she and Dad weren't together for years before she died. But after her death, on I think the third time when I was here, the photo appeared in an ornate silver frame.

Mum was a principal dancer at the Royal Southern Ballet. She had two loves. Ballet and rock climbing.

She died doing what she loved.

I need to get back to Roseheart.

I know there's no way Dad will let me go back, not after Thursday's confirmation of the diagnosis and the procedure that says you must rest after it. So, I wait until he's gone to bed on Monday evening, and then I walk out of the house. I'm still in pain, and each step hurts, but it's not far to the train station. I know the route off the back of my hand.

Halfway there, I see a group of teenagers. Probably about my age or a bit younger. They're dressed in baggy clothes and the air smells like weed around them. They're shouting, and my shoulders tighten, and my whole body feels heavier as I pass them. I wish I could walk faster, more normally. My heart pounds and doesn't stop pounding until I'm away from them, at the train station.

It makes me wonder if I can even run in a life-threatening situation now. If they'd pulled a knife on me, I'd have been outnumbered, and I'd have had to run. Yet would I then drop down dead from that?

I buy a ticket on the Trainline app on my phone because the ticket booth is closed, and I scan the e-ticket at the gate barrier. Once on the train, I feel calmer. Even though my phone rings. It's Dad. Didn't take him long to realize I've gone then. I ignore the call. I'll message him once I'm there. Once I'm there and safely in my room where he can't stop me. And he can't drag me back. Not when he thinks I'm doing a choreography course and I've told him the staff will adapt it to suit my medical needs.

But I'm doing the right thing, I think, as I stare at the window. Half of my reflection is visible. Staring back at me. The other half of me is the night sky, and, as the train rumbles on, I swallow more and more darkness.

It's easier to get back into Roseheart than I'd thought it would be at night. But I just walk in, use my keycard. No alarms go off or anything. I make my way to my room. I sit on my bed, holding my canvas flats. Just an old pair. Probably from a few years ago. But I never liked throwing the old ones out, even though I was forever buying replacements.

I stare at the box of them at the foot of my bed, then at the pair in my lap. They tell a story. My story. They're my journey through this. My steps. And my journey isn't going to stop, just because some doctors think they can dictate what I do. My journey only stops when I stop.

THIRTY-EIGHT

Taryn

I stay five nights at Mum's, until Tessa is settled back at home, and Mum has calmed down and doesn't keep disappearing. Giovanni had to leave on the Sunday, and Mum was in pieces after all that. Grandad said he needed me there for a bit longer, so I stayed, even though I was aching to go back. I need to get back to training. Just one day off can make a difference, let alone five. Although the Roseheart Romantic Dance Company usually only has classes or rehearsals only or weekdays, I know most professional dancers train seven days a week. You have to. Your muscles suffer if you miss one day, and we need to constantly be in shape. And now I've missed so many days, even though I've been stretching and practicing as much as I can in my room at Mum's house, using an old pair of pointe shoes that I must've brought back here at some time, and going for runs.

But I need to get back. I need to get this position, even with Jaidev as my partner.

I need to make sure my lies to my mum don't remain lies. Need to get this place on the tour with Jaidev.

"Are you sure?" Mum asks. "You have to go back now?"

I nod, but I heard the hesitation in her voice. Like she wanted me to stay so we could maybe have a massive heart to heart, so we could become closer again. But it's always like this. That emotion is only ever in her voice when I say I'm going to go; before that, it's just like she keeps me at a distance, doesn't really let me in.

She wrings her hands together at the sink. When she looks at me, there's a vacant expression in her eyes. "It must be difficult, there. Doing this without your sister."

My mouth dries, and I think of Helena's shoes. The missing ones. The stolen ones. But I can't tell my mum her shoes have gone. Been stolen. They're the only thing I have that belongs to my twin. Shortly after she died, Mum removed all her toys, her clothes, her ballet shoes. I managed to keep that pair of pointe shoes for myself, hiding them away with my shoes.

"No one there knows about Helena, though." I try to keep my voice neutral, even though I know someone does know. The lipstick-note-writer. "That makes it easier. Because they don't ask. I can just be me there."

I prefer it at Roseheart. Because at this house, I'm *not* just me. I'm one half of the twins. I'm a constant reminder to my mum. And the house itself is a haunting presence. A number of times, I've thought I've seen Helena in the last two days. A shadow in the corner. A presence in front of the mantelpiece. A dim shape at the kitchen table.

"What are you talking about? They do know," Mum says.

I stare at her, feel the pit of my stomach shift down. "What?"

"Your friend, Sibylle. She phoned me once and asked what had happened. Said she wasn't sure whether to ask you directly."

"How… How did she find out?" I take a deep breath. Grainy, horizontal lines appear in my vision. Sibylle only asked me once about Helena, after she said I'd whispered her name when I was asleep. When I'd said I didn't know who I'd been talking about, she'd left it, not said anything more.

"She said she'd Googled it," Mum says. "She worked out you were twins by the info given online for Helena's age, and I think she saw a photo of Helena too. She wanted my advice of whether she should say anything to you, offer you condolences. Or whether that would make things worse."

Sibylle knows about Helena.

She's seen stuff online—oh God. I know what's online. I know the story that Adelaide James, that wicked journalist, spun.

No. This can't be happening.

But Sibylle *knows*, and someone is sending messages saying *I know you're a murderer.* They are aimed at me, not Jaidev, these messages—just like I'd originally thought.

And they're from the girl who's the closest thing to a best friend that I have now.

Like I'm in a film or something, the first person I see when I get back to Roseheart is Sibylle. So, she's finally back from her stay in Berlin—or maybe she got back the day I left. She's smiling at me, holding her arms wide like she wants a hug.

We never hug.

I stare at her.

"I got in!" she says.

"Got in?" I blink.

"Yes, Berlin State Ballet. It was amazing, and they let me train at their studios too, even when it wasn't the day of my audition. Isn't that just great? They're so nice there." She's staring at me expectantly, like she wants me to celebrate with her. But how can I when she's targeting me?

Still, she doesn't know that I know, and I want to keep it that way for now. I need to work out what I'm going to do. I need time to plan.

"But how's your sister?" she asks. "Sorry, I'm being so insensitive."

My sister. The dead one that she shouldn't know about.

But I clear my head, force my voice to sound light and airy. "She's doing better, thanks." I told her in detail via WhatsApp before, giving updates, but suddenly I feel guarded around her. She shouldn't know about Helena, but she does, and now I want to hold both Tessa and Tammy close to me, away from her.

"Police are still about," she says. "They talked to Jaidev a lot while you were away. They're treating this seriously. Mr. Eldridge asked me to tell you that they want to talk to you when you're back, too. You're to let him know when you're here, and he'll contact them."

"Oh." I stare at her. She's happy for the police to waste their time on this, believing someone is targeting Jaidev when really, it's her just messing with me? "Well, I'd better go and let Mr. Eldridge know I'm back then."

I half expect her to try and stop me, but she doesn't. She just says she'll meet me for dinner afterward.

I drop my bag and coat off at my room and then make my way to the administration building for the Roseheart Institution. It's in the company's half of the grounds. Mr. Eldridge's office is at the top of the block, up six flights of stairs. There is a strong smell of air freshener in the corridor outside his office, reminding me of how some elderly ladies walk around in clouds of perfume. I wrinkle my nose, then knock.

No answer.

I knock again, then call out his name.

Still nothing.

But the door next time opens, making me jump. A mousy looking man peers out.

"Oh, it's you." Apparently, he knows me. "Mr. Eldridge is out at the moment. Can I take a message?"

"Uh, yeah, I heard he wanted to know when I'm back so he can arrange a meeting between me and the police?" My mouth dries. It sounds so formal. And I'm going to have to tell them about Sibylle, let them know they are wasting their time. Will Sibylle get charged with wasting police time then?

The man nods. "Okay." He shuts his door.

I don't feel like eating dinner with Sibylle or at all, so I head to the studio instead, retrieving a pair of my pointes on the way. I've got a practice with Jaidev in two hours, which I messaged him to say I'd be present for, but I feel out of shape, so I use this time to train. My muscles feel tight, and I know that two hours isn't going to remedy five days of no proper ballet, but I have to try.

I'm so engrossed in combinations that I don't notice when Jaidev arrives.

I just glance up at one point, and in the mirror, I see him leaning in the doorway, smiling a little. His eyes meet mine, still in the mirror, and he jolts.

"I'm not being creepy, watching you," he says. "I just didn't want to disturb you."

"It's fine." I push back the stray pieces of hair that have escaped my bun and turn to face him. "Let's start."

He enters the studio and shuts the door behind him. His hair is damp like he's just showered recently.

"Uh." He falters. "Are we okay? Because I just want to make sure I've not ruined things between us. And I don't want you to feel pressured or whatever. I hope I haven't made this awkward."

"You haven't. We're fine," I say. I overreacted. Jaidev is a good guy.

"I'm just…sorry." He looks down at the polished floor. "You've no idea how many times I've kicked myself since then."

"Jaidev, stop. It's fine."

"And I won't take it personally. I know you and Teddy are—"

"Are what?"

"Close," he says. "And I know it's not ideal, you dancing with me and not him."

"We're not together."

I see the way hope lights up his eyes. *Oh no.*

I take a deep breath. "I'm… Look, I'm aroace, okay?" The words burst from me, but the power with which they leave is mismatched by the weakness of my tone. I've never really had to come out like this before. Teddy and I just sort of learnt it together. I've never told anyone in person, like this. And I know I shouldn't feel like I have to. I don't have to justify my lack of interest in Jaidev. Or anyone.

But I don't want to be inadvertently leading him on.

He squints a little. "Ace… Asexual?"

I nod. "And aromantic. But don't tell anyone. I don't want people knowing, because it could affect whether I'm chosen for this position. And being aromantic doesn't mean I can't connect with you for the dance. I managed it with Teddy, and I can do it with others. In my first year here, I had to dance a pas de deux with Xavier. Madame Cachelle said she could feel the romance. So, I can do this. But that's why I can't get together with you. It's nothing to do with being with someone else, okay? But I'm not faking something and going against who I am just to try and get better at dance."

He nods. "Yeah. Okay. Uh, just so you know, I didn't mean we'd fake anything. I was genuine about me saying that I like you. But I wasn't just saying all of that to make you sleep with me. That's what Hazma said it could've sounded like."

"You've discussed this with Hazma?"

"We're kind of friends," he says. "And Trent, too. I mean, they've both honestly been quite invested in this whole thing."

I don't even know what to say to that. "Let's just dance."

THIRTY-NINE

Taryn

I find Sibylle in our room after the session with Jaidev in the studio, and I realize I'm just going to have to have it out with her. I hate confrontation, and I've always worked to avoid it as much as I can, but I can't do that this time.

"You didn't come to dinner?" she says as I drop my training stuff at the foot of my bed.

"No, I needed to be practicing." I sit down and carefully examine my left foot. While I've avoided getting any of the push pins in my flesh, checking each pair every time, my foot is hurting a lot. The knuckle of my big toe looks red and inflamed. I need to go and see Ross, the physio, ideally.

"So, you're eating later?" Sibylle asks. "With Jaidev?"

"I don't know." I flex my toe. I know I'm concentrating on it simply to try and delay what I have to say to her. And that just makes me even more nervous. I swallow hard and look at her. "Can I have them back?"

"What back?"

"The stolen shoes. *Helena's* shoes."

Sibylle frowns. "I haven't got them. What are you saying?"

"I know it was you." I look back at my toe. "So why did you do it? Because you think you should be in the company, right?"

"No! Taryn, I haven't got them. I wouldn't steal from you—especially not something that belonged to your sister. And I've said all along you deserve that space with the company. Why would I be doing this?"

"Because you know about my sister. They're her shoes, those ones. The missing ones. And you *know*."

Her frown gets deeper, but there's hurt in her eyes too. "I don't know what you're meaning. Why would I do this because I know about her?"

"Look, I'm not stupid. I know the messages the police are investigating about Jaidev are actually aimed at me. And that they're about Helena's death." I can hardly say the words.

"What?" Sibylle's staring at me.

"And someone's stolen her shoes, put pushpins in all of mine, and ripped up my photo board."

"And you think that was me?" Her voice cracks.

I swallow the lump in my throat. "You're the only one who knows about Helena. You're my roommate. You have access to my things, and then they get ruined or go missing."

"Oh, so you're going to question Ivelisse, too? Seeing as she's our roommate, too."

"Look, I'm not a murderer, Sibylle. That journalist spun it that way, and it wasn't true."

Her face crumples. "I wouldn't do that to you. You're my friend. And I'm not the only one."

"What?"

"I'm not the only one who knows about Helena. A lot of people here do. Definitely everyone in our year. I don't know about the company dancers, but people talk. And it's not exactly hard to find. If anyone Googles your name, those articles come up."

My stomach twists. "Oh."

"Yeah," she says, her voice hard and cutting. "I thought we were friends."

"We are. I'm sorry."

She snorts.

"I'm going to go and get some food," I say, numb, even though eating feels like the last thing I could possibly do. But I just need to get away.

"You do that." Sibylle doesn't even look at me.

I get some carrot and potato soup from the canteen and sit alone, staring into it, stirring my spoon. I should've trusted my gut when I thought that Sibylle would not do that to me. She is my friend. Or was.

And it turns out everyone knows. It could be anyone.

"Ah, Taryn, you're in here."

I look up to see Madame Cachelle poking her head in the entrance to the canteen.

"Mr. Eldridge wants to speak to you," she says. "He's just down at the reception now, but he's got to leave shortly again. You could catch him now if you're quick."

I rise, leaving my soup. Mr. Eldridge is still at reception when I get there. It only takes me a few minutes as it's the same building as the canteen. He tells me that the police have arranged a time to speak with me—in two days.

"We're waiting until I'm back from business," he says. "I want to be sitting in. As you're not yet eighteen, you can also have a parent or guardian there. Or one of the staff here, if you'd prefer."

"Hold on," I say. "I haven't done anything wrong. This sounds like I have if I need an adult there?"

"No. Just procedure. I'm doing everything by the books."

I return to the canteen, more unsettled. I've never really spoken to the police before. Despite what journalists said, there was no evidence that Helena's death wasn't an accident or that I was involved, so the police never talked to me. But Mr. Eldridge almost made it sound like I was a suspect. Like *I'd* be sending racist messages to my own partner.

Or sending threats to myself. Taking my own stuff, ripping up my photo board Though, of course, he and the police don't know about those things. Yet.

A couple of younger students are in the canteen now. They watch me with wide eyes as I sit back down. There's no steam lifting off my soup now, and I still don't really feel hungry as I pick back up my spoon.

"I wouldn't eat that," a petit rat says to me. She's got delicate curls and long eyelashes. Probably about eight or something. "You're the one with the sugar allergy, right?"

"Well, fructose. Yeah." It's too difficult to explain it's a malabsorption issue, and I just haven't got the energy for that right now.

"I saw someone put a load of sugar in there," she says.

"Someone?" I turn to look at her.

"It was either sugar or a laxative. I don't know. But he didn't want anyone to see."

He? The person after me is a guy?

"Who was it?" I stare at her.

The other girls are looking at her, a little in awe, a little scared. Because she's ratting on someone.

She shrugs. "I don't know. He was wearing dark clothes and a hat. A beanie."

A beanie.

There's one person I know who always wears a beanie.

FORTY

Taryn

I move to the common room in a daze. Sibylle's by the entrance, and she casts a long glance at me that almost makes me want to turn and run. But I hold my own, and I try to appear confident.

I need to find him.

And there he is. With it on. The beanie. God, he hasn't even taken it off.

But why would he? He always wears it.

Lightheadedness pulls at me. I can't believe he'd do something like this. Him, of all people.

I look around the room, trying to find something to focus on so I can steady myself. Everyone is here though, all those on the diploma, of all the years, and it seems too crowded now.

"So did it hurt at all, at the time?" Peter is asking.

Teddy shakes his head. "Nah, I was out of it during the actual procedure."

"Obviously," Xavier says.

I clear my throat. I'm right behind them, and I don't remember walking up to them. It's almost like I didn't. Like there's been some glitch, and I'm just suddenly here.

Teddy turns to me. "Taryn!" His enthusiasm doesn't betray any ounce of his deception.

"Hi." My voice is a squeal.

I don't understand. Why would he be after me?

Peter's eyes widen when he sees me, and then he's leaning across to Robert and Xavier, saying something behind his hand in an obviously theatrical way. Has Teddy told them already about trying to trick me into eating fructose? Or laxatives?

They're all looking at me. Expecting me to have diarrhea or something right now?

I feel sick.

But why would Teddy of all people be trying to sabotage me?

Wait. The messages started *before* he returned to the academy after his injury.

And a beanie doesn't mean it's him.

Anyone can wear one. It's not patented to Teddy.

But they're all looking at me. And now they're laughing too.

"Yep, she's frigid," a second-year student says.

Frigid?

I freeze.

"Nah, she's with Teddy," another says.

"Yeah, but they never do anything." Peter's face has never looked so crimson. "Do you, Teds?"

Teddy goes red, rivalling Peter's hue. He looks at me, his eyes wide. "I never said any of this."

There's a low hoot of laughter from Xavier. "But we know it's true. You were my roommate, and you never brought her back there—you know, *properly*—the whole time."

"Because she wouldn't let you?" Peter looks like he's about to burst with excitement from this conversation.

"Well, I know why," Freya says suddenly, from a sofa on the other side of the room. "She's *asexual*."

FORTY-ONE

Taryn

I freeze.

Everyone is laughing.

"I always thought there was something weird about her," Freya is saying, like I'm not here. "I mean, it's one thing to be nervous about sex for your first time. But quite another to declare that you're different to everyone. Like you're not even subject to basic human desires. Like you're not even human!"

"Hey!" Teddy's voice is sharp. "There is nothing inhuman about being asexual."

"Well at least you know now why she was frigid, mate." Peter slaps Teddy on the arm. "So, it wasn't anything to do with you."

"How'd you even know this?" Someone points at Freya.

"Victoria told me."

"What?" Teddy shouts. "She…"

Victoria. My head spins.

"How does she know?" It takes me a second to realize I've said those words.

Teddy's gone even redder.

"You told her?" I stare at him. How does he even know her?

"Well," he says. "It wasn't like I meant to. She just… But it's fine. She promised not to say anything because she's ace-spec, too." He looks to Freya, frowning. "She told you?"

"Victoria said Taryn was like her," Freya says with a shrug. "And then I figured out she was meaning the whole asexual thing. Wasn't difficult."

"Oh my God, it's spreading," Peter says. He raises his hands above his head, cowering in pretense. "Don't infect me too with this!"

"Shut up!" Teddy yells, standing up. His fists are balled into fists.

"Careful. Don't get angry, mate. You don't want to have a heart attack." Peter laughs even deeper, like it's the most hilarious thing he's ever said.

"Then shut the hell up," says a new voice. Ivelisse. "You always go way too far, Peter. You're not funny."

"I'm not trying to be funny." He points at me. "She's the one denying she's got basic human feelings. I mean, Taryn. You're just frigid and now trying to cover it up to make you seem less of—"

"Being ace is valid," I snap at him. Tears blind me, but I feel rage. Proper rage.

The door opens, and someone else slips in. Jaidev. He takes a step back as the energy in here apparently hits him.

"And I'm asexual too," Teddy yells. He puts his arm around me. I can feel him shaking.

Peter hoots. "Oh my God. Do you all hear this? This is just ridiculous."

"I'm getting Madame," Sibylle says, standing.

Peter yells something else, but I can't make out his words. They're just a sail of fog that flies over me—and then Peter flies back.

"Yes, fight!" a first-year shouts, and a second later, everyone's chanting it. *Fight, fight, fight.*

Jaidev. Jaidev's being held back by Xavier and Advik.

Peter rises from the ground, holding his face. There's blood streaming from his nose.

Jaidev's punched Peter?

Oh my God.

My head pounds, and everything inside me is screaming for me to leave, to get out, to go. And yes, I need to.

Victoria. I need to find Victoria. She's been outed by all this, too, in front of everyone. I need to tell her, warn her. Oh God. She's going to hate me even more. But I can't not tell her. I'd want to know if it was me.

"Taryn! It's okay!" Sibylle's voice.

Sibylle who hates me is trying to help, but I can't stop. I need to let Victoria know what's happened as soon as I can. Even though she hates me, because I know now she can't be the person after me. The petit rat said the person who tampered with my food was a guy. Sibylle said everyone in our year knows about my sister. Possibly the first-year diploma students do, too. But there's no way the company dancers can. And anyone from the academy could've slipped into the company studios to write those notes.

But only academy students can get into the academy dorms with keycards. I think of my photo board and the pushpins in my shoes and Helena's stolen shoes. It's someone in the diploma. A guy. It has to be. But I can concentrate on that later, on working out who it is. I haven't got time now.

I run to the company buildings and let myself in.

My shoes slap on the linoleum, like a countdown. But where will Victoria be now? I falter. I don't know where she hangs out. Her accommodation block? I won't be able to go in there.

"Right, we'll finish up now then," a voice says. Mr. Vikas. "Good work."

The studio to my left. I race to the door. He'll know where Victoria is, won't he? I'm clutching at straws, I know. But I can't, and—

And there she is. *In* the studio with Mr. Vikas and Harry and Marion. They're just finishing a session, by the sounds of it, and—

I go cold as I see them.

Helena's shoes. That burnt orange color. On Victoria's feet.

FORTY-TWO

Teddy

I lose sight of Taryn and I've no idea where she is. Shit. I run in the direction I think she went, but there's no sign of her. I call her name, and nothing.

Oh God.

My phone buzzes.

Where are you? The text is from Victoria. *You're late.*

Late? My eyes widen and I check the time and date. Shit, she'll be waiting for me now. Her practice with Mr. Vikas finished five minutes ago. For a second, I consider telling her I'll be even later than I'd be if I went straight there now. Or that I won't be going there at all. Only I know I can't do that again.

So, I rush to my room, grab my canvas flats, and then head down to Studio 7.

"Sorry," I say when I arrive. "A lot has been happening."

Victoria is stretching out at the barre. Her back is to me, and through her leotard I can see the nodules of her spine. They're like water droplets dripping down her back.

"A lot is always happening around here," she says. "So, it's no excuse. If you want to learn all the choreography, you need to practice. So come on. You already cancelled our last four sessions, so if you're as serious about getting into the company as I am, then you need to actually do the work."

I nod. I don't tell her I cancelled the last sessions because I was in hospital. I don't want her pity. I don't want her thinking I'm fragile and treating me differently. I'm a dancer. A professional dancer. And this is work. I am healthy, and I am strong. What is going on with my personal life won't come into it. I mean, they're wrong anyway. That collapse was a one-off. I had just misjudged my food intake, that's all. I've been dancing since then, and training hard, and I haven't collapsed any more, or even come close to it, so that's proof. I am healthy.

I change into my flats and join her at the barre, warming up. She's now doing grand *pliés*. I wonder if I should tell her that I've just outed her, but fear gets the better of me. I've heard from the others what she's been like with Taryn. I know it's selfish, but I don't want her turning on me.

We are silent as we stretch. When it's time to start dancing, Victoria takes control. She barks instructions at me, telling me what to do and walking me through the choreography again for the divertissement pas de deux.

"Start in first, but keep your lines clean with your arms… No, that's too slow, and you're wobbling. Start again… Yes, that's better but you need to do it quicker. The music is faster here. You're going to be several beats too slow."

Huh. She'd make a good teacher.

We dance and dance, going over the same combinations for nearly an hour. Then we have a quick break. Delicately, Victoria takes a few sips of water from a purple bottle. I don't need any water.

"Cops think I've been sending Jaidev those messages," she says with a shrug. Her voice startles me. "They keep asking me all these questions, all sly like."

"And have you been sending them?"

"No." She scowls at me. "And you're supposed to be on my side. We're friends now, Teddy. I look out for you, so you look out for me. That's fair, isn't it?"

I nod. "Yes."

"Good. Now let's get back to it."

I push myself harder and harder in the studio with Victoria—and it's proof I'm fine. The doctors were wrong. I've not got this heart condition because I'm not collapsing. That was just a one-off. I hadn't eaten then.

And I ate earlier today and now I'm fine. So that proves it.

FORTY-THREE

Taryn

Of course, Mr. Eldridge is away, so I end up waiting outside Madame Cachelle's office for her to return from whatever class she's teaching.

"I know who's sending the messages," I say the moment she is here. "The ones that the police are investigating. Because it's not just messages, and it's not aimed at Jaidev. It's aimed at me."

She stares at me, her eyes wide.

"I've been targeted," I say. "Had things stolen, things vandalized. And I've got proof. It's Victoria. Possibly Marion, too. Maybe Harry? Those three seem to be good friends."

Madame Cachelle holds her hands up and tells me to calm down. "Deep breaths, my gem. Now, come and take a seat and tell me everything, starting at the beginning."

I do, and I tell her everything. Even about what happened in the common room, the outing of my sexuality, and Victoria's too. Peter's words. Freya's. The muscles around

Madame Cachelle's mouth tighten but she says nothing, just waits for me to finish.

And when I do, this feels like a relief. Like all of this will be over now, because it has to be—well, the stuff with Victoria, anyway. And there's going to be some sort of punishment for Peter's and Freya's words about asexuality and how so many of the others laughed. Not to mention Victoria and I were outed. But even if Freya and Peter are asked to leave immediately or something, not everyone who laughed will be. People will still know, still be whispering.

"Thank you, Taryn," Madame Cachelle says. "We will sort this."

I go to my room because I can't face going back to the common room—and that's when I find Jaidev outside. Waiting for me.

"Are you okay?" His eyes hold concern. Make him look worried and tender.

I nod.

He's massaging his hand.

"Did you get in trouble?" I ask. "For punching Peter?"

He shakes his head. "Well, not yet."

"You should ice that though." A hand injury is all we need. Especially when we've got our final assessment on August 26th, at the end of the eighth week of training. We'll be dancing in a full performance of the ballet, a week before the tour starts that will decide if we're in it. In the company. And this assessment is in exactly one month's time.

Jaidev nods. "The canteen?"

I let out a small smile. "I was thinking more about the nurse's office. Or Ross. He's the physio."

"Ah."

We stand and turn around, heading to the exit of the dorms.

"Are they all talking about me?" I ask.

Jaidev's eyes do a little darting motion as he looks at me and then past me. "They are talking," he says. "But after you left, it really died down. Ivelisse had a big go at Peter, told everyone his secret too and that definitely took the attention off you."

"His secret?"

"He has a stuffed toy that he still sleeps with."

I don't like the idea of anyone being shamed for that, but I also don't like Peter. I smile a little. The thought of people laughing at him, focusing on him rather than me, does make me feel a lot better.

"That way," I say, pointing to the right as we exit the building.

The night is dark now, cold—but there are people. Madame Cachelle and Mr. Aleks and two police officers.

And Victoria.

"I didn't do anything!" Victoria screams. "This is ridiculous! You're taking the word of her over..." She sees me.

I freeze. Jaidev steps closer to me.

"You better stop lying and tell them the truth," she says. "Because this wasn't me. And I haven't done a single thing to you."

"Everyone heard you being mean to me," I say. "And you really expect me to believe someone else hates me too?"

"Well, they clearly do. And what I was saying was nothing. We always give new recruits a hard time. Ask *anyone*."

"Victoria, it's over," Jaidev says.

She laughs. "Is it?" Her gaze is cold and steely, like she's boring a hole into me.

I shudder, stepping back against Jaidev, and then Victoria lunges at me.

The officers and Madame Cachelle move to grab her, but she spits in my face.

I freeze, rooted to the spot, feeling the way her saliva clings to my face.

Something hot and angry rises up inside me.

"Now we can get you for assault, too," an officer says, and he pulls her back.

"Let's go," Jaidev says, his voice all dark.

I let him lead me away, and I know it's going to be better now. All of this bullying is over.

FORTY-FOUR

Jaidev

A week has passed since Victoria was arrested, and I'm still keeping a close eye on Taryn, a protective eye. If I hear people talking about her, I say something. I'm not the only one either. Ivelisse is very vocal about it, and so is Sibylle, to an extent— though I notice there's a little tension between her and Taryn that I don't understand and that neither girl explains.

But I stick close to Taryn, as much as I can without seeming creepy, and she does seem genuinely appreciative of it. Teddy's around a lot too, but I almost don't mind that as much now. He nods at me, manages to even hold a small conversation, without glaring.

And with the messages explained and Victoria away, things feel better for me and Taryn. She's definitely more relaxed, less tension in her shoulders every time we're in a studio, dancing and training. She's not jumpy, and she even goes into one of her flexibility classes smiling when I walk her to it after our solo class with the pas de deux teacher.

We haven't heard what's happened to Victoria, but Trent tells me that Marion and Harry were also both called into the police station the morning after Victoria was taken in. There are rumors they're all being charged, rumors they've been kicked out of Roseheart, even rumors that their ballet reputations are over.

"And they deserve it," Netty Florence says. "What they did to you, Taryn, was awful."

Taryn nods.

We're sitting in the café, just before a group rehearsal for the tour. Netty Florence and Hazma will then go to do their own rehearsal for their pas de deux. The two principals are side by side, then there's me and Taryn on one side of the table, and Li Hua and Trent on the other. It's nice, sitting as a group.

"I still can't believe we are now Oberon and Titania in the *Midsummer* tour," Li Hua says, smiling at Trent.

Yesterday evening, we all heard that Victoria, Marion, and Harry are officially out of the tour. It's unclear if there'll be able to return to Roseheart at all.

Trent fist-pumps the air. "My gran's going to the Liverpool showing of it, too. She's going to be made up. Guess it really does pay to be the understudy for a lead role."

"Wonder how they'll recast the other roles though," I say. With Li Hua and Trent now having lead roles, Helena and Demetrius should now be played by their understudies—but I heard yesterday that they both got injured during a lift.

Zara, the understudy for Marion's character is okay though, and Zara's original role was a small one anyway that apparently she can still do alongside playing Hippolyta. But now new dancers are going to need to learn the dances for Helena and Demetrius.

"They might bring Nora in," Netty Florence says. "She played Helena a few years ago, when we also did the *Midsummer* tour, so she'd be familiar with it, too. Especially at such short notice. A dancer's muscles never forget, and I'm sure choreography won't have changed too much."

Taryn nods.

"And I'm sure there's a guy who can learn Demetrius at short notice," Netty Florence continues. "You've still got a few weeks anyway. Not like it's two days before."

"Well, we'd better get going," Taryn says. "We don't want to be late."

We've still got ten minutes before the next group rehearsal begins, but we amble along at a comfortable speed. A few others are there when we arrive, and then we're all warming up together.

"Okay, new casting." Mr. Vikas clears his throat and claps his hands before unfolding a piece of paper from the breast-pocket of his jacket. "Dancers, gather round. Li Hua and Trent and Zara are of course now Oberon and Titania and Hippolyta. Li Hua and Trent's previous roles of Helena and Demetrius will now go to Jaidev and Taryn. There is still enough time for you two to learn that choreography. The divertissement will of course go to the planned understudies, Emma-Leigh and Rhys."

My eyes widen. We're Demetrius and Helena? I look at Taryn. She's frozen.

"New understudies are also as follows: Taryn and Jaidev will also understudy the roles of Titania and Oberon."

I inhale sharply. We're understudies of the main roles as well?

"Emma-Leigh, you will also understudy Hippolyta. If need be, you can play both her and the role in the divertissement. With five cast members now out, we will have to double up on more roles." He reads out more changes to casting, then looks at us all. "We're going to need you all taking on extra rehearsals to make sure you're ready. We've not had to make such big changes to casting before, especially so soon before a tour starts, and we need to make this work. And Taryn." Mr. Vikas pauses, touching her shoulder lightly. She tenses up. "I'm sorry about what some of our dancers put you through. That is unacceptable."

She nods and says thank you.

And then Mr. Vikas starts the rehearsal, beginning with the choreography for Oberon and Titania. Li Hua and Trent are already very fluid with it, having already been practicing it as understudies, and Taryn and I watch from the sidelines. We know Mr. Vikas doesn't like the understudies dancing at the edges of the studio when he's assessing the dancers cast for the roles, so we remain as invisible as possible, until he has finished advising Li Hua and Trent. Then he and Evangeline move over to us, explaining the choreography for Helena and Demetrius. As the previous dancers for the roles, Li Hua and Trent are asked to demonstrate their marriage pas de deux for it.

"Though of course you'll be on stage with the two other couples for the wedding scene," he tells us. "But it's not so much a pas de six as rather three separate pas de deux happening on stage at the same time, as we don't directly interact with the other couples."

I nod.

Then I realize it, realize what being in these roles, as Demetrius and Helena, means for us.

Taryn and I will have to kiss.

But she won't want to.

Oh God.

It's about all I can think of when I'm supposed to be concentrating on the instructions Li Hua and Trent are now giving us, after Mr. Vikas has finished with us and has moved to advise the next dancers who are now learning completely new roles, alongside Evangeline.

"I'm sure we can choreograph it a bit differently for the kiss," I say when Taryn and I start running through movements and combinations, after the session, when it's just the two of us. "I don't want to make you uncomfortable. What if I turned my back more on the audience and just lent toward you? If I just got this close—" I stop an inch from her face. "I don't think anyone would notice."

"We can't do that in rehearsals though, or for the final assessment," she says. "Mr. Vikas and Mr. Aleks would notice. Look, it's okay. I can kiss on stage. I don't want special treatment. I've had to do it before. With Teddy and Advik and Xavier. It's just kissing. It doesn't really mean anything."

But still, it makes me uncomfortable. Especially when I suggested to her before that we get together. She's going to think I'm getting what I wanted—even though it's about as far as I can imagine from what I wanted.

We stay late, practicing the new choreography. We'd thought eight weeks to learn choreography was hard enough. Now it's all changed. New roles to learn as Helena and Demetrius, as well as our understudy roles of Titania and Oberon.

Suddenly, it makes us seem so much more important to the tour, so much more vital. We matter for this tour. We're important.

And there's so much to learn.

"Shall we try it then? The routine where Helena and Demetrius get married?" Taryn asks.

My breath catches in my throat. This is the one containing the kiss, the triple wedding in the scene, with Lysander and Hermia and Theseus and his bride, as well as our characters. "Are you sure?"

"It's part of the job, nothing more," she says.

I nod. But I'm nervous. *Of course* I'm nervous. I can't just turn off my feelings, but I respect her, and I tell myself this won't be anything more. It's purely professional.

We dance, our steps light, and my heart thumping. We get closer and closer. I can smell her shampoo as I stare into her eyes.

I hold her, tight.

Kissing her isn't how I thought it would be—before I knew she was aroace. When I'd been talking to Trent about how much I liked her, I'd let myself get carried away. I'd imagined how soft and tender kissing her would be, and I'd thought about how she'd kiss me back, wrapping her arms around me.

But this is a short kiss. A quick one. Me kissing her. She doesn't really kiss back—not in the way Camille did.

"Okay?" I ask, pulling back.

She nods, and I see movement behind her in the window of the door. It's Teddy.

Even from here I can see the smoldering hurt in his eyes.

FORTY-FIVE

Teddy

She…she lied. That's all I can think as I see them, through the window in the door. See them kiss. Taryn and Jaidev. Jaidev who I was only just beginning to get used to, to like even. Because he did punch Peter when he was saying all that shit about Taryn. But now his motivation for doing that is clear.

And she kissed him back. That's what it looked like. I mean, she didn't push him away. And that's what I just can't understand.

Taryn told me she was repulsed by kissing. We managed it for auditions and shows, and I was always so careful with her, but now she's doing this? And there's no reason for her to kiss Jaidev. They've not got a kissing part. I know their choreography. I've got it right here, and it doesn't involve that.

And she was kissing him *back*. She looked like she was enjoying it. So, it was just me she didn't want to kiss or was repulsed by?

I feel sick. I turn.

She lied. Hell, maybe she even pretended she was aro and ace too. This whole time, was she just going along with it, laughing at me?

And all this time I've been putting my all into training, so I can dance with her!

Anger takes over me, and I punch the wall. Pain erupts through my hand. My knuckles throb.

Maybe I don't even want to dance with Taryn—which means I don't need to get into Roseheart. There are hundreds of other places across the world I could apply to as a solo dancer.

Yes. I'll do that.

I don't want to be around Taryn anyway. Not when she lied.

The door swings open. It's Taryn.

"Hey," she says. "We were just finishing."

"Were you?" My voice is dry. She's just going to pretend like she's not hooking up with Jaidev? I mean, how stupid does she think I am?

"Yeah. But we're ready now. We're going to go and get dinner now. You coming?"

The lightness in her voice gets to me.

"No."

"Oh, have you eaten already?"

"Yes," I lie. But there's no way I'm sitting there, at the same table as them!

I head to the studio. I need to practice more, get better if I'm going to get into a New York company, I decide. Then we'll see who's laughing.

FORTY-SIX

Taryn

I dream of my sister, Helena, that night.

"Why are you trying to be me?" she asks, and her voice is haunting and soft, twisting round and round me. She knows about the recasting, but I don't think she's angry. Maybe just curious.

We're on a stage, dancing, the two of us. Her face is a mirror to mine, even though she's forever a twelve-year-old. But her body is translucent. She's fading in and out of apparition. She wears a simple gray dress with a raggedy skirt. I am wearing the same outfit, but it is newer, cleaner, and my body is firmer, stronger.

We don't look like twins. We look like a before and after. *Before and after death.*

"I'm not trying to be you," I whisper, but my words aren't strong. They get lost as we pirouette together on stage. I feel like I'm not in control of my body, my actions. We are both dolls being commanded by something else. An otherworldly force.

Then there's an audience. It's just suddenly there, but each person in it is Mum. Each of her faces is expressionless, neutral, a smooth pane. Helena and I keep dancing.

"Do you like being me?" Helena asks.

Somewhere, there is music. But it's not a piano. It's a lullaby. I hear a triangle striking a note.

"I wish you were here," I say.

The triangle gets louder, sharper tings that hurt my ears.

"Do you like living for me?" she asks.

"I wish you were here." It's all I can say, and it feels like a script. Like I've been programmed to say the words. But I don't like that because it suggests they're not sincere. But they are, I can feel it in every step I take by her side.

I wish you were here. I wish you were here.

I wake, mouthing the words.

I wish you were here.

The next morning, I wake to the sounds of vomiting. Sibylle's in her bed. Ivelisse's not.

Oh no. I jump up. Not again.

I wait a few seconds outside the en suite's door before calling through, asking if she's okay. She looks scared and small when she comes out. She holds her arms over her stomach, protectively. Or like she's blocking it from my view.

"Don't tell anyone," she whispers, her voice pleading.

I know I'm supposed to report this though. We all know that—and if it was a stomach bug, Ivelisse wouldn't be insisting on secrecy. But I see the fear in her eyes.

But maybe it *is* just another stomach bug. I mean, she's going to have weak immunity, isn't she? Maybe she's just embarrassed. Doesn't want people knowing she's sick?

"I'm getting this sorted," she says. "I will. It's not too late. It can't be too late."

I try to give her a sympathetic look without seeming patronizing. "Look, I'm here for you, if you want to talk or anything."

She just nods. She's already dressed, I realize. Baggy jumper and leggings.

"Look, uh, I… I need you to cover for me tonight." She fidgets. "Maybe tomorrow too."

"What? Why?"

"I've got to go out. But I'll be back, I just don't know how long it'll take. And Madame Cachelle shouldn't ask for me, but my therapist is going to expect to see me tonight, and I don't know if I'll make it. But, uh, if I'm not back, can you just cover for me?"

"Cover? Like, do what?"

"I don't know. Just say I'm sick or something, headache. Nothing to make them come and check on me though. It'll only be one session I miss, tonight. If I do. And please tell Sibylle when she's up too, so she says the same. I've got to go now, else I'd tell her myself."

"Okay," I say. "But are you all right?"

"I'm fine. And don't speak a word of this conversation. Okay? Please?"

"Okay." I nod.

She leaves.

I sit at my desk for a bit. I've got an hour or so before a flexibility lesson, but I don't want to leave until Sibylle is awake. I still feel like I need to apologize to her again. Not that I haven't already apologized a lot—I mean, I have, of course I have—but I can't help but feel like I've shattered whatever fragile friendship we'd begun to have.

But after ten minutes of waiting, I get a message from Nora, asking if I want to meet up before the flexibility class to go and try on the costumes. *They're ready for all the tours now*, she tells me, *as dress rehearsals are starting soon and Allie wants everyone to drop by today or tomorrow.*

I take a look at Sibylle, still sleeping, then decide, yes, I'll go.

It doesn't take me long to get to Allie's office, and Nora meets me outside. Allie must hear our greetings to each other because she calls out for us to come on in. We do so.

Her whole office is covered in various swathes of fabric and glitter. Lots of glitter.

"Nora and Taryn! My favorite girls!" Allie beams from behind a sewing machine that's only half put together.

"You say that to all the girls," Nora says with a smile.

"And why not?" She directs us to find our costumes for our tours. "*Midsummer* is over there, *Don Quixote* at the back."

I feel apprehensive as I lift down the costume for Helena. Like, somehow, I'm stepping on my dead sister's toes, even though she didn't seem angry in my dream. But I take a deep breath. It's just a name, nothing more.

The dress is off-white. A simple bodice piece with a stunning sheen to it. The skirt is made of several layers of chiffon in varying shades of grey and peach. The edges have been left unhemmed, more ragged in places than others. A bit like the dress I dreamed my sister was wearing. A small lump appears in my throat, makes my eyes smart, makes me want to choke; the dress is simple and no way near as magical as the divertissement dress I was measured for originally, but this one feels rawer. It captures the desperation of Shakespeare's Helena, arguably one of the most romantic characters, and I know visually that this dress will work with my routine as I depict Helena's desperation for Demetrius to return the love.

I wonder if my sister will be watching me from wherever she is.

"Taryn, I already altered this one to fit your measurements, so it should also be perfect," Allie says. "We just need to make sure, so if you pop it on. Yours too, Nora."

Nora immediately looks worried.

"What is it?" Allie asks.

Nora shifts her weight from foot to foot. "Nothing."

"No, tell me. Is it the design?"

Nora gives a weak smile. "It's nothing like that. I just get nervous doing the final trying on. At my old school, the one I was at until I was sixteen, they were quite…harsh. They made costumes like five months before they were needed and refused to do any alterations closer to the time. And one time

I'd put on weight slightly, only a little in a few months, really, but the costumes were made to be skintight and then mine didn't fit right. It was obvious I was fatter, and the ballet master pointed it out to everyone."

"That's horrible," I whisper.

Allie's mouth has dropped open.

Nora nods. "He took me out of the show completely. Said I had to learn to be disciplined and that only disciplined girls could dance for him. It was only like five pounds too. Something silly. But it made me so nervous. I restricted so much after that, and then the next time when I had a costume made, between it being finished and the tour starting it was another three-month period. Only, I lost weight that time. A lot of it. And they wouldn't make any alterations to my costume or let me wear it as it was. So, I didn't get to perform then either."

"Nothing like that happens here," Allie says.

"I know. I've been here for years. Roseheart is actually good. It's nice that not all the dancers are stick-thin here."

I shift a little. Is she meaning me? I mean, she has to be. I take in a breath a little too deeply, and it makes my chest ache. I wonder if many of them think I'm fat. Or if I make them feel better about their bodies. Maybe that's what Ivelisse thinks when she sees me.

Ivelisse. I frown. I've still no idea what I'm covering for her for, but there's a bad feeling in my gut.

"Well, there's nothing to worry about," Allie says, smiling. "It's only August 4th now, right, and the tour doesn't begin until September 2nd. Plenty of time for me to make adjustments. And rest assured, I'll even remake costumes the morning of a show if needed. Now, let's see how these dresses are looking."

Trying on my dress for the role of Helena feels strange. It's not like any other costume I've worn where the garments allow me to become a different person, a different part of myself. It's *more* than that. Because it makes me think of my sister, and it also makes me think of her desperation—desperation to do ballet. Desperation to play the big roles. Desperation to fall in love.

I jolt a little.

Helena loved fairytales and love stories. I wonder if she'd have got her love story, if she'd lived. I wonder what she'd have said about me being aro. I wonder if maybe she would've been aro too. Is romantic orientation bound within genetics? What about sexuality? Would she too have been sex-repulsed?

Before I can ponder any more, Allie starts doing some more measurements on me, noting down adjustments to be made.

"The color really suits you," she says.

It would've suited my sister too.

I try to smile brightly, but I feel like I'm weighed down. We've got full dress rehearsals starting soon, and I pray that becoming this character fully isn't going to distract me.

"Thanks for coming with me," Nora says afterward, as we leave. "I'm always so nervous about costumes. Even though I know it's fine here."

"It's no problem." I smile.

We head to our flexibility class. A grueling ninety-minute class with one of the strictest ballet teachers I've ever met. My muscles are sore, but I'm pleased with my progress by the end of the class. The teacher even gives me a compliment, and I'm still glowing as I leave, heading down the corridor when a door opens, and I come face to face with Teddy.

"Hi," I say.

I look past him into the studio he's just left. "Oh, is it a choreography training thing in there?"

"Choreography training thing?" He snorts. "You couldn't sound more patronizing if you tried."

"Oh, I wasn't meaning that." I laugh lightly, but the air suddenly feels thick, heavy. The other girls from my class filter past me, until it's just me and Teddy here. "Um, are you okay?" I ask.

"Sure." But his eyes are narrowed.

"Teddy?" I stare at him. I don't get why he's being off. He was fine with me yesterday morning and then yesterday evening he was just…off. "What's the matter? Are you not feeling well?"

He glares at me. "Why's it always got to be something going on with me? I'm really getting fed up with people assuming it's something to do with my heart , like it can't just be that it's everyone else being dicks."

My shoulders tighten. "You think it's me? Being a dick?"

His eyes are steely. "You tell me."

I fold my arms. "Look, I've got no idea what any of this is about."

"You don't get it?" Teddy shouts. "You don't get why I'm upset? You *kissed* him."

"Jaidev?" I nearly laugh. "Yeah, I know. I remember."

I've been trying not to think about it—how weird someone's lips feel pressed against my own. How it makes me shudder, makes me feel like part of me is curling up and writhing every time I do it. Even when I can feel the romance of a dance and I'm playing a romantic character and manage to kiss with no one realizing how repulsed I am, and I appear to be *loved up,* as Madame would say, I never really *enjoy* the actual kiss. It's the one part of a dance that can take me out of character. It feels like it's crossing a line. But that's why I'm glad that ballet kisses are just short. Just a second at the most, and then it's over. A second of discomfort in order to make the audience believe in the romance. And that is my job.

"Oh, you remember, do you?" Teddy snorts. "How gallant of you not to deny it."

"Why would I deny it?"

"Oh, I don't know, Taryn."

I don't like the way he says my name. Like it's something bad and rotting.

"Maybe because you said you were aro, like me. And ace. And sex-repulsed, which includes kissing. That's what you said! So, what was that? All just lies to make me feel better?"

I don't know whether to laugh. This is just… "It's a part," I say. "That's all." I stare at him. I don't get this. He never had a problem when I had to kiss Xavier or Advik before for routines. In fact, he was nice then. Asking me if I was okay afterward. Saying that my personal feelings on kissing didn't come through in the dance, that I was still able to capture the romance of it all. He was encouraging and supportive, but not now.

"Because we talked about being aro," he says. "What it meant for each of us. But one look from Hot Asian Guy and you're shoving your tongue down his throat. Next, you'll be jumping into bed, too. Guess you were just a pity aro."

"A pity aro? Oh my God, can you hear yourself?" I hold up my finger. "Firstly, that's racist, what you've just said about Jaidev. Secondly, it's part of our routine. Nothing more."

"It's not! I know your choreography."

I shake my head. "We were recast. We're Helena and Demetrius." I'm not sure, but I think his eyes widen a little at that. "You know, one of the couples who gets married in the wedding scene? Well, it's part of *that* routine. Thirdly, I don't have to justify myself to you, even if we used to be best friends. Fourthly, you have no right over what I do or don't do. And fifthly, you have no right to insult me like that and say I'm not aro or ace. It's *my* identity. I decide it." My words all tumble out so quickly, and there's something about my speech that makes me feel strange. Like it feels too formal, too rehearsed, what with the numbering. But once I started doing that, I couldn't stop.

"Well," Teddy says, "you've clearly decided you're not aro or ace."

"Oh my God. You're just unbelievable. And even if it wasn't part of the routine, which it is, it wouldn't mean you've got any right to question who I am. Kissing someone doesn't mean you're not ace or aro. It's a spectrum—and labels and identities change anyway. It also doesn't mean I'm not repulsed by kissing. It's not up to you to tell someone what they are. You can't just say all that and completely invalidate my identity. It's not fair and it's damaging." As I say the words, I feel everything inside of me sinking. I never thought I'd have to say any of this to him.

"Damaging?" He snorts. "I'll tell you what's damaging—knowing your best friend has lied to you all this time."

"I haven't been lying. You're just not listening because you're being stubborn and determined you're right." I'm aware of how patronizing my own voice is now, but I feel like he deserves it. Even if he has had a terrible diagnosis and the path of his life has changed, it doesn't give him the right to speak to me like this, like he has to authorize what I do or don't do.

He folds his arms. "You were practically drooling back there over him."

"You can't invalidate someone just because of their actions. Especially when you're jumping to conclusions." I mean, seriously? Actions are different to attraction—he should know this! "But I don't need to justify my actions to you. And you're being a dick."

He turns and goes into the studio, so I follow him. He heads to the barre and starts practicing. Practicing *properly*. Like he's a dancer. Not a choreographer.

"You shouldn't be doing that," I say. "Right?"

"Like you care."

"I do."

"Just mind your own business." His voice is still cold. So cold.

"Fine." And with that, I walk away.

He doesn't make any effort to shout after me. And I don't turn around to give him satisfaction of my looking. I haven't got time for this. I need to practice.

I head toward the studios on the lower side of the building. I'm meeting Jaidev at Studio 11, and fury propels me quicker and quicker. God, I can't believe what a dick Teddy is being. And Jaidev will agree, I know that! I just need to let off steam and—

Someone grabs me and shoves me to the right. I see a dark hoody and a balaclava over their face as I scream, trip. My head slams against the wall.

"Just get in there," an angry voice shouts.

A male voice is all I have to think before the person pushes me through the doorway, into the women's toilets.

Then the door locks.

"Well," says the voice. "I think you need to learn a lesson."

FORTY-SEVEN

Taryn

The person—the man, it's a man—shoves me toward a cubicle. I trip and fall heavily, catching my shin. I cry out and spin round, trying to get away.

He's not speaking now. The man. Do I know his voice? It's not Teddy or Jaidev, I know that. Trent's voice is too high. But…but I can't think as fear courses through my veins.

The man grabs my arm, yanking me to the right and then backward.

I scream and fight against him, but—the toilet. He's pushing me toward the toilet.

"Get off me! Help!"

The toilet bowl gets closer. The lid is up.

No! But I know what he's going to try and do. Know because I've seen it in films and books. The stereotype of bullying that I never thought actually happens.

But this, oh God. This is going to happen.

He grabs my shoulders and hauls me up. I try to twist and manage to scratch his wrists and one of his arms. He swears at me. Then he grabs me by my hair, a fistful, forcing my head closer, closer, closer.

Fear floods me.

He is going to do it.

Scream!

Maybe Teddy will hear me. Or someone.

But the thought of opening my mouth, so close to the toilet bowl, has me shaking even more.

"You think you're so clever, don't you?" An accent. Irish. A bad Irish accent? He's putting it on? When he grabbed me in the corridor, I don't think he spoke with an accent. Or if he did, I didn't notice it. "Think you can just dance your way to the top, even though I know what you are? And soon, everyone will."

My chest rises and falls too quickly.

"Please," I whisper, then clamp my mouth tightly shut again. I get ready to hold my breath, but my chest shudders, and then I'm crying.

He laughs.

His hands shove me forward, and I scream involuntarily, try to move, but he forces my head into the bowl. *No, no, no!* I try to move away, throwing all my weight backward, but he's pressing right against me. The cold rim of the ceramic bowl presses into the base of my throat, hard, bruising. The stench of piss fills my nostrils and—

Water. Spraying. The roar of it in my ears. Pouring over me.

I scream, another instinctual reaction. Cold water invades me. More and more of it. So much of it. I can't breathe. Water in my throat, my lungs. Choking, spluttering. Gasping for breath, more water.

Stinging. My eyes. Can't breathe.

Can't breathe.

I try and move away, but he's still there. I struggle against him—another torrent of water around my head.

More and more of it.

Until it…stops.

I fall back, shaking, crying. Water on the floor, everywhere. My hair—suddenly I feel it all in my hair. The toilet water and…and bacteria and….

My vision is blurry. But I see him, standing over me. A dark shape. The black balaclava. White skin around his eyes. He's laughing. But then he stops.

"Don't tell anyone about this," he snarls. Still that stupid attempt at an Irish accent. He moves away, out of the cubicle, out of sight.

His footsteps disappear.

Then the outer door clicks. Shuts again.

I listen, my heart pounding.

Am I alone?

My tears come fast. Huge, shuddering tears. Tears I can't stop.

And it sounds silly, but suddenly I feel my sister's presence. Feel her concern. Her anger. Her annoyance at me.

You were wrong, she says.

And I know I was.

It wasn't Marion or Victoria, because whoever has this vendetta against me is still at Roseheart.

FORTY-EIGHT

Taryn

No one sees me as I leave the bathroom, two hours later. I feel Helena walking with me as I go to the dorm, as I reach my room. It's just the two of us.

I get into the shower, still dressed in my ballet clothes from the flexibility class. I turn it onto its hottest setting and stand there, forcing myself not to move as the water sears me. Helena waits…nearby. Somewhere. I'm not sure, because now it feels like my brain is turning round and round, ever so slowly like the ballerina in the music box that Helena and I had when we were little. I'm realizing what has happened. *What* I'm covered in.

I can hardly touch my hair. My skin. My clothes. I can't take them off. Can't touch them because the toilet water, the urine and the stuff I don't even want to think about, it still feels like it's on me. *Still.*

I open the cubicle door, shower still running, and reach across, spilling water all across the floor as I grab the antibacterial soap from the sink. I squirt it from the bottle onto my head, my face, uncaring when it stings my eyes. But I still can't bring myself to touch my hair. I just can't. But I need to lather it up.

I scream and scream and scream, like there's something inside my soul cracking and breaking and falling and crumbling as more and more steam fills the en suite.

I wait for Helena to tell me all will be okay, but she's silent. She's gone now.

And I just keep standing here, crying.

"Taryn?" The voice is foggy through the pounding in my ears, the water. "Taryn?"

There's a pounding on the bathroom door, but I can't see it for the steam.

"Taryn! Are you okay? Is that you in there?"

There's more pounding.

But then it stops.

I'm still crying. I can't stop crying, and I don't know how long I've been in here.

Then the door flies open—I see the movement. And, a second later, Sibylle's face is up close to the shower cubicle. She pulls the door open.

I jolt, trying to cover myself until I remember I'm still fully clothed. In *these* clothes. My stomach twists. I rush past her and vomit into the toilet.

Exhaustion and dizziness pull at me.

I look around the room, blinking, peering. Someone turns the shower off, but it's not Sibylle, because with a jolt, I realize she's holding my hand. There's someone else here.

"What's happening?" Sibylle's voice is low.

"Should I get a doctor?" another voice asks.

Jaidev. Jaidev's here?

"I don't know," Sibylle says. "Taryn? Uh, let's just get into the bedroom, okay? I can't see. My glasses have steamed up."

They lead me out. Someone wraps me in a towel and then a dressing gown. I'm still clutching the bottle of antibacterial soap. It's empty now, the plastic slippery. I have a vague memory of squirting it, over and over, forty, fifty times, scrubbing my face again and again because that was the only thing I could manage.

Sibylle tries to lead me to my bed, but I resist. I can't sit down there. I'm still dirty.

"What's happened?" Li Hua's here too.

And Nora.

I gulp. Is everyone just meeting in my room now?

"Taryn?" That's Jaidev again.

Don't tell anyone about this.

But I can't not. I dissolve into tears, and I tell them about the attack.

Jaidev's face is like thunder.

"Right, we're telling Mr. Eldridge," Li Hua says.

"The police should know about it, too," Nora says.

I shake my head. "He said not to tell anyone! He'll know I have and…"

"He's not getting away with this," Li Hua says.

"Nora is right. We should go straight to the police now," Jaidev says. "We'll go with you."

I shake my head. "I just… I just need to get clean." My sobs start again. "I couldn't get clean."

"It's okay," Sibylle says. "We'll help you."

I stare at her. How can she still be so kind to me?

But she is.

"Now?" I whisper.

She nods.

"You can use our bathroom," Alma says. *Alma*. When did she get here? People just seem to be popping up out of nowhere. "It's pretty steamy in yours. Too hard to see. Come on."

She and Sibylle lead me away.

"We'll wait here," Nora says, indicating her and Jaidev and Li Hua.

I barely nod.

Alma and Sibylle take me to Alma's bathroom. They unwrap me from my towel and dressing gown. Alma peels my clothes off and puts them in a plastic bag.

"Oh my God, your skin is *red*." Sibylle's voice is soft. She looks at Alma. "Maybe we need the nurse in here?"

I stare at myself in the mirror. My skin is red. I am red. Like I've been severely sunburnt. "No nurse. No more people," I whisper.

Alma and Sibylle share a look.

"Okay, so we'll do cool water," Alma says.

They help me wash. Both of them. I'm too exhausted and numb to feel self-conscious, naked in front of them. Alma washes my hair twice, using her expensive strawberry-scented shampoo. Then she combs the conditioner through it.

Sibylle has towels ready when I step out, then Alma supplies me with body butter and moisturizer.

"There, all clean now. All gone." Alma smiles. "I'll get you some of my clothes, okay? And we can put this bag in the wash." She points at the carrier bag with my sopping, discarded clothes.

"No. Throw them away." I can't bear the thought of having to wear them again. "And the shoes." Even if they are a pair of pointe shoes that I've customized well. "Just...just everything."

"Okay."

Alma disappears and returns a moment later with an armful of fresh, dry clothes. As I put them on, I catch sight of Sibylle's anxious face in the mirror.

Then there's a knock on the door. We all jump.

Alma answers it, and my heart sinks when I hear Madame Cachelle's voice. Because I know. She *knows*. Jaidev or Nora or Li Hua have told the staff what's happened.

"He's going to be after me even more," I whisper.

Madame Cachelle shakes her head. Mr. Aleks, Mr. Vikas, and Mr. Eldridge are in the office too, along with several members of the board. They all look grim.

Sibylle and Alma are still with me, and I grip each of their hands tightly.

My head spins. Everything seems to have happened in the last few hours since Madame Cachelle knocked on Alma's door. Police interviews and public announcements. Jaidev and Trent going around questioning everyone. Teachers looking at the bookings for studios earlier in the day and CCTV for the company building.

It feels like everyone has tried to speak to me. Everyone except Teddy.

But it wasn't him. I'd have known if it was him.

"One of us will be with you at all times," Sibylle says, her voice fierce.

"We will make sure you're safe here," Mr. Eldridge says. "Safety of our dancers is of paramount importance."

"We will find this person," Mr. Aleks says. "The police are looking at the CCTV now with Miss Tavi. We will find them. And they will be dealt with accordingly."

That seems to be the end of the meeting. Because then we're moving. Sibylle says we should get dinner. None of us have eaten and it's late now.

Dinner time.

I frown. Ivelisse. Is she back? I murmur her name, looking around for her when we reach the canteen. If she's not here, I need to tell her therapist something. But I... My head pounds. I can't think. Can't...

So, I just eat the jacket potato and cheese that Sibylle gets for me.

"That's all right, isn't it?" she asks. "No fructose in it?"

"It's good, thanks." I force myself to eat.

Sibylle and Alma both eat with me, picking through salads with tuna. Jaidev arrives with Trent and Hazma after a while, and they eat with us, as well. Everyone talks in hushed voices, asking for updates and if anyone's heard anything.

At eleven, Sibylle, Alma, and I head to our dorm. Jaidev comes, too.

"I'm going to sit outside," he says. "In the corridor." His eyes meet mine. "Make sure you're safe. That no one comes."

I smile weakly. "Thanks."

"Won't you risk getting in trouble for that?" Alma asks.

"Not in these circumstances," he says. "And I won't be *in* the room. Just keeping watch."

That does make me feel better.

Alma heads to her room. Freya's waiting outside it. Her eyes are wide as she sees me—she's heard, everyone has heard—but she doesn't say anything. I don't want to speak to her. I still haven't forgiven her for outing me, but I haven't got the energy to deal with that now.

Sibylle and I head inside our room. Ivelisse's not here.

Someone has tidied up our en suite. There's no steam, fresh soap by the sink, and all the water I spilled on the floor has been mopped up.

Sibylle keeps asking if I'm okay. I keep nodding. We get ready for bed. I message Jaidev to see if he's still there.

I am. Why?

I just wanted to check, I reply. *Thanks.*

My phone screen lights up with another message the moment I've sent it.

But it's not another from Jaidev.

It's Ivelisse.

Taryn, I need your help. I've done something stupid.

FORTY-NINE

Taryn

I call Ivelisse immediately, and she answers. Her breath is labored.

"I've done something stupid…" Her voice doesn't sound right. She's speaking too fast, and her breathing is heavy. Like she's in pain. "I'm sending you my location now. I…"

"Taryn?" Sibylle's looking at me, but I hold my hand up at her.

There's a gulp from Ivelisse, and I don't know whether the phone line twists it so it sounds tinny or whether she's choking or something.

"Don't tell the teachers, please," Ivelisse whispers, then the call clicks off.

I stare at my phone, then I call her again. It goes straight to voicemail, but a second later her location pings to my phone.

"It's Ivelisse," I say, turning to Sibylle. The few bites of potato I managed to eat suddenly feel like they're stuck at the base of my throat. "She's... She said she's done something stupid and needs help. She's sent me her location."

"Then we give it to the teachers or the police." Sibylle rubs her left eye.

"No, she said not to tell anyone."

"Well, what can we do?" Sibylle asks.

"Go and find her," I whisper, my voice cracking. "Help her. She's asked for my help. And she wanted me to cover for her."

"Cover?"

God, that conversation seems like a lifetime ago. Not just this morning. And I never updated Sibylle on Ivelisse's plan. I tell her quickly. Her eyes widen more and more.

"Okay. But we're not going on our own."

"Jaidev's outside," I say.

"Good." She grabs her coat.

I put Alma's clothes back on and grab my coat, then pull on my trainers. I shove my phone into the pocket of my jeans.

Sibylle opens the door, updates Jaidev. I hear him swear under his breath. Then the three of us are running down the corridor.

"Where are you going?" Freya is suddenly here, blocking her way.

Xavier is behind her. His hair is disheveled, and his lips are red. Freya's too. I wonder if they were kissing.

"Just move," Sibylle pants.

"No, he can help," I say, looking at Xavier. "We don't know what's happened to Ivelisse. If she's in trouble, if people have her or have hurt her, we're going to need more strength. Jaidev *and* Xavier."

"And Freya," Freya says.

"Five is better than three," I say.

"So, what's going on?" Xavier's frowning.

Sibylle tells him quickly.

Then the five of us run.

Rain hammers down, bouncing on pavements, throwing darkness everywhere, obscuring my vision. Sibylle clings to my left hand and my right hand is in Jaidev's. I think Freya is clinging to him and Xavier. We're all huddled together, all trying to run.

"Is it this way?" Freya yells. "Down there?"

I squint into the darkness. There are barely any streetlights here.

"Let's see your phone again," Jaidev says.

I hand it to him. He peers at the map I've got up on it, trying to shield the screen from the worst of the weather. Then he nods and hands my phone back to me.

We run faster and faster. My skin burns under the rain.

Water.

No. I try not to think, to remember.

I just keep running.

Must keep running.

We're in a part of London I don't know; we got two buses here, and we've been running since. We pass the odd person—usually someone bundled in layers, sitting in a doorway. The shopfronts aren't posh, and there are lots of broken windows. None of them are boarded. The air smells strongly of smoke, but it's stale smoke. My lungs burn.

Sibylle trips and stumbles, but I right her. She squeezes my hand.

"This way," Jaidev says.

We turn left. The rain pounds down heavier. My clothes cling to me. There's a hole in my left trainer, and my socked foot squelches against the sodden insole with every step.

A streetlight flickers ahead—there's only the one, casting a weak glow.

"Wait, is that her?" I point to the right of the streetlight where what I think a figure is slumped by something dark. A doorway? I can't tell.

"Oh my God," Sibylle says.

We move forward, faster. It's a girl. I can see it's a girl. A girl with lots of dark hair tumbling down over her face and her chest.

"Ivelisse?" Fear grabs me, and then I break away from the others, running faster and faster. "Ivelisse!"

She stirs, opens her eyes. Then she groans, holding her stomach. She's been sick on her clothes and the stench wraps around me. She looks up at me through bloodshot eyes. "Something's gone wrong."

I crouch next to her. "Gone wrong? With what?"

"I…" Tears pour down her face. She looks behind me and freezes.

Jaidev's here, and the others, but Ivelisse shrinks back a bit.

"It's okay," I say. "We're here to help." I push her hair back from her face. "What's happened?"

She gulps. "I...went to this...person. She said she could help me."

"Help you?" My heart pounds. With her anorexia? I thought she had therapists and doctors for that. I don't understand why she's out here.

Unless she's not talking about that. Has she got money problems?

Oh God. How didn't I notice anything? I'm her *roommate*.

"Is it gangs?" Jaidev asks. He crouches next to me. "Did they give you drugs? Because they did that to Bastien, my brother, and—"

Ivelisse shakes her head and looks at me. "Because of... In June."

"June?"

She shakes her head. "The party, remember the party I went to? In June."

I don't. I didn't know she went to a party.

"They were drunk, there. Everyone was drunk at the party." Her words tumble out, crashing into one another. "I had one, just one, but they wouldn't leave me alone. Two men. And... I thought it would be better after, but then the test was positive. And this, this person I saw today, she said she'd help get...get rid of it."

Get rid of it.

"No," Sibylle whispers.

The streetlight flickers more.

I found a pregnancy test in the toilets of the lower school.

I go cold.

"A backstreet abortion?" Freya's voice shakes. I see her face. She's gone white. Xavier grabs hold of her.

"It's gone wrong," Ivelisse whispers, and I turn back to her, just as she slumps forward.

I let out a scream.

Dead. Another girl *dead.*

My sister, my friend. No!

"Hey, Ivelisse?" Jaidev pushes me away. He shakes her gently, then he places his fingers against her neck. "Okay. Uh, recovery position. Taryn, help me."

He barks out directions to me, telling me how to position Ivelisse. He knows what to do, that's clear. We lay Ivelisse on her left side. Freya and Xavier both have their phone flashlights on now, and they shine them on her. I can see the blood appears to be coming from her crotch.

"Lift her head up a bit," Jaidev says. "Make sure her windpipe is… Ah, what's the word?" But he takes over and carefully and gently maneuvers her head. "We have to watch her, in case she starts vomiting." Then he looks directly at me. "Call an ambulance."

"Already doing it," Sibylle says.

FIFTY

Taryn

"Why wouldn't she just go to the doctor for that?" Freya looks at all of us. We're in the waiting room of the nearest hospital. "It's not like it's illegal in this country. And it's free with the NHS."

"I don't think she realized," Sibylle says. She looks at me. "Remember when she had that infected tooth and didn't go to the dentist for ages because she said it would be expensive?"

I nod. That was in the first year of the diploma.

"Maybe she didn't want it on her medical records," Xavier says. "Not when Roseheart could kick her out."

"Even though she's graduated now and is leaving?"

"We hadn't graduated when that teacher found the pregnancy test though," I point out. "And Ivelisse's trying to get auditions with other companies, right? If news that she was pregnant got out, it could harm her chances. She might've just wanted to pretend none of this was happening.

No official records. Especially…" I can't even say the words. Ivelisse was assaulted at a party?

"She might not want her family knowing about any of it," Jaidev says. "Are they very religious? They could be more pro-life than pro-choice. I know Avril is. Ivelisse might have thought it was best to hide all this."

We've never really known much about Ivelisse's family. She's mentioned a mother and two brothers, and how they all moved from Puerto Rico to New York when she was eight. She doesn't go back every holiday because plane tickets are expensive, but that's about as much as I know.

Still, I don't know if I even asked her. Maybe I didn't, because I didn't want it to reflect questions onto me about my own family.

"Bloody stupid, whatever it was," Freya says. "I didn't think she even got her period anyway?"

"Amenorrhea can give a false sense of security that you can't get pregnant." Next to me, Sibylle lets out a long breath. "What time is Madame Cachelle getting here?"

"Should be soon."

Right after Sibylle called the ambulance, I called Madame, using the emergency number she gave us all when we started the diploma. She said it was important we knew we could call her at any time, day or night, if there was an emergency.

Madame said she and someone else from the academy would meet us at the hospital. Sibylle went in the ambulance with Ivelisse, and the rest of us got an Uber. Jaidev had sat in the front, and I was squashed between Freya and Xavier. None of us had really spoken, apart from Jaidev who was trying to amenably answer the Uber driver's chatty questions. He'd been very interested to learn we were all dancers, though I noticed Jaidev didn't tell him we were ballet dancers.

"I'm going to get some coffee," Freya says, yawning. "I simply cannot stay awake any longer without it. Anyone want any?"

I shake my head. I don't like coffee at the best of times and so often the machine coffee at hospitals has sugar automatically added to it. Jaidev says he will, Xavier says no, and Sibylle shakes her head.

"I'll help you," Jaidev says, even though I'm sure Freya can manage to handle two coffees on her own.

I lean against Sibylle. She looks down at me, smiles a little.

"What a day, eh?" she says. "Didn't think anything could add more drama to earlier. Or, well, yesterday. Wow, it's late."

I nod. "Thanks, though. For being there for me, yesterday."

"What are friends for?"

"Even though I'd accused you of all that stuff."

"What stuff?" Xavier asks.

"She thought I was the Victoria," Sibylle says. It sounds weird the way she says *the Victoria*. Almost comical. "Only it would appear that Victoria wasn't actually the Victoria."

I nod. "It was a guy." I look across at Xavier. "You heard what happened, right?"

He nods. "Could've been a company dancer working with Victoria, though? Getting revenge for you getting her locked up? Who's her partner?"

"Harry. No, he might be Marion's. I don't know. But the three of them are not at Roseheart now anyway, so it can't be him."

"But you didn't see his face?" Xavier asks. "Robert said something about a balaclava?"

"Yeah, he was wearing one." I shrug. "Could only see that the skin around his eyes was light. He was strong—but then all the dancers are. Doesn't really narrow it down."

"What about the voice? Did you recognize it?"

I shake my head. "He was putting on a terrible accent."

Xavier laughs, then he stops quickly when neither Sibylle nor I join in. He's saved from any awkwardness though as Madame Cachelle and Ross arrive. Madame sweeps straight over to us while Ross calls at the reception desk.

"Any news?" Madame asks us.

"We don't know what's happening now," I say.

"She was taken straight through from the ambulance," Sibylle says. "We think she'd tried to get an illegal abortion. She was bleeding, kind of a lot. And she'd been sick. She mentioned a party she went to in June. It kind of sounded like she might've been…raped there." Her voice is even quieter. "She was mostly unconscious in the ambulance. The paramedics put an IV line in her or something, and they were really worried about infection as well."

Madame nods, gravely. "Poor child."

I can't imagine dealing with all of this. Being assaulted, and then having to try and sort out an abortion in secret. But abortion—is that what the strict rules at Roseheart lead to? There are always rumors of dancers visiting clinics. But those are always NHS clinics. Or at least legal ones. Not like this place Ivelisse went to. Not that I know of.

I think of what Jaidev was saying. I take out my phone and Google whether abortion is legal in the US. It is, but after reading a little, I realize what a polarizing issue it is. Maybe Ivelisse was worried about her career, so she wanted an abortion, but she was worried what her family would think of it, so she didn't do it through the NHS so there'd be no paper record. She could've been scared of repercussions. But I'm just grasping at straws, I know that. I don't know what her family situation is like, whether she's close to them—or why she even chose a ballet school so far away. She's never really said, and they've never visited to watch performances.

Still, mine haven't either.

Ross joins us, says the staff at the desk aren't able to give any information. It's just a case of waiting—something I've been doing all too much of in hospitals recently. Tessa. Teddy. Now Ivelisse.

I try not to think about Teddy. Even when news of the attack on me was flying around the whole institution, not once did he ask if I was okay. He seemed to just be staying out of the way.

I look at Xavier. "Did you see Teddy in the dorms earlier?"

He shakes his head.

I hope that doesn't mean he's still in the studio, doing ballet. Or worse.

Lying in a heap on the floor, by the barre.

No.

That's just my imagination. I'm tired. I'm traumatized, by everything.

Freya and Jaidev return with their coffees. Madame greets them politely. Ross nods. Freya asks if they want coffee too, but they shake their heads.

"Has Ivelisse's family been contacted?" Sibylle asks.

Madame nods. "Her mother is flying over on the next available flight. I don't know where from though"

Sibylle nods. "She's in New York, I think."

"Well, I do not know what time she will be here. Hopefully, we'll have good news to give her. But we could be here for a while, so I suggest you all go back. Ross will drive you." She glances briefly at Ross who nods. "I will wait here."

That seems to be the plan and it's not something to argue with, going by the way Madame makes eye contact with each of us. It's strange leaving the hospital without knowing.

"She could already be dead or something," Freya says.

"Shut up," Sibylle hisses, just as I'm about to say something too.

"What? Just being realistic."

We're silent all the drive back to Roseheart. Ross turns the radio on, and we listen to traffic reports for roads we're definitely not driving on nor will be.

It's nearly 3 a.m. by the time we get back. Sibylle and I climb straight into bed. I didn't think I'd sleep easily—but I do.

My alarm goes off at eight, and I struggle to open my eyes. Sibylle murmurs something then pulls her duvet over her head. I hit the 'off' button on the alarm clock and slowly, having to use all my energy, pull myself out of bed.

Fatigue and tiredness wash over me. Every part of me is sore, my muscles feeling like they're super strained. My skin's hurting more too, this morning, and in the bathroom mirror, I see just how red it is.

There's a text on my phone from Jaidev.

I'll meet you outside your room and walk you to class.

I start to smile, until I remember why it's necessary. Someone here is still after me. And the next three weeks are going to be the most important ones so far. We've got to get everything perfect before the final assessment. The one that will decide whether Jaidev and I can dance in the company, whether we'll get issued with permanent contracts. In just under a month's time, we could be starting the first leg of the tour, in the south of England. Or we could be preparing for another year at the academy, training with Madame to really perfect our pas de deux together.

Jaidev looks just as tired as I feel when he arrives to collect me. We make small talk.

Neither of us has heard an update on Ivelisse.

"Well, we'd better just distract ourselves with ballet," he says.

And it does work surprisingly well. I throw myself into pointe class. Netty Florence, Nora, and Li Hua form a protective ring around me during the class, and they walk with me to the group rehearsal. Jaidev's there as well, so I feel a bit better with his presence—but also at the group rehearsal are all the guys on the *Midsummer* tour. And that makes me nervous.

I look from one to another as we dance and run through several different acts, with Mr. Vikas giving correction after correction and getting us all to start again at various stages.

My attacker could be one of the guys here. Or it could be someone else. Another company dancer who isn't even on this tour. Or an academy student.

A teacher? A staff member? All I've got really to go on is the white skin color—but that doesn't really narrow it down, only excluding a handful of people thanks to how predominantly white Roseheart is.

We practice and practice. When group rehearsals are over, Mr. Vikas and Evangeline ask the leads and understudies to stay behind for another session. Then it's endurance training and finally a flexibility class.

By the time evening draws around, no one's made a move to hurt me, but I've not been on my own at all—Netty Florence and Li Hua even accompanied me to the toilets each time I wanted to go, and we made sure not to go in the ones where I'd been attacked—but we also haven't heard an update on Ivelisse. My texts to her haven't been answered. My WhatsApp messages have been delivered but are unread.

We don't see Madame Cachelle at Roseheart again until the next morning, and all she can tell us is Ivelisse's mother is at the hospital now. The hospital staff haven't given an update to the school due to data protection and confidentiality, and Madame doesn't want to bother Ivelisse's family at this very stressful time.

I hate not knowing but knowing isn't within my control right now. All that I can control is my training. And so that's what I do. I put my all into it, day in, day out. We get into a routine. Jaidev, Netty Florence, Li Hua, Xavier, and Sibylle stick to me like glue. There's always at least one of them with me.

A week passes, and Jaidev and I take part in our first dress rehearsal. Still, we haven't heard anything about or from Ivelisse. There's just…nothing. Even Madame doesn't know.

We keep dancing.

Teddy still ignores me.

Sibylle and my friends accompany me everywhere.

And, finally, Madame utters the words that allow me to breathe a huge sigh of relief: "Ivelisse's okay."

Jaidev and I dance easier with that knowledge.

Another week passes, the days just zooming by. My attacker still hasn't been caught, but I feel safe with my friends around me. I trust them.

"Right," Mr. Vikas says, clapping as we come to the end of another rehearsal of the wedding scene. "That's better.

Taryn, keep your lines as elegant as possible. Jaidev, watch your arms. Come on, everyone. We have thirteen days until the tour starts!"

Thirteen days. I gulp. The tour starts on September 2nd, but our eight weeks of training end on August 26th. That's six days away. We've got six days until our final assessment—and I know we can practice after that, before the tour starts, but that'll only apply if we *pass* the final assessment. Nora said the company will have created the window between the assessment and the tour start-date in case we don't make it and the dancers need to re-choreograph certain scenes so they make sense without us, with even fewer dancers.

In these last six days, we do full rehearsals, on stage, under the glaring, hot lights. We use industrial-strength deodorants, but still, they're not enough. The theatres are heat-traps.

We pack more and more practices in. Excitement builds among the company, and Jaidev and I become more and more tense. Mr. Aleks tells us all, in a group session, that the *Midsummer* tour has now sold out. Everyone cheers, before we're back to work.

And then it's here—the final evening before our fate is decided.

Jaidev and I go to the graveyard. I tell him about how I dance for Helena there. We both dance there, for her, slow, sweeping moves.

"Tomorrow will be beautiful," he says. "You'll see."

I nod. All I can do is hope he's right. Hope we've done enough. Hope this works.

FIFTY-ONE

Taryn

This is it. The day of the final assessment. I'm nervous—so nervous—and Jaidev and I cram in another session. The whole cast for the Midsummer tour will perform the ballet from start to finish today—a showcase for academy staff and dancers' families—and we've been told Jaidev and I will be assessed based on our roles as Helena and Demetrius. I'm glad for that. We're still working on making our understudy routines as smooth as possible—and if we're selected today, we'll have another week to perfect those before the fall tour starts. I wonder if it will be easier to train then, without the pressure of knowing it could all end in a heartbeat. Or whether the pressure will be even worse, knowing it's a certainty. That we *will* be dancing the *Midsummer* tour.

"What are your plans now then?" Jaidev asks. "Before the showcase?"

I breathe hard. Teddy. I need to find him. I need to try and sort things out with him. He's stubborn, of course he is, so he's not made any move to actually contact me. Not even to see if I'm okay. I've barely seen him for the last few week. Just glimpses of him here and there. Walking through a corridor. Leaving a studio. Talking to choreographers. Sibylle says she saw him in the library at one point.

I tell Jaidev I need to talk to him, and he nods.

"Xavier said he was in one of the academy studios earlier."

We go there. And Teddy *is* there. He's dancing. And it doesn't look like it's to work out choreographies. It looks intense, like he's pushing himself. Exactly what he shouldn't be doing.

"I've got to just phone Avril," Jaidev says. "But if you can get Teddy to walk you back to the costuming, then I'll meet you there. Don't go on your own."

I nod. We've got to get fully costumed and made up before the showcase—like it's a proper performance on one of the tour shows. And that whole process can easily take a few hours in the academy. We've been warned that it takes even longer for the company.

I watch Teddy for a few more minutes before I open the door. His movements are strong and precise, calculated, positions held with poise and determination and familiarity and—

It's one of Demetrius's solos that he's dancing. Jaidev's dance. My eyes widen, and I watch Teddy dance more, knowing the movements that will come. He's learnt it.

When I open the door, Teddy notices—he must do because the door creaks—but he doesn't stop dancing. Just keeps pirouetting. I hear him counting as he does. He's slightly off time, I can tell that because I'm so familiar with the music, but I guess he's not practiced with music at all. My shoulders tighten. He shouldn't be doing this.

After a few minutes, when it becomes apparent that he's not going to stop just because I'm here, I clear my throat. He can't really just be planning to ignore me, can he?

He stops after a long moment, then makes a few notes in a notebook that he's got at the side of the room, under one of the barres.

I venture forward. The roof of my mouth feels too dry. Suddenly, and I don't know what to say. Eventually, I force words out. "How are you?"

"Good." His voice is monotone, and he doesn't even look at me. Instead, he goes back to the center of the studio and starts pirouetting again.

I approach him. "Look, Teddy. Can you just stop?"

He does so, but he sighs loudly. "What?"

My stomach roils, and my chest feels all fluttery, too light, like part of me will just drift away. "Um, are you still angry at me? Because I've done nothing wrong."

He lets out a snort. Somehow, the snort sounds sarcastic. "I suppose a liar wouldn't think that *lying* is doing anything wrong."

"Oh my God." I stare at him, feeling my temper rise, irritation flowing through my blood. "I can't believe you. After all this, and you're still het up on that?"

"Yes, because I have things I stand for. Things I believe in. You clearly don't."

I throw my hands up in the air. "Look, I came here to try and clear the air—not that I have done anything wrong. It's all you, but here's me trying to sort things out, being the bigger person and all that."

"Oh, that's rich." He wipes his hands on his shorts.

"What is?"

"Saying you're the bigger person."

I sigh. I haven't got time for this. "I'm not putting up with this, Teddy. I've got the most important assessment of my life later today."

"Lucky you."

"Look, I know you're upset about your diagnosis—and I guess that this is probably what all this is about?"

"You don't know anything about me."

"And whose fault is that? Who's completely shut me out of their life?"

"You did that all by yourself," he says. "You've had no time for anyone else, it's just all been about you and Jaidev."

"That's not true," I say. "And you know that. You know what I've been going through—that attack, and the police still don't know who did it. You never once asked me about it."

He shrugs. "I'm sure your boyfriend's looking after you plenty. I've seen him doing his bodyguard act."

"Oh my God. Can you just listen to yourself? I'm trying to be nice here. We used to be friends, and for some reason, I still want your support."

"How nice of you. Now," he says, turning away from me. "I've got somewhere else to be. You've completely ruined the vibe of this room. How do you expect someone to do good dance if the air's all bad?"

I want to scream and scream at him, make him see sense. But I know a lost cause.

"You've done that all yourself," I say. "And you shouldn't even be dancing."

"Then tell the world." He lets out a high-pitched bout of laughter that doesn't sound anything like him and then gathers his notebook and pencil. He picks up his trainers. And he walks out—just like that. Doesn't even change out of his flats first.

I stare after him, almost unable to believe it. It's like he's a completely different person now. Like I don't know him at all. And this new Teddy? Well, there's no way I want to be friends with him.

Tears pierce the corners of my eyes and I try to blink them back. I take deep breaths. I mustn't be getting upset—I've got to keep calm. You can't cry and be stressed before a big performance. But Teddy's made me like this.

I gulp and gulp. Then I hear the door opening again. He's coming back?

I turn, hopeful. But it's not him. It's Xavier.

He looks surprised to see me here. "Oh, hi. I thought you'd be in the company buildings? Don't their make-up sessions take, like, five hours?"

I nod and quickly wipe my eyes.

"Hey, what's wrong?" He crosses the floor swiftly and reaches me. "Taryn?"

I shake my head. I don't want to talk about it.

Xavier hugs me—he does it so quickly, without warning, and I can't do anything to stop him. I just tense up.

When the hug's over, he pulls back and readjusts his hoody.

"I was just coming into practice here," he says. "I've got an audition tomorrow. Last-minute thing. With a classical company, and I wanted to get a session in. You don't mind, do you?"

"Oh no, I can go," I say as he pulls his hoody off.

He's wearing a tank top underneath—and I see a scar on his inner left arm. It looks pretty nasty, only then I see that there are more of them. Scars all up and down both of his arms and around his wrists. Faded red lines. Maybe three weeks old.

Three weeks.

My throat squeezes.

They're the scars I made.

He was the one who put my head in the toilet.

My mouth dries. Xavier? *Xavier?* My head spins. Why would he do that?

"Great," he says, smiling. "You can give me feedback, right? Let me just shut the door properly. This one always sticks a bit, you know, but if it doesn't fully shut then you get the wind whistling through. Proper distracting it is."

My head spins as he heads toward the door. It's Xavier. *Xavier!* And I'm in here with him.

Oh, God. I need to get out. Need to get out right away. Now.

I start to move toward the door—after him—getting ready to say how I actually need to go to costumes and makeup. That I can't be late. Maybe I'll laugh and say he's right, it does take five hours.

"Woah," he says, turning around. He finds me right behind him. "What are you doing?"

"I…" I shift my weight from foot to foot. But all the words I'd planned to say just get stuck. They're pebbles in my throat, and I can't get them out.

I scurry backward, turning around. Windows. I can get out the windows—and I run for the other side of the room. Thick curtains have been drawn the full length of the wall, and I lunge for the left one and pull it back. No window. Of course. A lot of the academy studios don't. Not like the company studios where many back onto courtyards and gardens or have windows overlooking the lake.

"What are you doing?" Xavier's voice is cold, all signs of the earlier warmth now gone, and his words echo slightly. He knows I know. I feel it like a stab to my gut.

I turn, my feet skidding. He's still by the door. It's shut—looks properly shut now. He's holding a key. Locked it? Already?

My heart sinks.

I raise my hands up. I don't know if I'm going for a surrender gesture or if I'm getting ready to fight him, as ridiculous as it seems. "Please." My voice shakes. "Look, I don't know what you want or why you're doing this."

"You don't know?" He stares at me. His lips curl. "You don't know? Are you having a laugh or something?"

My heart pounds. Should I scream? "I… Well, you want to be in the company." I mean, it has to be that. "But it's not my fault," I say. "I didn't stop you."

He laughs. "You didn't stop me? Is that really what you think?"

"Xavier, I didn't."

"If you weren't so goody-two-shoes and *utterly perfect* at dancing, they'd have let me in. They'd have paired us together. Or maybe even have admitted me and Sibylle. But it's *you*. You stopped both of those happening."

He's angry because I'm better than him?

"No," I say. My breaths come in short, sharp bursts. I need help. He's already physically attacked me once. I don't know what he's capable of. My phone is in my pocket, and I turn so my side-profile is to him, and so my phone should be hidden from his sight. I try to slide it out of the pocket of my leggings. "I didn't stop you."

"You did!" he roars. "That was *my* place and you're not even the male dancer, but you took it away from me and gave it to a dancer who didn't even train here."

"Xavier, *please*." I take a deep breath. My phone is in my hand now, and I try to keep it angled away behind him. From memory, I try to unlock it, typing in my passcode. My heart pounds. "Look, I wasn't taking anything from you. It's a fair audition."

"It's not fair when they bend their rules to suit you. They'd never do that for anyone else. But they do it for you."

But it's because I'm really good, I want to say. But I don't. That won't help, and I need to be careful.

He moves closer to me. Two steps. "They do it for you, thinking they know you, thinking you're this amazing dancer, but they don't know you at all. No one knows you, do they?"

I take a step back as he advances toward me. Then another step. My fingers are frantic, tapping on my phone. Have I opened contacts now? I can't tell without looking, but I can't risk looking away from Xavier.

"I know what you did," he says. "I know you murdered your sister."

"I didn't."

He laughs. "*Of course* a murderer would deny it. And for some reason, I thought you wouldn't want that getting out. I thought you'd take the message and go. But you didn't."

"Because I'm not a murderer. I didn't kill her. She fell off that balcony."

"Fell off or was pushed off?"

"She fell off." My voice is hard.

"There should've been a whole investigation done into you," he says. "But of course no one suspects the pretty little ballerina is actually a *murderous* little ballerina. I mean, I didn't either. I knew you'd lost a sibling, too. I felt close to you before, because of that. It never occurred to me to actually look up how your sister died. And when I did, it all became clear. Good thing some journalists tell the truth, eh?" He steps right up to me. So close I can see every pore on his skin. "It's disgusting, how some people think they can just take the life of another and get away with it?"

My chest rises and falls too quickly. He's right in front of me, inches away. His breath is hot on my face. I need to look at my phone. My head pounds.

I lift my hand with the phone up and around him, holding it behind his shoulder so I can see the screen. I try to focus on him, look at his face, into his eyes, so he doesn't realize what I'm doing, but I'm shaking, and my vision is blurring. I glance at the screen. Jaidev's contact. *There.*

"Good things shouldn't happen to bad people." He says the word slowly. He hasn't cleaned his teeth, and I see food caught in them. I can smell his breath. Slightly bad.

"Xavier, look. I know about your brother, okay?" I click onto Jaidev's contact. "I know what happened to him was terrible and unfair and it was murder." I click the call button. "But this isn't that. Helena wasn't—"

He spits at my face. I scream and recoil back. My phone clatters down somewhere, but then Xavier's right in front of me. He shoves me, and I fall back. The back of my head hits the floor. Pain. Dark spots in my eyes, but then he's on top of me.

I shriek and scream, trying to throw him off me.

"Help! Help me!" I scream as I claw at his arms, drawing more blood. I try to swipe at his head. My phone. The call to Jaidev. Did it connect? But I can't see my phone and—

"I'm going to make sure you get what you deserve," Xavier says. "I don't like liars. And I don't like murderers. And Taryn Foster, I don't like you."

He moves his arm suddenly, and then there's a knife in his hand. The blade glistens.

I scream.

FIFTY-TWO

Jaidev

"Avril? Can you hear me? The signal's not good."

"I…yes…problem…" Her voice is full of static.

"Hold on." I move down the corridor. "Is this better?"

"Yes, and we've got a problem. I've been trying to call you all morning. Camille's mother has been in touch."

Everything stops.

"No…" My voice breaks. "What… What does she want?"

"She's got tickets to your show today. I was just speaking to Madame Cachelle, and she mentioned there's quite an audience for this performance. I enquired as to who would be there, and she mentioned Gabrielle Blanc, and that is Camille's mother, is it not?"

I take a deep breath. Yes, it is. We both know that. "Is she going to…"

"I don't know what her plan is, son. But I've been trying to warn you. As far as I know, Gabrielle Blanc has never been to any Roseheart shows before. And it's been widely publicized here you are dancing now."

It has?

My head spins as I try to work out what Gabrielle Blanc's plan could be. To cause trouble? To get revenge? Because that was the last thing she said to me. When I was at the hospital, trying to see Camille. When the police arrested me.

"You'll pay for this," Gabrielle Blanc had screamed at me, before some other people had stopped her. Maybe they'd restrained her, too. My back was to her, my hands cuffed by the cops. Maybe she'd been trying to get to me.

Maybe tonight she will.

"I've left a message for Madame Cachelle about this," Avril continues, "but I do not know if she's seen it, and so I suggest you tell one of the company staff. Possibly security. They have security guards, right? Because I do not like this. We all know how unstable the Blancs are."

"Stop," I try to say. Camille was never unstable. But I saw how the other dancers ganged up on her, gaslit her, made her think she was going crazy.

"There's no other reason for her to be at this show. No other reason to hang around ballet companies. She certainly didn't approve of Camille dancing."

Camille had had an uphill struggle with her mother the whole time. Gabrielle Blanc never understood how ballet is a part of a dancer's soul, how you can't just stop.

"Well, no, I think she's got a relative at Roseheart's company. Victoria," I say. Didn't Victoria say she was related to Camille when she threatened me? She'd said *family*, I'm sure, and at the time I assumed she just meant how all dancers are family. But this would make sense. "Maybe a cousin of Camille or something. Gabrielle could have already got tickets to see her, not knowing she'd be removed from the tour."

"Then there's no reason for her still to attend."

"Well, maybe she doesn't want to waste the money." I look at my watch. "Look, Avril, I really have to go now and get ready. I've still got to go to costuming and makeup. But I'm sure this isn't going to be a problem. I mean, she can hardly do anything."

Or is that just me wishful thinking?

But Gabrielle Blanc can't do anything.

Except I've suddenly got visions of her interrupting the ballet to tell everyone I murdered her daughter.

And I didn't.

It was an accident. I never meant to drop her.

"Just be careful," Avril says.

I promise her that I will and that I'll call tonight, let her know how it's gone. My phone buzzes as I end the call. There's a voicemail message on my phone. I roll my eyes. It's probably just Avril panicking. She must've tried to phone me earlier. If there's one thing that woman does well, it's panicking.

I click on to listen, getting ready to press the button to delete it as soon as I hear Avril's voice.

But it's not Avril's voice.

It's Taryn's. And she's screaming.

"*Help! Help me!*"

There's a clattering noise. Fast breathing.

And then: "*I'm going to make sure you get what you deserve.*" But that's not her. That's a guy. That's Xavier? "*I don't like liars. And I don't like murderers. And Taryn Foster, I don't like you.*"

My head pounds. There's more screaming, screaming from Taryn. I can hear her begging him not to do…something? I don't know what. Oh God.

The voicemail ends just as she screams again.

Nausea rises in me. My blood rushes to my ears. I feel sicker and I dial her number. It rings and rings. No answer.

I curse.

"You all right, mate?"

I look up to see Trent.

"It's Taryn," I say. "She's being attacked. Call the police, get help. Uh, the academy studios. I think she's there." And before he can say or do anything, I'm running.

The academy grounds have never felt so far away from the company as they do right now. I'm strong, a good sprinter, but time seems to run in slow motion as I rush to the studios. Everything inside me pounds.

What if I'm too late?

No. I can't think about that.

I yank open the building door and skid inside, gravel flying in with me. I run faster and faster, harder and harder.

"Taryn?" I shout. Shit, which studio was it she and Teddy were in?

Teddy.

Did he lure her there? He and Xavier were roommates, friends. I inhale too deeply, nearly end up choking and—

A scream cuts through the air.

I force myself to go faster. Turn right. All the doors are open to all the studios, except one. *That* one. The door of the one I dropped Taryn off before is now shut.

I run for it. "Taryn? Taryn, are you in there?" I grab the handle. It doesn't open. Shit. It's locked.

I pound on the door, screaming.

"Let me in!"

I can hear movement inside. And a voice. A man's voice. Muffled. Xavier's.

"Xavier, I know it's you! We all know. So just unlock this door and let her out. It's over."

"It's not over until I say it's over." His words drive fear into me.

I listen, listen for sounds from Taryn. But there's nothing. *Nothing.*

She… she fell…
I dropped her.
Slipped.
The sickening crack.
Her neck.
Labored breathing.
No scream.
Too silent.

Too much.

Too much nothingness.

"Xavier!" I scream. "Open this bloody door."

I wait a second. But there are no sounds.

I step back from the door. My chest rises and falls too quickly. I'm breathing too fast, but I know what to do.

Another girl will not die.

I will not lose another of my dance partners.

I won't lose Taryn.

I kick the door. Splintering wood.

I grunt and kick it again. And again, and again. I throw all my force and strength at it.

The door flies open.

Inside, Xavier is staring at me. I see something in his hand, something shiny and long that the light glints off.

A knife?

Taryn.

My heart pounds. I rush through the doorway, nearly stumbling on the shards of wood on the floor. And I see her. To the right. A slumped figure, curled up on the floor.

"Taryn!" I run straight for her. "Taryn, oh God."

She moves, looks up at me. Her face is tear-stained and bloody.

Xavier shouts something, and I jerk toward him, getting ready, putting my hands up. Is he going to come at me with the knife? Hurt me?

But he's looking toward the doorway. The doorway where Trent and Hazma and Mr. Vikas now are.

"Drop the weapon now," Mr. Vikas shouts.

I run to Taryn, dropping down next to her. Her eyes are wild, full of fear.

"It's all right," I whisper to her. "I've got you."

FIFTY-THREE

Teddy

It's not working.

I can't do it.

I need to practice with someone and the one person who knew about this, who I could practice with, has gone, is no longer here. Taryn sent Victoria away. She's trying to ruin everything.

Distantly, there's a voice telling me that that deduction is wrong.

That I'm not thinking properly. That joining Roseheart isn't even my goal now. But I ignore that voice because what does it know? I am in control. I know what's going on, and I can't do this routine. I'm not good enough.

Frustration builds up inside me.

"Do it again," I tell myself.

But I'm useless at it now. I can't… It feels like I'm not myself. I've let all those doctors' warnings get in my head, and now their words are stopping me. *I'm* stopping me.

"Do it again!" I growl. "Do it better."

I wipe the back of my hand across my forehead, trying to swipe the sweat away. It's too hot in here. Why the hell have they got the heating on at the end of August? Utterly ridiculous.

"Right." I start the routine again. I count in my head, keeping time. It's the pas de deux, but I have to dance on my own.

I stretch my arms out, but my chest feels tight. I look in the mirror. My lines are all wrong. And I look awful. I look *unprofessional.* My face is red, and sweat is dripping off me.

And it's not good enough. I'm not good enough.

I start the routine again. I push myself harder and harder, imagining all the ballet teachers are looking at me, watching me, judging me. I need to do this. I need to prove to them that I deserve this. I deserve to dance.

I should be dancing with Taryn. Not him!

No, that's not right. Taryn's not who she said she was…

But my head's foggy, and I can't think… What was it she said? Or did? And aren't I aiming for New York now?

I rub my chest. It still feels tight. And my neck feels strained. I must've pulled something. Did I warm up sufficiently today?

God, I can't remember.

I look around the studio, but it's all blurring, all of a sudden. Like I'm looking at a photograph but there's water on it. Shapes are moving. The barre wobbles toward me. Was this the studio I was always in? Earlier? I… It doesn't look right.

Start again!

I try to lift my arms up, to start another pirouette. But my arms are heavy. They're stone. They're weighing me down. The room tilts around me. I break formation, throw my arms out, to grab something, but my hands bat at empty air. There's nothing here.

I breathe deeply, dark spots hovering in front of me. My skin's tacky. My shirt is sticking to me. I'm sweating so much.

A window. I need to open a window.

I turn around, and…

Darkness swirls toward me, sweeping over my skin, engulfing me.

And then there's nothing.

FIFTY-FOUR

Taryn

"Are you sure you want to do this?" Mr. Vikas hovers in front of me. "Given the circumstances, we can definitely just admit you to the company. The board is already satisfied that you and Jaidev are good enough for the company—we knew that when we gave you the parts of Helena and Demetrius—and the final assessment is more of a formality to follow the plan we came up with due to the newness of the situation. So, it can be changed."

"No. I want to do this," I say. "I can do this. And I'm all right."

That's what the doctor said. Xavier only cut my face a little. A small cut that bled a lot, covering me in blood. But I am fine. The doctor cleared me for dancing, and I want to do it. I don't want to let Xavier win, even in the slightest.

The police took him off.

"Well, we'd better get you into costuming, and hair and makeup then," Mr. Vikas says.

I stand backstage, by the curtain, waiting for my signal. It feels like a lifetime ago, the last time I was standing backstage before a show, waiting to see if I could dance for this company.

And now I am. Now I will.

Li Hua and Sibylle are both back here. Li Hua, ready for her next scene as Titania, Sibylle here for encouragement. Li Hua and Trent are stunning as leads, alongside Pierre, much smoother and with more fluidity than Victoria and Harry were. I was mesmerized earlier, watching.

On the other side of backstage, I see Jaidev. He flashes a grin at me. He looks great. A jewel-adorned off-white leotard and leggings that also match the color of my skirt. I know we look great together, like we belong. I smooth my costume down with my hands. I'm ready.

Mr. Vikas whispers my name. He's behind Sibylle. And he gives me a nod. And this is it. My first dance as Helena.

Jaidev and I make our way onto stage, graceful. There are two spotlights swinging onto stage now, and we meet in the center, a light on each of us. We hold still in our positions, our faces both turned out to the audience.

The pianist starts playing, and we become Helena and Demetrius. I am Helena, and I am desperate for Demetrius's love and attention. I dance around him, and I feel the emotion, feel her desperation to be loved. I keep my lines strong and flowing as Jaidev and I dance what Mr. Vikas calls the rejection pas de deux, where Helena is jilted.

Jaidev and I transition into a lift and when I land, softly, I drop to the ground, my arms lifting over my head, almost like a shield—because Helena knows what is coming and she's trying to protect herself—as I look up at Jaidev, as Helena begs him to love her. To return her feelings. He lifts his arms and turns his head away. His steps are high and purposeful as he moves away toward where the dancer who plays Hermia now pirouettes.

The music softens, becoming deeper, more tragic as the lights dim until there is only one spotlight lighting up Demetrius and Hermia, leaving me—Helena—alone in the dark.

Hidden, I exit the stage.

Mr. Vikas nods at me, and then time speeds up again. Backstage, directions and instructions are shouted. In record time, Allie fixes a dress which has torn. I take sips of water, before I'm back on for my next scene, and my next. By the time it's my solo—a brief part where Helena is convinced that Demetrius, Lysander, and Hermia have grouped together to ridicule her—I feel like a true professional dancer. This is what I was supposed to do, and I ride the endorphins until we get to Helena's last scene. The triple wedding.

The lighting is soft and pink, and rose petals are projected onto the backdrop of the stage. Petals that glide over our skin as Jaidev and I dance our pas de deux, Helena and Demetrius now reunited thanks to love potions. The other two marrying couples join us on stage, and I feel alive, and, somewhere, I'm sure my sister is smiling.

It's weird how quickly it seems to be over.

All that we've worked toward for the last eight weeks. And then it's done.

We leave the stage.

"Beautiful," Mr. Vikas says, then he's moving forward to direct the next couples who are on after the next scene, in which Trent is currently doing a solo.

And just like that, I'm swept up in the buzz of it all. After Trent's solo, there's a quick break before the second act, then it's the group dances. I can't smile widely enough as Jaidev and I dance with our friends.

The whole ballet passes in a blur, then we're all taking our bows at the end. I smile and squeeze Jaidev's hand, and the stage lights up.

Mr. Vikas makes his way to the center spot.

"And now we have our important announcement to make," he says. "Congratulations go to both Mr. Jaidev Ngo and Miss Taryn Foster, for here we formally offer them places with the Roseheart Romantic Dance Company."

The applause that erupts is deafening. I become dizzy with excitement, smiling and smiling. Jaidev is grinning. Cheers from the audience, everywhere. Other dancers flood the stage—the company dancers and Sibylle. There are tears in her eyes.

"I did it!"

"We'll just do some promo photos in the studio," a photographer says, appearing so suddenly.

Time's moving at a jolting speed, and Jaidev and I are directed through to a studio. I've never felt so alive as we walk there. Everyone's chatting, all excited. Sibylle's behind us, and a lot of the teachers are too. I wonder what the promo images will be. Us doing our best lifts?

Mr. Vikas opens the door for us to the chosen studio.

I step in, smiling and—

"Teddy!" I scream when I see him. He's motionless. He's…

I scream, and I cannot stop screaming.

FIFTY-FIVE

Jaidev

I try to reassure Taryn as we sit at the hospital, even though for some inexplicable reason, I want to make a joke. Something about how we've spent too long in hospitals recently, between the two of us. Well, three if you count Teddy. He was barely breathing when we found him, and for a moment, I'd really thought he was dead.

I'd grabbed hold of Taryn, to try and stop her running to him, but she'd gotten free of me. Her screams were awful.

The ambulance arrived quickly, though.

"He'll be okay," I tell her.

"It's my fault," she says.

"No," I say, "you didn't make him dance."

But she looks at me with big, tear-filled eyes. "I knew. I… I saw him practicing. I should've told someone. I mean, I told him to stop, but I should've told someone. I was just only thinking about what Xavier had done, when you guys got to me, and I should've remembered what I'd seen about Teddy. I... I could've stopped all this."

"No, you didn't make him dance," I say. "This isn't your fault."

"It is. He's my friend. I know we fell out, but I should've still been there for him."

"You can't be there for someone who doesn't want to be helped in that moment," I think of Bastien, about what it was like every time I tried to help him. He only really started to get slightly clean any time he was put into rehab—but after coming out, he'd be back on the drugs. He wasn't ready for our help then. And a person has to want to be helped for it to work properly.

I wonder how soon that will be the case for Bastien. If it will be soon. Maybe Avril will ship him off again, so she can tell herself he is getting better. Even though it's not worked before. Recovery isn't easy. Nothing is.

We're told Teddy is alive but in a critical condition. A man who Taryn tells me is Teddy's father arrives with red-rimmed eyes and a blotchy face. He's led off by a doctor to see Teddy. Close relatives only. Taryn isn't allowed.

One of the ballet teachers gives us a lift back to Roseheart. It's strange walking back, knowing we're in the company now. I want to celebrate, but I can't. Taryn looks deflated, like the life's been let out of her and she's just a flimsy outline now.

Slight annoyance rises in me. She should be celebrating, yet she's not. Because of him. I wasn't even there the first time Teddy's condition messed up Taryn's admittance to the company. But he's doing it again.

I know it's not his fault, him having this. I shouldn't be angry. But he knew what he was doing. He chose to push himself, to dance.

"See you later then," Taryn says. "I'm just going to go back to my room. Sibs said she's there."

It feels weird, watching Taryn go on her own. I am so used to thinking she needs someone with her at all times. But that's over now.

When I get back to my room, there's a letter pushed under the door. My name is written on it in an elegant hand. I open it.

Jaider,

I saw you dancing today, and you were great. I always knew you would be.

I want you to know that I do not hold any grudges against you. Nor harbor any bad feeling for what happened to my daughter. I've been meaning to write this to you for a long, long time, but the longer I left it, the harder it became.

I know you loved my daughter greatly. And we all know she died doing what she loved, with someone she loved. Camille cared about you greatly. Anyone knew that.

We're always told that ballet is dangerous for dancers' bodies. But they always make it sound like any physical damage will be self-inflicted and not life-limiting or life-taking. And it was.

But she knew that, too. You all know that.

I am glad you're dancing again.

I wish you all the best,

Gabrielle Blanc.

FIFTY-SIX

Teddy

"You've been exceptionally lucky, Teddy," Dr. Reimbert says. "But we can't have a repeat of this. You nearly died. I need you to understand how serious this is. If there's a third time where you're brought in like this, we may not be able to save you. You were also seriously dehydrated with dangerous electrolyte imbalances."

It's strange. I'd kind of convinced myself that I didn't care if I died so long as I was still dancing. But lying here in the hospital again, I realize I was wrong. I don't mean that I've had a massive revelation and now want to live. There's still not that strong feeling of wanting to live *without dance* in me. But I know now that I don't want to *die*. Maybe I want to find out what I can be. What can happen now.

But I don't want this to be over.

"Thank you, Doctor," Dad says. He's next to me in the chair. He's been here all night.

Dr. Reimbert is still looking at me. "We're going to be sorting out some psychiatric help for you."

I sit up a little. "What?"

"A shrink?" my dad blurts.

"Getting used to a new diagnosis like this can be very difficult," she says. "We all understand that, and we understand the impact of being told you can't do what you love. Some patients need extra help with this, and we will provide it. But we have also just been made aware of some extra information regarding your health from one of your teachers."

Joe.

I close my eyes.

"What's this?" Dad asks.

Dr Reimbert looks at me. "I'll let you tell your dad," she says. "I'll be back shortly with your latest blood test results. We'll discuss long-term management of the HCM, too."

Long-term management. I know from the booklet and all my research and the doctors' prior words that likely means some kind of pacemaker or implanted defibrillator.

"Well, son?" Dad says once the doctor's left. "What is she talking about? You got another diagnosis? One that needs a shrink?"

I don't like the way he says *shrink*. "No." Technically, it's not a lie. Joe isn't a psychiatrist. He can't diagnose me. He can only suspect.

"So, what the hell was she on about?"

I take a deep breath. I can feel the words inside me, but I can't catch them, don't want to catch them.

"Is Taryn there?" I ask. The question surprises me.

Dad shakes his head. "She was. Yesterday. But the academy sent her back. And the other dancer, too. But don't change the subject."

"The other dancer?"

"Asian guy. But what was that doctor—"

"Jaidev? He was here?" I don't know how I feel about that. Angry? Annoyed? Upset. Or just…. empty.

I don't really think I'm feeling anything. Other than knowing I want to live.

I can't even remember most of yesterday. Doctors told me that Taryn and some others found me in a studio, unconscious. The only thing I can recall is getting up yesterday morning and going to the canteen but being too disgusted by the amount of grease on the bacon to eat any. Not just to eat any bacon but to eat *anything* at all. I felt as though the grease had contaminated all the food in the room. An invisible layer of fat on everything. I couldn't even pick up a banana, so I didn't.

And there was something empowering about that feeling that I loved. Walking out of there hungry but knowing I was strong. Knowing I was being healthy.

And then my memory is hazy, foggy. Like there's a translucent wash over everything. I catch the odd glimpse of faces—Mrs. Nolan and Taryn and Madame Cachelle. And then I was here.

"Talk to me," Dad says.

I look at him, and I feel lost and alone and fragile. And scared.

"I'm scared. So scared."

"I know, son," is all he says

I hold his hand. I can't remember the last time I held his hand. Even as a child, it was always Mum's hand I held. Never Dad's. He was the scary parent. The parent who did the disciplining. I never went to him for comfort, but right now, he's all I have got. The only parent here.

"I'm going to leave ballet behind," I say. "It's too painful, trying to still hold on to what I cannot have."

"I think that's a sensible thing to do."

"And…" I look at him. "I need help. I've got an eating disorder, and I need help for it."

In the evening, I finally do it. I take out my phone and text Taryn.

I'm so sorry for being so horrible to you and not being there for you with all the stuff with the company dancer bullying you. I should've helped you more, but I believed it wasn't Victoria when she swore she'd not done anything to you other than snide comments in class and out and about. But I should've trusted you. I'm so sorry.

Her reply is almost instant. *Teddy! How are you? What's going on? And don't be silly, you don't need to apologize. None of this was you or your fault. And it wasn't Victoria. It was Xavier. Well, he did the big stuff. She still said some mean things.*

Xavier? My roommate. Former roommate? What the hell?

I phone her.

"Hey." She sounds the same. Just like my best friend always does.

"Hi." My throat feels dry. "Sorry, easier to talk than text. But it was *Xavier*?"

"Yeah. I'm not sure how much you know, but he stole my sister's shoes and gave them to Victoria, that's what the police told me in their update just now. He admitted to writing the threatening notes. And attacking me twice."

"*Twice*?"

"Yeah. Before the showcase, he tried to stab me."

I swear. "But you're okay?"

"Yeah. He locked me in the studio with him, but Jaidev broke the door down. It all happened so quickly, really."

"Wow." For several moments, I just don't know what to say. I hate how things aren't like they used to be. I'd always thought, deep down, that Taryn and I would stay best friends all our lives. We'd found each other. We are like soulmates. Non-romantic and non-sexual soulmates. But we were close, just as close as others who have those relationships. But close in a different way.

"Yeah." Her voice is soft.

"Did you do it? Get into the company?" I ask.

"We did."

We. It hurts me the way she says it.

"I'm glad. Really, I am. You deserve it. And you're going to be amazing, Taryn. You know that, right? You're amazing."

I think she's smiling.

"But just do one thing for me, yeah?" I whisper. "Dance for me too. Dance for me, and I'll feel it. I'll feel it here." I touch my heart, though she can't see it. "Dance for both of us. And I'll do something for both of us, too. Accounting, maybe."

She laughs. "You're terrible at adding up."

"I know," I say. "But I'm going to learn what else I'm good at."

Long after we've ended the call, I'm still thinking about her. I want to be close with her. And I know that can't happen now I'm not going back to Roseheart. Now my dancing career, and any career linked to it, is over.

I'll have to let Taryn go.

Even if we are soulmates.

Even if....

But a plan begins to form. A plan that makes me smile.

It might work.

FIFTY-SEVEN

Taryn

Two nights before the tour officially starts, it's my birthday. Sibylle, Nora, Li Hua, and Jaidev arranged for Roseheart to hold a party for me, and then it sort of turned into a celebration for everyone. I don't mind though.

The party is huge. Mum is even here, and she's smiling and telling everyone who'll listen that I'm her daughter. I've never seen her look so proud. Even some of the other diploma graduates are here. As soon as the news of mine and Jaidev's success broke, Freya and Peter left. But everyone else is here for the party. Including Ivelisse. It's the first time any of us have seen her since that night.

"How are you?" I ask her.

She looks different, in a baggy hoody and skinny jeans. I don't think I've seen her not in sportswear before. "Good. Well, doing okay. Just resting."

She doesn't offer anything more than that, and I don't push her. Instead, we talk about the music that's currently playing. Some sort of pop. She doesn't like it.

Then Mum's flitting back over, another glass of wine in her hand. The red liquid sloshes over the sides as she slings an arm around me. The gesture makes me jump. Ivelisse backs away, and I see Alma and Ella swoop toward her, swarm around her, like they're protecting her.

"I'm proud of you," she says. She doesn't sound particularly drunk, but I'm wary.

When Mum has gotten drunk before, she blamed Helena's death on me. And the worst part about her words then is that they have an ounce of truth in them. My sister's death is my fault because I was the one who suggested we open all the doors to the balconies for our game of hide and seek. If I hadn't said that, Helena would still be here.

"I know I haven't always been the most supportive of your career as a dancer," she says. "But I am proud. You know that, don't you? I just find it hard, being here."

"Because of Helena," I say, and what I'm sure Mum means is it's not specifically Roseheart she finds difficult going to, it's anywhere where I am.

Mum nods. "It must be harder for you, though. When I found out I was pregnant with the two of you, I read book after book about twins. I didn't know you were identical then, but all these child psychologists stressed the special bond twins would have—and the even more special bond that identicals have. It's been strange, Taryn. Because I know it was years ago, but to me, in here—" She taps her temple. "It still feels like it was last week. It's still close, it's still raw."

I don't know what to say.

"But I guess it's worse for you," she says. "Not having the person you were closest to."

Tears well up, and I try to blink them away. But I can't.

"It was my fault," I whisper to Mum. "About Helena. I…" I gulp. "I knew we weren't supposed to go on the balconies. But we were both bored and we were playing hide and seek. And I… I suggested we used the balconies too. From all the rooms. I thought it would be fun. I didn't realize she'd…"

Didn't realize she'd try and climb behind the railings to hide there. Didn't realize until I was looking for her. Until I saw her—there.

And somehow as I opened the glass door when I saw her and stepped out onto the balcony, she stumbled back in her crouching position. Her hand shot out to reach for me. And I tried. I ran forward. But my fingers never touched hers. Gravity had already taken her from me by the time I reached the railings.

"Oh, Taryn," Mum says. "Darling, it wasn't your fault." She hugs me tightly.

Darling. I can't remember the last time she called me that since Helena's death. But before, before she always called me that. We were both her *darlings*. I hadn't realized she'd even stopped saying it until now.

I choke up.

"I should've been keeping a closer eye on you. I was only downstairs." She exhales a long sigh and then sips her wine. "It wasn't your fault. But we have to keep living." She gives my hand a squeeze, a distant look drifting into her eyes, and I know the conversation is over.

We have to keep living.

She disappears off into the swathes of people. I hope she's not getting another drink.

"I can't believe the tour is finally next week," Li Hua says, apparently appearing out of nowhere. She's wearing an emerald-green cocktail dress and her black hair is styled in ringlets. "I love your makeup, Taryn!"

I blink. I'd almost forgotten that Sibylle had done some amazing smokey eyes for me. "Thanks."

Li Hua and I head over to the buffet table. I keep an eye on my mother. She's chatting away to Allie now. I've never seen my mother so sociable. It's weird, having her here.

Allie catches my eye and smiles. After the announcement on stage, after the performance, Jaidev and I officially signed our contracts—Mum also did an e-signature on mine for the four days when I was still a minor—and then we received our spaces in the costume room, our names on the wall. It finally feels right having the gold star from Allie now.

Just as I'm grabbing a paper plate and reaching for the carrot sticks—there's not a lot at this buffet table that is low-fructose—I see a figure slip into the room through the side door.

It's Teddy.

I head over to him, and he smiles. He looks paler than I remember. His eyes are a bit duller too. He's not dressed up like we all are here, barring Ivelisse, but he looks more comfortable in his jumper and jeans than I feel in this dress. It's too low cut. Sibylle helped me choose it a few days ago. We went out shopping, and she said I absolutely had to go for it. So, I did.

"Hey," I say to Teddy. "You're out of hospital."

"Just for a few hours," he says. "I'm... I'm having an ICD fitted tomorrow."

"Then you'll be out after?"

He shakes his head. "They're setting up inpatient treatment for me." He looks around. "Can we go somewhere quieter?"

"Sure."

We walk out into a small courtyard at the side of Roseheart's grounds. The lake stretches out, a couple hundred yards away, and the moonlight glistens from its rippling surface. It's breezy out here, and I shiver a little.

"Taryn, I wanted to see you before you leave for the tour," Teddy says. He goes very red.

"What is it? Are you okay?"

He nods. "Just nervous."

"Nervous? Of me?" I laugh.

He laughs too, but it's weak. "I'm sorry." He looks at the ground for a moment before meeting my gaze. "I shouldn't have called you a hypocrite or a liar for kissing Jaidev. I... I do get it. I know you were just doing it for the performance."

"Even if I hadn't been, it wouldn't have meant I wasn't aro," I tell him. "Some aro people do enjoy it. It's a spectrum, like all of this."

He nods. "I shouldn't have questioned your identity, I know that. I just felt... betrayed. Because I've realized something, Taryn, and I need to tell you. I... I want to be with you, and I don't mind that you're dancing with Jaidev permanently now. I just want to be with you."

He wants to be with me? I feel like all the breaths been squeezed out of my lungs.

"Teddy, stop."

"No, please, listen. You're the only one who gets me. We're both aroace, so we know we'd work well together. And we *would*. We're best friends, and I know we've had a blip, but that's because everything around us was changing and we had no control over it. But I've been thinking about it a lot. About you, about us, and I know we'd be great together. We can raise kids together too and…"

"Kids?" I stare at him. "I don't want kids, Teddy. I've told you that."

"But we'd be great parents. And a lot of people do this. A lot of aro people do this together, become a family. *We* can have a family."

I hold my hands up. "Just stop."

"But we're meant to be together. See, we were paired as primary dancers for the diploma for a *reason*. Because we're both aroace—it was fate."

"Look, Teddy. Just because we're both aroace, it doesn't mean we have to be together. I mean, I'm happy as I am. You're my best friend, yes, but I like being on my own. I like being single."

"Okay." His eyes take on a shifty look. "We can continue as we are. As friends."

But I can see the hope in his eyes. The hope of how I might change my mind. And he's put his cards on the table now.

"No, look. Teddy, I know you want a partner. You want a family, I get it. And I…"

"But *you're* my family."

"Teddy. I'm your friend, but I can't be the family you want. Not in the *way* you want. Not *raising children*."

"We don't have to have children. We don't even have to live together." He's speaking too quickly, his words crashing into each other.

"Teddy, that wouldn't be fair on you. You deserve to find someone who wants the same things you do."

"But how will I find another person who's aroace?" His voice cracks.

"You'll find your person. You will. And maybe they won't be ace and aro, but you'll find someone. You deserve to get what you want. You've always wanted kids, you always said that, but that's not me. And you deserve that life."

And I don't think being around a dancer would be good for him. But I don't add that last bit, can't bring myself to say those words because I don't want to see him any more crushed than he already is.

He nods. "I'm going back inside. It's cold." His voice is neutral. He's trying hard not to show any emotion.

I watch him head inside. I did the right thing, I know that.

"I'm happy as I am," I say, and I don't know why I say it out loud. But I am. I've got my mum and I've got Sibylle, and I've got Jaidev. I've got the support of the company, and I've got friends who are company dancers: Li Hua and Nora and Netty Florence. I get to dance professionally with Jaidev. And though things are awkward with Teddy right now and probably will be for a while, our friendship might last. I'll have to give him time first, back off a little, because I don't want to give him false hope. But maybe we can still remain friends.

Maybe.

The door Teddy went through opens, and, for a second, I think he's coming back out. But it's not him. A woman with chestnut hair and a short, pale-blue satin dress steps out. She's wearing big heels and her hair is immaculate, I can tell that even from here.

Victoria.

My mouth dries.

Her heels clip-clop as she approaches me, then she stops a few feet away.

"Taryn."

I nod at her. "You're… You're back?"

"*Of course* I'm back. I didn't do anything. And so, you need to watch out," she says. "You've nearly ruined my career with your accusations, with jumping to conclusions. You've removed me from my first tour where I had a lead role, and I don't like you now. And I should warn you that people I don't like have a habit of getting hurt."

I stare at her, unsure whether to laugh. "Is that a threat?"

"It's whatever you want to interpret it as. Just remember I'm the queen around here." She smiles brightly suddenly. The change in her expression is jarring. "But have a good tour, won't you? Good luck. You're going to need it."

END OF BOOK ONE

BOOK TWO, *SWANS IN THE DARK*,

WILL HIT SHELVES IN SUMMER 2022.

NOTE FROM THE AUTHOR

One of my favorite things about writing characters who fall on the asexual spectrum is how I can explore the many different identities that this umbrella encompasses. My first three novels with ace representation—*In My Dreams, My Heart to Find,* and *It's Always Been You*—are romances and are part of the Aces in Love series (written as Elin Annalise). In each of those books, I explored different ace identities and when I first began writing *The Rhythm of My Soul*, I thought this would be another one for that series. But, in writing Taryn's story, it became clear to me that she was aromantic as well as asexual.

I am asexual myself, and while I used to believe I was aromantic too, I've recently discovered that the term 'demiromantic' is a better fit for me as I only really feel romantic attraction after I've formed a strong emotional connection. Identities are fluid and some people find theirs changes over time or they then discover a new term that fits them better—yet writing Taryn's story gave me a challenge. While her experiences are authentic to my past experiences, and a lot of her feelings surrounding how society dictates what 'acceptable' relationships look like mirror my own feelings, I wondered a lot about whether I should rewrite Taryn as demiromantic, to better match who I am now.

Ultimately, I decided against this as I didn't want to be inadvertently suggesting that all aro people will end up being demiromantic. So, I stuck to my gut and wrote Taryn as someone who embodied my previous aro identity.

In order to make sure that my portrayal of aromanticism in this novel wasn't inadvertently problematic—and understanding that one person's experience doesn't represent all who use that term—I employed a number of sensitivity readers who read for aro representation (along with sensitivity readers for the other diversities explored in this book).

The more I wrote of Taryn and the Roseheart Ballet Academy, the more I realized I wanted to write more in this world. The moment I finished the draft of this book, I was desperate to continue the story. I'd already been thinking that because *The Rhythm of My Soul* definitely wasn't a romance, I'd need to separate it from my Aces in Love series, and this motivation to write more of Taryn and the Roseheart Ballet Academy gave me the permission I needed to say that *The*

Rhythm of My Soul would be the first novel in the Roseheart Ballet series.

Readers, I hope you enjoyed the story of Taryn, Teddy, and Jaidev and that you will look out for book two. We've got more desperate ballet dancers, morally gray characters, and dark secrets coming!

Acknowledgments

The Rhythm of My Soul is a book I've wanted to write for a long, long time. I've always been fascinated by ballet, and my idea for a story about elite ballet dancers competing in a rather cutthroat industry just would not stop simmering in my mind. I was always a bit apprehensive about writing this book though, as I knew little about the industry from an insider's perspective.

Luckily, in writing this book, I met some amazing ballet dancers who helped me with my research: Sabine Deixler, Lilli Nocon, Garret McNally, Krystal Descano, Andrea Valeria, Larissa Loren Walker, and Sien H. To all of you: thank you so much for taking the time to not only answer all my questions but to also read extracts to comment on authenticity and for telling me about your own experiences. I couldn't have written this story without you!

A huge thank you goes to my sensitivity readers and the experts I consulted: Elisabeth TenBrink Kelley, Chelsea

Hindle, Maria Guglielmo, Kaitlin Maynard, Leaf Domantas, Marisa Manuel, Sarah Clark, Sefanya Hiennadi, Jennifer Webb, Debbie Hamilton, John Kalb, Amy Moran, Becky Smith, and Tripp Smith.

I must also thank my wonderful beta-readers: Linda Izquierdo Ross, Imogen Grant, Sarah Anderson, and Kate Kenzie. Writing this book was certainly a daunting process, and all of you made it so much easier.

I'm also so lucky that one of my beta-readers is my cover designer; Sarah Anderson, not only are you one of the kindest people I know, but you're so talented. I love the designs you created for *The Rhythm of My Soul*!

To all the writers in my writing circles and critique groups: thank you so much for always being supportive, for encouraging me, for organizing writing sprints, and more.

To my family: Mum, Dad, Sam, Grandad, and Gill. Thank you for always supporting me.

And to my partner, Michael: thank you for always being so encouraging.

About the Author

Elin Dyer lives on a farm in the southwest of England, where she hangs out with her Shetland ponies and writes dark and twisty young adult books. She is pursuing her MA in Creative Writing from Kingston University, having obtained a BA honors degree in English from the University of Exeter. Elin has a strong love for anything dystopian or ghostly, and she can frequently be found exploring wild places. At least one notebook is known to follow her wherever she goes.

The Rhythm of My Soul is her fourteenth book.

She also writes as Madeline Dyer and Elin Annalise.

CPSIA information can be obtained
at www.ICGtesting.com
Printed in the USA
LVHW111251070922
727689LV00002B/82